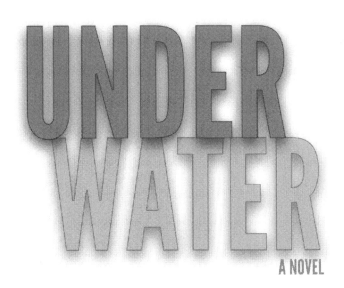

A NOVEL

RACHEL CALLAGHAN

Editor: Laurie Knight
Developmental Editor: Amy Delcambre
Cover Design: Kristina Edstrom
Cover Photography: Juan Vidal/Addison Wolfe Real Estate

An Imprint for GracePoint Publishing (www.GracePointPublishing.com)

GracePoint Matrix, LLC
624 S. Cascade Ave., Suite 201, Colorado Springs, CO 80903
www.GracePointMatrix.com
Email: Admin@GracePointMatrix.com
SAN # 991-6032

A Library of Congress Control Number has been requested and is pending.

ISBN: (Paperback) 978-1-955272-40-7
eISBN: 978-0-9893336-6-5

Books may be purchased for educational, business, or sales promotional use. For bulk order requests and price schedule contact:
Orders@GracePointPublishing.com

Table of contents

On realestately.com:

Amazing opportunity to own this peaceful bit of Highgrove's history. This stately Victorian farmhouse dates from 1895 and is set on 2.63 acres of mixed meadow and woods. The second-floor main bedroom's deck is perfect for watching the wildlife. The kitchen has handmade maple cabinets and the dining room, a huge fireplace. The stone-floored conservatory is bright and inviting with its glass roof; the massive living room, resplendent with oak floors and a cozy fireplace.

Make this property your dream come true! All the above PLUS a quiet, peaceful pond to sit beside on lazy summer days!

Chapter 1

"**WHAT THE HELL DID** you get us into?" Benny said as they stepped into the dank and musty house. It was a disaster: ancient pine floors creaky, antique wiring, mildew-mottled plaster, mouse droppings, and corroded pipes.

The website's photos had been taken with the magic camera realtors use to attract the unsuspecting. Those photos had lured Iris and Benny all the way from California.

Iris put a soothing hand on his shoulder. "Imagine how beautiful we can make this place."

Benny looked like he'd been smacked with a dead trout. "Imagine us bankrupt." He pivoted on his heels. "Air conditioning before summer or we're gone." He returned to the car for the luggage.

Iris didn't protest. Better to have a bit of time and distance when they disagreed—forty-some years of marriage taught her that. Though, in the back of her mind, she'd thought of the move as a fresh start for their marriage, a way back to each other.

Two months later, on a humid June day, men arrived to shovel out the muck beneath the duckweed in the backyard pond. Unlike the online photos, the water was murky green, a mosquito nursery. Obviously, the circulating pump wasn't on. *Peaceful, my ass!* she thought.

As she led the way, frogs leaped, landing in the water with pleasant little plops. Iris loved frogs, especially the tiny ones discovering dry land on newly grown legs. At the very least, frogs meant tadpoles to eat most of the mosquito wrigglers hatching beneath the weeds. But the stone-lined pond was yet another thing to return to health.

"Bought this place online, huh?" Paul, owner of Paul's Ponds, slammed the gate of his gold-logoed truck.

"Yes, a long-distance purchase. COVID, you know, all those quarantines, flying impossible. We had lots of inspections done. Everything checked out okay."

Paul grinned. Iris imagined him thinking, *One born every minute.* His smile disappeared when he eyeballed Iris's German shepherd running from the barn. "That dog aggressive?"

For a brief second, Iris wished Freddy was. "Only if you really upset me."

She took Freddy into the house to mix some tuna for lunch, Benny's favorite. The dog would get to lick the cans.

An hour later, she went back out the kitchen door. Paul lay on the grass, overseeing his men. Iris thought, *He could get off his ass and work alongside his employees!* but said nothing aloud—she didn't want to be that kind of newcomer to the county. Meanwhile, the hourly charges for the work added up in her mind like a New York taxi meter—*tick, tick, tick.*

"The pump's broken. Too old to be worth fixing," Paul said, scratching his sweaty receding hairline. "Just so you know."

She was about to ask why he'd stayed mum about this in bidding the job, when one of the men lifted his shovel and said, "What the fuck?"

On the end of the shovel lay a filthy cloth bag—the size of a supermarket sack—closed with a ragged tartan ribbon.

"Put it on the ground," Paul said, rising from his seat. "Sometimes they hid coins and stuff under water. Could be valuable."

Iris clambered up over the low wall and joined him. The bag was stained with mud, its original color indeterminate until, as more water leaked out, the grimy ribbon shifted, exposing unstained cloth of a remarkable violet color.

"This bit looks new," Iris bent over to peer closer.

"Yeah, well, that muck's been accumulating for a long, long time. Decades at least. Thick and sticky... stuff."

She could tell Paul would have said *shit* if she had not been there. Or if he didn't think of her as *old*.

"Should I open it?" the worker asked, wiping his hand across his already saturated jeans.

Paul looked at Iris. "Your pond, your call."

She shrugged. "Why not?"

The young man tugged at the knot, releasing it before jumping back, yelping, "Jesus Christ."

With a small gush of water, an infant's corpse slid from the bag, mud brown but perfectly preserved, as if in endless slumber.

Aoife

1863

The screams awoke her; open-mouthed shrieks jolted her upright. "Wake, William! Wake!" Aoife shook him to break the nightmare's spell.

That did little good. Instead of awakening, he shrieked, "No, no, no," and clung to his terror as if to an old and dear friend.

She took his arm again, only to have him moan and struggle, raining blows on her head and shoulders. All the while, he remained deep in the blackness of sleep.

He fell back and was quiet, but moments later he again stirred, muttering commands softly and then with mounting agitation, "*Fire! Fall back, they are too many!*" As his voice peaked, his hands twisted at the cloth of her nightdress, like a bridegroom ready to part her limbs and push himself inside her.

But William was no longer an eager bridegroom and never would be again. *He feels not a man, and that is what drives his madness.*

At last, he seemed to tire, his arms sagging, the blows softening, sliding off her body. The words became mutterings and then soft moans as his struggle subsided. Finally, he slumped down against her.

"Hush, hush," she murmured. To soothe his soldier's heart, she sang the lullaby her mam once crooned to her. Outside in the pond behind the house, the frogs sang along.

Fleeing the bed would have been easy, but staying was her duty. She was his wife, and she was what he needed. And, at daybreak, he was his true self again.

"Morning, love." She cradled his head against her bosom, kissing the high rise of his cheek and smoothing back the light brown hair over his brow.

We were in love once, and still are, in our way. She closed her eyes, wishing for a bit more sleep, then let them snap open again and thought, *At least, in the light of day.*

"Thomas is already in the fields with the oxen, William, and the cows are lowing. Do you hear them? I must leave you now for the milk shed. For just a little while. I'll bring your breakfast porridge and an egg the minute the cream is separated."

He turned his stony face to the wall as she rose to dress for the day.

Making her way down the stairs, she groaned, as the day was already warm and with promise to be suffocating later. If she wanted the cows to produce, she'd have to wet them with buckets of water and let them linger in the shade of their byre, timothy hay in their rack. Keep the barn doors open to

4

encourage the breeze. *Thank the Lord, I do not have to pull up bucket after bucket from the well!*

* * *

After they'd wed, two years before the war, William said, "Wife…"

Oh, upon my soul, I do love that word! Aoife had put her arms about his middle.

"… from now, you will not be servant to anyone, and I have kept money aside for what would ease your life." He rested his chin lightly on her head. His warm breath blowing across the tight pull of her parted hair set a ripple deep inside her. "I will hire a maidservant for the heavy work."

How she'd smiled, pressing tighter against him. He'd already provided her a pump instead of an oaken bucket and rope—the first house in the township to have one. But a maid?

"No, husband…" She loved that word, too. "… household work is nothing new to me. I wish to share our home with no one else." *Certainly, no other maid, not ever, unless someone old and stout like your mother.* She did not doubt his love and devotion but wished to show herself frugal and grateful. "I shall manage the milking and tend the kitchen garden, cook, and keep the house." She smiled up into his face and winked. "Perhaps get me a servant when we have many little ones underfoot."

William Sprigett had honored her by taking her hand in marriage, an unbelievable stroke of luck for her. William was born a gentleman with an inheritance of good land. Money, too; more than adequate to start and with the promise of more to come when his mother followed her husband to the grave.

Which, Lord forgive me, cannot come fast enough. Aoife tamped down that thought like a spark spat from the fireplace onto her rag rug. It was unchristian to wish for anyone's death, no matter how deserved.

William had wooed her and refused to marry another. It was their marriage that led to the break with his family. He was in love and, being so, willingly took a tumble down the ladder of respectability and wealth.

I was in love, too, with his handsome face and the long clean limbs that gathered me to him. And charming he was, able to lift my heart when I grew sad for my lost mam. Aye, she thought, *I married a treasure.*

There had been too much farm work for William alone. Thankfully, his hired man, Thomas Walker, was hardworking and trustworthy, married to the town's washwoman. He lived in the village and, before coming to the farm, earned his way with odd chores and seasonal labor. He and William put in the crops—corn, wheat, and hemp—and harvested them to be ground down beneath the millstone on Mill Road. Together, they herded the livestock, both cattle and sheep, the flock, a fancy of William's father whose English ancestors had once held great estates in Ireland. It was the likes of them that had driven Aoife's family from their croft to starve by the road. All to better the hunting for the rich.

After William and Aoife married, any loneliness she felt, any desire for the company of other women, she pushed away from her busy mind. *William is more than enough for me.*

Especially when he came into the house at midday, leaving Thomas in the fields. Another woman in the house would have spoiled their time. The very thought made her cover her blush-warm face with the apron skirt.

Aoife paused at the door to the barn. Those happy days glowed like gold in her memory.

And then came the war.

Thomas

1863

Looking across the field toward the house, Thomas shook his head slowly, unconsciously imitating the movement of the oxen he drove. The missus, Aoife, was slow getting to her chores. *Mr. William must have kept her up in the night.* He still couldn't call him William for all that they'd once worked side by side. That was too familiar to feel safe, not while the memory of the Philadelphia riots lingered in peoples' minds. And not while there was resentment of the war, what with so many men dead or crippled like Mr. William, but one like Thomas safe, working for the farmland he'd been promised for his labors.

The gate opened and the cows came out into new pasture at the far end of the field, Thomas's dog Hero nipping at their heels. Aoife drove them with a pole, her work dress hanging loose in the still morning air. Caring for her husband through his restless nights wore the flesh off her.

Longing for a place of his own, a place to escape the seething mass of the city, was why Thomas had taken the work. A few acres, enough to farm, enough to raise a family with his Lettie. Fresh vegetables to live on in the summer and fruit in the fall, all sufficient to put up sealed with wax for the winter. A cow or two for when the babies came and a spring house to hang the bacon.

He had roamed north of the city, looking for likely property, and spied a piece close by Mill Creek, a bit uphill to be spared all but the worst flooding. At one end, there was an apple tree, old, but still producing. A cherry, too—someone must have had a cabin there long before. *That parcel is as sweet a piece of land as can be found on God's Earth.*

"Call me William," the land's owner had said.

Thomas shook his head. That was too familiar to feel safe, though it was more than a decade since the fighting in the streets of Philadelphia. He'd been a boy in 1842, not even six years old, but he still saw, in the faint light between sleep and wakefulness, the fearful vision of his trembling mother barricading their door.

"Get down on your knees, son," she'd said. "Stay below the window ledge and pray your daddy gets home safely."

The softness of her voice alarmed him, so used to her usual gruffness. He snuggled against her large and powerful back, believing her bulk, as great as most workmen's, would keep him safer from the crowds roaring back and forth in the street—from the *thunk* of wood against shanty walls and the clang of iron against metal, of fists against flesh—than the old dresser she'd shoved up against their door.

That time of hiding behind her body, cowering against the cold plaster wall of their kitchen, had been easily the most frightening experience he'd ever known.

The city had been quiet since then, but what had come before and come again, could repeat a third time. And so, despite moving to this peaceful rural community, he'd decided, no, no Christian name, baldly and disrespectfully spoken. Thomas called his employer "Mr. William."

The Sprigett family's property had been granted more than 150 years before. Folk in the city listed them among Penn's aristocracy, once persecuted Quaker stock. Though no longer one of the Society of Friends, William Sprigett still thought in their brotherly way enough to hire Thomas on and treat him well.

That kindness, that decency, made Thomas half ashamed, since, being ignorant of farming, Mr. William didn't realize the worth of the parcel and was letting it go easy. *Or,* Thomas pondered, *maybe he just has so damn much land, it doesn't matter to him.*

For several years, Thomas had worked side by side with Mr. William, teaching him as respectfully as Thomas could, though his employer's impulsive ignorance was a challenge—Mr. William had been bound for the law until his older brother died of diphtheria and there was no one else to inherit the Sprigett land.

Each noontime, Mr. William's wife, Aoife, would walk out from the house, carrying a basket with their midday meal. She hadn't been much of a cook, truth be told, her chicken dry and bread hard, but what she brought had more thought to it than Lettie's. She tended her garden well and so they might find biscuits with a dollop of jam in the spring, before fruiting season, or fresh berries in the summer with cream from the cows she milked.

Coming up through the field, she surely had been something to see, though, with her red-gold hair shining in the sun, her long skirt billowing in the wind, and a colorful cloth over that basket. Thomas looked away from the sight of her. She was Mr. William's and so Thomas kept her a stranger.

Since the war, she now had Mr. William—just as Thomas had his Lettie—as a yoke about her neck, a burden, and yet still beloved. Thomas sighed and ordered the oxen to pull. Goliath, the boss of smaller Hercules, shook his head and bellowed, leaned into the weight of the plow behind, and started off again.

He'd be with Lettie on Sunday, after a few morning chores. Lettie had never settled well in the North; she was lonely without family. Thomas understood. She'd spent her childhood sleeping on one pallet with her brothers and sisters, curled naked against each other like rabbit kits down a hole, depending on each other for warmth. In some ways, in her mind, she was forever unsafe, as if still hiding from the fierceness of their mother. Their fathers had been scattered

9

hither and yon, some wolfishly mean as the mother, some just gone, and all as defenseless as that mother was from the greater wolves of the world.

And those greater wolves had done their damage, pursuing Lettie and her sister Sary when they fled the South. How could Thomas not love her? Not help her? He had been born free and so owed a debt to those who'd been enslaved.

He'd plowed this field for years. Season followed season, unchanging, time going slowly by, until, from far to the west, from wild Illinois, came a long lanky man, a man they called rough and unshapely, a callused-hand rail splitter, and Thomas wished his father had waited to name him so he could have been Abraham, in his honor. For what he did for Thomas's people.

After him came the war.

Chapter 2

IRIS SCREAMED AS THE BABY SLID from the bag, and so did one of the muscular young workers. And then he turned away, face red and neck muscles straining, to vomit into the bamboo. Iris immediately thought to get him a glass of cold water and a clean towel. But she couldn't force her legs to move.

Paul pulled out his cell phone and called 911. He sent his men to wait at the truck. The guy who'd been sick staggered a bit.

Iris closed her eyes. Saw a tiny lace gown and cap, waterlogged and slimy. Saw little fingers splayed out like baby squid startled by the sudden warmth of the air and seeming to grasp at nothing. But the face... she couldn't picture the face. Lost, as if she'd never seen it.

When she opened her eyes again, the treetops swirled around her vision as if she might faint, but her knees stayed locked, supporting her upright, frozen like a department store dummy.

Paul helped her down to the path and sat her on the low stone wall. The sun hadn't reached it and the nighttime chill worked its way through her jeans.

A few minutes later, the police arrived. The officers, both men, followed Paul's pointing finger and walked to the pond. For a few silent minutes, they leaned over the body, appearing puzzled. Then the older one said, "Call forensics," and headed across the path to Iris and Paul. Meanwhile the younger tapped a number in his phone and said, "Yeah, we need the lab."

"This is really unusual," said the older cop, who stood between Iris and the pond, blocking her from again seeing the baby's body. His words were flat, uninflected.

"I should hope so," Iris said.

To his credit, neither his expression nor his voice changed at her sarcasm. "You'd be surprised what can be found in the bottom of ponds and old wells, but a baby? Never before. My guess is, that poor tyke's been down there a long, long time."

A long, long time echoed in her head until a bright red cardinal flew into one of the big oaks and trilled, *Cheer! Cheer! Cheer!*

Iris's heart thrummed erratically, periodic beats landing like a hammer blow against her breastbone. She forced herself to focus on what the police officer had to say.

"We don't get much crime around here…" He looked taken aback by his own words. "… not that I'm saying this is crime related. Mostly we handle speeding tickets, accidents, the occasional drug bust. It's a safe, quiet area."

There was something else nagging at her mind. Something she could barely stand to think about.

Grabbing hold of a little maple's trunk for support, she forced her focus back to the officer, but his words were garbled, muffled, hanging disjointed in the air, like skywriting when it breaks apart, its message lost. Only his appearance seemed to make sense. She could use that to keep from sinking into the past.

He must have been outright handsome in his youth, with the bone structure that resisted aging. His attractiveness, and the realization he was trying so hard to put her at ease, brought a flush up her neck. That was something Benny hadn't done in a long, long time. Not with his panic attacks. They had made him curve in on himself like a fetus, growing less attentive to anyone else.

Focus on the present, Iris!

This detective was most likely a decade younger than Benny, and his looks would have piqued Iris's flirty side if a dead baby hadn't just been found at her new home. The dead baby… "What is it?" she asked.

The officer looked startled. "What is it?"

"Is it a boy or a girl?" She needed to know, to give it a fitting name, to think of it as real, as a person. It was in her pond. It belonged to her, in a way.

As if naming made a difference. Dead was dead.

The policeman took in a sudden breath, shook his head, and walked back to his partner. He motioned the other aside and lifted the edge of the baby's clothing with a pen. When he returned, he said, "A boy."

Iris nearly fainted with relief. "A John Doe," she said. "Nobody knows his name."

"So far, no, ma'am."

Little John Doe, baby John Doe, is what the papers would call him, until they found out who he was, if they ever did. John was a perfectly good name. Nickname Jack if a member of the family, someone who belonged to you. Was he, this little baby boy, was he safely hers, without the pain of remembering him alive?

The baby she and Benny lost had been a girl. So long ago but never forgotten. A baby girl would have been too close to home.

Aoife

1861

"I have already paid good money for someone to take your place, William, for there is talk of conscription coming, should sufficient men fail to volunteer. 'Tis all arranged through Colonel Thompson, your father's great friend, the one who lost his son from yellow fever in Veracruz." Mother Sprigett's stout frame shook, the jiggling of her arms scarce hidden by the silk of her bishop sleeves.

Those are arms that never saw work. Aoife could just see into the parlor from where she was hidden in the short hall to the kitchen. She wished to hear her husband's retort though it was odd to feel on the side of her mother-in-law in an argument.

William stood firm. "Stay out of this, Mother. I will go. You have no power to stop me, save you have me crippled somehow."

Mother Sprigett grew beetroot red, and her trembling grew at his words.

Aoife almost laughed at his audacity and disrespect. Audacity she expected, for he had broken with his family to marry her. But always before, he had treated his mother with respect and courtesy. No wonder she was in such a fury. Aoife glanced toward the mantel holding her one good vase—given her by the same Mother Sprigett when another of the maids knocked it over and made a tiny chip in its base. *Good thing she is not like my dadai when angered, prone to flinging anything at hand.*

"Rhetoric, son, from the likes of that Stowe woman up in Connecticut. Her own son is too young to be sacrificed, and so she can pen a dime novel to beat the drums of war. She has not my mother's heart! Have you learnt melodrama from your Irish wife? Such theater is all the rage with her kind, though at least she, when in my service, was never rude to me!"

"I have determined to be a man, Mother, to fight for an end to slavery and to preserve the Union." William's shoulders straightened further, and his chin lifted in defiance.

For all that I wish his answer would be different, he's a noble sight. Aoife didn't give a fig what cause moved him to risk life and limb. She wanted him, the two of them, to remain as they were. If only she could run into the room and cry, "For once, husband, the old woman's right!"

Aoife could barely understand selling life and health so cheap, all for the freedom of others. *It is a sign one had never been a drudge or ever suffered.* After near starving in the Great Famine, when the potato crop in Ireland rotted in the ground, her mam and dadai had emigrated, only to be worked to death, servants in the New World. Their dying had left her, their only daughter, no course but to be a servant herself.

Once she failed—again—to have her son obey her will, Mother Sprigett did what she could. She went to her dead husband's friends and had William made lieutenant, though he'd no training. Then she set about buying the best woolen cloth and trimmings, standing over William's young wife, tsking with her tongue as if Aoife was still her maid, overseeing the sewing of a uniform for him.

"No factory-made machine-stitching for my son!" Her bulk crowded the light.

Aoife gulped air through her mouth like a fish dying on a bank, as if that would tamp down the anger rising in her gorge. Then she remembered, *That is what I want for William too! When he dies—if he dies—it to be as a well-kitted gentleman. See him honored proper though he'd taken a servant for his wife.*

"Lock your stitches," Mother Sprigett said. "Turn the seams over and sew them secure with binding. I'll not have them come down and be raggedy. There's enough cloth bought for proper sewing, you can be sure." Still in widow's weeds but with a tongue as sharp as when her husband had lived, and she'd been Queen of the May. As William's mother stood over the sewing, there was soft clanking of the fine jewelry she'd vowed to have buried with her, so as to never leave it to her younger son's wife.

Mother Sprigett still mourned both her eldest boy and the bride he'd had no time to take. When the old woman turned for a second to take a handkerchief from the reticule she kept on her arm, Aoife quickly crossed herself and silently begged the Lord's forgiveness for both desiring the gems and for resenting a mother's love. She bent to her task and finished his trousers.

Mother Sprigett gave William the best horse they had, a blood bay gelding with a proud arched neck; its saddle, bridle, and bags of fine leather stained black. As he rode off, all in blue on that gleaming horse, as pretty a picture as ever seen, Aoife wished her mam had lived to see him as there was no one else to share the pride swelling her heart.

Standing on tiptoes, Mother Sprigett and Aoife waved white handkerchiefs from the roadside until he was gone from sight. Then the old woman turned and said, "Much as I love my son, more do I despise you for ruining his future, his chance for a suitable match. Do not bother coming to me for anything. I would rather see you starve." Then she returned to her buggy.

Perhaps, if I'd given her a grandchild, born in wedlock to her son, she would have softened toward me. Aoife sniffed and thought, *But mayhap not, the old bitch.*

Thomas

1861

Babes, the seeds that might grow into a family of their own, would have bound Thomas and Lettie together—would have healed her, *that* he truly believed. That was what he prayed for.

Lettie loved babies despite her work washing shit-stained diaper cloths for the townspeople. She took every opportunity to hold a babe against her breast, all those pink and white little darlings, and refused the pay she was offered for minding them, though the money might be saved for their farm. She'd shake her head, swearing, "I'll have my babe, not be no mammy to another woman's child. Not for all the tea in China!"

Thomas was glad, fearing attachments that would grow only to be broken, and her will with them. He loved her too much to watch as her spirit was trampled beneath other people's good fortune, her happiness diminished every time the Lord blessed them, only to have her body betray her and the bleeding return. The losses took her first to the edge of despair. And then to the frontier of madness. Sometimes it made her seem to hate Thomas as if he'd magicked their children away. *Better than hating herself*, he thought.

Lettie wore her knees out, praying and weeping, and he knew she considered fleeing, as if bad luck was something she could escape from. But fear she'd be found out put a stop to her dreams of flight. Fear she'd wind up like her sister, dead on a wooded path, killed by the hunters while Lettie hid in the bushes.

At first, she came to help Mr. William's wife with the sheets and the table linens, but something stuck in her craw, and she'd no longer abide it. She still did their wash, but only if Thomas brought the dirty to her and returned the clean and pressed to the farm. Even then, buttons went missing and small rends unrepaired, until he lied to her and said they'd no longer send her work if one more thing was wrong.

Truth be told, Mr. William's wife was too kind, too shy, or too little used to things done for her, and she had done the mending herself. That had made no softening in Lettie's opinion. She said, "Just mean that red-headed woman's a fool," and refused to take the farm's worn-out clothes. Worse ones from others were welcomed, to be cut and turned into crazy quilts and babies' nightgowns and sold in the market.

Lettie hated the wife but not the husband. Thomas saw the shine in her eyes when William Sprigett set off in that blue tunic, the sword by his side tapping the bright bay colt's side as he led his troops from the town. Jealousy did not occur to Thomas, but envy did, and he told Lettie he was joining up to go along and serve Mr. William. Said it was his duty. She turned on Thomas then, saying, "You gave enough, as have I. To all of them. Let those who never suffered pay the price. Home you'll bide." There was no more discourse on that. Mr. William rode off and Thomas stayed behind.

Despite her refusal to let him go, the war's start brought Lettie a small degree of heartsease, the first since he'd met her. "At least someone's fighting against the slavers, even if not for our freedom," she said.

"Some are," Thomas told her, but she only responded with a harsh exhalation.

Chapter 3

IRIS'S THROAT TIGHTENED AND seemed to trap her breath. Sudden longing for her husband overwhelmed her. Where the heck was Benny? Was his damn appointment at the ophthalmologist really taking two hours? Then she remembered he planned on going to Costco. It was almost on his way home.

She couldn't wait to lean against him, be comforted by his embrace and have everything feel securely normal—if that's how he'd react to their new house being a potential crime scene, even one decades old.

Had there been a crime? The baby was dressed with care, the gown and cap trimmed in lace that must have taken hours to tat. The bag was fine velvet, hand stitched. Someone had gotten to hold him. Someone had loved him. "Or someone felt guilty," she murmured.

"Sorry?" the officer said.

"Nothing. Just shock, I guess." No sense putting the police off by seeming odd or uncaring. Or nuts. But her thoughts accused: *Crazy, changing possible infanticide to a loving gesture. Was the poor thing drowned like an unwanted kitten? A baby, a dead baby—who the fuck puts a baby in a pond?*

She imagined the child suspended deep in the murky womb of the pond. Could it have been an act of love, putting the baby in the still and malodorous water beneath the duckweed, unchanging, protected from roaming dogs and wild foxes? *Derelict or not, this garden is a peaceful place to spend eternity.*

A safe, quiet area. A safe, peaceful internment. Who thinks like that? What was wrong with her? The previous thoughts had been deranged. "Amazing what the mind can do," she murmured, careful no one could hear but herself. It had become a bad habit, saying aloud what she should keep to herself. Sometimes people *were* listening.

That fine lace gown and cap, carefully tied beneath the face that remained blurred out in her mind, obscured like the faces of children in news photos beneath headlines like, "Father Kills Toddlers Then Shoots Self."

Iris shook her head. Perhaps her mind was fooling her, altering perception. Picking away at the veneer on the disasters in their lives, illnesses, losses, and mistakes, including the house purchase leading to this Edward Gorey/Tim Burton moment. Self-preservation ruining what should be her natural reaction, that of horror.

An image of Benny's face rose in her mind. He loved and supported her despite everything, and what had she done in repayment for his trust? What had she done to his peaceful retirement? Uprooting them, buying a derelict house. The man was almost seventy, for Christ's sake.

Perhaps she could blame it on brain damage. On aging. Or on all the weed they'd smoked back in the good old days. He'd started toking in Vietnam—most of the vets they knew did—and afterward, it calmed him and gave them a way to relax together. As free-spirited as Iris had been, she'd never been into it, until Benny needed her to keep him company.

Little Jack Doe was a boy. That was comforting. Perhaps that would let her talk with Benny about their baby in the way she longed to, if he was ever open to that discussion. It had never, not in decades, seemed the right time. She sighed with relief at the possibility.

So many couples we know have ended their marriages after a tragedy. But others have been brought closer. I wonder how many stay together out of love or habit, how many because there's no one else. I guess grief wears people out, one way or another, so we're not alone. It was a strangely comforting thought, that many couples go through day after day not really talking.

Aoife

1861

They would have lost everything had it not been for Thomas—not another worker for hire, not anywhere. The men were gone, leaving only boys too young and stiff-legged pensioners too old to be of use. All marched off, willing or no. Aoife feared seeing Thomas run off too, going as an aide to those fighting for the Union, despite they'd not call him soldier nor grant him pay. Each time a unit marched by, her heart shrank in fear. She could not manage the farm without him but knew why someone like him would feel the need to go.

After William set off on his fine horse and the dust from his mother's carriage had blown across the creek, Aoife went to Thomas. "Here," she said, blue bundle in her arms, "cloth left from that bought for my husband's uniform, enough for trousers and a vest at least. If you join the troops let it be in clothes that need no patches."

He shook his head. "No, ma'am, I won't take such fine goods. It wouldn't be fitting."

"Why not? Your woman sews well, better than myself. She could have them done in a trice."

"Lettie won't sew me a uniform. She won't let me go. And I'm needed here—I promised Mr. William to keep the farm safe. You as well." And he stuck to his work like a tick to a hound, even slept nights in the barn to be sure no foxes were at the chickens, no bears or wolves molesting the other stock. He kept his shotgun beside him, William's old long rifle leaning against the straw pile.

Sunday mornings, he hitched their plow horse Maisy to the wagon and went to be with his Lettie, who had refused to work for Aoife once William left.

The woods were uncanny quiet while Aoife was alone, with only the hooting of owls and the screams of rabbits dying in the dark to keep her company. She shivered then, with remembrance of childhood terrors. When her mam's lullaby had failed to bring sleep, she kept her child abed with fear, what with her tales of the Banshee—the wailing ghosts—and the Abhartach, the drinker of blood.

Thomas always returned long after nightfall from his visits to Lettie. Aoife was glad of it, though he seemed sunk deep in thought. Or sad. She knew he was near wore out, what with the work of two men and so falling behind. One day, she went to him with his morning meal rather than have him come to the kitchen door. "Thomas, teach me to hitch Maisy to the light new plow, so you can take the oxen. We can then cover both fields."

He stood rubbing his eyes, used to rising an hour before her. "The mare is hard to handle, more skittish than I like for plowing, at least for someone weak or little used to the work."

"The oxen pull the heavy old plow easier, and you're strong enough to keep it on the straight. I've already milked and turned the cows to pasture. Fed the chickens, too." Aoife allowed no more argument. "Eat first. There's ham and eggs and coffee in the pail. I'll tidy the kitchen and return." She took two steps away and added, "Having myself been a servant, I'm used to work and stronger than you think. Keep the cloth I offered. It's said to be a harsh winter."

When she returned to find the food eaten, the egg sopped up with a slice of bread, he was ready.

"I'll hitch her," he said.

"No. I need to learn it all, should the farm work fall on me alone." A shiver ran through her at the thought of William dying far away and leaving her alone forever. There was no other she would wed. "Who knows what the future will bring? They may yet draft you and the other colored men."

Thomas shrugged and brought the hames collar. He laid it at her feet.

"Oof," she cried, lifting it toward Maisy's neck. It was fearsome heavy.

"Lot of iron under the leather," Thomas said. "Keeps the pulling even and so keeps from chafing the horse's hide." And then, "Damn her!" as the mare tossed her head and half reared.

Aoife dropped the collar as the mare's hooves came down.

"She is little used to you," Thomas said. "Horses hate to work and so make everything hard. They're stupid beasts, injure themselves every chance they get. Too much like some people."

Aoife gave him a look and hoisted the collar again with both hands, but Maisy shied away once more, despite the crossties. He covered laughter with a cough and shook his head. "Don't let her get away with it. Jerk her head back down. Hold it close. Show her you're the mistress."

All his laugh had done was increase her determination to show he wasn't her better, that her wishing to work wasn't feminine folly, that, William or no, she was indeed mistress over more than the mare. Balancing the collar on the ground, against her skirt, she pulled on the halter to bring the horse's head around. The mare rolled her eyes like a wild thing, frightening Aoife, though she refused to show it. "Wait, didn't my husband put blinders on her when he worked her, to keep her from spooking?"

He laughed again, a bit more in the open. Had she been made a fool?

"Thomas!" She stamped her foot. "You'll not get me to quit, despite all the trickery in the world. The crops need to be in, and one man cannot do it alone."

His laugh burst out then and he bent over to breathe, his hands on his thighs. Seemed the thought of her working the farm was the funniest thing in the world.

Aoife insisted. "Thomas, I am owner here, and manager of the farm in my husband's absence." Her words served well. His laughter ceased and, at last, he nodded.

That morning he walked with her behind the plow, helping guide the mare to keep the furrows straight. After midday, he left Maisy and Aoife alone in the field and returned with the oxen hitched to the old plow. While he was gone, she'd ripped cloth from her worn petticoat to wrap the blisters on her hands.

Thomas

1861

Every Sunday Thomas went to the little church by the river with his Lettie, though he hated how the women wailed like lost souls and fell to the ground, senseless. An education provided him by the Quakers had taught the value of silence.

He remained deep in thought on the solitary drive back to the farm, only using his dusty voice to say, "Giddap, Maisy," pulling the reins to keep her from cropping the roadside weeds. His thoughts were much on his situation and its contrast with his employer's.

Mr. William's wife went at the farm work with grit and determination and was to be admired for that. Sometimes envy stabbed his heart at the sight of her, half-stumbling behind her plow, even falling on one knee every now and then, but getting up and moving on. Not that he begrudged Mr. William such a wife, going off as he did, so eager to fight.

Thomas wished he and Lettie were, like Mr. William and his wife, a team, yoked through life like the two oxen to the plow, working to gain something of their own. But Lettie was not such a partner and never would be. He knew that it was what made her Lettie, and so put such thoughts aside. He loved her, even the anger running through her like a vein of gold in the darkness of a mine. Her anger was well-earned.

Thomas mourned for who she had been. He longed for that Lettie and the future which had gleamed before them at the start, when they first met in Philadelphia, close by the Quaker school where he'd been taught to read and write and make his parents proud. It was sunny, but only minutes after rain had fallen, and the cobblestones still shone wet. Walking down those stones was a small, slender girl struggling to close a tattered umbrella.

"Miss, may I assist you?" He walked toward her, drawn by the warmth of her tawny skin and the dark tangle of her russet hair. As he did, a tinge, like the blush on a ripe Maryland peach, rose to her cheeks. And when he saw her eyes—like polished chalcedony—he felt his heart stop with desire. He bowed and she handed over the umbrella, and soon herself, to him.

But now, much as Thomas loved his Lettie, her anger tired him. He was often glad to leave her in their little room in town, while he stayed in the barn and got his meals handed out the back door. Until the day William's missus wanted to learn how to work like a man. The day Aoife came to where he slept and brought his food to him.

Chapter 4

AFTER THE POLICE LEFT, Iris watched the crimson cardinal until it was chased by a pair of jays, both vividly blue. It seemed to her the birds here were cartoon-colored, as if designed to be uplifting, sudden bursts of brilliance in a drab world, their appearance echoing the cardinal's happy sound.

As a courtesy, the police officer returned a day later to speak with Iris and Benny. From all evidence, including the discoloration of the skin, the clothes in which the baby had been dressed, and the bag's cloth, the coroner immediately felt he was about one hundred and sixty or so years dead. A complete autopsy and further tests would potentially narrow down when the child died. They said no more.

The county dredged the pond for more remains and any other artifacts. "Sorry for the disturbance." The head technician was a tall, stoop-shouldered man with a Van Dyke like Benny's but not as gray. He was polite but vaguely pompous, reminding Iris of the Geico gecko. "We simply can't assume the baby was the only one interred." He shrugged. "It also might be that we're wrong about how long ago he died."

They brought up bent, hand-forged nails, coins, animal bones, pottery shards, and other detritus, but found nothing they could link to the child. It seemed they were at a standstill when it came to clues about what had transpired or who the baby was.

Once they were told the autopsy determined the child's death had occurred more than a hundred years ago, Benny found the baby fascinating. "I always thought peat bog bodies were only in Europe," he said, coming down from his study, where he now spent hours researching online. "I just discovered America had them, too, in Florida. Native Americans from 7,000 years ago. Perfectly preserved bones! And now we have one of our own, a real peat bogger." He nearly bounced on his toes with excitement. "Our pond must have been shaded enough to make conditions right. Down deep in the silt the water's probably acidic. Anaerobic, to boot. Nothing organic rots much without oxygen."

Benny settled into the armchair across from where Iris sat knitting him a new wool sweater—his favorite deep blue—for the East Coast winters. They'd needed nothing as warm in California and Benny loved when she made things for him.

"Would you like some tea?" she asked from her own, her favorite, chair, the one with millefleur tapestry, expensive and handwoven in Italy. "We have that local wildflower honey."

"Actually, I think I'd like a Scotch and soda," he replied, though he rarely drank. The research had put him in a celebratory mood.

She went to the cabinet in the crumbling, outdated kitchen, a temporary place to store liquor until their good furniture could be brought in, returned with the Scotch, and resumed her knitting. But even one drink made him loquacious. He prattled on about interesting findings vis-à-vis those deaths safely dated eons ago. That the pool on their property was the site of an interment seemed not to faze him at all. Instead, it was merely the gateway to contemplation that took his mind off the plumber failing to show.

Their little Baby Doe—the local press preferred that to John Doe—began to attract attention. A serious-looking youngish woman with a white streak in her long curly russet hair, a doctoral candidate in the cultural anthropology and history of Southeast Pennsylvania, and an overweight woman near their age who introduced herself as a "bestselling writer" were especially persistent. The older one was more than persistent. Pushy, really.

They might have wanted to see the corpse, but Iris had moved quickly after the coroner's office concluded no recent crime was involved, that a good faith attempt to locate relatives would be useless, and the cost of formal interment wasn't something the county would pay. She couldn't let the tiny body or the baby's ashes linger in a drawer or be placed in an unmarked grave. She almost placed the urn in the ground by the pond but couldn't imagine doing that without a long and upsetting discussion with Benny, if it was even legal. She knew it was definitely illegal back in California.

Iris paid for a DNA sample—the report to be sent to her—and drove the backroads to find a serene graveyard in whose shade she could imagine sitting quietly, reading or knitting. Keeping the baby company. She found the ideal spot—the yard of the oldest church in the area—and had the baby's ashes buried in an antique silver urn. A gravestone could be ordered later—maybe it was possible to get a weathered antique marble one, even if the engraving would look new.

Built in 1749 and still in use, the brick church's life spanned the time the baby would have been buried if he'd had a proper grave instead of being submerged in their pond. In a way, Iris thought it was like she was standing in for the mother he should have had.

After the burial, Iris visited the florist in town, wishing she already had a garden to plunder, one overgrown with heirloom flowers, one she'd tended herself. She dithered for a while, uncertain, and finally bought the most elegant, the most fragrant tuberoses, an armload of them, and a Victorian-looking glass vase to hold them. She nestled the vase in the not-yet-settled dirt of the grave and packed some around the bottom to keep it upright. Kneeling, she said a prayer, something she hadn't done in decades.

After stopping at the supermarket on the way home, she began to fret. Her floral choice seemed off, all wrong. What infant ever responded to white flowers? She should have picked a riot of colors, all bright: red, blue, yellow, orange, clashing with each other, dazzling to the eye. She pictured the infant alive, imagined him already grown into a chubby toddler sitting on the grass beneath the oaks, reaching out with dimpled fingers, ready to crush blooms and cram them in his mouth.

Iris knew if such a child were hers, she would laugh and take the little dimpled wrist in her hand, peel open the fingers one by one until the broken petals all dropped to the ground and substitute a teething cookie. *A mother is always prepared,* she chuckled ironically to herself. *Just like a scout.*

She arrived home to find the workers gone, leaving a scrim of stone grit and sawdust over every surface in the kitchen. Plastic obscured the dining room windows, clouding the sunlight and making the already dark-paneled space even gloomier. It was hard to hold onto the image in her mind of the walls painted a soft, aged white, the big oak table set, candles at the ready, and wine glasses out for guests. The rusted radiators boomed hollowly, and the house seemed to brood as if resenting the changes.

Benny wasn't alone in the living room. The writer was with him; her broad bottom, upholstered in an unflattering and loud tropical print, was cozily settled in Iris's armchair. The one Iris loved. The woman's dyed head—a bright improbably-youthful gold—was nodding to something Benny was saying. They each had mugs of tea, and Freddy lay between them.

"Hello, nice to see you again," the woman said without rising, as if the house was her home, the carefully upholstered chair hers, and Iris just a visitor.

"Likewise." Iris felt her lips tighten, more into a grimace than a welcoming smile. The pressure shot into her teeth and jaw joints—if she wasn't careful, she'd wind up with a headache. "Sorry, but I've forgotten your name."

Without waiting to hear a response, she went into the kitchen with a bag of food cradled in her arms, bumping the door open with her behind. She called over her shoulder, "Benny, there's more in the car. They're heavy."

"In a minute," he said. "We're in the middle of something."

"It's hot out and I bought frozen stuff." Her answer and the tone in which it was said made her feel like a shrew. She wasn't sure why the writer irked her so much. Hadn't she told Benny she wanted them to reach out, meet new people here, have friends? She sniffed several times, a habit of hers whenever she was uncertain, and began to put away the groceries.

When Freddy pushed open the door with his nose, hoping she'd gotten something for him, she looked down and said, "Disloyal dog!" His tail drooped and he went to his water bowl as if that had been his aim all along.

Their unrenovated kitchen darkened her mood. It was the worst, most derelict room in the house and dimly lit, which made cutting vegetables and meat dangerous at Iris's age—she was constantly nicking herself. The dark-stained wood cabinets, handmade by a previous owner with little skill at carpentry and a fetish for mid-fifties country scrollwork decor, had doors hanging askew and insides disintegrating into sawdust. The designer Iris hired had created plans for a beautiful galley kitchen, but the contractors all were backlogged, some up to two years. The quarantine had interrupted work on many projects and slowed it on others, what with trouble getting workers and supply chain issues for everything. Especially her big range with double ovens, back ordered six months.

Things were going as well as they could, considering; then why was she so ill at ease and testy?

She couldn't complain to Benny about something she'd gotten them into, and she sure couldn't blame him for it. But somehow her irritation with him had grown with all the curious people coming to view the pond—an intrusion into their marriage, their privacy. This writer was the worst, invading the small area of the house they'd cleared out for some of their furniture, the small area that felt homey. The rest was taken up with drywall sheets, buckets of paint and general dereliction.

And the baby from their pond wasn't the way to make friends or to meet new people. He wasn't a curiosity; he was someone's tragedy, like their own little girl. Why couldn't Benny understand that?

And yet, she knew why. His best friend, who served with him in the Tet Offensive, had committed suicide thirty years after the war, and his second-best buddy waited only another five to follow suit. Friends were tough for Benny. Especially male friends. He often dreamed about them, awakening sweaty and confused in the middle of the night.

But this woman irked her. Round as she was, she still seemed to have sharp, intrusive, dangerous corners. Benny seemed more relaxed with her than he did with Iris lately.

When Benny brought the remaining bags to the kitchen, Iris asked, "Is she vaccinated? She's not wearing a mask."

He leaned his hip against the counter and crossed his arms. "Since when are you so particular?"

"Me? Particular?" Iris turned, feeling a sudden flash of anger.

Benny's breath quickened and one hand slid stealthily up to press the side of his chest. "It's rude to keep referring to her as *she*. Her name's Jessica Hartnup. We've had a great discussion about researching the body from our pond. Jessica wants to write about it."

It? Iris thought. *He's not an it. He's not this Jessica woman's baby. This isn't her place. You're not her husband.*

To Iris, Jessica Hartnup, who described herself as penning "cozy mysteries," whatever that meant, was a ghoul, coming to their house to use the child as a plot for a popular novel.

Aoife

1861

Never had she slept so deeply, despite being alone in their bed, worried about her dear, her William. It was the work, of course. When she'd been a maidservant, she'd carried buckets of water, heated in the kitchen, up the stairs to Mother Sprigett's room for filling her tin bath. And later emptying that bath as, every morning, she carried down her mistress's sloshing, stinking chamber pot. She'd hauled away the ashes and laid the fires, scrubbed the floors and swept the dust off the carpets. But she'd never sweated a full day under the sun, forcing a heavy plow to stay upright. She'd never stayed awake at night, helping birth a calf turned wrong in its mother's belly.

Thomas in the barn, gun at the ready, his dog on guard, was the other reason she got her rest, rather than lying awake fearing strangers roaming the woods. Each time she turned her head on the pillow she thought, *Bless him.*

And *Bless my loving husband, for making sure I am so protected.*

Aoife hoped for post from William, as such would be proof that he was alive, but for days none arrived. She went to town for news and heard his unit had gone down to Virginia, to a place called Manassas, where there was to be a great battle. Being ignorant of the distance, she inquired of the folk gathered 'round the posted broadsheet, though the ladies moved together and used their crinolines to close rank against her. It seemed Manassas was a great march away, but there William and his fellows would meet many others, and that gave her hope. She had always been told there was safety in numbers for fish in a shoal, for birds in a flock, and for men in a war.

At last, the postal office had a letter for her. From William, of course, for there was none else to write. She put it safe in the bosom of her dress, longing for word her dear was safe.

On her way home, letting Maisy walk as she would, it was fearsome hot, and sweat ran down her neck beneath her high collar. The damp between her breasts prickled most unpleasantly. Fearing the letter would be ruined, she opened two buttons again to draw the paper out.

She broke the seal and opened it. Drawings of brown canvas tents, sagging some in the middle, fronted by little cook fires picked out in red ink, and on the paper's other side, sketches of uniformed men, lined up, rifles over their shoulders. Writing, too, which squirmed across the page going down and then sideways, perhaps to save space. Even could she read, sure it all would have made her head spin. Being unable to read made the day hotter and the mustiness beneath her arms worsen, until she could barely stand her own stink.

The cart squeaked along, stop and start, stop and start. She was always quick to grab her chance, was their Maisy. As they moved on the mud of the road, jouncing in the ruts, the mare swung her head from one side to the other for a bite of thistle, chewing as she straggled on her way back to the barn. Aoife paid no heed to her sloth—tears dropped down to her lap until she saw the letters bleed and hastened to put the paper aside.

Thomas had said the fighting at Manassas, now called Bull Run for the close-by creek, was sure to be fierce, with many losses and wounds. Her William would face—might already have faced—the enemy, far from her sight. Might be he lay bleeding and his wife, his loving Aoife, would not be knowing. Might be he'd written the letter full of false cheer and dangerous bravery.

Reaching her house, Aoife handed the reins to Thomas and, carrying the letter tight in her hand, ran to the big house, to William's mother herself.

She banged on the door and called out. A maid answered, one she'd tried to befriend when she, too, had worked in the big house.

"If it ain't Miss High and Mighty," the girl said. "What's yer want?"

"Is Mother Sprigett at home?"

"Mother Sprigett it is now? No longer *ma'am* or *the mistress?*"

"Please, has she news of William? May I see her? I have a letter." Aoife held up the missive.

"She has said, should you come, you are to be turned away." The door was slammed in her face.

Aoife wandered slow back home, her sobs nearly taking her breath away, her steps unsteady, her eyes shedding many a tear.

At any hour, she might find herself widowed.

Thomas

1861

Thomas unhitched the mare once the carriage was sheltered in the barn. He put Maisy into the paddock just outside her stall and brought a full bucket to her trough, keeping an eye on the missus, who'd returned from the big Sprigett house with eyes swollen and red. She had seated herself on the steps to the kitchen door, appearing to him like a sack that had been emptied out.

Thomas went back into the barn and brushed Maisy's gray coat, flaking away the mud. All the while, his mind was troubled by the distress of Mr. William's wife. He knew she loved her husband and missed him sorely, but before this, she'd shown little outward sign. Perhaps that was pride. It was not his place to ask. He resolved to keep his distance until she returned to herself.

The day wore on, growing hotter under the sullen sky, which seemed to press down and flatten the crops in the fields and still the birds in the sky, buzzards drifting in lazy circles looking for something dead. *They would have better luck over the battlefields.*

The dog had helped him move the sheep to fresh pasture and bring the cows into the barn's shade for Aoife, who had, for the first time, neglected their care, though the weather might stop their milk, and there were late calves still needing that milk to thrive and grow enough for slaughter. It was only good husbandry to be cautious—the army paid top dollar for salted beef and decent hides.

Midday came and went, but not the midday meal. Evening was approaching, and still William's wife hadn't moved. Thomas's stomach growled with hunger until, at last, he went to her, holding his hat in hand. "Missus," he said, "would it trouble you too much for me to have a bit of bread?"

It took a moment for her eyes to lift to his and during that moment, he saw her face was reddened until small blisters had risen on her nose and chin. "You'd best go in the kitchen yourself and put butter on your face, for it is burnt. Unlike my own, your skin is not made for the summer sun."

Her hands went to her cheeks. She almost stood but her legs shook, perhaps from sitting so long. He had never touched her before, but now took her arm in his hand and made certain she didn't fall. She shook his hand off as if it had caused her offense.

He stepped back. "Sorry, ma'am."

"Come with me," was her response. She led him into the kitchen.

"Butter?" He hoped she could spread it on the burned area herself, missing no area to blain and fester. No area to scar and mar her skin.

She went to the table where a butter keeper stood. "Wait here. I need my mirror." She took the butter and went from the room. Her footsteps echoed as she climbed stairs.

The kitchen was a well-kept room, the great hearth had been swept and wood for a new fire laid. Dishes stood upright on a rack in a wall-hung cabinet and clean cloths hung below on a dowel. It was a homey place and once again, he envied her husband.

"Thomas." She had returned, her face dotted here and there with yellow flecks of butter. "Here is a heel of bread with cheese. And..." She put her hand up to her cheek as if to think, and said, "Oh!" when it came away slick with grease. "In fretting about your hunger, I had forgotten."

He laughed, not meaning to as it felt disrespectful to her, not when she had been so sad. She still was, it seemed, though her feelings were hidden beneath a shiny layer reflecting the lamplight, and her face showed nothing. "Thank you, ma'am," he said. "Let me go check the byre and see if they need feed."

They didn't. He'd checked not an hour before.

She glanced at the table and up at him, and with a sigh said, "Come to the door when you're done, then. For a proper supper, what with the missing of midday."

When he returned and glanced in the door, there was a new-lit fire, despite the heat. A chicken, plucked and gutted, was hanging from the crane. Beneath it, a frying pan to catch the fat. He smiled to himself—it seemed she practiced her cookery, perhaps to please her husband once he returned.

"Rest you on the steps a while," she said to him. "Let me put the potatoes in the drippings and go to the garden for celery. 'Tis good to have a bit of salad."

Chapter 5

"**HOW OLD IS THIS HOUSE?**" Jessica Hartnup asked. Her tea had been drunk and she now held a glass with ice clinking moistly amid a good amount of Scotch. From the bottle of Benny's best. Benny had the same. Her ass was even more deeply settled into Iris's armchair. "Do you know?"

"Not really," Iris said. "It looks late Victorian to me. The high ceilings and all."

Benny added, "When we bought it, we were told 1890s or there about."

"Oh, no," Jessica's voice sounded disingenuous, as if imitating a dove's coo. She pointed to the floor beyond the rug. "I think you got a real oldie-but-goody, Ben. Look at all those different sized square-head nails in the pumpkin pine. Nails like that were made one by one. In the second half of the 1800s, mass-produced nails were too available to make that kind of effort worthwhile. And the large fireplace for cooking at the west end of the dining room also makes it a lot older than late Victorian. They mostly used cookstoves by then."

"Really?" Benny sat forward. "You think my house is that old?"

My house? Iris thought. Sitting on the hard chair made her back hurt.

"Yup. The hearth has the hand-forged iron crane to hang roasting meat and stews in their pots, bubbling away."

Bubbling away? The damn woman even talks like a cheesy novel. But she'd thought some of Jessica Hartnup's comments herself, without mentioning them. After all, the burned-on stains on the back of the fireplace were dense enough to be hundreds of years old. Their real-estate agent and his website could have been wrong, misled by almost three centuries of additions.

Before this Hartnup woman, Benny would have corrected Iris if she'd told him she believed the house was pre-Revolutionary War. He'd have told her again what the real-estate agent had said, despite those handmade nails and the eighteen-inch-thick walls of the square center of the house. Before this writer showed up, he'd had no interest in their home's history. In response to her enthusiasm, he always replied, "You like charm and I like modern plumbing," his tone implying this time she'd gotten her way.

But now he was taking proud ownership of their "derelict money pit."

Iris sniffed.

"Well," Jessica said, "I suppose I'll just go to the county recorder and look it up to make sure. I should be able to come back here in the next month or so." She smiled in Benny's direction and then was quiet for a moment, as if deep in thought. "It may take quite a long time researching, as the oldest deeds were hand recorded. Most have never been uploaded."

The mystery writer told them she lived almost an hour away, outside Princeton. She frequently went to New York to meet with her editor and, regretfully, that would also keep her from coming sooner.

Iris spent the rest of the visit trying to be hospitable, even asking if Jessica would like to have dinner with them, but the writer interlaced her thick fingers and replied with a tinkly little laugh, "My dinner tonight is at Le Folio. A producer is wooing me for my latest." And then, as if such a backwater resident wouldn't know, she added, "Le Folio is the hottest new place in Manhattan."

Iris and Benny had been invited to dine at Le Folio by old friends but had yet to go. She shot a narrowed-eye glance at her husband, silently demanding he tell Jessica about the invitation, but he remained oblivious, happily chatting. She followed suit, declining to appear petty or competitive. Not wanting to give Jessica the satisfaction of having provoked her.

After Jessica left, Benny went to the kitchen to prepare himself another drink, which he obviously viewed as a celebratory one. "It's nice to have such a well-known author as a friend, isn't it? Someone like her, intellectual, like the people we knew back home. Such a fascinating woman, interested in history. I could talk with her all night." He laughed, "Who knows, Washington could have slept here before crossing the Delaware."

"We just met her, Benny."

He swirled the liquor in his glass. "And to think you were so adventuresome when I met you, a free spirit, up for anything and anybody. You were supposed to bring fun back into my life." He reached down to pat the dog and his expression softened. "Sorry. I shouldn't be so testy. Let's make up."

That evening, Iris and Benny fed Freddy then headed out to a restaurant close by the river, an upscale place with outdoor seating to accommodate diners during the pandemic.

"Hey!" Benny pointed at a huge building as they drove. It was all stone to the roof. "I remember a picture of that barn in your family album. I thought it was odd, a barn not painted red like all the ones you see in magazines." He'd been raised in Baltimore and still saw everything rural as stereotypically cute, something out of *Green Acres* reruns.

Seeing the barn, Iris felt a wave of nostalgia wash over her, a flash of memory, of sitting small in the backseat of the family Ford. Though she barely reached the top of the dash, she'd seen the barn through the split windshield. *When did cars stop dividing the driver's view of the world from the passengers'?*

The gray wool upholstery had itched her bare legs in the sweltering heat, her bladder ached with the need to pee. Her mother, Gwen, rarely stopped on the drive up from Philadelphia and then only for a farm stand in season. One time Iris wet the seat and her mother said, "I told you to go before we left home. Now you'll sit in it until we head back."

She'd seen the barn on several trips and noticed the horses in the paddock next to it. Arabs, rare at the time but, even from a distance, beautiful with delicate scoop-nosed heads and arched necks. "Stop!" she'd yelled to her mother.

Horses were the things she loved best in the world after her long-lost cat, a mostly orange calico, who had mysteriously disappeared after using the bathtub as a toilet. "That was a sign she wanted to move," her mother said when little Iris asked, taking a break from stirring a pot to light another Marlboro. "Didn't like it here."

Something in her mother's voice had been funny then and wasn't funny that day in the car; it wasn't just that her words had made no sense, since the calico loved sleeping in bed with Iris and catching mice in the damp, scary basement. But one thing the memory of her mother's tone made clear—there would be no stopping for the horses. Before her mother drove by, Iris had lifted her Brownie box camera and taken an image blurred by speed, just to remember the one thing she'd loved about drives in the country, drives she didn't want to take. That was the photo in the album.

Whenever she thought of that barn, those Arabians, she vowed to be a better mother than her own had been. One who'd stop and ask if her kid could pet the horses. If their little girl had lived, Iris would have stopped for anything and everything she wanted.

Iris was touched that Benny remembered the photo. They hadn't looked at her family album in years, not since before all those things happened. Maybe the barn had stood out to him since most of the other photos featured her mother—her pretty face prominent in each shot. In the decades before selfies, little Iris had been Gwen's portraitist.

An artist, a nervy, chain-smoking beauty, Gwen had produced scant artwork, but in the '60s, she still had friends in New Hope's dwindling colony of painters. She took frequent trips to visit them, bringing her daughter unwillingly along.

When it came to her art, nothing stood in Gwen's way. She believed creativity made its possessors special, deserving of whatever they wanted. Ordinary people, the peons, includeing Iris's father—already working two jobs to make the mortgage—needed to give to the creative and provide for them, expecting nothing in return.

Iris often joked about kids being traumatized, hearing animal noises coming from their parents' bedrooms. "All I ever heard was my mother saying, 'Well, Dean, are you done yet?' Which from an adult point of view was even more traumatizing."

Now, Iris worried that Benny was like her father, newly in thrall to a woman who, he believed, would bring something elevated, something non-pedestrian, something creative to his life. In thrall—even in a minor way—to Jessica Hartnup, *cozy mystery writer.*

Rather than cede anything to the writer, Iris resolved to do her own research on the house and its owners now that the renovations were—at least temporarily—at a stage where little could go wrong. Maybe it would be possible to find clues to the baby's family along with the property's history. Going to the county recorder and bothering busy clerks seemed a bit daunting, so she planned to start at the library, where she could also check out Jessica Hartnup's books. No way would she pay for them.

Aoife

1861

Aoife came near to asking Thomas to sit at table with her, just to have a body for conversing a bit. Not as William and she had done, laughing and touching each other on the cheek, taking hands across the table. Kissing. His body pressing hard against her as she stood at the basin, teasing arms about her waist as she washed the plates.

The thought of William's hands on her, his body, brought feelings like liquid from the well on a hot day, dripping and dripping until the pump brought it all in a gush. All pouring down to one spot between her thighs, the spot that sprang to life with his touch.

William was far, far away. What she longed for was not to be had. She was here, alone, with no one to console her. She had even lost the company of Mrs. Sprigett's other servants. Scarcely friendly before, they had not the energy for visits. Their free time was spent at prayer or in much-needed sleep.

Time to time, Aoife thought of attending mass, hoping that, among the Catholics were some who, like her mam and dadai, had come fleeing the Great Famine and so understood hard choices. But most around here were English Catholic, come more than a hundred years before, and now were respectable. Her mouth closed up near any of those and shyness overtook her.

It wasn't just longing for a few friendly words, or a story about the beasts out in the fields, their well-being and care. The letter's coming hung heavy in her heart. Its paper, folded along the lines her William had made, his fingers pressing down, was now under the wooden box which held the silver comb and brush set he'd bought for her long rose-gold hair.

The letter was so dear to Aoife that she wished to spend the day kissing each word, but kisses would soften the stiff paper, dampen it, and cause it to fall to bits, still unread. And so, the days slowly passed.

Thomas

1861

Thomas spent Sunday, as usual, with his Lettie, bringing fresh produce from the kitchen garden, which the missus gave him, despite Lettie being so unfriendly to her. He had also a part-eaten ham from the spring house, the full bone for her to boil up greens, and plenty of meat left besides. This he'd taken of his own accord, bold as that seemed. If the missus mentioned it later, he'd apologize if she made mention of it being missing.

The room he'd rented for Lettie was small, almost a lean-to, at the back of a brick house in the tiny colored section of the town, but he had installed a small stove for cooking and heating. The laundry Lettie took in was boiled in a big cauldron in the courtyard, beside the well.

Thomas put down the food when he reached the room but otherwise kept his counsel, though his heart sank upon seeing Lettie. She didn't leap up as she'd done time to time in the past, dancing about with joy at the sight of him or offering hugs and kisses. Even the full lips that had been so enchanting were shrunken. She seemed melted away in soul and body, limp and wilted, sitting on their narrow bed as if nailed in place.

Thomas knew Lettie was in another of her black moods and doing only what she must, neglecting her work as a laundress. He opened the tin in which they kept their savings and found little had been added and again, made no comment. The dream of a home of their own was all to depend on him alone.

He thought of William's wife, a small figure on the kitchen steps, letting herself burn in the sun, ruining her pale skin, all for the love of her husband.

"Thomas," Lettie said at last, without turning her great gray eyes to him, "the war goes badly. The South will win. They will come here after me."

He sat beside her on the bed and put an arm around her shoulder. "Just one battle lost, Lettie. One battle lost doesn't mean the war is lost."

"We hear news on the street..." Her fingers picked at the quilt. A small area was already frayed, near bare like the cloth the missus used to make cheese. "If you were here, you could read the broadsheets aloud to me."

"I cannot be here, not and get the land I was promised." A small flame of anger sparked in his heart. "Though I would have gone to war, had you but let me."

"They won't let you be a soldier," Lettie went on, her words nearly poisonous with bitterness.

What she said was true. If he had joined, Thomas would be only a servant to an officer. But if the officer was Mr. William, Thomas might help keep him alive and he and his missus might be generous in gratitude.

Lettie's bitterness drove her words, "Their hearts ain't in the fight for us but to preserve their precious Union. I'll never see my brothers again, unless..."

So the old fear, that they would come for her again, would get her this time as they'd gotten her sister, was back full force. "Lettie, I am sure the Union, with so many more men and equipment will, in due time, sweep the field and the war will be brief. The folks 'round here will never let the catchers come again. Never. They're good people; they've hidden more than you know."

She stiffened under his arm. "Didn't hide me or my sister."

"You two had yet to reach here. You were still down in Maryland."

She didn't say more, but the tears running down her face spoke for her as her gaze went unfocused, far into the past. His Lettie was back in her mind, again hiding deep in a flowery bush, watching the riders cut her sister down.

Thomas had hoped his affection, his loving touch, would bring calm, but when he reached for her, she sighed, laid back and let him have his weekly release. She never turned to him as she once had done, with eager and greedy desire.

The little room was tense as a breath held, and he easily realized for what it was bated, and that was for Lettie's tattered remains of family, scattered though they be.

It pained his heart to leave her when Sunday's sun waned in the sky, but Thomas stuck to his goal and returned to his work for Mr. William and his wife. Should Mr. William's Union win, and Lettie's family be freed, they'd need a place to welcome and to shelter them.

Chapter 6

THE RESTAURANT HAD LOVELY outdoor seating, bushes shielding them from the road, the waitstaff carefully masked for the waning pandemic.

Benny ordered a pork chop with gremolata; Iris, wild mushroom stroganoff made with oat milk sour cream. While they waited for the food to come, he held her hand across the table, rubbing her knuckles with his left thumb. "You know, honey," he said after a sip of his Cabernet Franc, "I think I'm going to be very happy living here."

"I hope so," Iris replied, again eager to try making her optimism contagious. "Our house could really be lovely. A showplace you'll be proud of. We can do some planting soon. Forsythia and redbud. Maybe lilacs if we can fence out the deer."

"Could be lovely?" Benny lifted his head to emphasize the irony. "I have complete confidence you'll make it so."

Their dishes were put on the table, pausing their discussion. Iris hoped the interruption wouldn't snap the thread of pleasant conversation.

Benny thanked the waiter and picked up his fork and knife. His pork chop was huge, glistening with liquid from the parsley topping. He cut a bit of meat and put it into his mouth.

"Good?" she asked. She was quite enjoying her earthy mushroom dish.

He nodded, then looked at the table again as his fork stabbed into her cream-covered noodles. He chewed for a moment. "Not bad. I was wondering if the oat milk stuff would be god-awful. It looks kind of grayish."

Benny taking bites of her food without asking had never bothered Iris, but she could have done without the commentary. Her dish now looked as if it had been made with dishwater. She concentrated on her side salad and the rather good bread and butter.

They ate in silence for a while and then Benny, over a slice of cake with coffee *crème anglaise*, looked up into her eyes. "I was talking with Hal about our mysterious pond find."

Though Benny seemed comfortable when someone else was talking about the body they'd found, he was still uncomfortable talking about it himself, even to their adopted son, Hal. Even with her. Especially referring to her little John Doe as "a dead baby."

"How is Hal?" A little stab of guilt struck her. After failing to adopt an infant, they'd taken Hal when he was a teen, impressed by his achievement in school, in staying out of trouble despite being homeless and with an addict mother who'd lost custody of him. Iris loved him, she really did, but he'd kept her at arms' length saying, "I already got me a mom."

"Have a mom," she'd corrected without thinking.

Time—and the death of his birth mother—had strengthened their relationship. Grown up now, a university graduate with a good job in technology, he called her "mom" and his kids called her "grandma," but they were never as close as he and Benny, the only father Hal had ever known.

"He's doing great. Coincidentally, he read one of Jessica's novels. Ruthie bought it on her Kindle. Hal had insomnia one night and nothing else to read. Said it wasn't bad." Benny took another sip of his coffee. "Oh, and they're trying for another baby."

Hal had married Ruthie, who looked almost exactly like a young Iris. For quite a while, Benny and Iris had pondered whether that was strange, but as the marriage flourished, that concern faded. And now Ruthie and Hal had two children, both with café au lait skin, blue-gray eyes, and tight blond curls.

Iris was diverted from thoughts of Hal as Benny again took her hand, rubbing the most sensitive part of her palm. When they were young, that had always been his way of indicating the desire for sex. Iris was surprised he remembered the maneuver. *How long had it been?*

"More coffee?" the server asked. Her downcast eyes above the obscuring mask made Iris think of *The Story of O*, lending a vaguely erotic air of privacy, anonymity, and danger.

Iris shook her head and the girl left.

"I really like your hair the way it is now—it's pretty, kind of like pewter. It shines, but discretely, with dignity. I'm glad you don't dye it." Benny's thumb was circling her palm lightly. It almost tickled. "And you don't wear makeup like lots of women. Some of them trowel it on."

Iris was wearing foundation, lipstick, eyeliner, and mascara. She smiled at him, deciding not to wonder if he really looked at her anymore or, like so many men, he just had no idea. The pressure of his thumb on her hand had increased.

The drive home was short. They took a different road than the one by the old barn. Iris looked at the passing landscape for anything else she remembered. At the midpoint of the trip, Benny put his hand on Iris's thigh and squeezed. "What d'ya say?"

Iris didn't answer but she didn't move her leg away either.

Benny skipped his usual nightcap. Instead, he dropped his coat on the sofa next to Iris's, and they went straight to bed.

She was up for an hour after Benny had fallen asleep, listening to him snore, thanking God that he'd been able to perform. For a long while, he'd had trouble, tense nights when, despite every approach she made, his penis lay in her hand like a rain-bloated worm. *What exactly had enabled him tonight? Who or what was different from the years so recently passed?*

She slipped into sleep. Her last conscious thought was, *Damn it, being old is so fucking tough.*

The next day, Benny, heading out to the postbox, winked and said, "Well, you really brought fun into my life last night!" The screen door slammed shut behind him.

He returned with the mail. The DNA report on their little John Doe had come in a large flat envelope. "Open it," he said, dropping next to her on the couch. "I'm really curious."

Iris slid her finger under the flap. "Ow!" she squealed at the paper cut that immediately dropped a spot on the paper. Benny handed her a tissue from the box on the coffee table. She wrapped the tissue tightly around her fingertip.

"Here, let me. You'll get blood all over it." Benny pulled the report from Iris's hands and read it silently.

"So what does it say?" Iris asked, poking Benny in his side. They were both in a good, jokey mood after last night. Approaching seventy or not, sex was still a bonding agent between them.

"The kid's George Washington's son." He grinned.

Iris laughed and batted him with her open hand. "No, really!"

"Okay. The DNA is 50 percent Irish descent. Southern Irish, that is, plus about a 25 percent mixed European, English and Northern French, and about 25 percent African American."

"Huh." The numbers made no sense for a moment. "So our baby boy was quite a mix."

"Yeah, but back then he'd only been thought of as black." He snorted a laugh. "Hell, probably the same today. Ask Hal."

What if he was born into slavery? The thought spun into Iris's mind like a blazing Catherines wheel. She voiced the worry aloud.

Benny, as usual, had an answer. "Didn't they give the outside time of his birth as about 1840? There basically weren't any slaves in Pennsylvania then."

Iris's shoulders relaxed. "Thank God."

"Well," he went on with an oddly cheerful air, "he could have been born to a runaway. Jessica told me about the Runaway Slave Act passed in 1850. Even if a slave on the lam was found in a free state—like Pennsylvania—they had to be returned to their owner."

Jessica? Was she the one to stir his interest in Iris's little John Doe? She decided to act enthused. "Do you think our house could have been on the Underground Railroad?"

Benny looked at her with something akin to the pity of one who knew better. "No, Iris. That was in the western part of the state. Get to the midpoint of Lake Erie and bingo! You're in Canada home free." He seemed to pause to let his newly acquired knowledge, delivered with grating condescension, sink in. And then he said, "Hey, what if he's older, maybe born to a slave and she didn't want him to suffer like her, so she drowned him? Seems that happened a good bit in Barbados, in the sugarcane fields. An act of desperation, I'd guess."

Iris refused to let herself start an argument, just because she again wondered if Benny and Jessica Hartnup were forming an exclusive little history club. Instead of letting her irritation get the better of her, she said, "I wonder if the DNA would help find living relatives, if there are any."

"Don't you think the detectives would have looked into that if it was important?"

Iris shook her head. "They told me the county wouldn't do genetic testing when a body was that old, with no identification, even if they thought it was murder. Too expensive for simple curiosity and the guilty party would be long dead."

"Well then, maybe it was a waste for us to get this report if it was too expensive for the county. Not to mention burying him in the cemetery. That was thousands. And what with all the work on the house..."

At least money was more important to him than Jessica and her celebrity! Iris wasn't sure how to respond. The morning's jovial camaraderie was gone. Outside, a jackhammer sounded; stonecutters had arrived to make more dust finishing the steps up to their guesthouse-potential barn. At the same time, Freddy began furiously barking at a knock on the door—workers had arrived with their buckets and white-stained tees, ready to smooth the inside walls.

The jackhammer and stone saw, combined with the workers' blaring music, made staying in the house intolerable. Her head felt like a balloon about to burst. She left the landscapers hard at work outside shaping bluestone and the plasterers up on ladders in the living room; took her laptop and headed to the library. Even if there was nothing about her property, general information about the county and the township in the mid-1800s would be interesting. Especially after the DNA results.

On the drive over, she realized Benny hadn't made a big deal about Jessica Hartnup in the morning's discussion. He had, instead, simply mentioned her in an aside showing his newly gained information. While it still irked Iris that he considered Jessica's opinion so important, when the writer had no degree and no legitimate claim to expertise, at least he seemed eager to learn more about the house he had instantly hated.

Was his interest in Jessica's opinion just that, interest in a friend who could make their property more intriguing, maybe even more valuable? Whatever, she'd still take out one or two of the woman's novels to get a clue of how anyone could envision getting a *cozy* mystery from the finding of a dead baby, even a long-ago death.

Iris parked at the library and sat in the car with her eyes closed. An image of a baby's face swam into her mind. The baby's face, one she never saw alive. His expression held a dreamlike quality beneath the mud's brown staining—delicate eyelids covering the globes, rosebud mouth slightly pursed as if ready to suck life from his mother's breast. Her baby, her and Benny's, must have looked like that, dreaming of being born.

Thomas

1861

William's wife had not cried again in front of Thomas, but still a pall of sadness dulled and blurred her in his sight. She kept busy and did not sink deep into melancholy as did his Lettie, who often spent days sitting at the window, looking to the south for something lost, or more like, something that never existed.

Lettie's eyes haunted him, strange pale as they were, nigh unto gray. They were like the ocean he visited once, just to see what their ancestors had been so unwillingly brought across. Instead of the evil blackness he had anticipated, in the sea he found something so huge, so untamed, as to make all the problems of humanity seem trivial. Or maybe in the ocean's sigh there lived profound regret in the folly of those who ruined the paradise they'd been granted by God Himself.

And yet the Atlantic's wild magnificence did not change his feelings. It only reminded him of Lettie's dark moods. Huge and untamed, that is how his love's sadness was, a wild and stormy thing inhabiting her soul, a vast wave always threatening to pull her under.

The missus's sorrow was different. It dwelt private, quiet, deep in her heart, hidden from Thomas. As she went about her work, her mouth moved with no sound, again and again. Her silent prayer was easy to parse out, "Please, Lord, please, Lord." It was not his place to ask for explanation, or to indicate he understood the unspoken words. He knew they referred to her beloved's safety.

For the reason of his two ladies' grief, he returned to the farm on that warm summer night, ready to offer some very salutary news—as no cotton was coming from the South, and scant English cloth making it through the blockades, the Army of the Potomac was desperate short of cloth. Wool from the flock could bring in enough for any improvements wished, from adding to the barn, or a new summer kitchen to make life easier for cooking during the hottest time.

And his extra effort to increase the wealth of young Mr. William Sprigett and his sweet-natured wife could mean extra pay for Thomas and so more security for Lettie. Mr. William might let the parcel go sooner or allow building a cottage upon it before it was even purchased. Hoping it wouldn't seem presumptuous, Thomas asked, "Perhaps in the next letter, you might apprise Mr. William? He'd be glad to know that those who scoffed at his father's flock were foolish."

"The next letter? I know not when that might be. 'Tis rare that I go into the town but each time, I check the post. Only one letter arrived from my husband, and in return I have sent none." She next said, "He drew me the camp, knowing his mother would not read his letters to me nor write any for me. And I have no other who would. Should he die, the old *bitseach bhradach* will keep that from me as well."

Her bitter words were more than surprising. Thomas hadn't considered she could neither read nor write—every grown person about could do so. There had been no reason for him to see her skill put to the test and so reveal her deficiency. Not until the war and her husband's absence.

Surprise must have marked his countenance, as she flushed, her sunburnt face growing redder. "William did try to teach me, but it wouldn't stick. Anyway, with no family or friends, what use had I for reading? My mam and dadai could neither read nor write. It was not seeming for me to be better than they."

She seemed so distressed that Thomas was thankful when she gave a little laugh. She asked, "Can you imagine me on a windowsill, curled up with a book as if one of William's sisters, raised to be idle? Whilst the roast sat raw on the table and the dishes on the sideboard? The rabbits making free with my kitchen garden?"

The young Sprigett ladies were strangers to Thomas, but he knew their kind if they were anything like their mother, high and mighty and better than all. Worthless women, believing that others were born to do for them, with their stiff-starched crinolines, long gloves, and dainty parasols. He felt a flash of hatred toward them until he realized it was by no fault of their own. They had been raised to be ladies, useless but for breeding, like one of their father's ewes.

"Well," Thomas said to Mr. William's wife, "he may have known of your resourcefulness and been content that you would find a way to decipher the contents of his letters."

She brightened at that, though her brow drew together, doubting.

"And now there is reason for you to learn reading. And sums if you wish."

Her brow tightened more, angry furrows appearing above her drawn-together brows. "Thomas, I will have you know that I can already do sums in my head, quicker than William for all his years in school. Numbers are known to me, as they are to anyone poor and so needing to count coin. Many charlatans walk the Earth, looking to cheat those who seem like dumb beasts." A brief huff came from her lips. "I am not dull-witted, Thomas, though I cannot read. Not stupid but just poor and born so."

"I beg your pardon, ma'am. I never thought of you as anything like that." He couldn't say the word *stupid*, not in reference to her.

She softened then, her face losing its tightness, and turned to go back into her kitchen. Then she paused. "This one letter, could you read it to me?"

"Of course," Thomas said, without a thought that he should deny her this for propriety's sake.

"Ah!" she exclaimed like a pleased child. She ran off to get the missive. When she returned, she had the paper open flat and, coming close, held it out to him.

Thomas shook his head and said, "Missus, perhaps your lessons in reading should start this very moment. At the school I attended in Philadelphia, the students who did best were those eager to learn, reading what drew their interest rather than a dull primer."

"No!" She pulled back the letter and pressed it against her bosom. "That will take too long! I promise to learn, but not today, not this letter. Come sit at table and I will sit across and listen."

He hesitated again, with a feeling of needing to right his world.

"Please, Thomas!"

Her pleading tone forced him to relent. *At the table would be good*, he thought. *We'd not need to sit close. The window will provide enough light to not need the kerosene lamp, despite us being out of the sun.* And so, they went in.

Aoife

1861

Aoife could not keep herself from shaking, though not from fear. It was hard to wait through Thomas's *ahems* and his sips of tea to get the hay dust from his throat. Longing to hear William's words started a tremble in her shoulders and arms.

Thomas spread the paper out on the table.

"You see," she said, pointing to the drawings, "knowing I cannot read, he has taken the trouble to show me his life in the military. But still, I want his words."

Thomas took up his meat knife. "Follow along," he said, "even if the words make no sense now. Follow the lines and perhaps learn a bit by memory." He wiped the knife's blade on his shirt and, without touching the letter, moved the point along as he read.

"My dearest, my best, my wife," was how William's letter began. Those sweet words made her tears fall onto the scoured wood and Thomas stopped reading. But she bade him begin again.

My dearest, my best, my wife,

First, let me set your mind at ease. I am sound and well, though sore from long hours in the saddle.

As for my mind's ease, it gives me great cheer to be sure you are true to me, and that I shall again lie next to you, the sun's rays warming our counterpane, whilst outside our window, the cardinals call out notes of joy. I might say more of what I wish, if you have since conquered your fear of reading.

Unlike lucky me, several of my men have received letters from faithless wives, declaring the loneliness was too hard to bear. Somehow, amid the great shortage of men, these women have taken up with others, the elderly, the infirm, and the cowards. I swear, those women should be horsewhipped until their great buttocks glow like embers!

Seeing how those discarded men suffer, it would be wrong to flaunt the great fortune that is mine, so I do not share my image of you with your crown of wildflowers. That image I keep in the breast pocket of my long coat.

As for the War itself, such horrors, such blood and suffering! The Rebels fight like the catamounts that roam the woods, and, though their arms are inferior to our own, their officers are splendid, better than ours, most especially Thomas Jackson. He cuts a fine figure, standing firm against our best efforts, closing breaches in their line. But, Aoife, I can only wonder why the ordinary soldier amongst them fights like the devil for slavery, when they have no part of the rewards.

Still, they attack, yelling as the red Indians did, their cries echoing through the woods and causing my men to glance about fearfully, unable to see from whence they might burst. And in fighting, they kill and maim, like the uncivil savages. So many men, husbands, fathers, and sons, left on the field to rise no more. I will not detail further, for, doting husband that I am, I would not want you, my tender darling, to see in your mind's eye what I have seen in battle.

At that, Thomas's glance rose to Aoife's face. Although knowing herself no tender darling, she could not help but look down. The love swelling in her heart embarrassed her, with a flush that rose in her bosom, setting her breast tips to tingling. The room felt full of William. She would have sworn to the Lord that she smelt him, as she had when he rolled toward her in their bed, putting the coverlet in disarray, and the odor of his warmth rose like a sweet fog.

"Read on," she said, her breath tight. "Please you do, Thomas, and bless you."

"Missus, these words are meant for you and you, alone. Not for any other." He didn't look up as he pushed the letter toward her and his chair back from the table. "Especially not for me, his worker."

She feared he would leave and hastily cried, "Thomas, call me by my name, Aoife. Here we are not mistress and laborer but two friends, one doing a kindness to the other."

He stopped his rise, hands clenching and unclenching.

"Since my William knows I cannot read nor write, he made those little sketches, to let me feel I am there with him. He knows all else must be read to me. Better you than that great dragon of a Mrs. Sprigett."

"That may be true, but…" he halted for a bit. "Perhaps your husband, though being full of love, is surrounded by death and forgets himself in the moment."

"Read on. Do!" The words came out odd, like an animal's bleat. "Have no fear he will say something untoward. Read on."

Foolishly, she thought Thomas would obey such a command. But he did not. Color rose to deepen the maple-wood brown of his cheek. He drank more of his tea and cleared his throat instead of any speech. At last, he began again.

After an ignominious defeat with many lives wasted, we moved out. Thankfully, our march began in the morning ere the sun was hot, and I cannot say to where we headed, only that it was away from the smell of blood and death.

Dearest sweetheart of mine…

Thomas again hesitated. "Ma'am…"

"Oh, Thomas, go on! Though you speak, I hear his voice."

Dearest sweetheart of mine, I speak to my men when we bivouac—it is, after all, an officer's duty to provide comfort to his soldiers. They all similarly feel their deaths would be righteous and are content, all save those with children, who fear leaving orphans behind, unprovided for. Speaking to them, I think, perhaps God was wise to make us wait for our babies, so there is no chance you would raise them alone and fatherless. For the rest, I am happy knowing that you would be left well-propertied and with Thomas to help you.

My forever wife, I assure you that, despite the defeat and despite our losses, I have no doubts about the rightness of our cause. I have no fear my death, if it comes, will be for naught. My only regret, should I lay dying, is that I would never again see you on this Earth and never again hold you in my arms. Be assured my final thoughts will be of you. Never forget that your husband loves you.

Until we meet again, at home or in Heaven,
Your William.

At that, Thomas put the letter down on the table. Aoife put her hand atop his to show no resentment at his superiority in reading her husband's endearments for her. As in a shattered looking glass, his visage glittered through her tears, and she said, "Tomorrow, if you will, we shall start my schooling."

Chapter 7

IRIS ALMOST WENT TO THE recorder's office, but the thought of clerks directing her on how to use their computer system was too disheartening, at least for starting her quest, and she had a bit of time before the Hartnup woman returned. She headed to the local library instead. Looking up the neighborhood and the immediate area's history would give context to a search for Little Jack's history, more than the name of property owners from so long ago.

This was her first visit to the library. Next to it was a tempting museum, advertised as jam-packed with early Americana, both tools and household goods. The possibility of running her fingers down the carefully smoothed top rail of a cradle—made of beautiful chestnut wood, one that might have held Jack Doe—or along the rough lid of a tiny pine coffin, was almost irresistible. It would only make the baby, alive or dead, more real in her mind and herself more possessive of his memory. *Jesus! I'm already kind of nutty about him.*

She dithered on the walk turning from one entrance to the other, her arms crossed. The position grew increasingly un-comfortable, as a phantom weight rested against her breasts, more anticipated than something ever felt. She felt a drawing sensation in her nipples, which, so long ago, back when she was big with her only pregnancy, her experienced friends said would be brought on by the cry of her baby. The baby she'd never held, the baby she'd resolutely pushed from her mind until little John Doe was dredged up from the distant past.

The weight came with a fearful sense of loss as if a wave from the stormy Atlantic had boiled across eighty miles of land to sweep everything away. She shut her eyes, pictured the calm, sailboat-filled waters of the San Francisco Bay, and the feeling slowly left her.

Turning away from the museum, she walked toward the library. The inside was filled with light from a multi-story window. A sharply peaked roof followed the window's outline down the length of the structure. Iris liked the feel of the building—like a cathedral, like the one in Philadelphia her mother had taken her to years ago.

Little Jack was part Irish. Would he have been brought up Catholic if he'd lived? Was she wrong to bury him in the yard of that simple rural Protestant church?

She shook her head free of distracting thoughts and got back to the task at hand.

The library's wide room held round tables where readers sat—a few wearing masks but most ignoring the Please Practice Social Distancing signs—rows of books, and a desk for the librarians.

Iris stepped up to the desk. "Where can I find information on local history?"

"What in particular?" the librarian asked.

"Something on the types of people who lived around here long ago. Not the Native Americans, though. Say the 1800s? Police investigations? Old crimes?"

Before the woman could answer, someone behind her said, "Excuse me, aren't you the lady who bought the white house on the hill? The one with the pond?"

"The one in the news?" the librarian's round face lit up with the question, squinting with delight and curiosity.

Iris turned, ready to deliver a retort at the interruption. But to her surprise, the speaker was the PhD candidate who had come to the house, if she remembered correctly from the frizzy white streak in the woman's tightly curled, reddish hair. The younger woman had appeared almost the same time as Jessica Hartnup, just after word had gotten out about the pond's secret.

"You stopped coming around. Disappeared," Iris said. She drew in a breath, realizing she sounded both accusatory and opening of a discourse, though, perhaps, an unpleasant one. She'd meant to be simply off-putting.

"Yes, sorry, I should have been in contact again but I wasn't sure you and your husband would be receptive. I'm Charlotte, by the way. Charlotte Moore. I wonder, would you possibly want to chat? I'd really like to speak with you."

"Well, I was about to look up something."

"Yes, I overheard." Charlotte blushed. "I wasn't eavesdropping, just returning a few books." She brightened. "I could help you research if you want."

Iris moved away a bit. "I don't know you and not sure I need help... Or have you already looked up stuff on my house? You came around because of the baby..."

Perhaps because she had been cut out of the conversation, the librarian frowned and put a shushing finger to her lips.

"Please, if you'd just let me explain for a moment." Charlotte took Iris's arm.

Iris shook her off. "We can't talk here. It's disturbing the quiet."

The young woman's lips pursed slightly. "You're right." She turned to the librarian behind the desk and put on a subtly exaggerated, apologetic smile. "Sorry."

They really hadn't been loud or said much. Iris chuckled, detecting an undercurrent of sarcasm, which made her feel instantly comfortable, at home. Charlotte Moore shared a trait that not many people—especially Benny—appreciated.

Besides, she was curious about Charlotte's reasons for being so persistent. Was Little Jack to be a hook for her paper, used to grab the reader's attention? Did such hooks have a place in academic papers?

Her stomach grumbled, wanting food. She patted it discreetly, to calm the rumbling and realized she'd forgotten to eat that morning. She'd listen to the young woman for a brief time and then slip away. Truth be told, she wouldn't mind having someone do a lot of the work. Hating research was one reason she'd avoided grad school. That and the desire to marry Benny and have a family.

Charlotte took her arm again—this time, she wasn't shaken off—and led her to the door. "There's a nice garden here, with benches."

The brick-paved sitting area was right outside the door, but the humid heat weighed on Iris immediately. If only she had a parasol like the ones women used in the 1800s to keep the sun from their heads. It would be fitting in her new town, as most of the houses were from that time—tiny, cramped places, really, but each with a plaque declaring its "ye olde" vintage.

Iris sank gratefully onto a concrete bench, still cool from the fast-receding shade of a tree. The sun was near its zenith.

Charlotte moved easily with the cocky attitude of someone adjusted to the local weather, not to mention being thirty years younger.

"You said you were getting a doctorate?" Iris asked.

The younger woman became even more animated, even more youthful. "Yeah, in history and cultural anthropology. Early feminist study, focusing on this area, starting from the Lenape, until they were pushed out by the colonists…" Her eyes lost focus, as if her attention had shifted inward. "Their women were very empowered. They owned their houses, the wigwams..."

"Wigwams? I thought that was a made-up word, a joke," Iris said.

"Nope. It's from the Algonquian *wikewam*. The local natives, the Lenni Lenape, were one of the five Algonquian tribes. My doctoral dissertation is a contrast of the roles of women in the Native society to those of the early European settlers—the Dutch, Swedes, and Germans—where women were supposed to be subservient to their fathers and then their husbands. And then I compare both to the gender roles of the early Quakers."

Iris nodded to show she was paying attention and at least knew something of history.

"And with the Quakers, women had more power again, right?" It was always safe to laud the Society of Friends. They were now everybody's cuddly do-good unorthodox religious types, despite their historic persecution. She kicked a matted leaf wad off the path in front of the bench. *An iced drink, that's what I want.* It was too sultry for anything hot. And, God, despite the heat, she was hungry.

Charlotte bent over and picked up a handful of gravel from the flowerbed, shaking it in her hand. It sounded like a teething rattle.

Without waiting for her to explain or toss the gravel back on the path, Iris asked, "So why are you interested in the baby in my pond? He died way after the time period you're re-searching."

Charlotte's mouth opened, but she didn't speak. The cars on the road beyond the grass stopped, glittering with reflected sunlight. Two teen girls, squawking in laughter like jays and pushing each other, crossed slowly. Iris would have honked if she'd been in one of the cars, but the local drivers tended to be polite.

"And if you're still interested, why did you never come back?" Iris wiped her brow with the back of her hand.

The young woman looked at Iris and scowled. "You seem really, really hot. Why don't we get out of the sun?"

Good idea, thoughtful—something Iris didn't expect these days. A realization that made her feel even older. But she wanted to continue the chat without angering the librarian and without suggesting a café. Not until she knew what Charlotte wanted from her. If she wanted to leave without offending the girl, it would be awkward to be seated at a table, trapped by a yet-to-be consumed iced latte. "Maybe we can stand inside the entrance of the museum?"

"Yeah, smart. It's got air conditioning and the attendants probably don't care, long as we're pretty quiet."

They walked the short distance to the museum and Charlotte opened the door. Iris caught a glimpse of herself in the glass and hesitated. Her middle was getting thicker while the rest of her was growing thin. *Shit! I've got to get back to working out. I look like my mother. At least she got to be a mother.* Then she pushed her hair out of her eyes and that thought out of her mind as she stepped into the blessedly cool foyer.

Inside, Iris's stomach rumbled again. Charlotte said nothing, though she'd certainly heard. The noise wasn't something you pointed out to a new acquaintance.

"To tell the truth," Charlotte said, moving to lean against the cool sandstone wall, "the reason I didn't come back to your house was because I was intimidated by that writer, Jessica Hartnup. She seems like the sort to steamroll over anyone in her way. I figured you'd rather deal with someone sort of famous, and she's all over the bestseller lists." She sighed and paused for a moment. "Pretty sad, right? A PhD candidate not having the courage to get the info I want." She jiggled the gravel in her closed hand. The attendant, behind her glass enclosure, looked up at the noise, but quickly lost interest.

"It suits me. I'm happy you aren't pushy—I'm not sure I want too much publicity. Imagine the curious reading her novel and then coming to view the pond, like lookie-loos do at crime scenes, when my husband and I are having a quiet day at home." They were both silent for an uncomfortable moment. "Which makes me ask again, why did you come?"

Charlotte moved the gravel from one hand to another.

During the pause in conversation, Iris had time to think. *If Charlotte got to the story first, she could be the perfect antidote for Benny's attraction to that odious Hartnup woman.* She chuckled. *Not having the courage indeed...* Charlotte just might have ingratiated her way into exactly that.

One bit of gravel escaped. Charlotte bent to pick it up, not yet answering the questions.

Iris knew about young women's artfulness in dodging the revelation of their secrets. When she'd held parent-teacher conferences, it was usually the mothers coming in, even when they worked, though the fathers prided themselves on doing their share in childcare. Those mothers would divert the conversation in some way—rummage in their purses, need to make a sudden call—when anything unpleasant arose, lest she blame them for misbehaving offspring. "Nope," she went on, leaning away. "I think there's something else on your mind."

Charlotte blushed, highlighting the freckles scattered across her cheeks and nose. "Okay. I'm here because I'd love to help figure out a mystery. My dissertation topic is interesting and all, but kind of dry in the way it's supposed to be presented. If I'm honest, it doesn't have much appeal outside academia."

Iris laughed. "You mean you crave something marketable, like the Salem Witch Trials? Something to give you a little touch of being Jessica Hartnup, even if just for a magazine article?" She almost went on with, *You want to write something people actually want to read?* But she and Benny had known enough academics to realize their egos bruised easily, especially when people's eyes glazed over on hearing the topic of their dissertation. Or someone said, *Oh! I thought you were becoming a real doctor.*

"The money she makes wouldn't be bad," Charlotte said, "but I'm not sure I could deal with the celebrity." Her mouth turned down as if the disappointment in herself was almost too much to bear.

"Well," Iris said, "to tell the truth, being unlike her is a trait that appeals to me, so you've got an advantage there. Make a case for why I should let you on my property and in my home."

"I'd help with the research. Maybe look into who lived in the house around the time the baby died. And I have some idea how to trace the owners of an old house around here. It's tough."

"Let me think about it a little," Iris said.

On the way back to the library, Iris realized she hadn't mentioned the DNA results and was pleased. She wasn't sure why, but it was something she wanted to keep to herself.

Aoife

1862

The letter having been read, Thomas left to his chores. Aoife went to the doorway to be cooled by the breeze from the north, a welcome relief from the sweltering heat. No sooner was he gone into the barn than a black phaeton rolled into the yard, Mrs. Sprigett driving, her face shaded by the carriage's fringed top. She pulled the horse up short when she reached her son's wife.

Aoife stood her ground, wanting to cause no quarrel by turning away. The old woman was William's mother and so her kin, like it or not, and their nearest neighbor. *Upon my husband's return, he would be pleased to find the rift between us closed.*

Mrs. Sprigett leaned forward, just enough that her scowling face could be seen plain and could cast her cold blue eyeballs over Aoife. "Call your man to hand me down!" she said by way of greeting.

"Mother Sprigett, if you please," Aoife said, approaching The Dragon with hem lifted in to seem ladylike, "let me assist you. Thomas is in the barn cleaning the stalls and would not be fit to go near your skirts."

"Harumph," she answered. As Aoife gave her no choice but to take an offered hand or stay in the carriage behind the black gelding's arse, Mrs. Sprigett held out her leather-gloved fingers and rose. Stepping down, she leaned on her daughter-in-law as little as possible. Once on the ground, she handed Aoife the reins to tie, while she herself swept into the house as if it were hers, nose tilted upward. She looked like The Famine Queen, Victoria, who also hated the Irish and who also was absent a chin. Truth be, they both reminded Aoife of Saint Scholastica, her bossiest hen, but, as neither the old queen nor old Lady Sprigett were laying eggs, not as useful.

Following behind William's mother, Aoife breathed in little puffs to tamp down the anger in her bosom.

Inside, Mother Sprigett stood looking about, no doubt hoping to find fault. But the fire was nicely banked, the table cleared and scrubbed, the plates in their rack, and a clean cloth lying over the basin. She nodded. "You are keeping my son's house well. It seems you remember the skills learned as my maid." She looked about again. "Though the clapboard outside needs whitewashing."

Aoife folded her hands before her waist, intending to keep silent, but a tickle in her windpipe interfered. She cleared it, more loudly than she'd anticipated.

"Seems as if you need to moisten your throat with some tea," Mother Sprigett said, "or were you not planning to offer me a cup?"

"Of course I am, with fresh cream if you wish." Aoife went to the tea chest for the leaves.

"You do not keep it locked up properly?" Her mother-in-law's face was stern as a schoolmarm's.

The heat came to Aoife's cheeks. "There is no one here to steal."

"Bring the tray to the parlor." Mother Sprigett turned and left the kitchen.

At her command, Aoife's resolve frayed like an old rag. She felt much as she had when pulling Mrs. Sprigett's stinking chamber pot from under the bed and carrying it down the servants' stairs. That is, she felt shabby, ignorant, unworthy... And Irish.

William's mother was sitting on the fine horsehair couch, the best piece of furniture they had, skirts spread out across the seat so there was room for her alone. Her gloves were still on her fat, busy little hands.

Aoife was glad to note the cornflower eyes, of which Mother Sprigett took such pride, were red-veined, the lids thickened and discolored, with great bulging pouches beneath, like the sacks in which she doled out her servants' scanty wages.

Since William left, his mother had aged a decade. Perhaps she feared losing him, as she had her older son to diphtheria, not two years before William and Aoife wed.

Aoife knew how she liked her cup and so prepared it for her, pouring the milk first to show the cup was porcelain and not disrespectful ordinary ware. Mrs. Sprigett put it aside without a sip. "My son has written you?"

"Yes, Mother Sprigett." Aoife didn't sit. Maid or daughter-in-law, she had never sat in her former employer's presence.

"He has not written me." She tightened her thin-lipped mouth further. "May I see the letter?"

William's letter was back up the stairs, for it had been put away directly upon being read, to keep it safe. Aoife could not deny it to his mother, not if fences were ever to be mended. "Of course." She ran to get it.

Mother Sprigett looked it over quickly. "Do you wish me to tell you what he says? The other maidservants say you can neither read nor write."

"No, thank you." Aoife silently cursed their disloyalty. And then she made a deadly mistake. "Thomas has read it to me."

"Thomas?" William's mother looked up, her piggish eyes narrowed to near slits. "Thomas read a letter from my son, your husband?" She crumpled the letter like something filthy, heathen. "You let him? Ignorant, foolish girl! How dare you!"

With a gasp, Aoife put a hand up to her lips. "Whatever do you mean? There was nothing in that letter…" And then she remembered Thomas's hesitation.

"There is talk concerning unseemly behavior between you and that, that…" She rose from the seat. "I demand you discharge him. Send him away."

"We have done nothing…"

Her jowls wobbled in anger. "Just now, he was in your house alone with you. Do not deny it. Anyone on the roadway could see him come out with you close behind."

She held onto that, to use as a weapon against me. "Mother Sprigett, William hired Thomas and made him vow to help

71

and protect me, which he has done. He has been promised land in return for his work. There is, nor has been, nor will be, anything untoward between us." Aoife straightened further. "I will not discharge him."

Mother Sprigett shook out her skirts and said, "Send him away. I'll not have my son's good name dirtied by you."

"No. Without him I would lose this farm. *William* would lose this farm."

"William will not. I shall write to him." And with that, Mother Sprigett stood, tightening the string of her reticule about her wrist. Her turn was abrupt; her wide batiste skirt *whooshed* angrily against the door frame as she left. Aoife followed, as the fat old woman would need a hand up into her carriage.

A hand up Aoife did give, though Mother Sprigett seemed twice as heavy as when she came. Her face red enough to presage a stroke, she whipped up her horse and left in a cloud of dust.

Aoife watched her go without waving. *I know my William well, better than his mother does! Even though he be far away, he will surely set her right.*

When the carriage was safely gone, Aoife smoothed the letter and put it under the weight of William's Bible, the better to get the creases out.

Thomas
1862

It had rained mightily that first winter of the war. The foul weather did not help the mood of the people—glum—as the war was going poorly for the Union. Thomas read the posted broadsheets and every paper he could get his hands on when he went to purchase supplies and he heard gossip in the streets on Sundays. There was a smattering of victories, but not a few defeats and many losses.

Standing a respectful distance from the top-hatted gentlemen discussing the campaigns, he was too far back to read all but the largest print. The men took their time, discussing each point and he grew anxious, as he was due back with liniment for the bull's swollen hock. All home remedies had failed.

A stout, gray-haired woman spoke earnestly to the elderly man accompanying her, "John, just yesterday, I heard General Lyon was killed in Missouri. Struck by a hail of bullets to his heart and brain!"

A woman standing to the side, thinner and less richly dressed, snorted. "'Tis old news, that. He died in August."

The old man shook his head at the rough speech. He made as to protest, but a gust lifted his bowler. Grabbing at the hat, he missed, crying, "No!" as it fell. Windswept, it danced down the wet street. Thomas darted after, successfully, wiping it on his sleeve as he walked back. He returned the bowler to its owner.

"Thank thee kindly, friend," the man said. "Read the news with us. No doubt it interests you greatly." He gestured to Thomas to stand beside him before turning back to the notice. "And now Colonel Baker has been lost in Virginia."

With a narrow-eyed glance at Thomas, the rude woman turned, banging his side with the market basket she held. She left, muttering to herself, dragging her skirt across the glistening bricks.

The stout woman moved closer to the broadsheet. She pulled the chain about her neck, retrieving silver-wired pince-nez from inside her coat. Despite the spectacles, her vision still seemed poor, as she leaned in to read. "It says, many of the routed men drowned beneath the icy Potomac." She clapped her hand over the bosom of her coat.

The man put a sheltering arm about her and led her away. *As if she was my Lettie and at risk of the war being lost!* Thomas chided himself for the thought. The news was enough to make anyone discouraged and downhearted. *Should the Union losses continue, Lettie and I might need run to Canada.*

But that would mean leaving the farm… and leaving Mr. William's wife alone.

It wasn't until January of 1862 that things turned from constant defeat to victories at Forts Henry and Donelson.

Late that winter, Thomas returned to the town square. He moved restlessly through a small crowd surrounding the latest posting. Those reading the news were more mixed than usual. All ages and, seemingly, all the strata of local society were there. Interest in the distant battles was rising with fresh victories.

A lad of about thirteen leaped in the air, waving his cap. "Yahoo!" he cried. "Another win brought by General Unconditional Surrender!"

Thomas didn't join in the gaiety—it seemed too precarious to celebrate the success of the short, cigar-smoking general, Ulysses S. Grant. It was a surprise that all joined in, even the ladies known for their temperance leanings. *Grant is said to be a drunken sot. Could such a whiskey-lover possibly save the Union?*

Though every farmer and every farm wife—especially those who had sons or brothers at risk—followed the war closely, they knew their task was to provide for the army and those waiting behind. Everyone did their share, though rumors grew of price gouging and inferior or spoiled meat being sold to the military, profiting both the sellers and those in position to purchase. It was rumored that some grew rich, cheating the men fighting to preserve them.

There were crop worries aplenty that winter and spring. The unseasonable warmth and the downpours together meant creeks swelled and ran over their banks, livestock became mired in mud, and tall grass rotted on the ground.

Foreseeing some of this, Thomas had stored excess feed for the cold weather and in spring kept the ewes and cows in to birth their young. But by the end of April the hay was gone. They had to let the animals out to graze on the near-ruined fields.

The sheep fared better than the cattle, though their close grazing did damage to the sprouting grasses. The cows grew thin; there was little milk to send to town for sale and what they gave needed to be left for their young. The best grazing went to the cows which had borne heifers. Thomas and Aoife were forced to sacrifice two bull calves before they reached full flesh—better than have them grow weedy and die. They were not wasted. Thomas butchered them and Aoife boiled and salted the flesh to seal in barrels for sale to the army. The meat brought a good price as they were known for the care they took, ensuring the meat didn't spoil.

Despite the weather, they made it through better than most. Come high spring, with lambs bounding in the field beside their dams, it was apparent that they had increased Mr. William's flock.

They sold some sheep's milk to a family's cook to make into cheese. An old Negro man known to Thomas, the cook had come up from Philadelphia to the country, his goal to buy fresh produce for his employers. There was no real shortage of food in the city, but still much was going to the Union forces.

"The French man who employs me is so mad particular about their victuals, you could believe him a woman!" He laughed, a great belly-rolling sound. "An aristocrat, they say, rich as the kings of Araby. And yet they'll have me make soft cheese from this filthy stuff. *Phaw!*" His broad nose wrinkled. "It smells of raw wool and mutton." Then he laid his money down, more than Thomas hoped for. "We must hang together or hang alone," he said as he left.

With his share of that money, Thomas bought a National School Primer from parents in Lettie's church. Their son had left them and his schooling, off to be a drummer boy.

When the animals were secured for the night, Thomas and Aoife sat at the table, now with the lamps well-lit, while Aoife struggled with reading. Her progress was slow, near a standstill.

"Sure, and the letters do squirm on the page like serpents in a pit. You read off clear as day but for me, all is rawmaish, nonsense." She put her hands over her face. "My eyes grow weary. Mayhap they could fit me some eyeglasses and that would make all stay still on the page."

Thomas shook his head. "I doubt the problem is with your eyesight. Too often, I have seen you thread the smallest needle with the finest thread, no trouble at all. And you spot storm clouds coming from far off, much sooner than I do."

"What is it then? Am I just thick? An eejit?" And she raised a fist and thumped herself on the side of the head.

He grabbed her wrist to stop her before she did herself hurt.

"Leave off! I would pound some sense into my thick skull!" Her face bright with fury, she moved to use her other hand. "No one in my family could read and now I know why. Muttonheads, all, as the English said about us."

"No," he took her other wrist, too. "You are right. You do sums in your head better than others do with pen and paper. I cannot say why reading escapes you, Aoife, but it is not because you are thick."

Chapter 8

IRIS HAD ALWAYS KNOWN the area surrounding her house was rich in history, with George Washington's December 1776 headquarters less than a half-hour's drive and, even closer—a scant few miles north—was the tavern from which Nathaniel Greene ordered the boats for crossing the Delaware.

Despite all the notable, well-documented past of the area, nothing at the library indicated there was anything special about her house, or about any of the other antique stone structures along her road. Only their age made them remarkable—all built before the mid-eighteenth century. Most, like hers, had been added onto higgledy-piggledy over the ensuing centuries.

As expected, searching brought historical reports of local industry, farming, and the actions of the county's men from the French and Indian War on. But if there had ever been note taken of a crime against an infant or about a missing child, the tale had been lost or considered too unimportant to be recorded.

How could a baby die and disappear as if he had never been? Then Iris remembered the churchyard where she'd interred little Jack's ashes. He was scarcely the only child buried there. Many children lay beneath the soil there, under moldering gray granite and marble nearly effaced by moss, lots of stones engraved "Beloved son of..." and "Beloved daughter of..." Many of the dead hadn't even reached five years of age. Some had only lived a day or perhaps had never drawn a breath. And quite a few were buried with their mothers. *Media vita in morte sumus,* she supposed. *Though possibly amended to "Media nativitas in morte sumus."* The process of delivery fatal to both. She had known the conceit of taking Latin might come in handy one day.

Maybe I got off lucky. Survived giving birth. Modern medical miracles and all. But it didn't feel that way. Since her daughter vanished, sight unseen—and, with her, Iris's plans for being a mom, all those tiny clothes knit, that bassinet never uncrated, the rainbow and unicorn wall mural painted over—it felt as if she'd tried on prospective futures, one after another, searching for the way out of a maze of disappointment. Benny had been little help—they hadn't even discussed the root of her rootlessness.

"Hell," Iris said to Charlotte, when the two again met at the library. "Now I remember why I became an elementary school teacher instead of finishing my graduate studies like I wanted. Because of a profound hatred of research."

Charlotte threw back her head and laughed, mouth wide. "I totally understand. Bet that's why you've put off going to the Clerk and Recorders. It's bound to be a total bore."

"Yeah. A few hours shuffling through their records, and I'll be ready to drown myself in the pond." The thought of interacting with people who spent all day inputting forms gave her the heebie-jeebies. But to do an end run around Jessica, she'd be forced to. She looked at her phone. "Eleven-forty. Almost two more hours of this to go. I've got to be back at the house by one-thirty to answer questions for the contractors. Tile, baseboard trim…" Iris rubbed her eyes and thought of Freddy, probably waiting patiently by the backdoor for her, his main treat-giver and his walker when Benny was tired.

Her stomach rumbled and she felt lightheaded. *Damn! I forgot to eat today. Again.* And then realized that lately she only felt hunger during the days she spent with Charlotte. She fed Benny—and the dog—but was herself indifferent at mealtimes.

She had a brief frisson of worry. She'd had spells like this before, of neglecting to care for herself. Their family physician had even talked to her about anorexia. She'd put her foot down and refused to allow it when Doctor Silverman wanted to inform Benny.

No sense letting things get that far now—that would only throw a wrench in the works. And she craved an excuse to delay returning to the house's problems. "How about we go somewhere for lunch? It will give me the strength to take the dog out later. My treat."

Charlotte practically bounced in her seat with eagerness. "Sure. What would you like?"

"Any good Chinese or Thai restaurants close by?" She needed something different, something that would satisfy the cravings of her mouth, not just quiet her stomach.

When Iris and Benny had first arrived at the house, before any kitchenware was unboxed, they'd gone crazy eating hoagies and cheesesteaks. Getting good ones had been impossible in California. Something was always slightly off—the sandwich off-puttingly gourmet with excessive "inven-tive" ingredients, or the roll was too crusty and hard to bite. The sandwich craze had passed and now the difficulty was finding good Asian restaurants locally. They'd thought themselves immune to the Bay Area obsession with food, but it turned out that being holier-than-thou about disliking food frippery was a conceit in itself.

"I do know a place with a killer Szechuan fish fillet," Charlotte said. "A mere two-minute walk away."

At the restaurant, Kung-Pao Palace, Iris requested spicy rather than medium and Charlotte agreed after the briefest hesitation.

When the food arrived, Charlotte served Iris pieces of the fish, which floated with slices of tofu in an aggressive and oily red sauce, loaded with chilis.

The dish delivered on its promise. It was burningly hot with the distinct mouth-numbing of Szechuan peppercorns. The food immediately lifted Iris's mood—she'd heard eating the peppercorns increased endorphins—and made her feel almost at home in her new town.

"Tell you what," Charlotte said. "There's an Asian market about twenty-five minutes away. I could take you there." She stirred the soupy fish stew for a moment, looking into the bowl as if unknown treasures might surface. "And I could go to the recorder of deeds for you. See if it's possible to find out who lived in the house back in the 1800s."

Iris had been about to take another piece of fish. She paused, taking time to consider the offer.

"It will probably be a tedious job," Charlotte went on. "I've tried to trace ownership of places around here before, and it involves a lot of cross-referencing of numbers. Parcels were divided up and sold in pieces and sometimes there was nothing to indicate where structures had been. Some of the info's computerized now, but for the really old records, it might take hours and hours of pulling handwritten transactions to find anything. In fact, might not be possible to go all the way back to when your house was built. Back then, many property transfers were handshake deals or in-family transfers. It wasn't until the Land Ordinance Act of 1785 that there were title documents for the legal transfer of property."

She sure is doing a sell job, Iris thought. The feeling that Charlotte had something personal at stake, something she was reluctant to divulge, kept Iris wondering. But the earnestness of the younger woman's words reminded her of the kids she used to teach. She did nothing to hide her eagerness, and the absence of cunning was endearing, so different from Jessica Hartnup's manipulativeness. "It all sounds like a lot of work." She moved a few red-stained grains of rice across her plate. "Could I pay you to research? It's no secret young grad students don't have much money."

"No, that's okay. I live cheap and I've got a pretty good stipend. Plus, money saved from working after my BA. I'm not really so young anymore. Running out of time, in fact." She flagged the waiter, waving her empty glass. "So, enough about me. I'd love to learn more about you. Any kids?"

Iris's chopsticks hovered in midair for a moment before she put them down. "Yes." She reached into her purse for her wallet and pulled out the photo of Hal. His bright brown smiling face.

Charlotte's eyebrows lifted momentarily.

"Adopted," Iris said. "And here is his family." She held out another photo watching Charlotte's face. "Our daughter-in-law and our grandkids."

To her surprise, the young woman smiled at the sight of Hal's white wife and his pretty green-eyed children, their coloring so intermediate between his and Ruthie's. Iris had expected neutrality at the least, if not another gesture of surprise. She didn't want to identify Hal as adopted, as if that made him not really hers and made her not really a mother. But the smile made her, momentarily, wish to discuss her loss. She couldn't put her finger on why.

"Nice family." Charlotte stared at the photo. "Cute kids. But why did you and your husband move here?"

"I grew up in Philly, and…" Iris searched for a way to explain while giving little away. "We were tired of the high cost of the Bay Area and just wanted a change." Needed a fresh start was the truth. Thought things would be easier.

"Hmm." Charlotte handed Iris the picture and was back to business. "Right. All I need is your—and your husband's—permission to do a paper about your property and the baby in the pond. And... and I think hopefully find out whatever happened to his mother..." She twisted in her seat, looking for the waiter. "... I keep thinking, how awful to go through pregnancy and labor only to have the baby die. And, well, there might have been a crime around his death, or the pregnancy, or just what happened to women back then, but it's important for people to learn about the history..."

Jesus, Iris thought, shivering at the range of possibilities, glad she hadn't divulged her own past. *A lot of things happen to women. Some of those are best forgotten.*

"... and for that I'd have to do a lot of research anyway."

The waiter still hadn't refilled Charlotte's glass. Iris pushed over her own drink, which she hadn't touched, though the fish was very spicy.

Charlotte took a gulp. "Anyway, someone should search through the state archives and go to the state historical and museum commission, see what they've got. And maybe, if it's okay with you for me to poke around the property, I might find something that would give some extra clues. I always did like archaeology but didn't major in it. It's hard to find a position. Shame there are so few professorships."

"You want to be a professor?" Iris had once dreamed of that, despite her hatred of research. She had often mused about being important, lecturing to an audience of eager faces, but marriage had come first, marriage and the plans for a family. She'd wound up teaching, herding rambunctious small children, hoping to make a difference in their lives.

"I love teaching college level. It gives me lots of time to natter on about subjects I love."

"I can tell." Iris smiled. She found enthusiasm in a young person infectious. "What the heck, let's see what you can dig up, in the archives and under the ground." She still wasn't ready to hand over the DNA results. On the other hand, she didn't want Jessica to get them from Benny first.

That thought stopped her with a slippery bit of fish halfway to her mouth. It seemed to her now as if there was some sort of weird childish game, with opposing sides, hers and Jessica Hartnup's. Or was it hers and Benny's? After forty-six years of marriage, of being lovers and companions, now antagonists because of another woman? A horrid thought.

All she'd wanted to know was how that poor mud-stained baby wound up at her house, in her pool, and who his people were. Make a connection with her disastrous purchase and the area to which they'd moved, as if she and Benny had always been part of their house's history. As if they were, once again, at home.

Aoife

1862

Despite Thomas trying so hard to teach her, she gave up on learning how to read. Letters still came from William, all lacking affixed stamps. By Thomas's telling, the government had wisely declared no postage was needed, should the words "soldier's letter" be written on the outside fold.

Thomas read William's letters aloud, giving her no more quibbles concerning privacy. Aoife depended on his friendship and discretion, though sometimes what was written made them both blush, and then she begged him to read those endearments again. They wasted much kerosene in the lamp, sitting in the warm summer nights.

It is good to have Thomas know how very fond my husband was of me and that I am not abandoned to soldiering. William will return. His words kept her feeling womanly, despite the earth under her fingernails, the roughness of her skin, and how the work had made her ribs jut from her body. She prayed the changes in her would be forgiven by William, if, and when, he came back home to her.

She was shamed to realize how long it took to inquire about Thomas's Lettie. *How easily the elevated fall into seeing workers as without the same feelings we have! No matter that I have lately been a servant.*

Aoife resolved to be more thoughtful of poor Thomas, who loved his Lettie as well as she loved her William, as things were more troubled between them. Lettie, he said, was prone to fits of melancholy.

"Why?"

"It seems partly the way she is made," he replied. "Her moods seem to shift with the wind." His shoulders slumped as if he supported a great weight.

"Why?" Aoife asked again. "That cannot explain, nor can the war, which has scarcely reached here. No woman who has a man such as you can be sad without cause. A man, devoted and hardworking, who turns from the drink? Why you are like my William! Tell me your story, that I might help in some way."

Thomas
1862

He worried that telling Aoife would betray Lettie, lay her bare to judgment by someone she didn't like or trust, but what else was there to do? Who else was there to tell? She had no friends in Pennsylvania or, as much as he knew, anywhere. She detested the ladies in the town, even the Quakers, and even the few other Negroes, fearing they looked upon her as a charity. Family she had none—her mother had never been kind, her brothers still enslaved, deep in the South. Only her sister had ever been close to her heart. Thomas was a man, Lettie's man, but had failed to relieve his woman's misery.

And now, she had lost another baby ere she'd told Thomas she was with child.

All he knew was that her suffering, her melancholy, made her like a pond in winter, frozen in place, hiding secrets, and treacherous to tread upon. She stopped gathering the town's wash and no longer frequented the shops. Her flesh fell away until her bones seemed to clack together. Always a tiny thing Thomas could lift and swing about with ease, she now seemed weightless, a wraith or shadow. The velvet skin he loved to touch, so lately a rich, bright brown, paled, grew dry and ashen as if the spirit had burned out of her. He feared she would grow too weak to stand and blow away with the slightest of winds, leaving him alone.

Lettie pushed against his attempts at comforting twice as hard when he offered to stay in town and care for her. Demanding his presence before, she now refused him lingering with her, saying, "No, Thomas, you must not sacrifice your dreams. Not for me. I am not worth them." And so, despite her despair and his, he believed she loved him still.

What else could he do but look for help? Confide in the only woman who might not turn away from them.

Aoife's high forehead wrinkled in consternation as if struggling to understand his words. She rolled the old teacup in her hand like a gypsy about to read the leaves. "You are important to me, Thomas, but I know little of you and less of your woman. Please, start with the story of Thomas and then move on to that of Thomas and Lettie, for like me and my William, at the end there need be no separate he and she but two together making one."

Thomas and Aoife sat down together at the table in her kitchen, as was their custom. Most times, he had read her Mr. William's letters, new ones if they came, otherwise the same over again until the folds of the paper grew thin and ragged at the edges. This night was different.

And so, he began. "My great-grandfather was a mulatto man. It's rumored that he came with the French to fight the British, serving under Lafayette, but my father always said he was at least part Wampanoag, maybe pure-blooded. My great-grandmother, his wife, was a slave manumitted just after the Revolution when the sentiment for freedom was high.

"By my father's time, they were well-established in Philadelphia, where Negroes found a bit of sanctuary. As the city grew, Father found work for a builder, digging ditches and laying stone. Mother cooked for the men in the crew, and so we got our meals with no outlay of cash.

"They both were doting parents, though very strict. Church people, believers in the Golden Rule and The Commandments, in God's righteousness, with no thought for slights or grievances done to them.

"They wanted more for their son, more than they had ever had. Instead of sending me for rough, punishing work in the housing trade, they begged the Quakers to educate me. They wished me attend normal school and teach amongst our community, but my father was injured when a falling beam crushed his leg and he needed me to work.

"The Friends stepped in again, not wanting my teaching wasted on a laborer. Their money fed us and apprenticed me to a watchmaker, who would pay back a trifle if I swept the shop when the usual work was slow. He was a German man and treated me fairly, as if I was no different from his other apprentice."

"Aye, that is good," Aoife said with her sweet little smile.

"Good?" He could but laugh. "White or not, fairly to him meant his apprentice was his slave. We worked by candlelight, even in the day, for the shops were close by one other. The one bright window at the master's was the front by the street, where the people passing might see him at work, surrounded by the timepieces he had already repaired.

"It seemed my life was becoming something I never wanted, as if I had fallen into a mantrap, confined in a dusty place away from sunlight and air. Time was ticking away to the sound of the many clocks all wound but just offset enough that there was never silence. I feared the dim light, the work, and the endless chiming would drive me mad."

On what impulse Thomas couldn't say, Aoife chuffed in a great breath and leaned toward him crying, "For Heaven's sake, Thomas, get on with your story and get to Lettie!"

Outside in the dark farmyard, the dog began a mad barking.

"Something is after my chickens!" she screamed and gathered her skirts to rush out, as did Thomas with his rifle.

Chapter 9

"WOULD YOU POSSIBLY LET me see the autopsy report?" Charlotte asked, without looking up. She stood at one of the computers in the recorder's office, patiently searching for parcel numbers and matching them to names, rechecking surveyors' records, going back year by year to match the house's location, despite divisions of the land.

Iris glanced up from the book she was looking through, one containing deeds from the early nineteenth century. The information it contained had never been entered into a computer or even put on microfiche. The pages were filled with elegant copperplate script that approached hieroglyphics in readability. "Ye Olde," she muttered under her breath. Out loud, the words might arouse the ire of the locals, who took their antique history seriously. *You don't really have a leg to bitch on*, she thought. *You wanted a quaint old house... with a pond.*

Charlotte's question about the autopsy was a welcome interruption.

"You know, I didn't get a report, just a statement from the detective. The whole dead-baby-in-my-pond thing was so unsettling that I wasn't sure I wanted to know any specifics." Not if the baby was already dead—or still alive—when submerged in the murky water, nothing about any trauma, nothing... except the ancestry, of course. "So, I didn't pursue it further."

There was no clue that could say who was the culprit, if any, in the death or in placing the body in the pond. Not a damn thing would guarantee the child was loved and wanted. All she wanted to know was who the child belonged to. A name, or two, and perhaps, with enough digging, a photo would be unearthed. Even one with the baby being held in his mother's arms.

"I read on some clickbait," Iris said, "that even if the baby was dead, there might be a daguerreotype—or whatever picture-taking stuff came after them—of him. Seems the Victorians were fond of ghostly death portraits. I've even seen some that had the corpse sitting in the mother's lap, even with her covered to hold the child up." She paused to see if that ghoulish tidbit affected Charlotte. It didn't. "And even more creepy to me was saving strands of dead people's hair, braiding it to keep inside lockets. If anyone told them to forget their dead, they just ignored the advice."

"I think I saw some of those videos on YouTube, so that must be true." Charlotte winked. "But really, they didn't often let grieving affect their daily lives—couldn't afford to unless they were rich enough, or a queen like Victoria, who wore black for forty years. But most had to work in the house or on a farm or factory. They lived parallel to their mourning, their dead not always before them nor left behind, but walking alongside, unseen."

Iris shivered as the words echoed in her head. *Not left behind, but alongside, always, unseen.*

She hadn't held her baby. All she had was the memory of quickening—if she closed her eyes and concentrated, she could feel the ghost of a movement deep in her lower belly. Fluttering, like a small, restless bird or butterfly. That was the beginning. The middle was the sensation of pressure against her bladder waking her, sending her to the toilet three, four, even five times a night and making her curse Benny's peaceful slumber. Just weeks later came the sensation of a vigorous sea creature inside her, flipping over, striking out against the confines of her womb. At one point, that creature turned into a person whose little foot, stuck straight out just below Iris's belly button, could clearly be seen to have five perfect little toes.

"This kid's gonna be a real handful," she'd told Benny. "Doesn't give me a moment's peace. Next time the kicking starts up, I'm snuggling up against your back so you can be kept awake. You'll be kicked in the kidneys."

He laughed in response and held her tight. "Sounds fair. I'm the one that got you in this predicament." He had paused to grin widely. "At least I hope I'm responsible!"

She'd agreed to being heavily sedated when the doctors convinced Benny that seeing the body would be traumatic for her. That it would be too hard to go through the labor induction awake, only to deliver a corpse. Her baby had died mysteriously, silently... one moment there, the next winked out like a distant star gone nova, leaving dense, dark nothingness behind.

And after she delivered, her baby was whisked away and disposed of somehow, some way.

Only the doctor was there when she awoke. He was the one who told her. Benny had gone to call their parents. When he returned, she was mute, the words dying in her throat. She stayed that way for two months, her chest aching with the thwarted desire to use her voice.

And then, one morning, sitting on the deck of their house in the bright California sun, the bay glittering in the distance, she asked Benny to pour her more orange juice. Without saying a word about her sudden ability to speak, he obliged.

Iris and Benny had not discussed what had happened in the hospital. As time went by, it became more and more difficult to think of doing so. It was like something had hardened around each of them, a shell that, if broken, would lead them to be defenseless, the delicate connection between them shattered. So, Iris hadn't revealed the depth of the despair she felt, the loss and loneliness. But truth be told, her baby never did give her a moment's peace.

* * *

Charlotte moved impatiently and Iris realized how long she'd been frozen—book open on the counter at the same page—deep in the reverie of memory.

"If you're ready to learn more..." Charlotte said.

"I am now." Iris was sure of that.

"Well, if you weren't given a full autopsy report, why don't we call—or even better, visit the medical examiner—and get one?"

"Will it cost a lot you think?" If it did, how would she justify it to Benny?

"I bet it's just a nominal fee. And they might not charge anything. They're government employees after all. The report could tell us so much." Charlotte shrugged. "Like how he died."

"Maybe he was never really alive."

"It could tell us that, too, even after all these years." Charlotte clicked in a few more numbers. "Shit!" She turned to Iris. "Oh, sorry, I don't usually have a foul mouth."

Charlotte obviously hadn't met any of Iris's pupils in Oakland. Young as they were, their cursing was way more creative. "If you think that's a bad word..." Iris leaned toward Charlotte and grinned. "Is it because I'm old?"

Charlotte blushed. "You're not old."

"Come on now. You're what, forty?" Iris thought she was shaving a few years off the younger woman's age.

"Thirty-six." She plucked at the single streak in the midst of her red. "My family goes gray early."

One of the office workers, an overdressed, overweight blonde, walked toward them, tucking her flowered blouse into her waistband. "Excuse me, ladies, but someone else needs the computer."

Charlotte stepped away from the keyboard. "Sorry. We've been here for quite a while. Don't want to wear out our welcome."

"No, I'm the one who's sorry," the woman said. "Usually, we let people use our resources as long as they want. It's just that demand has been high, what with our offices being closed during the quarantines. Please come back again."

Jesus, Iris thought, *they're so pleasant here.* There would have been a strict time limit and hostile workers back in California, even if no one was waiting.

Aoife

1862

Out they ran to save the chickens. Ran pell-mell, so deep in their talk had they been that their minds seemed scrambled, not able to see what was real. The night world was strange and uncanny with the sound of Aoife's birds screaming in fright. And the dog, loosed from his tether, snarling and howling in pursuit of a fox, like something Devil-sent.

Aoife slipped and put down her hand to break the fall. She wasn't hurt. But when she again looked up Thomas was on one knee, rifle barrel up, aiming.

The shot was sharp; it echoed from the trees. But not true. He returned to where she stood with no fox to skin. "Shame," Aoife said, to jibe at him, "for had you returned with a pretty red pelt, white-tipped at the tail end, sure, and you'd be making a winter muff to warm your love's hands!"

As they walked toward the house, the clouds parted, the night sky grew brighter, and the moon could be seen looking down on them. "Oh, look!" she cried. "The man in the moon smiles down upon us."

Thomas stopped, stock-still. "You continue to jest with me."

"Thomas, it is no lie. If he smiles on you, it is a portent of good."

"There is no such thing as a man in the moon. A superstition, Aoife, not fit for a Christian. Though I have heard the Irish are fond of such heathen delusions."

Anger rose in her chest. Who was he to put down her race, for all he was more educated than she? With her voice as cold as it had ever been to him, Aoife said, "Everyone knows there is a man, even the English. Look up, see his face."

Thomas stopped and said, "When I was just a boy, a nephew of the great scientist Bertram, who studied the flora of America and was a friend to Franklin, took an interest in me. He had a telescope powerful enough to see the moon, nearly so close it seemed I could reach out and touch its cold and lonely surface. Nothing living moved there and the face you see was just a figment of shadows thrown together."

The night was warm, the air alive with the mysterious flies that glowed greenly. She caught one in her cupped hands, then opened the trap slowly, one finger at a time. The little creature climbed to the tip of the longest finger, spread its wings and flashed farewell.

The Lord, or her common sense, spoke silently at this omen, this warning that a rupture with Thomas could ruin all. Aoife would not be a hothead like her dadai had been, tossing tea in her mam's face, should it not be hot enough. For friends do have words between them, yet soldier on, being friends. And she was curious as a cat to learn about Lettie.

Instead of anger, she laughed. "I suppose you might see me loose that little flying creature and imagine I think, 'There are none such flies in Eire, so it must be a fairy.' Sure, and you know the Irish are fierce mad for fairies."

His shoulders eased at her good humor.

"And would you find it sweet were the Pennsylvania woods full of such little winged creatures? Swarming with fairies?"

"Sweet?" She stopped walking at the very thought. "Fairies are no such, Thomas. They are mischief makers, uncanny beings who do not live full in our world but have their own. They are not concerned with us but still are often spiteful. My mam told me, should they be good and never evil, they would have driven out the British. Laugh if you will but respect them."

Then she sauntered on, singing what she'd heard the English soldiers sing when she was small:

> *"Oh, our man in the moon drinks claret,*
> *With powder beef, turnip, and carrot,*
> *If he doth so, why should not you,*
> *Drink until the sky looks blue!"*

Both laughing now—Aoife so hard she could barely finish the ditty; they had reached the kitchen door and gone in, companions, the pieces of the world in place again. The stew hanging on the crane had thickened down, smelling of meat well-browned and once-good ale gone too flat and sour to drink. She took one of her best bowls, not the tin ones she served Thomas in most nights, cut a slice of bread and put it on the table for him to dunk in, and sat across.

And Thomas said, "Lord, it does smell good." He spooned a bit over the bread and put it in his mouth. "Tastes good, too."

"So," she said, "it seems my practice at cookery has paid off. And seems for all your fancy education, you can still talk with your mouth full of mutton!"

He laughed and grabbed another slice of her bread.

She waited until he'd eaten a good bit. "Tell me of your Lettie, Thomas. How fares she, the one for whom you should have shot that fox?"

He put down his spoon and dropped the bread in the bowl. "Lettie is always sad now and doesn't care whether I journey to see her or not."

"Was she always thus?" And added, because his eyes grew moist, "Does she cry?" She feared her eyes would dampen too, though she didn't know why. *All for missing my William, mayhap.*

"Cry? No, she is becoming dry, like stone, like kindling, ready to be burned away. No, not always thus. Lettie was different at the start. She almost danced as she walked and seemed to me sweet, a sprite."

He smiled at Aoife. "I do believe there are good fairies, too."

"Thomas, you have not yet explained her melancholy."

He ate again but she was not convinced hunger—and her food—was what closed his mouth.

"Thomas."

He squirmed in his seat like a babe with a wet nappy. "Mistress Aoife, it seems disloyal to say aloud but I fear it is part her nature, going from happy to sad, with no immediate cause for the alteration. But certainly, what happened to her on her journey to Philadelphia changed the balance of her mood to deep melancholy."

"Well," Aoife said, "how God saw fit to make her cannot be changed, but what has happened to her might be softened with kindness."

He looked at her in doubt, as if to say, "From whom?"

She lifted her chin. "From such as myself."

95

Thomas
1862

Thomas began the story of his melancholy love. "Lettie was born in slavery, in the state of Alabama. Not only a slave, but child of a mother harsh, and even cruel. A mother who treated her children—all six of them—as the overseers treated her. The mother had borne six children from five different fathers, all unknown to their offspring.

"Lettie at ten was trained in mending and laundering the bed-clothes and soaking sheets in turpentine to whiten them—the fumes choking her and raising headaches near blinding in their ferocity, she has them still—and then boiling the wash in a cauldron near as high as she was, standing on a bucket to do so. Her older sister, Sary, then fourteen but skilled with a needle, was tasked with the finer things. Working together, they grew closer and closer, enough to hatch the plan of escape from the tedium and tiring tasks, if not from slavery itself.

"They ran three years later, when Lettie was thirteen, as full-grown as she would ever be, joining a band already on the move under the guiding of a man who never gave his true name. For security, they called him only Robin.

"As perilous as flight might be from Virginia or Maryland, their journey was manyfold more, miles and miles patrolled by slave hunters. But they were lucky until they reached the Delaware border, meeting many kind and hospitable folk along the way. There, Lettie twisted an ankle and was to be left behind alone, until Sary broke from the group and ran back to protect her. Alone the next night, and with Lettie slow and limping, they tried to follow but lost their way as the moon was hid behind clouds. They headed east instead of northwest toward the great lake where boats awaited that would take them to Canada and surety of freedom."

He paused the story then and said, "The telling is difficult and 'twill get far worse, especially for a lady."

Aoife cocked her head. *How like a little bird she can be,* he thought. And then she gave him a measured smile. "Thomas, you flatter me. I am no lady and never was, for all that I am a gentleman's wife."

And so, he soldiered on. "This is just as Lettie told me, for the words stuck with me, so powerful, they live in my mind like poisonous serpents.

"Sary broke little branches from a tree limb fallen in the winter storms and gave them to her sister. With them, Lettie could take steps like a hobbled mule. And so, they moved on together, slow, blind in the dark, Sary with another stick, sweeping back and forth to keep them from tripping on roots or falling into bushes.

"When day broke, they hid as deep as they could and ate the little food Lettie had when she was left behind by the others. Water Sary got from horse troughs and streams, oft'times leaving Lettie hidden until she returned with some in a little bottle hung about her neck.

"They made scant progress. Lettie feared for her sister. She argued with Sary, 'Two should not be sacrificed when one alone might satisfy the hunters.' But Sary would not leave her, not even to save herself. Lettie begged her to go, to run and escape to freedom. So much faith did she have in Sary, she was certain her sister would return to find her, somehow, some day.

"That night, heavy rain came, washing their path and causing them to shiver in the wet with nothing to cover them. From a distance, they heard the baying howl of dogs, and so they ducked into deep brush. Sary whispered, 'Perhaps they all be coon hunters looking for a meal.'

"Sary might have hoped her sister was convinced by her false cheer, but Lettie believes it not, as Sary kept her hand over Lettie's mouth, fearing she would cry out."

Thomas swallowed, hard, the words a lump in his throat. "She tells me she can still taste the mud, the sweat, and the fear on the soft, damp mound of flesh at the base of Sary's thumb.

"As the hounds drew closer and closer, Sary whispered, 'They have scented us!' She pulled Lettie's cheek against her own rain-soaked breast, and her heart beat wild in Lettie's ear. Then she jumped up suddenly, pushing Lettie down, and ran further on the path to lead the dogs away.

"She did not get far, just far enough to save her sister. 'Here I be!' She cried and soon they were upon her, the hounds and then the three men, one after another, as she fought, kicking and screaming, her arms flailing at them. All the while, Lettie peered through the brush, afraid to turn away and lose the last sight of Sary.

"At last, the third man stood, pulling at his drawers, only to be slapped by another. 'Damn you,' he said. 'That's six hundred dollars gone.'

"It was a while after they'd mounted their horses and left, a while before Lettie could rise from her crouch and go find her Sary drowned in the mud."

Chapter 10

IRIS DISCOVERED THAT, when inquiring about a death, there was an online form to be printed, filled out, and mailed to the county coroner. It surprised her to find no indication the dead person had to be related to the information seeker—it seemed a potential invasion of privacy, for surviving relatives if not for the dead.

She filled out every line, explaining that the baby was reported to have died over one hundred years ago, that he was found on Iris's property, that she had paid to have him interred at a local cemetery, and had sent DNA but had no idea to whom he might be related. She wanted all the information on him possible. She enclosed the one-hundred-dollar fee, waffling about a toxicology report. Why would anyone need to poison a newborn? They died so easily.

When Benny came home from walking Freddy, she told him about sending the check. All he said was, "What's for dinner? Not chicken again!"

"If you wanted something special, you could have started it."

Benny turned to leave the room. For a moment, as he pressed his hand to his chest, he looked ill, neglected, like an old man with no one to care for him. And then Iris blinked, and he was just Benny again, healthy and young-looking for his age and his medical history.

Good. For a moment, it seemed he was about to have another of his anxiety spells.

He came back to her a moment later. "Let's start the evening over. I was lonesome for you today. I was here with the contractors, who, though you haven't asked, have finished repairing the back wall. And you were off doing I don't know what."

"Didn't Ms. Hartnup have time for you?" *Where did that come from?*

"Aw, don't be silly," he said, reaching for her hand and pulling her to him. "Did you spend the day by yourself?" He kissed the top of her head in the part of the gray hair he'd admired—and that she feared was getting thin. "How about we just have salad with the leftover chicken…"

She turned, angry, breaking his hold. "You don't listen to me, but I listen to you. You just said you were sick of chicken."

"I was kidding. You know I love chicken. Why don't we open a bottle of wine and eat out on the wall by the pond?"

"The pond?" Iris was surprised and a bit ashamed. She'd turned his olive branch—or drumstick—into a possible fight and he'd been the bigger person, refusing to be triggered.

"Yeah, time to reclaim it as ours." He embraced her again and she leaned her cheek, hot with a blush of shame, against his chest.

Ours. Not the baby's. How would Benny have handled things if I'd buried my little Jack by the pond?

Maybe it was better she'd paid for a place to visit, private, away from the house, rather than have Benny interrupt every time she went out the back door, asking, "Where are you going?" He always knew damn well.

And the beautiful old cemetery chosen was certainly better than the cremated remains sitting in an urn on the dining room mantel. Or Jack being a box of ashes stored in the attic, near forgotten. But still, either way, there would still be something.

Of her, *their* own baby, nothing remained. Benny had seen to that.

She broke away from him, loath to escalate things and further ruin the day. Bending over the shelves of their tiny temporary fridge, she asked, "How about I make the chicken into salad the way you like? Mexican flavors?" She pulled out the chicken, the remainder of a red onion, mayonnaise, and celery.

Benny grinned. "Yeah, wow, I really like that. Shame we can't get good tortillas around here."

For a moment, he looked almost as he did when she'd met him. *Minus the bell bottoms and long hair. Minus almost all the hair, in fact.*

Iris began to chop the vegetables but stopped, knife raised. "Maybe we could take lunch over to the churchyard where I buried him?"

"Him? The body from the pond? That would be creepy." He sat at the table and scrolled through his phone. "Not like it's our kid."

"*It*" again? She chopped with greater force. Benny didn't seem to realize why little Jack's death—his burial site—was so important to her. *Why didn't—why doesn't—he ever talk about our kid?*

She had been the one who'd carried their baby, the one who'd gone through labor. He'd been out calling family, having coffee, abandoning her when she most needed him, leaving it to the doctor to tell her what they hadn't had: a little girl.

"So, did you spend the day alone?"

Iris took a deep breath before answering. "I was in the library, looking for more history on the area, maybe even the story of our house. That young woman we met—the one who came over after we found the baby—was there. She's not a cozy mystery writer or anything..." Iris paused for effect and to stir in the mayonnaise. "She wants to do a paper on our house and the baby in the pond. She offered to help me do research. I told her we wouldn't give anyone else any information we had before we let her write it up." She added taco seasoning and some oregano to the chicken salad, squeezed half a lime on top, and plopped the Tupperware container down on the table hard enough for a dollop of yellow-stained mayo to spatter. "I told her you and I were always partial to students. You want some greens with that?"

Benny looked up at her, his mouth slightly agape. "What about Jessica?"

"Jessica? Ben, I thought you'd be happier having someone academic involved, a real expert on the area. Someone with facts about history and cultural anthropology. You could really be proud of that, right? Imagine calling and telling everyone back home…"

"There is no back home, Iris. Not anymore." Benny pushed the chicken salad to the side of the table. "You moved us here, where we didn't know a soul. I talk to the workmen, because someone's got to watch over them and make sure things are going right. But Jessica Hartnup's the first friend I've had in years. The only person to talk to about real stuff…"

The only person you to talk to? Iris cut a lemon in half. A tiny abrasion on her finger, one she hadn't realized she had, stung with the juice. *And what's "real stuff"?*

"You're always wrapped up in…"

"The student's name is Charlotte in case she drops over." Iris went back to the refrigerator. "I think you should have a bit of arugula and tomato. I'll dress them with lemon juice. Most dressing is too high in sodium. Not good when you get old." She put the salad together and set the plate in front of him.

Benny sighed and spooned out mayonnaise-y chicken salad on top of the greens.

102

Fury was building within Iris, cutting off her breath, a band about her chest. She wheeled about, a pitcher of water in her hand, took two steps and *crash!* Only the handle remained in her hand. She'd banged the pitcher against the counter's edge and shattered it. "Oh, Benny!" She burst into tears. "What the fuck is the matter with me?"

He rose so suddenly that his chair clattered to the floor and came to embrace her, murmuring, "Shh, shh, love. I know. I know."

Aoife

1862

"My Lettie's sadness comes not just from losing her Sary but from the many times she lost a baby. She longs to be a mother." Thomas sighed and blew his nose into a bright red scrap of cloth he used as a handkerchief. "A child might tether her to sanity."

Aoife sat silent for a while. After all, what was there to say to him? How could any gesture of kindness or friendship help such grieving?

"If she but had women friends or attachments in the town and had not ceased doing her work, her mind might have been eased," Thomas said. He sat across from Aoife, their silence making the tick-tock of the parlor's mantel clock that much louder. She regretted her diligence in winding it, for it seemed to make the slow passage of time more burdensome.

Until this moment, she'd been proud of that mantel clock, French with bits of inlaid malachite and a lovely chime. She had loved to wind it, as her mother would have, she who never had a timepiece of her own. But now, as they sat together, morbid thoughts crept into her mind to dart about, muddling her feelings.

Time is king. The past forms the present, as the child forms the man.

In Ireland, with no timepieces, they'd relied on the sun and the crowing of the rooster. The only *tick, tick, tick* in the cottage came from the beetles infesting the ancient oak timbers above Aoife's straw bed. Her widowed great-grandmother had shared that bed with her. With that old woman's tales, the beetles' ticking made her heart clench up with fear.

Thomas's fear for Lettie's changing sanity seemed to burrow into Aoife's being. She felt the same as when she was a small child, alone in bed with that daft old woman.

"You hear that? You hear that?" the toothless crone would whisper, deep in the dark of night. Her words were mushy soft as the oats soaking for the morning porridge. "Sure 'tis the omen of my death, child."

"No, no, 'tis not!" Aoife had muffled her frightened cries with the blanket covering the two of them. She was careful not to waken her dadai from her parents' nearby bed, where he lay drunk with fatigue and the stinking barley *poitín* he made. He'd be as like to wallop her as to hit the old woman.

"Yes, 'tis. I did hear it at night before each of your baby brothers and sisters died. Sometimes I hear them round the door, weeping and begging to come back in." The old woman turned toward Aoife. "Listen!"

Aoife crammed her fist between her teeth to quiet the whimpering squeezed from her tight-closed throat.

"You hear them? Do you? Good thing I am so old and ready to go. Mayhap death has had enough with the young and will take me now. Mayhap, having had all the other little ones, he will pass you by. But mayhap not." She shrugged and pulled the blanket up over her mouth. Her breathing settled into snores.

Back so long ago and far away, Aoife had lain in the dark, her eyes searching the lightless room as the deathwatch beetles' steady click kept her awake all night.

Tonight, I will cram an old stocking within the works of that monstrous clock and still them, or I'll get no sleep at all.

Thomas still had not said a word.

Aoife broke the silence. "Lettie is haunted, Thomas, is what I would say." She pursed her mouth to think and then nodded as a memory came to her. "There might be the fixing of that. One day serving Mother Sprigett and her friends at whist, I heard of a woman who could summon the dead. Do you think she could help? Mayhap by reaching her Sary who, as she loved her sister, would say that Lettie should let her go and be at peace, as mourning too greatly keep the dead from rest."

Thomas's face passed through many changes, as if he thought of and then rejected ways to answer Aoife. At last, he shook his head. "I fear dealing with the uncanny would only worsen her condition."

She said no more about the medium, feeling Thomas was wrong, for someone like Lettie had to be bedeviled by the spirits of her sister or of the babies she'd lost. Aoife's own levelheaded mother had been. "Is there anything to cheer her? Sweetmeats from the confectionery?"

Thomas shook his head again. "She eats so little. I fear that any wind would blow her away."

Living alone might be a good bit of Lettie's sadness, and Aoife's heart wanted to say, *Go, Thomas, be with her now. What benefit shall property be if you have no one to share it? Solitude might drive her mad.*

Would that not be a kindness? To release Thomas from his vow to protect herself and the farm. But that kindness would betray William. He had entrusted her with the care of herself, his wife, and his property, to keep all safe for his return home. "Only one thing would do, then. Bring her here whilst the weather is fair. The countryside and the pleasant air might heal her disordered mind."

Thomas's eyes widened with surprise. "To your house?"

Aoife blushed. That had not occurred to her. That was something she did not want. "A bed could be put in the barn loft, and she would be welcome to whatever I cook for you. That way, she would no longer be alone. You could watch over her."

Thomas
1862

The second cutting was almost complete. The hay lay spread across the wide field. The sun beat down in a cloudless sky—promising the crop was not likely to be ruined—and the barn was full of the first cutting for their own livestock, the cows and oxen, which would later be grazing anyway. This richer hay needed to dry well, as it was to be sold in the city for the municipal horses—and if the weather held and they got a third cutting, it would go to the cavalry and racetracks, should any be buying. The Negro grooms and stall muckers had stood humbly shuffling, caps in hand, and convinced the officials that Thomas had the best and, more importantly, the cheapest, feed to be found. They were still proud of him, proud of his learning and his rising to prospective rural landowner. And his love for Lettie, his devotion to her—difficult as she was—had only improved his status among the local women, who helped sway the opinions of their menfolk.

It was gracious of the missus to offer shelter to Lettie, and Thomas planned to broach the possibility with Lettie little by little unless she became so frankly mad that his hand should be forced.

That Lettie hated Aoife was a worry, but worse worry was the missus's talk of mediums and séances for reaching the dead. Truth be told, if steering clear of William's wife by sheltering in the barn meant protection given to Lettie's mind, that would be a good thing. She could have kittens to dote upon, as the barn cat was near ready to deliver, and he himself could return many times in the day to make sure she was safe.

And with permission, Thomas could, in his spare time, throw up a lean-to against the back of the house and a small stove to keep it warm. They could winter over, at least until Mr. William returned. But Lettie had to live until he could bring her to the farm. She had to eat.

Honey. Lettie had been very fond of honey. There was a hive at the edge of the field of clover planted for the cattle. It mightn't please her as well as honey from the South, but the clover and wildflowers on which the bees foraged should make a tasty sweet to put atop her toast. He had meant to get it for the missus, for baking her sweet soda bread.

How poorly Lettie had looked the last he saw her! *Perhaps I could induce her to take it by the spoonful, like medicine.* He scratched his whiskery chin and thought, *I'd best shave before I visit her as she dislikes a beard and, should she let me near her, could rub her skin raw. I'll ask the missus for a jug of heated water.*

The very hope of lying with Lettie was something he had to tamp down.

"Thomas!" Aoife called from the barnyard. "I would go to the post office to see if William has written again. Is Maisy fit to carry me?"

It had been a while since word from her husband had come. Thomas feared that Mr. William's mother had some-how, through the interference of her dead husband's friends, intercepted arriving letters, perhaps diverting them to herself. He said nothing to Aoife about his suspicions, fearing a role in troublemaking and so more gossip.

Gossip could lead to more visits from Mother Sprigett.

Only a small segment of the field remained uncut. He left the mare standing, still hitched to the hay mower, and made his way to meet the missus.

"Would you prefer I leave the last bit be? I can bring Maisy and plow to the barn and hitch her to the cart." He wiped his brow on the hem of his shirt.

Aoife looked fretfully toward the horse, who stood in mid-furrow, head hanging. She twisted her hands in her apron. "I apologize, Thomas. 'Tis womanish of me to put my desire for news of William ahead of the farm work, and poor Maisy looks near played out." She sniffed loudly with her eyes downcast.

He suppressed a smile. She played on his sympathies, but it had been overlong since he'd had a letter to read her. "I would go for you if I could, since it's not far to walk if one's fast enough. Faster than Maisy goes unless you whip her up. I have seen you too softhearted to do so."

She turned her eyes up to the sky and sighed. "Best to get the hay cut."

"When the field is cleared—even before the evening meal—I'll go into town. There is a man who will sell me the newspaper cheaply, once he has read it."

"And you will look on the lists of those wounded and killed for the name William Sprigett and report back to me?"

Thomas nodded. "I'll do so, and better, bring the sheets back to read with you, though I've heard that those with influence, like the Sprigetts, will have news of their soldiers personally delivered. They would have no need to search through the newspaper lists. Would she not even be kind enough to let you know if Mr. William were injured?" He would never suggest the word *killed*.

Aoife's lips twisted wryly. "Mother Sprigett is not noted for her kindness, least of all to myself. Please, finish the fieldwork. Have no fear—my worry will still be with me when you finish."

"I will, missus. And will go to the town afterward." He smiled. "I planned to go to the bee tree today, but your concern is far more important. The honey would be sweet, but tears of worry might turn your cooking."

Aoife put her hand atop his. "You would raid a wild hive for me? Risk their angry stings? No, I would not have that. I have some stored now and over the winter I'll weave skeps as my granny did, and come spring, will lure a swarm to settle with us." She turned to go back to the kitchen but stopped midway. "And when we have our own honey, we shall sell that, too, with plenty over for us and for your Lettie."

Chapter 11

THE CONTRACTOR WAS RIPPING out the kitchen's dark and decrepit homemade cabinets, the 1970s range, and the rusty dishwasher Iris had never used, fearing that, if she opened it, she'd find dead mice and swarming ants, just as there had been under the 1970s range. Despite the heat, Iris wanted out of the house.

In the early afternoon, she walked Freddy down the long southern arm of the driveway and stood waiting in the sun as several cars passed, and it was safe to step out along the verge to the mailbox. The heat and the moisture-saturated air made it hard to breathe.

An official envelope from the county coroner was stuffed inside the box. The only other mail was flyers from the supermarkets and high-end catalogs, which had followed them, like unshakable imprinted ducklings, all the way from the Bay Area.

Walking back to the house from the mailbox, anxiously clutching the mail against her chest, Iris decided to wait for Charlotte before opening the autopsy report. Failing to disclose the DNA results made her feel a bit guilty, and uncertain as to why she'd held the information so close to her chest.

When the young woman called an hour later, Iris invited her to the house, planning to meet outside at the pond's newly fixed wall. She zipped down the road to the Italian bakery and bought pastries to go with a pot of coffee put up in the conservatory, which was serving as their temporary kitchen.

Waiting for Charlotte, Iris sat on the front steps, draping an arm over the neck of one of the lions that guarded the house's entrance. It was comfortable in the shade of the small portico, hidden behind two tall rhododendrons. As the moments ticked by, her heart beat faster in anticipation. Strange, but she was eagerly looking forward to this visit, in a way that seemed more than just the excitement of sharing further information about Baby Jack.

Something about the young woman made Iris comfortable. At the thought of seeing Charlotte, it seemed the difficulty getting air into her chest lessened and she could breathe more easily. The tightness she'd tried hard to ignore in the day but which—when she awoke beside Benny in the dead of the night—felt almost deadly.

It irked her that he could rouse her with his tortured dreams and yet immediately fall back to sleeping soundly.

The little old tin can of a Honda Civic rattled up the driveway's north end and parked by the steps up to the barn. Charlotte clambered out, wearing a pair of hideous old-lady sandals, the rawhide kind that made all feet look as if they sported lumpy hammertoes. Her long skirt, with its uneven hem, skimmed across the top strap.

God, why does she do that to herself? She looks like one of my mother's idiotic Bohemian friends. The kind who subsisted on dried fruits and nuts.

She was endearingly awkward.

"Charlotte!" she called, rising from the step. "Here!"

Charlotte waved and walked toward her.

"We're going around the back to the pond. There's a fresh pot of coffee and two cannoli with our names on them. And lookee here…" Iris waved the envelope, "… the autopsy report! I haven't opened it yet."

Charlotte's pace quickened. She reached for it.

"Uh-uh." Iris wiggled her index finger. "Wait 'til we're by the pond. It's only fitting."

They traipsed through the mud to the newly reconstructed stone wall behind the house, just below the pond. Iris put the envelope down and went for a tray, bringing the coffee and pastries.

"Go ahead," she said when she returned, "read it."

Charlotte pulled out the report. She scanned it silently, and said, with a gasp, "The baby…"

"Little Jack."

"Little Jack never took a breath. He was born dead."

Strange, Iris thought, *she sounds almost more upset than I am.* "At least he never suffered…"

"Didn't he?"

Iris shrugged.

Charlotte looked down at the report. "It says there are—were—other injuries found. An upper arm fracture, consistent with a breech birth… That would be feet first, right?"

Iris nodded. "Or butt first. Possibly—or usually—needing help to be delivered. Maybe needing to be pulled out. If the shoulders get stuck, sometimes the midwife has to break an arm."

"Break the baby's arm?" Charlotte's face registered horror.

"The baby has to be gotten out quick if the shoulders stick because the mother's blood can't get through to supply oxygen and the lungs aren't working yet. The head's still inside the birth canal, so no air's coming in the nose or mouth." Iris took the papers from Charlotte. She read on, "…and trauma to his neck."

"Like if he was strangled? There are always marks with strangling on crime shows."

"He wasn't born and then killed." Iris thought for a moment. "He was born dead. So, he never breathed, and if he never breathed but he had something wrapped tight around his neck..." The suffocating tightness in her chest returned.

She pushed her plate away. It hit her coffee cup, which shattered on the brick walkway below the wall. The pieces spun like flung ninja stars, and her mind conjured a horrifying image of them whirling and whirling, slicing baby froglets into ribbons of pale green flesh. She rose, swaying, and dropped back down on her seat.

"Iris?" Charlotte said. "Are you all right?"

She took deep breaths with her eyes shut, while Charlotte fanned her with the empty envelope until she again opened her eyes. Then Iris smiled at the young woman through the start of tears. "Just momentary dizziness. The heat, you know."

Charlotte bent and reached toward the scattered pieces of white china. "Yeah, it dehydrates you. Even gets to me sometimes, and I'm used to it."

"Leave it," Iris said. "I'll sweep it up later. I broke a pitcher before, in the kitchen. Crockery and glass seemed to be risky for me to handle these days."

"Are you really okay?"

Iris nodded. Charlotte looked dubious but bent and picked up the papers from the ground, smoothing them against her skirt. Iris had, without realizing, crushed them in her hands. "Strangled before taking a breath... that would probably be the umbilical cord?"

Iris coughed to excuse the tears starting in her eyes.

"I've read a lot about unusual births in the eighteenth and nineteenth centuries, breech and whatnot. The old settlers' superstition from the British Isles was that a breech baby would have healing powers. Been magical."

"Magical?" Iris looked at the duckweed floating on the pond's surface. A slight breeze had come up to move the green clusters about, as if a hand beneath the water was lazily waving. "I'd suppose if a breech birth was successful in live delivery, in an age of babies dying left and right, that would be unusual enough to seem magical. No ultrasounds or fetal heart monitors to figure things out ahead of time like we have…"

"Midwives were pretty good at their job back then, but you're right, the mortality was horrendous. That's part of my dissertation." Charlotte's voice rose with excitement. "Oh! It says they have the clothes. Maybe we can still get DNA, even though he was cremated. I was afraid that would be impossible."

Aoife

1862

Broadsheets were posted weekly. Thomas collected them and read aloud the names of the wounded and dead.

"It would be wondrous if William were to be lightly wounded," Aoife said, "just enough to be discharged but not enough to cripple him or risk his health."

"Samuel Johnson, Roland MacFayden, Lemuel Emerson" Thomas kept a finger on the last name so as not to lose his place. "Missus, knowing Mr. William, all that would mean is that he'd return to duty, crawling if necessary. I never knew a man as determinedly brave as he is."

Aoife sighed. "I suppose you are right. We must carry on our ghoulish reading, long as this war lasts. Sure, and I feel as if I am delighting in the misery of others with each name that is not my beloved's."

"Ezekiel Swartzkopf, Johnny Moore, Walter Sawyer…" The paper rustled as Thomas's finger moved along.

Aoife cried out, "Walter Sawyer? Who worked at wood-cutting? But he was a fine young man, little more than a boy." She held up her hand to break his recitation. "I can take no more today, Thomas. I will believe if you say William is not on the lists." She rose to dip water from the kitchen bucket for the kettle standing in the fireplace, for it had almost boiled dry. "The bread would be best toasted to have with stew. Would you cut two thick slices?"

Thomas nodded and rose, taking up the knife.

Aoife took the toasting fork from its hanging nail beside the fireplace. "I'll start the dough rising in the morning, and you should have fresh baked by midday. There will be an extra loaf to take to your Lettie." She stabbed the fork into the two pieces of bread and held them over the fire with one hand. With the other, she stirred the stew.

Thomas waited, knife in hand should she want more slices. "The hay crop's good. We have plenty for our stock once we take to market the beasts we wish to sell, and this second cutting is already spoken for. Two women from my community will help you gather and tie the sheaves, and I will stack them in the field. The dry weather seems to hold."

The bread was well browned. Aoife pulled it from the fork, pausing to blow on her burned fingertips, and set it on a small cloth on the table. "There is enough stew for three bowls, two for you. William would want you well-fed to keep up your strength, so handily do you manage the farm." She scooped stew into bowls and put one before him. "Have you spoken to Lettie? I have put aside quilts for her use in the barn. And a fine feather pillow, one of my best."

"I'll not discuss it with Lettie but simply bring her here with the help of the churchwomen. They have seen her steady downhill course, no longer feel they can help look after her, and will gladly assist me take her from town."

Aoife thought for a moment. "You must do what needs be done, even to take your Lettie by force."

Thomas

1862

It was set. Lettie would come, willing or not. He hoped she could find a way to be respectful of Aoife, who, though she was not quick to anger at slights, was still proud.

How sharp Lettie's tongue could be. Her rage has, at times, been directed at him. And stirred by envy mixed with madness, that tongue might be forked as a serpent's and sharp as that serpent's tooth.

Despite his worry, Thomas couldn't help but laugh, remembering that, long ago, his hands clean enough for handling books, he'd read Shakespeare's plays and Alighieri's *Divine Comedy*, and had been on his way to a profession. In a few more years he might have been a fine clockmaker, living in the city, with hope of further schooling and the opportunity to attend plays and concerts.

But then he'd walked that wet cobblestone street and seen a beautiful girl under a tattered umbrella. A girl, a country girl, out of place in the city.

He took the bedding from Aoife and brought it to the barn, storing it in an old chest that was free of mildew and vermin. It wouldn't do for the missus to be seen carrying such items for their use. No more eating in the kitchen once Lettie came, either. He'd get the food and eat in the barn once again.

It was an uncomfortable thought that Aoife would be left by herself in the evenings. Their convivial evenings together would be over—he couldn't risk sending Lettie into a fit. Their meetings would have to be in the barnyard, in full view of Lettie, if she roused enough to observe them. But there they could also be seen by any passerby.

He didn't relish another visit from Mrs. Sprigett, though Mr. William seemed to have set her straight. She had not come again and neither Thomas nor Aoife had heard more about discharging him. No, Mr. William had written Aoife that Thomas was to remain working on the farm and his mother, Mrs. Sprigett, had no say in the matter.

On Sunday, Thomas drove the farm cart into town and stopped in the square. Instead of going straight to the room he shared with Lettie, he went to the little church near the outskirts of the town.

"Preacher Matthews!" Thomas called.

A short, bearded man came from the small vestry off to the side of the main room. "Thomas." He held out his hand. "Good to see you."

"I've come to take Lettie away."

Matthews nodded. "I'll go round and bring the women from their work. They'll be relieved to no longer care for her, as she seems to sink further with each day, sometimes lucid, sometimes as deranged as anyone we have seen. They fear they will fail you at the task of keeping her safe, Thomas, and you are a great favorite with the ladies." He winked and slipped from the church while Thomas waited.

The three women who had kept watch over Lettie, and who now vowed to help him get her to the farm, arrived at the church. They all wore the ordinary dress in which they worked, two as laundresses and the other as a baker's assistant.

Thomas bowed to them. "One day, I hope to reward you with goods from my own farm, for there is no other way I can repay you."

"Jesus Himself rewards us," one of the laundresses said, "for He did say that if we visit the sick…"

Underwater

"… it is as if we do these things for Him instead," the baker's assistant broke in, "and it is promised that we will inherit His kingdom."

Pastor Matthews's smile made deep pocks in his ruddy-brown cheeks. "'Tis true, ladies. And 'tis true that Lettie will be well cared for. Perhaps that Sprigett woman will let us visit her of a Sunday, for charity's sake."

Thomas felt a flash of anger at Matthews referring to Aoife as "that Sprigett woman." He replied, "I'll ask Mrs. Sprigett, but am sure she shall have no objection."

But Lettie might.

Chapter 12

IRIS WAFFLED FOR A MOMENT before saying, "I forgot to tell you. I have a DNA report."

"You did? You do?" Charlotte's eyebrows nearly met her hairline.

Iris stood. "I'll just go get it from my husband's desk." She went into the house.

Benny sat in his office, watching a YouTube video on something having to do with programming. "'Sup?" he asked, his eyes fixed on the screen.

"I'm out by the pond with Charlotte…"

"Charlotte?"

She sighed and rummaged through the papers next to his keyboard. "Remember I told you that's the name of the doctoral student who wants to write about our little John Doe?"

"Oh, yeah." He didn't turn around. The video presenter's voice droned on with an Indian sub-continent accent. Men were strangely fascinated by these software videos, with their arcane acronyms and numbers.

Back out in the garden, Iris sat on the wall again and held out the envelope with the DNA results.

Charlotte pulled out the sheet and perused it. "Well, this confirms what I wondered about. The baby was mixed race."

"Why did you wonder that? The only photos made public were of the pond with the forensic lab people standing around…"

"Hey, speaking of photos, did you get any from the police or the coroner? I'm sure the police took some when they came, and a bunch must have been taken in the lab for the record and all. Not internal organs or anything, but the baby's face."

"It never occurred to me to ask." Requesting them sounded perilously close to being a morbid souvenir hunter, despite Iris's house being where the infant was found. Yet, she'd love to have at least one—she had been so bothered by the inability to picture little Jack's eyes and mouth, the curve of his cheek. "But you said you wondered if the baby wasn't white. What made you even think of that?"

"Well, uh…" Charlotte seemed to search for a reason to explain herself. "Well, he was in the pond, rather than in a proper grave. Hidden." Her eyes moved side-to-side a few times as if she was picking scattered words to string together. "But he was obviously loved, so well dressed, at least that's what I read in the news reports. Would still be great to see and touch the clothes. And, really, they're your property. We should get them back if they've still got them."

Iris thought for a moment. "I just remember the lace and how beautiful the stitching was on the little gown and bonnet." She shrugged. "I didn't think about the clothes when arranging to pay for his cremation. Much less expensive than burying a body, and I already had a silver urn that seemed appropriate. The graveyard's nearby—would you like to go visit him?"

"I'd love to, but we ought to check on the clothes first. Photos, if they'll give us any, can wait, but things like 150-year-old baby outfits would have a way of disappearing and winding up on eBay or Etsy."

It was getting on toward five o'clock. "I'll call first thing in the morning and go get them if they can still be found. But now, it's time for me to make dinner." She clapped her knees and stood.

Charlotte stood, too. "If it's okay, could I have the DNA report? It would make anything I write about this area, especially about the women, so much more intriguing."

Iris couldn't think of a reason to say no. Charlotte had already read it, anyway. "I'll go copy it on the printer."

"No need, really, not right away. A photo's fine." Charlotte rummaged in her worn canvas hobo bag and pulled out an iPhone.

Iris, reluctant to put the paper on the stone wall, held it up. Charlotte took a photo and, to Iris's surprise, hugged her tight after she put her phone away.

They walked together to Charlotte's car. After it disappeared down the drive, Iris went to the kitchen. She sautéed onions with garlic and tomatoes, leaving them on the stove to simmer. Once they were caramelized slightly, she added herbs and roughly chopped leftover arugula. Stirring always gave her time to think. As the strands of arugula went round and round, so did the thoughts in her head.

Why did Charlotte think little Jack might be mixed race? Because he was hidden away? Back in those days, any stillborn baby born to an unmarried or an adulterous woman would need to be quietly disposed of, no matter how loved. No matter how wanted.

Well, maybe she has a theory she doesn't want to share yet, something of more commercial than academic interest. She chuckled to herself. *As if I have aspirations in that direction!*

Benny came into the kitchen. "Making pasta sauce?"

"Yes, Captain Obvious." Benny did look a lot like the Hotels.com ad character, though his beard was smaller and whiter, and his expression was more exasperated.

"Want me to grate the Parmesan?" he asked. When she nodded, he added, "Did you have a nice time with Charlotte?"

"Sure." She turned down the burner.

He took out the electric grater and the Parmesan. "Jessica called. She'd like to take us out to dinner."

"Okay…" Her voice trailed off.

"But first, I think you and I should talk."

"That's a good idea." She sighed. "I really have been awful for a while now."

"Ever since that body was found in our pond."

The cheese grater began its high-pitched whirring, and steam rose as the pasta water started to boil.

Thomas

1862

The churchwomen came willingly with Thomas, eager to do a good deed. Though Lettie had held herself apart from them and so had much turned their sympathy to enmity, they were believers from her congregation, and he hoped they'd help convince her to leave town for the farm. Ruth, the bakery woman, was to bring Maisy's cart from the square and wait discreetly in the street.

Should Thomas's sweet talk fail, and neither the women's counsel nor the laudanum they planned to pour down her throat, should it be needed to subdue her, then their hands, strong from scrubbing clothes or kneading dough, would prove useful in taking her away. They would also help keep things quiet—he did not wish a public display made of his Lettie.

"It is good you have come for her, Thomas. She has accosted men in the street lately," Ruth said when she clambered into the cart behind Maisy and took up the reins. "Good Quaker gentlemen who have done nothing wrong. Called them *defiler*, *debaucher*, even *whoremonger*, chased them on the streets, pulling at their clothes and spitting. The constable says something must be done, or they'll put her in the lunatic asylum in Harrisburg. It reflects badly on our community. We know she is no real lunatic, simply a soul the world has treated too harshly."

Thomas put his hand on the mare's withers to reassure the animal and said to Ruth, "When I come, she sits quiet and still. Too quiet, perhaps."

"You calm her by your very presence, Thomas, though you might not see it."

"I hope the country air, the peaceful beasts, the green fields, and the birds singing will enable her to reflect on the Lord's bounty and bring her lasting calm. And Mrs. Sprigett has said she will make wholesome fare for her."

Ruth's eyes widened. "She will serve you and Lettie?"

"Mrs. Sprigett, for all being an Irish Papist, is a wife devoted to keeping her husband's farm safe. She knows there is not another worker to be found and will do what needs must. She already feeds me, quite well…"

Ruth chuckled. "Lettie was not known for her cookery. But be careful, Thomas, of such a woman as Mrs. Sprigett, whilst her husband is away at war." She ducked her head. "Best if we go in now and get her. The other ladies and I have the day's work to tend to."

Thomas's heart pounded hard at the thought of entering the room. So hard, it felt likely to escape the prison of his ribcage. One step after another, he and the two women climbed the stairs. This was the first time he'd done something that Lettie might see as bending her to his wishes.

"Courage, Thomas." One of the women touched his back lightly as he led the way. He turned and saw it was Nan, of whom Lettie once said, "She puts me in mind of Sary." Nan's compassion brought tears to his eyes. She was an uncomplaining wife, whose husband failed to support his children and often took his rage out on the nearest member of his family. To protect her babies, Nan made as sure as possible the nearest was herself.

Once he and Lettie had their own place, Nan and her babies would find refuge there, when needed.

The flight of stairs seemed too short to lead to what Lettie could view as a betrayal and what might cost him her trust. No matter, the asylum in Harrisburg was enough of a threat to put his own fears aside.

Lettie lay face up on the bed, her arm flung over her eyes.

"My darling…" He walked toward her slowly, so as not to alarm. Not a muscle twitched in her arm. He stepped closer, fearing her chest didn't rise or fall. *Is she not breathing?*

He touched her, fearing only cold flesh would meet his fingers, but she was as warm as always. Alive.

At his touch she spoke. "Thomas. This is not Sunday. I'm sleeping."

"No, Lettie, it's not Sunday, and you are not sleeping."

She curled on her side away from him, like a newborn who hadn't yet learned she was free to stretch her limbs.

"I've come to take you away with me to the farm."

"To your whore?"

Thomas sighed. "She is my employer, Lettie, and our chance for a farm of our own."

"Is her husband still away?"

To Thomas's surprise, she turned again and sat up, her head hanging on a neck that seemed too thin and frail to support even her curls or the tendrils that tumbled down her back from her untidy bun. Those curls, once glistening deep brown, capturing the sun in reddish hints, hung limp like burnt straw. He feared that, should he run his fingers through them as he'd loved to do, bits would break off and fall to the ground.

Lettie reached out and grabbed the iron of the bedpost. She staggered as she stood, and her face blanched further. "Leave me. I can care for myself here!" She swayed like a reed in a high wind.

Thomas caught her as she fainted dead away. The laudanum was not needed.

"She is very low. A woman should come with you, to nurse her," Nan said while gathering the few clothes Lettie possessed and putting them in a satchel. "But she has driven all from her. Anything dear to her here, a thing or two that might bring comfort when she opens her eyes?"

As he thought of their meager possessions, Thomas rocked Lettie in his arms like a baby. "That Bible—we signed our names in it soon as we were a 'we.' And that knotty string necklace with the arrowhead hanging from it." He silently blessed Nan. Lettie would have raged if the necklace had been left behind, since it had been Sary's most-prized possession.

He carried Lettie to the cart and laid her in its bed, her head on the satchel of clothing.

"The Lord be with you, Thomas, and may He return Lettie to soundness of mind," Ruth said as she stroked Maisy's neck, murmuring, "Good old girl."

The three women stood together, waving goodbye as Thomas slapped the reins on the mare's rump and headed back to the farm.

Aoife

1862

Aoife stood in the shade of the climbing rose; its branches still draped with faded yellow blooms. The rose clung to the stone wall just outside the kitchen door and, now that it had grown unruly from not being pruned, gave her a place to watch without being seen.

The muscles of her temples twitched, sending a sharp pain through her head. She sighed, partly with fear of Lettie's coming and partly regretting her own impulsive offering of the barn as shelter. But Thomas? Her generosity had come from concern for him. For his friendship and loyalty, she'd put up with being hated in her own home.

With nothing moving on the horizon, she slipped back inside. Grabbing the long-handled spoon, she stirred the beans simmering in the pot on the fireplace floor. The surface of the liquid glistened with fat—she'd put in big chunks of bacon.

There would have been more meat, had not Thomas taken most of a ham to Lettie. She didn't begrudge him that, though, with what he reported of Lettie's condition, it had most likely gone bad or been filched from the room Thomas rented.

Aoife stirred the beans, watching the bacon rise to the surface and, with the burst of a little bubble, disappear back down beneath the ale-rich broth, like mysterious portents. *It would be good if I could read the future in the beans, as my mam read it in the clouds, and know if bringing Lettie here would mean good or ill.*

Aoife kept her mind as far from her worry as she could, but she and Thomas had fallen into an easy rhythm of life on the farm—rising at the same hour, tending the beasts and the crops. Her body still ached in the night with longing for William's return, for the sweetness of kisses on awakening with the dawn and turning toward each other for the act, the very thought of which made her thighs quiver, weaken, and grow damp with sweat.

William's last letter had apologized for a time of silence.

My darling honey wife,
  I hope this letter finds you in good spirits and, of course, the best of health.

Many apologies for my neglect in writing. It was not for lack of love, simply seemed a better course, as you had no one to read you letters but Thomas, and that allowed my mother to poke her sharp nose into our affairs.

With the dying of the old postmaster, Mr. Wilkinson, she will have no chance of knowing when a letter comes to you. The new postmaster is someone who served under me and who had the misfortune of being crippled in action. I petitioned to have him given the position and so have someone loyal to me—to us—in place.

I have been safe, lately serving under General John G. Barnard, Chief Engineer of the Defenses of Washington, building trenches and walls about the east side of our nation's capital. We have come under no attack and, the best news of all, our forces now control the great Mississippi, all excepting that by Vicksburg. I am confident that our forces shall soon secure that branch of the river as well.

How fare the crops this year? The livestock? I do not fear that they suffer neglect. Thomas is a careful and prudent man. However, Aoife, word has come to me that you have been working in the fields behind Maisy. This must stop. Yes, this knowledge comes from my mother and her local network of spies. There has never been a woman more meddlesome than she, nor more clever at meddling! If she worked for the Confederacy, our nation's great cause would be imperiled. Please dear heart, do nothing to arouse her curiosity or cause further gossip to reach her ears.

There is money put away to hire another man or, if none can be found, to let this year's crops diminish. Beware, though, not to hire any deserter. You would not have one peacefully plowing whilst your husband was serving.

That you are well, and the farm is doing well under Thomas's direction has been a great salve to my mind and soul, both of which were ill at ease upon leaving you.

Now for my best news: I may be granted a furlough before we head out through Virginia. So, relying on God's grace, I soon shall hold you in my arms and again gaze upon your shining face.

With all my love,
Your husband
William

Aoife had already chosen to ignore his request that she cease working the farm alongside Thomas. Instead, she wove a broad-brimmed hat from clean straw and tied it on her head with a large scarf over the top, covering her cheeks. She knotted it tight beneath her chin. Her nose and chin, she covered with a paste of flour and water, and a worn pair of William's gloves flapped from her hands. She sweated fearfully and looked a comical fright, yet with luck, her efforts would mean some measure of her beauty would be preserved.

Thomas urged her to retire from all except the milking, the kitchen garden, and the chickens, but the thought of lessening her chores dismayed her. What would she do with her day, then? Melancholy would overwhelm her, and she would be no better off than Lettie.

Lettie. Now there was another matter. Should Mother Sprigett get wind of Thomas's woman, said to be mad, arriving at William's home, she would surely make her feelings known.

Down the hill, beneath the elm trees on either side of the road, a modest cloud of dust arose. Maisy, under the whip, was trotting with the cart behind.

Chapter 13

DINNER WAS OVER, the last dried strands of angel hair pulled from the sides of the pot. Benny was bringing the bowls to the sink and Iris was loading the dishwasher.

"Do you feel like talking, now?" Benny hugged her around her waist. "Tell me what's on your mind."

Cowardly, asking to talk and then depending on me to open the discussion. Iris took a step back from Benny's arms.

"Just give me something, hon."

"Okay." She took a deep breath. "Please, please don't refer to our little John Doe as *the body* or as *it* anymore. It brings it all back, that horrible time long ago. It makes me feel like you don't care now, just like you didn't care then."

"What? What are you talking about? How can you even say that?"

"You didn't care. If you had, you wouldn't have done what you did."

"What I did?" His breathing was faster and faster as he grabbed her shoulders and held her roughly at arms' length. "How dare you? Of course, I cared!"

He pushed her away and her back bumped painfully against the counter's edge beneath the kitchen's bay window.

They were interrupted by Freddy barking as a white van pulled up next to the barn. Taking advantage of the long summer day, several of the stucco workers had returned to remove the scaffolding from the new mudroom's finished walls. The sight of strangers at their home broke the spell and they paused airing their grievances with each other.

"The full crew was here today," Benny said, taking the empty coffee carafe and shaking it as if he wanted more.

Iris turned to gaze out the window, watching the young men climb from the truck and disappear around the front of the house. They seemed to stagger as if their dinner break had included a good bit of beer. They returned in just a minute, carrying the heavy metal pieces.

"Iris," Benny's voice was now soft and private, but he spoke through clenched teeth. His brows were set tight and desperate. "Tell me."

"Our baby was dead. She died inside of me." Iris poked her own chest, hard, with her index finger. Poked herself again and again for emphasis. "Me! Inside of me, not you, and you never talked to me about her. You never grieved her. You were too occupied with other things. Work… For you it was like she'd never existed."

Benny's face blanched. He looked gut-punched and as if he couldn't take another breath. He gasped, his mouth dropped open, like someone surfacing in the middle of drowning. His eyes rolled wildly.

For a moment, fear and confusion overwhelmed her. She took one step forward to support him but stopped herself. She wouldn't be that easy, not after all the time that had passed.

"That's not the way it was." His words came out in jagged bits that hurt her ears. "How could you? How could you? How could you?" His voice seemed stuck in a bitter rhythm.

"How could *I*? How could you be so trite, having that tawdry affair? Fucking someone in your office?"

He peddled backward, slumped into a chair, and leaned over with his hands pressed against his chest. He said, "Iris,

I'm sorry. I'm sorry. But how could you believe I haven't suffered, too?" He took two deep, gasping breaths, and slumped to the floor.

Ten to one, this is another panic attack. I'm sick of dealing with shit from that stupid war. "Come on, Ben, get up."

But Benny didn't get up. Iris called 911.

Aoife
1862

The cart rolled into the barnyard more rapidly than it had come down the road. Maisy no longer needed the whip. She wanted to return to her feed and water, as horses will, and threatened to pull the cart into the frame of the barn door.

"Whoa!" Thomas called. The obstinate Maisy ignored him. When she kept on, Aoife grabbed the traces and held the mare still so Thomas could climb down and lift Lettie from the cart's bed.

"I'll unhitch Maisy and water her. Tend to your Lettie." Aoife pulled on the reins and led the mare off. She was glad to have a task to delay coming near Lettie. The woman was cradled in Thomas's arms, draped across his chest like a rag doll whose sawdust stuffing had leaked out.

It was all real now, Thomas's Lettie had come, and life on the farm would be different. It felt as if the ground shifted beneath Aoife's feet.

She should have been more prepared. The barn should have been made ready. Waiting to do chores had never been her way.

After Maisy drank from her water bucket and ambled into her paddock, Aoife had no further excuse to avoid helping settle the woman Thomas had brought from town. She went into the barn and pulled the quilts from the box where Thomas had stored them, safe from vermin. They were fragrant still with the lavender water she'd sprinkled on them after washing.

The barn was so still and peaceful. Maisy and the cows were outside, so even their quiet chewing and the shuffle of their feet were missing. Only the whistle of bird wings was heard above the dusty rafters.

Aoife sorted through the hay for the sweetest smelling, which she heaped in the corner where Thomas slept on the ground, softened only by a blanket. She shaped the hay into the rough shape of a mattress, covered it with a quilt, and laid another quilt atop. As Thomas had described Lettie wasting away from not eating, it seemed that the woman might need covering on even the warmest days. Though the air remained hot and stifling through the night, Aoife had memories enough of starvation making sufferers chill down to the marrow of their bones. *But hot broth from the bean pot is rich and salty and should help restore her to herself.*

Aoife went outside again and said to Thomas, "Bring her to the bed I've made."

All the while, she wondered what Lettie, restored, would mean for herself.

Thomas

1862

Lettie hadn't stirred on the way to the farm, despite the jouncing of the cart. Thomas had glanced over his shoulder often to assure himself that she was still with him and still breathing. His heart ached at how low she looked, but his spirits had risen at the sight of Aoife, stepping out into the yard from her lurking spot behind the climbing rose.

As Thomas jumped down from the cart, Hero ran barking from the field where he'd been hunting mice beneath the cut hay. At a whispered "Hush," the dog immediately quieted.

Thomas gathered Lettie in his arms and carried her to his old rush-seated chair by the barn door. He sat, Lettie on his lap, her head against his chest where, hopefully, his heartbeat would keep her quiet, as a baby is soothed against a mother's bosom. Hero settled at his feet with a contented sigh— Thomas rarely sat still during the day, when a dog could enjoy the sun's warmth. The dog looked up at Thomas with adoration and leaned his head against Thomas's leg. *Though we feed and care for both, how superior is a dog to a horse in obedience and love for humankind.* But Hero's pleasure was brief, as Aoife quickly returned.

"Thomas, bring her," Aoife said when he'd failed to rise at her first summons. "Better to not keep her here in the sun. She will burn almost as easily as I. Her skin is pale honey to my whey." Aoife stood before him, brushing the loose hay from her skirt.

Whey? Thomas had a flash of memory of the hollow beneath Aoife's throat, the barely visible swell of her pale bosom's top as she leaned over the table, of the faint blue veins that coursed there. *Where the sunlight has yet to cause reddening, your skin is more like the freshest cream, not like watery whey. But yes, Lettie's was once honey sweet.* He felt a warm rush of affection for Aoife, as she praised Lettie's beauty and placed it before her own. He'd never heard another woman do such a thing.

He stood slowly; sitting so still had stiffened his joints. Stretched out one leg and then the other. Satisfied that his gait was steady, he brought Lettie inside the barn's shaded interior.

"I've put out the good feather pillow for her poor head." At that, Aoife turned and left for the house.

Thomas lay his woman on the straw bed. She opened her eyes and looked about but didn't grow agitated. He hoped it pleased her to be provided such an agreeable space, cool, lit by the sun's filtered rays, fragrant with hay, high roof rafters a-twitter with swallows. He longed to stretch out beside her but feared she might fly into a rage.

Aoife reappeared, looking like a specter with her wide straw hat, scarf, and gloves. She carried a tray holding a steaming bowl. "Bean broth. A starved stomach often cannot take solids right off." She placed the bowl on the barn's floor. "See if she'll sup a bit from the spoon." She headed toward the door.

"Wait," Thomas whispered to her, "begin binding the hay where I first cut, near the old apple orchard. The women come to help after midday when their town work is done." The bean broth's fragrant steam made his stomach rumble. He hadn't eaten since the previous night.

Aoife stifled her laugh with her hand and said, "Your belly might disturb her with its grumbling. Get a bowl for yourself with bread while she slumbers."

Lettie stirred after Aoife left and struggled to sit. When he helped her up, she spat into the dust of the floor. "Thomas, do not let that woman near me again."

Thomas's heart sank at her words. "Hush, my dear. Your mind is disordered and sees bad where there is good." He lifted a spoonful of the rich-smelling bean broth to her lips. "Now eat," he said, as sternly as he could.

Chapter 14

INSIDE THE HOSPITAL, waiting to find out what the doctors thought Benny's issue was, Iris realized how small her social network was now. She knew carpenters, plumbers, and masons, she had a new dentist and doctors, but had no close women friends. Everyone she'd known growing up in Philadelphia was either dead or had moved away. The house and little Jack Doe had eaten up so much of her time, she hadn't cultivated new acquaintances. Without Benny, she was alone.

The hospital was still under COVID rules and only patients were allowed into the treatment room. It felt so unnatural, so uncaring, having to wait for someone to come out through the locked doors to tell Iris what was wrong with Benny. Her husband of forty years. She should be at his bedside, holding his hand.

The intake area was crowded with patients waiting to be seen. Some held bloody pieces of cloth, paper towels, or other wrappings to various body parts, a few elevated a swollen ankle or cradled a wrist, several rocked while holding their heads, and others groaned, bending over their bellies. An elderly lady in a wheelchair, oxygen prongs in her nostrils, moaned and coughed, removing her mask to spit into a tissue. Few were unaccompanied.

The only person Iris could think to call was Charlotte, who said, "Of course. I'll be right there." She arrived in less than half an hour.

"It's so nice of you to come, Charlotte." Iris's voice was muffled by the mask the hospital still required. It had been a while since she'd worn one and, on arrival, she'd sorted desperately through her belongings fearing she would be turned away, though the hospital was awash with masks, if the littered parking lot was any indication. Thank goodness she found one stuffed in the center console of her SUV. It had a ketchup stain from a serving of french fries back somewhere in Illinois. What possible good could it do to protect her or anyone around her? The intake attendant said nothing about its inadequacy.

Charlotte wore one, too. A considerably cleaner one. "Glad to be here if you need me."

"Could be hours." Iris already felt wrong, having someone she'd known for such a short time. She should have family. Close friends. Benny.

Stop that! Hold it together. It's nice she came.

"That's okay. It gives us time to learn more about each other." She pointed to the other end of the room. "Look, if we move to that corner we can talk privately."

They went behind a pillar where two armchairs sat isolated from the rest of the crowded waiting area.

"Want tea or coffee?" Charlotte asked as she put her things on the small table in front of the chairs.

Iris shook her head, which felt numb and hollow, her thoughts echoing in the empty space. She remembered all the stories she heard from friends who'd lost someone they loved, all those, "My God, the last thing I said to him was said in anger, and now I can never set things right." Sooner or later, she figured, the guilt would overwhelm her, but for now, all she felt was fear. *What would life be like, fixing up the house alone? Eating and sleeping alone?*

The incipient guilt came next. *Oh shit, was that thought totally selfish?* And, *All those times his hand was over his heart. Were those warning signs dismissed because I was so angry?*

"Have you called your son? Hal, was it? Anyone else?" Charlotte asked. "Is there someone you'd want me to call?"

"No, no. They're fine and I'm waiting to tell them until I know something. Hal would jump on a plane right away and it might be... it hopefully would be over nothing." For all that bravery and proud talk of Hal's devotion, Iris wished like mad that he was with her. She sank deep in longing for his competence, warmth, and—even more—for one of his bear hugs.

"You and your husband never had..." Charlotte's voice dropped off. She hadn't finished her question with "children of your own."

She nearly snapped at Charlotte but stopped herself in time. The younger woman was just trying to be a friend, hell, *was* being a friend, giving up her time to sit in the hospital with someone she'd only recently met. And, insensitive as it might be, "Do you have kids?" was just something that people asked.

For Iris, that lack, those memories were the worst thing to bring up, especially now, when asked in caring innocence. "Just Hal. He may be adopted but he took a week off work to drive us old folks here. He's that kind of son."

"That's so nice!" Charlotte blushed and lapsed into silence, as if she didn't know what to say.

Iris looked around. The waiting area was unchanged. Not one new patient had been taken into the back. *What were they up to back there? Where was the damned doctor? Or a nurse? Anyone who would give an update on Benny?* She could barely sit still—her anxiety level was rising so fast. She itched all over like a thousand ants crawled on her skin beneath her clothes.

Desperately she blurted out, "I was pregnant once, a little girl. Stillborn. Died just before her due date."

"Oh." Charlotte shifted in her seat. The mask made it hard to read her expression.

As discomfited as the young woman seemed to be at such a bald revelation, telling someone at last made Iris's chest muscles relax. She could breathe more easily. *Confession really might be good for the soul.*

"I'm sorry."

"I was pregnant when we moved from here to California, thirty-some years ago. I grew up in these parts, you know. Well, down in Philadelphia."

"I did not know that." Charlotte's voice was blandly polite, as if she was uncertain what to say.

Iris rolled her sweaty palms up and down her thighs, wiping them on her pants. She willed herself to stop but her hands seemed to have a mind of their own. "Yeah. We wanted a fresh start, a more relaxed lifestyle, a warmer, friendlier place to raise a child. California seemed to fit the bill with all that sunshine and so on. The old cities in the East were a mess, just crime pits. We wanted to let our kid run around free. Most of the Bay Area was like that then, safe. Or seemed so." She laughed. "Except for the earthquakes and serial killers."

Charlotte nodded.

"So there we were, far from family, knowing no one, Benny in a new job that took up most of his time, but were in a good place, both of us gloriously happy to be in such a beautiful spot. And me getting everything ready to welcome the wonderful little being, swimming like a crazy happy dolphin inside me." She paused to work up saliva to moisten her dry throat. "And suddenly, I just knew everything was wrong."

"How could you tell?"

"I woke in the middle of the night and there was nothing there. No more somersaults, no more punching my liver or kicking my bladder. Nothing but deadly stillness. I had just turned thirty. We hadn't even had my planned birthday dinner yet—you know, when the whole gang of waiters comes out with a teeny sparkler-decorated cake and sings 'Happy Birthday'? Well, that never happened." Iris never again let Benny celebrate her birthday.

Someone called Iris's name. A nurse in Donald Duck scrubs, anonymous in an N95 mask that reminded her of plague doctors, stood scanning the room, holding a clipboard to her cartoon bedecked chest. Iris rose partway and waved. "Here!"

The woman walked over.

"It's nothing serious, just a panic attack, right? I told the EMT he's prone to them."

The nurse's face remained expressionless. "Your husband is resting now. So far, there's no confirmation of anything serious. Dr. dela Cruz is doing another ECG and set of labs and if they're normal, which the first set was, he'll be doing a treadmill test right here in our department. The good news is, if that's okay, you'll both be going home."

"How long before I can see him?" Iris asked, still half-standing, holding on to the chair's armrests for support.

"I can't tell you yet, but it will be at least two hours. Because of COVID regulations, you can't come into the treatment rooms." The nurse turned to leave then turned back again and put on a professionally sympathetic smile. "We'll keep you updated, of course."

Iris dropped back into her seat, so relieved that a flood of embarrassment swept over her. She turned to Charlotte. "It seems a shame to keep you. Why don't you go?"

Charlotte fiddled in her bag and finally pulled out a cell phone. "I do have somewhere I'm supposed to be, a family thing. But I hate to leave you."

"I'll be all right. Go on, then."

"Really, I feel bad." She trailed her fingers slowly along the back of her chair, in no hurry to leave.

"I'll call you tomorrow," Iris said. "We'll arrange a visit to the coroner for photos and hopefully Little Jack's clothes."

After Charlotte left, Iris scoured the room for something to read and found a few ancient magazines lying about on the tables. When she leaned over to take a few of them, the people nearby drew back from her as if *CONTAGIOUS* was branded on her forehead, though her mask was still in place. Even those wearing their own masks below their noses.

The good news from the nurse had made her mood ebullient. She kept herself back from saying something snide, but it took effort.

Aoife
1862

She did not need to be close to Lettie to know the woman didn't want her near, she could read it in her eyes, no matter how sunken from lack of food and drink. And, looking back before she left, Aoife had seen the spittle fly. Thick as it was, it must have taken a lot of hate to get from such a dry mouth.

Anger rose in her at being looked at like a scuttling roach in the pantry. And to be looked at so by Lettie! She had been glared at and then dismissed before, but that was by those to whom she was an inferior. What right did this woman have to treat her so?

Aoife stomped up into the hayfield, tripping on the stubble as she headed to the driest patch of cut hay. She began tying sheaves, wrapping one long stalk around a bundle of its fellows, holding them tight together. The sun was blazing, but both her coverings and her anger made her hotter than its rays.

I have only myself to blame, for I told Thomas to bring her here. By now, he is feeding her my good broth, like a nursemaid with a sick child. She scratched her scalp, which itched dreadfully under the woven straw.

An ancient wagon, pulled by a swayback gelding, rattled into the barnyard and two women climbed down. Thomas came from the barn and spoke to them, pointing up to where Aoife bent gathering the hay. She watched them from the corner of her eye, wondering if they would regard her as coldly as Lettie did. Her hands grabbed a bundle and bound it into a sheaf and then tied another as they approached.

Both women bobbed their heads in acknowledgment when they reached her. It did not seem to be mocking deference but simple politeness. "You be Mrs. Sprigett?" asked the taller and stouter of the two.

Aoife straightened, her hand going to her aching back. "That I am."

"Mamie." She pointed at her enormous bosom. "We come to help 'cause Thomas asked us. He said you and your man been good to him. And now you let him bring Lettie here."

Aoife couldn't help but roll her eyes beneath the shade of the hat's brim. The women laughed.

"You right! Lettie sure is hard to have around. Downright crazy and full of spite! Watch yourself. Stronger than she looks and..."

"My name is Nan," the smaller of the two interrupted. "We know all too well how Lettie can be and realize the burden on you. Poor thing, she's been through so much. She cannot help herself. Thomas is closest thing to a saint of any man alive. Thank you kindly for doing right by him."

The other woman, Mamie, spoke up again, quickly, her voice tight. "'Fore we forget, we each gets fifty-five cents for what's left of the day when our town work's done. Less if you give us board. Fifty-five cents, that is what we get. We'll work just as hard as a man, and a man would be twice as much." She paused. "For a full day, I know, but we'll get all the hay ready for stacking in…" She looked over the field, moving her lips as she assessed the labor. "… three days, working 'til we can't see no more."

"I can surely use the help and find fifty-five cents a day appears quite fair." Aoife held out her hand and shook on the deal. "And board will be included if you want beans flavored with ham. I have a full pot and two fresh loaves of bread to soak up the pot liquor."

"We'll get to work now," Nan said. "We know what to do. It grows dark, we'll come back to the yard to eat and then return to town."

They all began to gather the hay, Mamie and Nan each tying four sheaves to one of Aoife's. In less than an hour, Nan spoke up. "You go back and see to Thomas, maybe free him up to stack as we go. Best for the hay."

When Aoife failed to leave the field, the bigger woman snorted. "Go on now. Hay'll never be got in this way. We're faster than you but we need Thomas to stack. Someone has got to be down there if Lettie causes trouble. We would not willingly go near her."

Nan shot her a stern look and turned to Aoife. "If Lettie is such that you cannot handle, shout out and we'll come running."

Thomas

1862

He'd gotten some bean broth down Lettie's reluctant throat, though she'd sprayed nearly as much on his shirt. Now she lay exhausted, sleeping, her eyes moving beneath their lids like anxious birds fluttering in their cages.

The hay harvest was critical to the farm's success. The farm's success was critical to him getting the promised acreage and providing a home for the family he still hoped to have. He longed to be out working instead of sitting on the barn's floor, but he couldn't leave Lettie alone.

Aoife appeared at the barn door. He held a finger to his lips to keep her from speaking, rose, and stretched. He stepped out from the cool barn into the sun.

"The women feel I am not up to snuff and have sent me back to let you join them. They order me to remain by the barn should Lettie awaken."

Thomas smiled at her words. "They mean well. Does that suit you, Aoife? Playing nursemaid? It is more than I can expect." The hem of his shirt had come free. He tucked it into his pants.

"We need the hay safe, Thomas. That is what William expects from us. If my being here is better, so be it."

"I fear Lettie is… difficult."

"As a maid, I cared for Mother Sprigett, who was more like to throw her water glass at me as thank me for my efforts. Old and fat she be, yet still more fearsome than Lettie." Aoife's face was set in determination, her round little chin uplifted and firm. Her voice softened. "To tell the truth, with needing to cover so much of me, it is a relief to be out of the sun."

Thomas started to the field, ready to work alongside the townswomen. Something made him turn before he had gone through the yard's gate. Back by the barn, Aoife unhitched the women's elderly gelding from the wagon, patting his flank and speaking too low to be overheard. She led the horse to the watering trough. The gelding drank then swayed his back further to let loose an enormous stream of piss. Aoife jumped back, as a farmwife would, to save her skirts from the splatter, but held on to the reins. Thomas's heart seemed to swell in his bosom at the sight of her, a lady, so determined to make the farm succeed. Embarrassed, he turned back toward the field. Ahead, the women were working feverishly under the smoldering August sun.

"Thomas," Nan said when he reached them, "that lady acts Quaker though she talks Irish."

He laughed. "And she is generous, is she not? Wait until supper. Her beans are good, cooked through and well-seasoned. I cured the ham myself and there are generous bits throughout."

The women paused and looked at each other, shaking their kerchiefed heads. Nan spoke again. "You sound too much like a proud husband."

He picked up a pitchfork and stabbed it into the ground. Leaning heavily on the handle, he said, "I am no such thing. She is my employer yet works under my directions. That's all."

Nan bent and gathered hay to make another sheaf. "Take care, Thomas. People are talking. Not just the white ones, but our people, too."

"That risk is always in my thoughts." He pulled out the tool, turned away, and forked up several sheaves, forming them into the start of a stack.

Nan lay her sheaf on the ground and began another. "Remember, we are here for you, not for any fondness of Lettie."

Chapter 15

NO ONE HAD COME OUT from the ER in an hour. Iris wanted to go home to take Freddy out before he peed in the house. She had finished up the second magazine of diet recipes, flipped through all the *Architectural Digest*s, a *Times*, the single *Country Life*, and three *Highlights*. She was looking through her purse for the car keys when her name was called.

"Here!" She raised her hand like a schoolgirl.

This nurse wore scrubs with an all-over print of playful cats. Her mask also sported frolicking felines. "The doctor can speak with you now," she said. "Put this on." She handed Iris a clean surgical mask. She paused to glare at a man wearing his mask incorrectly but turned quicky back to Iris. "Over your nose, too."

When Iris changed her mask, the woman went back to the treatment area door, pausing to point her out to a short man in a white coat. Her anxiety spiked at the sight of that coat, which brought back unpleasant hospital memories and a sense of impending disaster. She began to shake.

The doctor introduced himself so quickly that Iris didn't catch his name, except to recognize his accent as possibly Filipino and assume he was Dr. dela Cruz. He didn't hold out his hand to shake hers. "You are Mister…" He paused to take a quick look at the chart he held. "… Pearl's family?"

Iris locked her knees to still her trembling. "His wife. And you're Dr. dela Cruz?"

He nodded.

"How is Benny and when can I see him?"

"Sorry for the wait. Mr. Pearl is resting and comfortable. All tests so far show nothing worrisome. In fact, everything is completely negative, and if we weren't so busy, he'd be on the treadmill right now." He bent ever so slightly toward her and asked, in a conspiratorial manner, "Does he often have those panic attacks?"

"That's what he had? Not a heart attack?"

Beady eyes searching her face, dela Cruz deadpanned through his mask, his voice blandly monotone. "His symptoms are consistent with a panic attack and severe heartburn. We've given him a GI cocktail—an antacid and a topical numbing agent. If he gets relief from that, it's more than likely heartburn. The older we get…" His tone became condescendingly sweet, and she wished his mask away, so she could see his expression. "… the less the lining of our swallowing tube and stomach can take spices. Did he by any chance have something spicy for dinner? Or maybe you gave him something too acidic, like tomato sauce?"

She stiffened. Was he saying it was her fault? "But he passed out…"

"Hyperventilation does that. He must have been under a lot of stress for some reason. Sometimes people need a lot more emotional support than they're getting."

He *was* blaming her, without knowing her at all. Iris was astonished and angry.

Fuck you, you little self-important twerp! She took a breath to keep from saying anything aloud. That attitude would get her nowhere, and, as Benny's doctor, he *was* important. Instead, she smiled her best meek *I'm old, too, but I love my husband too much to care about my ego now* smile. "Can I see him?"

"If we were admitting him, you'd be able to go to his room, but family is not allowed in the emergency treatment area." He cleared his throat. "He should be discharged in a short time, if the treadmill test is normal. By the way, he's a really likable guy. Told me a couple of jokes."

Iris returned to her chair. Even if Benny's problem was gastritis, she had triggered it. And it had been severe and painful enough to make him pass out. Usually, her hospital anxiety made her agitated but now she felt worse, more restless. She shifted in her seat and jiggled her right leg, taking note of who arrived to be evaluated and who left, satisfied or not. She wanted to bitch with someone about the wait and the staff's rude arrogance, but the mask restrictions made that tough. The other people kept their eyes down or looked about warily.

At last, the nurse in duck scrubs returned to say, "Dr. dela Cruz is coming to speak to you again. Wait there." She pointed to the door.

The doctor was quick to arrive. "Mrs. Pearl, I'm afraid your husband didn't do well on the treadmill. We've sent him straight to the cath lab. Cardiology will handle things from now on."

"What?" Iris took hold of the door to steady herself. "Has he had a heart attack?"

"I'm afraid we don't know that yet." Dela Cruz stepped back through the door, adding, "Sorry."

If only she'd asked Charlotte to stay with her. She called Hal, but it went straight to voicemail. She didn't leave a message. He wouldn't be able to leave until the morning and she'd know more by then. Instead, she went into the bathroom and vomited from nerves.

Two hours later, a voice echoed in her ear, "Mrs. Pearl?"

She jumped up, confused. She seemed to have drifted off without falling asleep. A tall man with an unruly shock of hair, like the crest of a crazed rooster, walked up to her. He wore blue scrubs, plain, no animals. "Yes, that's me."

"I have some very good news. Your husband is fine."

"There was nothing wrong with his heart? It was all a mistake?"

He wiped his forehead with the back of his hand, though he didn't seem to have been sweating. "No, not quite. He had almost complete blockage of the main artery to the largest pumping chamber of his heart, the left ventricle. He was in the early stages of a heart attack. But he was very lucky."

In what way is that lucky?

"We got to him in time. Stopped any damage from happening. That's really lucky because the most usual presentation with a heart attack from that blood vessel is sudden death. It's called the widow maker."

Iris took a sudden breath in. "But he's all right?"

Instead of answering the question directly, the doctor turned over two papers he held in his hand, saying, "Before and after." Each had a photo resembling a roadmap in white on the dark background. The biggest road, really a highway, on one, was missing on the other, cut off as if by a roadblock. "These are photos of his cath. This one..." He held the picture of the open road. "Is the after. Totally normal. The stent is supplying all the blood a normal artery would. Bloodwork and post-op ECGs confirm there has been no injury to heart muscle. He'll be discharged tomorrow, able to do anything he wants to."

"Anything?"

"Anything." He handed her the two papers, as souvenirs, it seemed. "You can go see him now."

After he left, Iris went up to the cardiac floor, to Benny's room. "Hi, honey," she said. "I'm so glad you're okay."

He was groggy, his voice weak. "Yeah, I'm okay. How are you doing?" He didn't wait for a reply. "Christ, you look exhausted. You've been here all day. Go home and get some food and rest."

Is he brushing me off? "No, I'm fine. Couldn't wait to see you."

"Don't know what they gave me, but all I want to do now is sleep."

"Should I call Hal?"

"He'll want to come but he can't take more time off now. And the kids… I'll be fine; no damage done. Really, just go on home."

She took her purse and stood, feeling strangely embarrassed, as if the nurses would judge her for leaving.

"Iris. Don't forget that I love you. We'll get through this."

The next morning, she waited for Benny to be discharged. When the attendant wheeled him out of the elevator, Iris jumped up to get the car. A few minutes later, she stood by the open passenger door as Benny was wheeled out.

They pulled out of the parking lot before he said anything. "They were very nice and efficient," were his first words.

"Uh-huh." She wanted to get home so they could be face-to-face and there was no traffic to distract her. "Though the ER doctor had the personality of a wet flounder."

"A wet flounder? Redundant. Flounders are always wet when they're alive." And then he was silent until they turned onto their road. "He seemed to think I was faking. *Heh*, I proved him wrong." A minute later he said, "It was humiliating."

"What?"

"Being wheeled around. Not being believed."

Iris parked the car at the top of their drive. "Let's go in and talk. I'll make some herbal tea." She reached across him to open his door.

He batted her hand away. "For Christ's sake, Iris, don't treat me like a fucking invalid. I'm fine."

She pulled her arm back so quickly that her elbow hit him in the chest.

"On the other hand, a sharp blow to the heart can kill you," he said, then, on seeing her stricken look, added, "Joking! Joking! We got nothing if we ain't got humor." He laughed. "We still don't have the new kitchen cabinets or a working range."

From inside the house, Freddy began frantic barking in his, "You've been gone for years and years!" hysteria.

Aoife

1862

After unhitching the women's horse and providing for him, Aoife stirred the beans. Scorching them would make them bitter and prove false Thomas's praise of her cooking. She moved the pot a bit further from the fire and went back to the barn.

There she found Lettie lying supine, hands resting on the top quilt, eyes open. Above them darting in the air about the rafters, the swallows caught flies and gnats. Their aerial dance was like the waltzes the older Sprigett girl had bragged about to her sister, who was too young to attend the balls in Philadelphia. *The swallows are softer, dearer creatures than those girls could ever hope to be.*

"It is peaceful here, is it not?" she asked the still figure lying under the quilt. "I think I shall bring my knitting and sit here for a while, listening to the birds."

Lettie did not reply.

"I could never bear to be idle." All of Aoife's being wanted to depart completely, even to return to the field and the hot sun. But for the sake of peace on William's property and to help Thomas, she would persevere. In a moment, she returned from the house with her basket of handiwork and sat on the chest with the long wooden needles, casting on yarn from the farm's flock.

She worked in silence for an hour, fashioning a new sweater for William, to gift him on his return. Blue as the sky, his favorite color. But she was exhausted from working in the sun, under her hot and heavy garments. When she felt herself nodding off in the pleasant dim light and hay-fragrant atmosphere, she gathered her things again, stood, and said, "I must go feed the chickens and make sure there is food enough for the workers. The cows and their babies need be turned out to graze in the evening cool. Between chores, you'll get tea with bread and fresh butter."

Thomas's woman remained almost completely still. She didn't turn to look at Aoife, only her lips began to move. Silently at first, but slowly becoming a whisper. Aoife inclined her body to be closer, straining to listen. Lettie spoke in a voice that didn't rise or fall with emotion. Instead, her tone was so flat, so unchanging, it was more of an insult than the evil words it conveyed. "The master had a parrot stolen from Africa to mock us, but that damned bird didn't talk as much as you, papist bitch. Coming up to my man like you're in heat. And him liking it, though you got a fine man of your own. Whore. You an' him can both leave me to myself. Leave me to die."

Thomas

1862

Thomas led the weary townswomen back to the farmhouse. While they sat for a moment on the chairs by the barn door, he pumped water into a pail, pouring it into the trough where he washed himself after fieldwork. "I have soap in my kit. I'll bring it for you. Then I'll keep myself to the barn with Lettie, leave you alone while you wash." He pumped another bucket and took it with him for his own ablutions.

Lettie lay as he'd left her, staring upward. She didn't stir when he took the soap out, nor when he returned.

"Did you have a good day, love? Sleep a bit?" He stripped off his sweat-soaked shirt and dipped a rag into the bucket. "It was very hot, but Nan and Mamie worked as hard as ever." He was determined to chatter even if just to keep her aware the world existed outside her mind. "Mrs. Sprigett went back to the house. She was kind enough to say she'd keep watch over you until I returned. She also offered meals with the generous pay she's giving your fellow church ladies. I'll be eating with them in a moment and bringing your supper back."

Something in Lettie's eyes, though they moved not at all save for her same slow blinking from time to time, let him know that she was listening closely. It took him a moment to realize they were focused on more than the birds above. That gave him hope this present spell was ending, as others had before.

Thomas pulled on a dry shirt hanging on a peg by the halters and put his work-stained one in its place for the next day's labor. He combed back his curls with his fingers and, before heading back out to where the two women waited, said, "Oh, Lettie, please be calm and good for Mrs. Sprigett. She is the one who bade me bring you to her farm." And then he left her for the yard.

Aoife appeared at the kitchen door, wiping her hands. When she smiled at the workers, Thomas feared she'd invite them all inside to eat at the kitchen table. Though he was sure they'd refuse, such a kindness might tell the women he was used to being in the house, alone with a white man's wife. Gossip in their community could only hurt Lettie more. And, if it came to the ears of William's mother, would hurt Mr. William and, most of all, Aoife.

He spoke quickly to the townswomen. "Ladies, please take your victuals and come sit outside with me. The sun is now low on the horizon. It is cool and pleasant there."

Aoife paused before speaking. "Your plates are filled. I'll bring them directly." She disappeared back into the kitchen and returned with a platter in each hand. After Nan and Mamie had taken theirs, Aoife handed Thomas his serving and left to eat alone inside.

"Nan," Mamie said, walking toward the barn, "There's beans and look! White celery, like the rich folks eats. Not only that, but pickled tongue."

Thomas caught up to them. "Mrs. Sprigett has a notable kitchen garden. She grows the celery covered. The tongue is from a calf bred and born here. Slaughtered in the spring."

Nan spoke low and quiet. "Mrs. Sprigett was a servant, was she not?"

Perhaps that will protect her a bit—that they realize she was not always a landowner's wife. As might her own way of not being overly grand. "Yes, a maid."

"And married the son..." Nan smiled. "I heard that set the grand old lady—or so she thinks of herself—right on her overfed ass. It's said she was a fury to work for after they ran off and married."

Thomas nodded. "And now he is gone as a soldier for the Union." *That would never hurt to remind them.* "... Leaving his young wife alone to run the farm."

The women settled on the two chairs by the barn door. Thomas slid down the siding to the ground, careful of his food. It was generous of Aoife to give of her celery, which sold for so much in the market, and the tongue, pickled well with spices and set to last the winter.

"And now young Mrs. Sprigett is giving haven to Lettie, so that I might both work and watch over her, too."

Famished by the day's work, Thomas and the women fell to eating silently in the evening gloom. He was always conscious of Lettie, only steps away inside the barn, lying beneath the quilt on her straw bed, but no sound came from her.

In the dimming light, he saw movement in the distance. A moment later, it was just possible to see a figure walking rapidly down the road. A woman, as the white apron atop a dark skirt revealed. And that apron, moving with her stride, wrapping itself about her legs, was what had attracted Thomas's attention.

He rose as the woman walked onto the way leading to the farmyard and house. Aoife had never had a visitor in the time he'd worked for her and Mr. William. "Excuse me, miss, are you looking for someone here?" he asked.

She drew closer, her chin lifted haughtily. "My business is with William Sprigett's wife, what used to be Aoife Kelly, and with no one else."

"Mrs. Sprigett's in the house. I'll call her for you."

Before he could reach the door, Aoife came out. She must have been keeping a close eye on the yard. "Bridie Summers! What brings you here?"

The woman looked at Thomas. He moved away but kept his senses focused on her. "I come to tell you Mr. William's mother has word he's been injured. Badly, I fear."

Aoife cried out, put her hands on her cheeks, and swooned. Before Thomas could move, Bridie stepped up and took her by her arms to support her.

At the barn, Nan and Mamie stood suddenly, like hares in the field sensing a fox come close. They put their plates on the chairs and froze as if they wished to disappear and become part of the stone wall, stolid and inanimate.

Bridie shook Aoife until she moaned and opened her eyes. "'Twas clear the mistress wouldn't tell you, out of spite if nothing else. We thought that wrong. We drew straws and to me fell the job of letting you know."

"How came she to find out and not me? Is it posted in the town?"

Bridie Summers shook her head. "The general, what was a friend of the old dragon's husband, looks out for her. He sent her notice, so she needn't check for news of her son in the papers like ordinary folk."

"Where is he?" Thomas asked on Aoife's behalf.

Bridie shot him an appraising look and smiled as if she might have news to bring back to the other maids, or worse, to Mother Sprigett. "He is at Sudley Church in the town of Manassas, getting care from Rebel doctors. But will be brought home to her once he can travel." She looked about as if her employer could see her. "I must hurry back before I am missed." She turned and ran up to the road.

Thomas went to Aoife, with no thought of the townswomen watching. He walked her to the house and into the kitchen to sit.

Aoife wailed over and over, rocking in her seat, scarcely pausing to breathe. "My William injured! And likely to die." She threw her apron over her head to hide her tears.

"It is lucky that woman brought you news, or you would stay in the dark."

She sniffed and pulled the apron down. "Much as they hated me for being elevated by William's love, the more they hate Mother Sprigett as a mean and unfeeling mistress. If that is luck, then I guess I am lucky."

155

"Good of her then, to bring news." *But though the news was heavy for that woman to tell, she seemed lightened by the joy of telling!*

"I don't know what I shall do, how I can help him," was Aoife's only reply.

By the time he came out to bring Lettie her supper, Nan and Mamie had hitched their nag to the wagon and gone.

Chapter 16

"WE SHOULD GO IN," Iris said, swatting a bug. "We'll be eaten up by mosquitos."

"I'll get the Off," Benny said as he slid his bottom from the stone wall by the pond. "But I think we really do need to keep sitting here, by the pond, as it seems so important to you. To us. We need to talk."

She put her hands atop the wall, preparing to rise, "I'll get it for you…"

He put a hand on her thigh, stopping her. "Again, Iris, no fucking Benny-the-invalid stuff." He left, only to return in a moment with the can. "Cover your eyes." When she obeyed, he misted her with repellent and said, "Now you do me."

She stood, coughing in the weirdly perfumed fog and sprayed him from head to toe. Benny was very allergic to mosquito bites, getting two-inch welts that kept him up nights, scratching desperately. Keeping her awake, too.

"Okay," he said, "before I so rudely—and melodrama-tically—interrupted our discussion…"

"Stop it!" She poked him. "It's not funny. I was terrified you were going to die."

"And I was terrified you were going to hate me forever. Terrified our marriage only seemed good on the surface. That we were trudging through, day by day, because we didn't know what else to do." He gave a little laugh. "I sure didn't know what to do! I think that's what caused my collapse."

Iris didn't respond. They sat silently together on the cooling stones, no longer warmed by the sun as it dropped below the horizon. The yard was lullingly peaceful, just a slight breeze stirring the leaves, and a few single chirps from the birds. With no movement to frighten it, the bullfrog began to croak.

"At least you being irritable wasn't due to PMS or even menopause. Way too late for those."

Is that an attempt at humor? Or getting back at me for some failing?

"Why didn't you tell me all that?" Iris said. "You used to tell me everything. How you felt, every detail of your day. We'd talk all night when we first met."

He looked at her quizzically, with his left eyebrow cocked. "Tell you what? That I was devastated when our baby died? When you nearly died from the bleeding and from the infection afterward? Shit, I was scared I was losing you, too." He turned away from her. "Jesus, Iris, I can't believe you never saw that."

"How can I believe you?"

Benny drew back. "What the fuck does that mean? How can you even begin to think I wasn't heartsick? For God's sake, I've been grieving for our baby girl the same as you have. Maybe I didn't know what it was like to carry her inside me, or to knit..." He began to hyperventilate.

Iris put out a hand to stop him, but he pulled further away.

"Iris, I started a college fund the minute you—*we*—conceived. Don't you remember me buying a crib and changing table and car seat? Iris, I sold my Corvette, for fuck's sake..."

When had that happened? When had she noticed it was gone? "You said you lent it to your friend Richie and he totaled it." She waited a moment, but he didn't answer. She dropped her voice. "I used to love riding in the 'vette with you."

"Well, it wasn't kid-safe and the baby was only a month away and we needed the money."

A month and forever.

"You weren't there in the hospital…" Her voice was now a whimper.

"Yes, Iris. Yes, I was. You were sedated but I was there. I even slept in the chair by your side the entire time. I only went home to shower."

"But when I woke up…" She felt for her rage, which had been her protector for so long, anger she'd carefully nurtured as a barrier to further hurt. But it was hidden somewhere, leaving a hollow feeling of lost and lonely years.

"You only woke up maybe twenty times in the months you were so sick. For Christ's sake, the doctors came in time and again to hang crepe, to say your kidneys were shutting down or your blood pressure wasn't stable, or your fever was rising again. I couldn't eat or sleep and there was no one I trusted to relieve me, so I sat on that crap chair in the corner and stared at you, just to fix you in my memory. I was there every moment but for the time you were finally lucid for good. How was I to know that douchebag doctor wouldn't wait for me to return but just blurt out that our baby was a girl? How was I to know you would remember that but not all the times you *seemed* awake, and I told you? Communication is a habit, Iris, one we've lost. I think we need to go to counseling."

Benny had always been against therapy, always the one to feel things would improve over time. Now, he stood and walked down the row of red-leafed maples. His chest heaved and his breath was so loud she thought she should rush to his side. But a queer languor had overcome her; she stayed seated and kept herself out of reach.

He didn't bring up the words they'd spoken at the end of their last argument. When in all of this had his affair begun?

Somewhere hidden in the cattails beside the pond, the bullfrog had quieted again.

Thomas
1862

Thomas helped Aoife up to her bedroom. The staircase was narrow, the pie steps curving. Her weight was almost fully on him as they ascended, the first time he'd climbed up to the bedroom.

He turned down the quilt and drew the curtains. "Perhaps you'll sleep tonight," he said, for want of other words. He stood over her bed, watching a small spot of blood appear on her lower lip as she bit into her own flesh. It wasn't until he was nearly out the door that her sobs were loud enough to reach his ears. He fled, giving her privacy, returning to the house only to bring in the dirty platters and slip them quietly into her wash basin. He made his way back the barn.

It was almost dark now, but Lettie seemed to glow with a pale fire. She reclined against the pillow, which she'd folded and set atop a small pile of hay. To his surprise, she was untangling hay from her long, curly hair, which was now loosed from the braid.

Up in the barn's rafters, the little white-faced owl sat, waiting for mice to creep from their hiding place in the hay. "It screams sometimes, Thomas. The owl screams." She pushed herself full upright. "Some might take fright at the sound, but I like it."

"Why is that, love?" He feared the answer might reveal more derangement of her thoughts, but the wild russet tendrils of hair about her face were too arousing. His fear became more and more mixed with desire, the longing to comb his fingers through those tresses and remember the way they'd seemed to catch fire in the sunlight, burning her image in his mind.

It had been so long since he'd had a woman. His woman.

"He is saying what I can't, Thomas. I try, but I can't."

Thomas sat beside her and made as if to touch her, but she pushed him away, crying, "No!"

Above them, the owl called out, flying from one rafter to the other. It dove suddenly, took a shrieking mouse, and held it beneath sharp talons as the curved beak ripped the little body apart. The savagery made Thomas gasp, but Lettie broke into a loud, crazed laugh, yelling, "Oh, Lord, yes!"

That, with the vehemence of her *No!* when he'd reached out, enraged him. He grabbed the long dark hair in his fist and pulled her back down onto the hay, placed his other hand over her mouth to keep her cries from ringing across the silent barnyard and waking Aoife.

Fierce desire swept over him, as did the driving, aching need for release. He resolved to take her. She was his woman, Lettie, who he had always protected and loved, who he had shaped his life and future to provide for. And she'd spurned him. He took his hand from her mouth and took her shoulders to pinion her.

"No," she said again, weakly. "No, no, no."

He rolled atop her, putting his lips just under her collarbone. He sucked in the soft, dry skin until it caught tight between his teeth.

She took a great shuddering breath and bit into his palm hard. The pain aroused him further. He pushed down the neckline of her nightdress and found her nipple. Starvation had brought that breast so close to her rib bones that, beneath his lips, he felt the beat of her heart, as fast and as fragile as that of the owl's prey.

Something jolted in him, and, as if they were no longer separate but one and the same, his mouth filled with the taste of his own flesh, as if his mouth was hers, filling with the bit of blood her teeth had raised, hot and tangy. He had a vision flash behind his eyes, bringing to life her tale of her sister's loss. Before him, shimmering in a ray of moonlight, was the ghost of Sary, her hand over Lettie's mouth, as his was now. Sary wanted only to protect her, not take something from her, as he did. Shame flooded him. He pushed up and away from her to sit at a distance.

"Forgive me," he whispered.

Lettie sat partway up, supported on her elbows. She stared at him with her great gray eyes, though, in the gloom, her stare was more felt than seen. "The owl is not sated. He is still hunting."

As if obeying her, the bird screamed again.

Confused, as remorse mixed with his thwarted desire, he stood, keeping his back to her and so concealing his arousal. He went to the barn door and opened both sides. The moon, waxy yellow, had come out in the overcast sky, washing the barnyard in eerie light. Everything—the fenceposts, the well pump, the watering trough, and the trees—stood in sharp relief with deep shadows flowing from them. The farmhouse across the yard was dark and silent.

The moonlight crept into the barn through the great open doors, flooding the floor. When Thomas looked down to the worn wooden surface, small, bare footprints marked the dust and the fact that Lettie had been up, observing and listening, before returning to bed. He glanced back to again see her eyes glitter. Was she acting the hysteric?

"So, Mr. William will be coming home." Her words were fairly larded with delight. He was dismayed at how much that stung him.

Aoife
1862

Aoife lay awake, a shaft of moonlight moving across the linens, advancing up her body, stalking her. Better the sky had remained overcast—the bedroom would be less gloomy than it was in the eldritch glow slipping from behind the clouds. She ran her hand down William's side of their marriage bed. It seemed even colder and emptier than before.

Her thoughts were jumbled, a disconcerting feeling in one used to seeing a clear path of action. William was injured, perhaps direly. He would need loving and devoted care to mend. She, the wife who loved him, would be best at tending to his needs.

A way had to be found to keep Mother Sprigett, that old she-bear, at bay. A way to bring her William, her husband, home to his own wife.

Sleep eluded her, though she desperately needed it. She swung her feet onto the floor and padded over to the window.

The clouds were scudding rapidly across the sky. Between them, the myriad stars appeared like sugar crystals spilt on a tabletop. Though the night was sultry, the moving shadows brought a shiver to her. She dragged the quilt from the bed to cover her shoulders.

With luck, a star would shoot across the sky, and she could make a wish. Her mam had always said such was sure to come true.

Down below, movement at the barn's door drew her attention. Thomas appeared, come to lean against one side of the great door, his arms crossed over his chest. Illumed by the stars' glow, he turned his gaze up to her window but blankly. She stood still, certain the angled light kept her in darkness, but not wanting to chance a flash of her white nightdress between the dark green shutters.

She rubbed her hands down the front of that gown and wished things were the way they had been before, when they were, at least, safe from Lettie's rage. When they could sit side by side at the table and offer each other comfort. When the great rotation of the heavens meant only the planning of the crops and the care of the animals.

Thomas's whore! The words still burned, enhancing Mother Sprigett's threats. Those words hung between Aoife and Thomas like a thick and dirty curtain. Though they had done nothing wrong, she wondered what further harm that woman would bring.

Chapter 17

"COUNSELING, BENNY? You feel things are that far gone?"

"Iris." Benny put his right arm around her shoulder. "I'm not good at discussions like this, so forgive me if what I said was clumsy. Finding the baby's body must have triggered memories for you—they did for me, too. I know that's why you're so attached to him and have gone on this… this quest to learn more."

Iris sighed. She wished the frogs were singing. The little frogs that made such an amusing chorus of sounds. All that she heard now was the rustle of leaves in the slight breeze.

"This is what happened. What I remember." Benny reached across her lap with his left hand and took hers. "We made the decision together for you to go through labor rather than have surgery. It seemed the best decision at the time, since they laid out the risks of a cesarean, with the scar and the problems when you got pregnant again. We agreed, even when they said the induced labor might be hard."

Her eyes filled, blurring her sight, and she was nearly overcome with the desire to stop his voice. It was ringing too true, awakening vague, misty recollections of so long ago.

"We didn't know… *they* didn't know… that an infection had started. Some insidious…"

"Not of the baby!" Iris had a horrid image of her infant crying, feverish in her womb.

"No, not of the baby." Benny said. His voice was so soothing, it occurred to Iris he might be lying, but what difference did it make now?

"She was perfect. It was the other tissue, the lining of the uterus, the fluid, the placenta, something..." He gave a short little laugh. "I couldn't handle getting too savvy about it all. Anyway, you didn't even have a fever for the first day or two, but your temperature suddenly spiked..." Benny's voice cracked then. He had to clear his throat before he went on.

He *had* been there, she remembered now. He'd sat on the horrid vinyl cot reading to her—so young he didn't need glasses to see the words. She remembered his knuckles pressed into the small of her back, a fulcrum for her writhing, somehow easing the agony. How eagerly she had arched into that tight fist, a grotesque simulation of the passion with which they'd conceived their doomed child. But then her memory failed and there was nothing but jumbled nightmare images: people and machines looming out of a fog, pain everywhere, strange noises. Recognizing no one. A time when she was more alone than she'd ever been.

"And you hemorrhaged suddenly into the bed and I yelled for the nurse and you started talking... not talking but *babbling*, making no sense at all, and then you were *gone*, Iris."

"Gone?" Had she died? Had Benny lived through her death and made her return to him? Her memory clouded in a mass of swirling images. Had she seen a light? The face of God? Or simply medical staff and cleaners, anonymous, alien in their masks and gowns?

"You were delirious. Your fever was so high, and everything was going wrong and whenever things got better, they got worse again. And over and over, they warned me you could die. They insisted only the surgery, only a hysterectomy, would save your life, and I had to give permission. So, I agreed."

I not only lost my baby, but the ability to try again. You made that decision, Benny. But her anger had weakened.

"It was weeks before you recognized me. Don't you remember any of this? You did surface every now and again and talk to me. Sometimes you seemed to know it was me."

"I did?" She blinked away the tears and looked into Benny's eyes.

He nodded. "Each time you asked me about the baby, I told you. I told you we'd had a girl." He released her hand to wipe his tears. "Shit, Iris, I was so afraid I'd lose you, too."

Weeks? Everything was hazy until... "All I remember is waking up and the doctor being there. He was the one who told me about the baby."

"Okay." Benny sighed. "If that's all you remember..."

"I didn't mean it like that. But we didn't talk..."

"*You* didn't talk. Even after you were stable and they were ready to release us, you were totally silent. In the hospital, going home in the car, and even in our house. God, I was so lonely without you."

He'd sat in the yellow leather loveseat in the bedroom of their classic Eichler, the light-filled California modern ranch of which they'd been so proud. She remembered Benny napping in that love-seat with the sun pouring in. Herself, sitting upright, alone in the bed, pillows piled behind her back, wanting to say something, anything, but being unable to force out a single word.

He'd slept in that chair nights, too. She remembered now the revulsion she'd felt at the thought of him touching her. Inside her had been nothing but rage. And its echo had persisted until now, untouched like a sore tooth that would be worsened by a probing tongue.

Thomas
1862

Thomas read the letter to her as soon as it arrived.

> *Ma'am,*
>
> *We soldiers what served under Captain Sprigett, who was to be made a Colonel but for his unfortunate injury, beg your pardon for addressing you direct, but we fear his wishes will not be honored. To wit: he does strongly desire to be taken home to you and not to his mother's house.*
>
> *To us fell the heavy labor of the earthen works about the Capital and, tho we are not fine Philadelphia gentlemen, Captain William treated us like we was good as him. And so we followed him when General Pope engaged the Rebs at Bull Run.*
>
> *Captain Sprigett's wounds are fearsome bad, but he has survived them so far—it has been six week—and we see more men die from being in hospital than we can count. Diseases spread from bed to bed, hopping from man to man like fleas in a pack of dogs.*
>
> *Three of us are planning to bring the captain home to you before winter sets in. He will be very weak and needing a bed and loving care. The way he speaks of you sets our hearts at ease, knowing his chances of getting better are best in his own home.*
>
> *He sends his love and begs you tell no one of this missive.*

"Is there no name signed?" Aoife asked.

Thomas shook his head.

"If only he'd told us who he and the others were! To be sure, I would raid Thomas's money box and send it to them.

That way we might guarantee a more comfortable journey. Are they coming by train?"

"I doubt it, Aoife. The rail lines are what are fought over now, for the control of the east-west routes to bring men and supplies. They must bring him as they can, in coaches or in wagons. And for certain, they fear what would happen if their plans were discovered. They would be deserters and branded as such, if not executed."

She went to the fireplace and removed a small, lidded pot from its tripod. "Take this to Lettie and make her eat. Warmed milk with fresh bread and blackberry preserves, sweet and wholesome for such as her. We need her well again. Keeping the farm and tending two invalids might break us." She spooned the pot's contents into a bowl. "Hurry now, lest it cool."

Thomas stood still for a while. "You are too good to her, Aoife. It is time Lettie knew that. Please come with me to the barn and tell her your husband is returning. She admired him greatly." *Too greatly, I fear, and I do not want it revealed how she spied upon you.*

Aoife laughed. "I had best pin my apron on or change into my oldest dress. For 'tis sure she will spit at me and stain the cloth."

Aoife

1862

Her heart soared like the swallows in the barn, high above every burden. She wouldn't allow herself to think of William's injuries or the risks of travel. Just of the one thought: Her William was coming home.

She stripped the bed of its coarse cotton bedclothes and took out the fine linen ones from the blanket chest. She put them on the goose-down mattress, smoothing the wide lace border she'd tatted just after their marriage and tucking the edges so he would not, in restlessness, lie uncovered. She sprinkled all with lavender water and the light, fresh scent rose in the air. It was sure to lift William's spirits.

The old bedclothes she put on the floor, atop the braided rag rug. She would sleep on them until he arrived, not knowing how long his journey would last and not wanting to be caught off guard. This would guarantee everything fresh and ready for William, whenever he arrived.

Aoife backed down to the kitchen, wiping each stair with a damp cloth as she went. She pumped a bucket of water and went back inside to scour the floor. *Nothing may be out of place. 'Twill not only be William but, sooner or later, his mother. I do not wish her here, but I'll not come between a mother and her son.*

And then her fretting gave way to a small shiver of delight. *With William coming home, mayhap soon we will have a son of our own.*

Mother Sprigett had made note of the need for whitewashing the house. While the kitchen floor was drying, Aoife went out and looked at the walls with a critical eye. Indeed, the old dragon was right and there were signs of neglect. Devotion to the farm work had done more damage than Aoife realized.

She'd have Thomas fetch the lime and the salt and mix it herself to mop on the wall and make it glow again. There was only enough lime to whitewash the kitchen side of the house but that would have to do for now. William would enter that way and the front parlor side was mostly obscured from the road by summer sweet bushes and dogwoods. It was a shame the dogwood was not still in bloom, but the summer sweet's honeysuckle-scented white flowers would do nicely in vases.

Aoife walked to the pigsty behind the barn and looked at the ten pink-snouted shoats clustered about their huge white mother. Thomas could slaughter one of the piglets upon

William's arrival. Roasted, there would be more than enough tender flesh to nourish an invalid's recovery. She planned a chicken stew as well, with carrots, potatoes, and onion.

She supposed that some would need be given to Lettie as well.

Lifting her whiskered snout, the sow eyed Aoife with suspicion, as if years of losing babies had alerted her to the evil intentions of humankind. "Sure, old lady, 'tis hard, but they are why you loll in the mud, staying cool, and why you get tasty slops every day, brought to you in a pail. And soon 'twill be acorn time, and we'll drive you all into the woods to fatten."

Aoife decided on the second biggest boar shoat, as the largest might one day breed true to size. The sow was noted locally for prize offspring.

The path alongside the barn was in shade and so she came down that way. Reaching the front corner, her gaze went to movement at the open door. Lettie stood almost hidden in the shadows with her feet bare, her tangled hair hanging to her waist, and her nightdress off one shoulder in a mockery of seduction. She looked mad enough to launch another attack on Aoife, this time with fists and feet instead of words.

Aoife's breath stopped with a loud gasp. At the sound Lettie lifted her head. "Mr. William returns, injured?"

She must have overheard the talk. Best that extra care is taken now she is moving about. "Yes."

Lettie arranged the neckline of her gown properly. She pushed back the disordered tendrils of hair, twisting some into a bun away from her face. "Would you do me a kindness?" she asked.

Aoife shrugged, still afraid to speak.

"Thomas can fetch me a pail of water to wash myself with but he is too rough at combing my hair. Would you brush out the knots?" Two hectic red blotches adorned Lettie's cheeks, but her affect was docile and childlike.

Aoife's shoulders relaxed.

"I fear my hairbrush was left in town, though." Lettie gave a pleasant little laugh. "Men are careless with such things."

Thomas is never careless. "I have an old one tucked away, still with enough bristles to do the job. I will seek it out for you and, yes, I will brush out your braid until it is such that you can dress it yourself."

Lettie smiled and, at the change in her demeanor, the beauty that had ensnared Thomas was evident. Her features were soft, rounded, and delicate. Perhaps the spell of melancholy had passed. Thomas had said that her moods were like quicksilver, and a period of calm would ease the work of William's return. With the Lord's grace, Lettie might keep stable.

Chapter 18

THEY RELAXED FOR THREE DAYS, being loving and careful with each other. Then they sat again, and Benny continued his recounting of their loss. "The doctors said your withdrawal was grief and even brain trauma from the time you spent in shock from blood loss. Maybe I shouldn't have taken it personally but..."

Iris tucked her face against his chest to keep him from saying how unloved he'd felt, hiding her burning cheeks, fearing it would break her heart. "But you always said we'd never need to see anyone. We loved each other so much; we'd always be able to work things out."

"Well, things have gone pretty far if you were so angry with me. If our realities are so far apart. If the gap between us is so huge."

"Oh, Benny..."

"You may not remember. I was alone more and more as friends—not really friends, you know I don't have friends, just the few people we knew in California—grew tired of showing up with food or flowers only to be turned away. Relatives flew in and left feeling the trip was a waste; I saw pity in their faces. Pity for me—rightly or wrongly, they felt you weren't trying. It was *months* of you being silent, of you turning away. I disgusted you—you shied from my touch like I was a monster, a rapist or something. The cause of all your pain."

She only remembered the blackness, the nightmare images. And the pain of loss.

"You were like an ice sculpture called Angry Woman Who Hates Her Husband. I was alone with you, Iris. And without you."

The affair. He was excusing the affair, blaming what had gone before. But she needed him. She had just almost lost him. She shook her head against his chest, trying to clear the tangled memories, the grief mixed with rage. Her voice muffled by his shirt, which was growing damp from her moist breath, she said, "I didn't mean to be like that." But she had. "I'm so sorry, Benny. I love you. I always have." But for a while, she hadn't.

His voice softened. "Your little John Doe brought it all back, didn't he?"

Iris nodded.

"And I understand your attachment to that grad student Charlotte. She must be pretty much the age our little girl would be if she'd had the chance to grow up."

Iris's mouth dropped open. That rang so true and yet was so unexpected. It had been thirty-six years. She pressed her lips together, realizing a small wet area of drool had formed on his front, though he was oblivious. "Benny…"

"No need to say anything now, Iris." He gently pushed her back until they could see each other clearly. "We'll look for someone to talk to, but meanwhile, I think you should call Charlotte and continue your research. You've got a mystery to unravel."

Iris sniffled a bit, overwhelmed with emotion. She nodded and picked up her cell phone. "We were supposed to go ask the coroner's office for photos and hopefully get the clothes he was wearing. Are you okay? Does it feel risky to be alone? Do you mind?"

He shook his head, a small smile on his lips.

She stood and headed toward the kitchen.

"Oh, Iris?" Benny called. "One more thing. Don't worry about me."

Shit. The self-congratulatory feeling of being a good, attentive wife evaporated.

*   *   *

Iris was the driver for the twenty-minute trip to the county forensic facility. Five minutes on the road, Charlotte announced that she hadn't eaten all day and was so hungry she was getting carsick.

Iris pulled into the drive through of a fast-food place. There was a long line of cars. Hopefully, this pitstop wouldn't make them late for their appointment. *It seems like when we're together, one or both of us realize that we're hungry.*

Benny had described Iris's hunger, but what was Charlotte's?

"I was surprised to see on the website that the coroner's a woman, and such a pretty one," Charlotte said after she'd gotten her food. "I expected an old man." She bit into a cheese and bean chalupa. "Oh, so good," she moaned, licking the melted cheese from her thumb. "I don't usually eat such fatty, salty crap, but it's so tasty."

I wonder how she'd react to the real Tex-Mex I make? Iris's heart warmed at the thought of preparing dinner for the young woman. *I think Benny would welcome her visits, now that he understands how I feel. He better!*

"Glad you're enjoying it."

Oily cheese, like luridly orange plastic, oozed from the folded dough, dripping down on Charlotte's skirt. *Maybe we should have taken her already messy car.*

But Charlotte's driving frightened Iris, who was known to exceed speed limits—sometimes excessively—but only when it seemed safe. In her rickety car, the younger woman sped and tailgated egregiously. Iris lapsed into silent thought, hoping Charlotte would pay close attention to the food and so save the SUV's leather seats from grease stains.

A propane truck passed in the opposite direction, its silvery tank distorting the reflection of the trees beside the road. Trucks that could explode always made her nervous. She watched it, sighing when it disappeared down the road, a risk only to strangers down the road.

Charlotte soon finished the food and was rapidly slurping up her iced tea as they pulled up at their destination.

*   *   *

The coroner's assistant, a young man with a wispy blond beard, asked, "Weren't you here before about the pond baby? Didn't you pick up the ashes?"

"I'm surprised you remember," Iris said.

He laughed. "How many perfectly preserved, hundred-seventy-year-old bodies do you think we get? Pretty memorable, I'd say." He pointed to a sitting area where Charlotte and Iris could wait and left to get the file and any effects from their little John Doe.

The attendant returned carrying a cardboard file box marked with Iris's address and the date the baby had been found. He put it on a table set in the middle of the room.

"Ahh!" Charlotte cried as he removed the lid. "Look, Iris, the clothes are still here."

The man shot her a resentful look and stiffened. "We're very careful with personal effects here."

Atop a few sheets of paper, a sealed clear plastic bag held the little gown and cap, pressed flat. Iris stroked the outside of the bag. "Is it mine to take?"

The attendant shrugged. "Found on your property, not part of a crime investigation, so, yeah, I guess."

"You guess?" Charlotte said.

He sighed. "You already took the body, so yes, go ahead and take the clothes. The coroner's throwing in a photocopy of the kid's face. You'd have to pay for copies of the full autopsy."

Charlotte nodded and moved to say something, but Iris shuddered. "No thanks." She smoothed the bag of clothes a bit more. They were still mud-stained, though dry—or at least without water squelching and bubbling out when she pressed the plasticine bag. "How do you take care of clothes like these?"

"Advice is above my pay grade." He watched her hands caressing the plastic, then leaned in conspiratorially. "Got a really good dry cleaner? Like someone you'd trust with silk? Your wedding gown? Just don't put them away dirty. Degrades them."

"Okay, thanks, I think." Iris regretted not thinking of this before and finding a local cloth conservator. It would be best to protect the clothes immediately. She held out the envelope she'd brought. "I have the DNA analysis. Is it of any use?"

He took it, put it in the box, and closed the lid. "Not to me. See you next time."

"No offense," Charlotte said, "but hope not."

Iris pulled her purse strap higher on her shoulder. "Let's go, Char."

In the car, Charlotte broke out in peals of laughter. She gasped, "Imagine him saying 'next time'!" Giggled again, her face red and shiny with perspiration. "Like a whole nursery of babies will be found in your pond."

"God forbid." Iris spit on the first two fingers of her right hand, saying, "Puh, puh, puh."

Charlotte leaned away, turning to look at Iris. "What was that?"

"Means *God forbid.* I've used it a lot during the renovation, not so much now the kitchen's usable and almost done. Benny's grandmother used to do it." Iris had forgotten Maida until, recently, she'd seen the gesture on a TV show and remembered the stooped old lady. "She never said, but I think it's a Jewish superstition." She laughed then. Maida had spit like that the first time Benny had brought Iris home. Of course, her own parents had never let her bring Benny home at all. *Maybe they would have done to see a grandchild.*

Charlotte's face morphed from amused to somber and she nodded, her gaze losing its focus. "Family's funny, isn't it? The things they tell you and the things they don't?"

Thomas
1862

Thomas headed to the barnyard with a load of fresh timothy hay, destined for sale in town. The sweet smell was always heady, an odor full of promise—almost of romance, of mid-summer nights when the cool damp rose from the ground. Of two bodies crushing the grass, releasing its scent.

Across the field, Nan and Mamie were bent over, hard at work. He sighed. They were right. It was a dangerous time for him, for Aoife, and for the community. Emotions were high and growing higher with every soldier's death, with every soldier's crippling. With every family losing a husband, a son, a brother, a wage earner.

Some claimed the local men were fighting to preserve the Union, but everyone knew the Union was fracturing over slavery. And though much of the populace, especially the Quakers, were abolitionists, Thomas had heard muttering in town when they saw him.

The bereft mothers and sweethearts of the casualties—small farmers, tradesmen, and impoverished mill workers—openly resented him, a hale and hearty black man who hadn't joined up, not even though enlistment was, so recently, opened to Negroes. Who, instead, was preserving the wealth of one of the rich landowners, a Sprigett.

Of course, there were those who suspected him of having designs, perhaps even realized designs, on Mr. William's beautiful Irish wife. He hoped the news that Lettie had joined him on the farm would seep through the town. That should help put such rumors to rest.

Being on the farm seemed to have soothed Lettie's tormented soul. There had been no violent rages since her arrival, no fits of profane screaming. Aoife brought her food and, as yet, had not complained of Lettie lashing out at her.

If there was any complaint to be made, any worry to be had, it was Lettie's craftiness at spying. And, he feared, with peaceful sleep and nutritious food, her debility was now more feigned than real. Soon he would have to introduce the idea of earning her keep. She could not expect the Sprigett farm to provide for her with no return.

He stopped the wagon and entered the barn which, though cooler than the outside, was still warm. Lettie was on her pallet in her nightdress, the quilt pushed to the side. Staring up at the rafters where, as usual, the swallows sported.

"They are graceful, are they not, Thomas? If fairies had mounts to take them through the air, it is certain they would be those birds. Lovely little fairies with cobweb wings on those lovely birds."

Fairies? He'd never heard her speak so lyrically before, nor of those creatures. Haints, yes, and ghost lights floating over the brackish swamps of the South, ready to lure the unwary, but never fairies. *Is she mocking Aoife as I once did?* "Fairies are not all lovely, Lettie. They can cause mischief for the unwary."

Lettie's smile was fetching beneath the neat crown of her hair, and her usually disheveled garments were tidy. "Perhaps that is true, Thomas, or perhaps mischief is caused by them what believe in fairies."

Her speech does mimic Aoife's, so I am right to worry. But what is her game? As he left, he saw that her neat gown's hem was dirty where it would have dragged on the ground.

Aoife

1862

She climbed the ladder carrying a sloshing bucket filled with whitewash. Her skirt was pulled between her legs and tucked into her waist to keep it from tangling her feet. Thomas had looked askance at her garments' arrangement, but she only responded, "William is on his way. I cannot afford modesty, with all that needs be done!"

The feel of the sun-warmed rungs beneath her naked soles brought back memories of climbing into the loft in the crofter's cottage of her childhood. She began to hum "The Wild Rover," the song her dadai sung, off-key, when he'd come home from a night of drinking. The memory made her laugh. Her father had always believed his voice was a fine Irish tenor, like that of his cousins and uncles. He had been so lonesome for them in America, for the chorus of their voices. With the grandam dead, no one excepting Aoife, her mam, and dadai had come on the journey. Instead, two cousins had been transported to Botany Bay for theft and two more had deserted their wives during the Famine, as they could not provide for their children. She never learned where those men had gone or if they survived their journey.

Would that someone had come here, to America. I might have family then, women to visit with. And then she silently chided herself for the complaint. Had she not her fine husband William and a farm of her own? A house with a parlor, a real second story and attic? And Thomas, of course.

Despite the heat, the great arcing of her arm sweeping the whitewash mop created a soothing rhythm. It was what lulled her into idle thoughts and wishes. She picked up the pace of her work and banished them from her mind.

All the while, she kept watch for a sign that William was arriving. Should she see the dust rising from the road, hear the neigh of coach horses, or the ringing of harness bells, her descent from the ladder would be as quick as her exhausted body could manage. She'd not allowed sleep to interrupt preparing for his return.

Nights, when she should have been long abed, she'd cut meat in bits and baked them in fat rendered with precious imported spices and homegrown herbs. Those baked morsels she pounded until paste-smooth, then cooled to wait for when sufficient butter had been churned for sealing the crocks to keep the contents from molding. She'd stood back and looked at the little pots, proud of her work—even now, atop the ladder, in the daylight, she was still pleased. That potted meat was nutritious food to help her beloved William recover. Potted meat and broth, ale, and wholesome bread.

Her vantage point atop the ladder let her almost see the covered bridge over Mill Creek. Late in the afternoon, a wagon, covered in dirty-brown canvas, emerged from the bridge like a chafer grub wriggling from the ground. Two spent horses, near stumbling with fatigue, pulled it down the road.

She scuttled down the ladder, released the hem of her skirt, and ran into the house for her shoes, twisting the loose strands of hair back into a bun as she went. In the kitchen, she grabbed a red rag and brought it outside to signal Thomas by jumping up and waving it, yelling, "Thomas! Thomas! William is come," as if he could hear her from the field.

The wagon pulled into the yard, driven by a man who wore civilian clothes instead of a uniform, as did the fresh-faced youth seated next to him. The driver removed his floppy hat, pressed it respectfully to his chest, and nodded at her. "You be Mrs. Sprigett?"

"Aye, that is me. Can I see my husband? Is he all right?" She stepped toward the rear of the wagon, ready to climb in. "William?"

His own dear voice answered weakly, "Aoife, no."

Her heart leaped up at the sound of his voice but stilled at his words.

Another stranger, one with a large and bushy moustache that drooped over his mouth, slid out from under the canvas top. He loudly bade her wait. "There's not room for you within, ma'am. Please, have you a bed ready for the captain?"

Something in his voice, the coarseness perhaps or the steel beneath his words, stopped her in her tracks.

"We'll bring him in to you, if you just go inside."

"But I need to see him!"

There was movement at her side. She turned to see that Thomas had come up alongside her. The man standing by the wagon's rear gave him a narrow-eyed look. His upper lip drew back, and Aoife saw his tongue working in the wide spaces where teeth were missing. He inclined his head toward them.

Thomas nodded in return as if he understood something she didn't. "I'll help them, Mrs. Sprigett."

"Thank you, Thomas." She stood rigid, wringing her hands.

He took her shoulder and gently pushed her in the direction of the kitchen door. "I'll help bring Mr. William in and then tend to the men's rig. You turn down the bed and make sure there is coffee and victuals. They've had a long and difficult journey."

"I mayn't see him out here, in the sunlight?"

"Best we get him situated first," the driver said, as he climbed down from the worn wooden seat. "This wagon is not the most comfortable bed, 'specially for an invalid." He patted the flank of one of the horses and tipped his hat. "I'm Captain Sprigett's second in command, ma'am, in charge of these men and Captain Sprigett's comfort."

It seemed there was nothing to be done but for her to go about her duties as best she could, though her heart's racing nearly stopping her breath. She left Thomas conferring with the men too quietly for her to hear. *How bad things must be if he keeps them hidden! But I will tend William, and all will be fine. He is alive, and that's the most important. He's come home to me.*

She started a pot of coffee, glad she'd ground a good amount that morning, and laid out two loaves of bread with a quantity of her best cheese on the table, along with a bowl of raspberries still beaded with morning dew. She lifted a basket of peaches, checking for worms.

"Raspberries and peaches are best with fresh cream." Though he'd spoken softly, Thomas's voice startled her—she hadn't heard him come inside the room. He nearly whispered to say, "Aoife, go to the springhouse and fetch the cream. When you return, we will have Mr. William in his bed."

She turned and when she saw the look on his earnest brown face, the peaches slipped from her hands and rolled, willy-nilly, across the floor.

Chapter 19

IRIS DROPPED CHARLOTTE AT her car and then headed to the most expensive dry cleaner in town. She placed the crinkly plastic bag on the counter and told the owner, "I can't emphasize enough how important these clothes are to me."

The woman behind the counter was elegantly outfitted with a silk blouse that sported an enormous bow. She spoke with a heavy Korean accent. "Ah, these your baby's clothes?" She glanced up at Iris for the first time. "From long ago?"

"Yes, from long ago, but, no, not my baby. Or my grandchild," Iris replied. "Still very important to me. I don't want anything to happen to them."

"Very old-fashioned. Very fine lace. Heirloom?"

Iris bent her head to examine the little gown's border more closely than she'd had opportunity to do before. Through the plastic it was easy to see small, tatted flowers joined together by a delicate network of mesh. She nodded. "Very old."

"Irish lace." The woman smiled. "On dress and on bonnet."

"You know that it's Irish? How?" As soon as she asked, Iris feared the questions would be taken wrong, even seem offensive.

But the owner's face remained smoothly bland. "In this business long, long time. Irish crochet lace is easy to spot. They crochet flowers, then join together. I collect lace, in fact, and offer to buy antique lace like this, if for sale."

Iris shook her head. "This isn't for sale."

The woman smiled. "Just meant to show I appreciate the fine work. So far look in good shape." She drew the clothes from the bag and smoothed them on the counter. "Oh! So dirty!"

"Yes, well…"

"Dried mud." The dry cleaner's forehead wrinkled in deep consternation. "I think I saw a picture of this baby gown online news. This is from the pond, from old house in Highgrove, right?"

There had been a photo of the gown once it was taken off Little Jack's body. Iris hoped that wouldn't mean opposition to the clothes being cleaned. She'd heard this laundry was the best.

"Yeobo!" the woman called.

A slender young girl, sporting ponytailed jet-black hair with a fuchsia streak, wearing a multi-pocketed maroon apron, came from the back. After a rapid exchange in Korean, she put the baby clothes back into the bag and whisked them away.

"I told her, 'Very special,'" the owner said. "Don't worry, they will be taken care by hand. Come back in a week and we have them wrapped in proper tissue, like for silk."

Leaving the clothes behind, with only the photo of little Jack in her hand to show he belonged to her, Iris felt bereft. She'd had nothing of her baby long ago, not even a picture, not even the memory of the weight in her arms.

What had Benny said? *You'd told me no way I'd understand. You said you hated me for not letting you hold the baby, but when I went over the doctors' heads and brought her to you, you pushed her away. There was no right thing for me to do.*

Remembrance flashed into her mind, as clear as a reflection in the pond. A memory of being in the hospital after her surgery, terrified. *Yelling at Ben, "I hate you! I hate that awful thing. Hate that you let my body be ripped apart." Pushing away from the little corpse, screaming, "Take it away, it's not mine! My baby isn't dead!"*

And she remembered Benny's face, stricken pale by her words.

Acid rose into her mouth, burning the area behind her molars. Why had she been so vicious to him? She'd had no reason then.

The reality overwhelmed her, and she wanted to pound herself on the head, as she'd done when she was little, arguing with her mother. In her mind, she heard her voice take on her mother's lecturing tone, saying, *Don't be stupid, Iris. You've read enough women's magazines and blogs to get the picture. Postpartum depression wasn't such a thing then, especially when there was no baby to bring home and make you sleep deprived, but the smart guess would be that's what you had.*

The Iris and Benny of nearly four decades past seemed more real than the two of them in the present. Benny was right—they couldn't return to just being two people going through the motions of being a couple, just making it through the days, one after another, smoothing over disappointments with superficialities. Two once in love, now just in habit.

Aoife

1862

She shook her head. "I'll not go to the springhouse. I will wait here." Her legs would scarcely take her from the room anyway. She leaned forward to support herself on the table, as now her chest was so tight that she could only gulp air through her open mouth. *What do they not wish me to see?*

Thomas sighed. "Let me help the men. Mr. William's valise and gear are in the wagon."

Before he could reach the door, one man entered sideways, the corporal, leader of the three. With a look of dismay at the sight of Aoife, his glance shot to Thomas.

Another man stepped in, and Aoife realized William was held between them, carried in their arms. A blanket was wrapped about him, heavy wool, despite the heat. It draped over his bowed head and then hung loose and empty a short way below his hips. His legs were missing.

She bit back a gasp, heedless to the risk of drawing blood from her lips. Her arms wobbled and her legs threatened to drop her. She steeled them, refusing to collapse, forced herself upright, back against the dry sink for support. Smiling at William, she cried, with as much delight as she could muster, "Oh, my husband, thank the Lord you are home!" She turned to Thomas. "Please, help these gentlemen take Mr. William up and settle him comfortably whilst I set out the coffee. The rest is already in place." She gestured toward the table. "In just a moment, I'll bring William a tray and beg you leave me with him. Alone."

The men carrying William started up the stairs after Thomas. As soon as they were out of sight, her legs gave way, dropping her to her knees. With the sign of the cross, she prayed for the strength to never let William see the horror she felt at that empty, dangling blanket, but only how glad she was to have him back with her again.

To gain time to collect herself, Aoife went for the cream. Hot as the outside air was, her breath eased for a moment and her limbs ceased their trembling.

As she hurried back from the springhouse, she saw Thomas's Lettie at the barn door, composed in her dress and hair, and with a bright daisy tucked above her ear. At the pretty sight, Aoife put a hand up to smooth the bun she'd so hastily shaped. William must know that she cared enough to be well kempt for him. As neat and appealing as the house she'd whitewashed and as the woman of his field hand. He must not see her too horrified by his wounds. Too distraught to be womanly for him.

In the kitchen the three soldiers were eating, but Thomas was nowhere in sight.

"Your hired man is up making the captain comfortable." The corporal, his words scarcely to be understood, gestured to the stairs with the knife in his hand. His mouth was crammed with bread, thickly smeared with her potted meat.

"What are your names so that I might properly thank you?"

He shook his head and pushed the food into his cheek. "No names, ma'am. Captain William's instructions. We'll not put you at risk." He went back to chewing, then swallowed with a gulp of coffee. "Mighty fine victuals. Been a long time since we ate."

"'Tis the least I can do. You have brought my husband home to me." She ran up the stairs to William.

Thomas
1862

The counterpane had been turned down; the fresh sheets smelled of lavender and summer sun. The blanket with which the wounded man was covered was filthy, coated with road dust and bits of hay. Thomas assumed the wagon, an old, ill-painted farmer's cart, had until recent been used to haul feed. The deserters must have stolen it. The horses had not come with the wagon—they were both branded "US" on their left shoulders. Property of the army.

Most distressing another smell, strong and gamey, challenged the lavender, making his nose crinkle. He pulled the blanket from William's shoulders. The wounded man was not much cleaner than the blanket that had wrapped him. His injuries were far graver than Thomas had feared.

"Thomas," William reached out to him, his hands desperately raking the air, "don't let my wife see me, not yet. Fetch a basin and pitcher and help me wash. At least she should not be offended at my rank odor." His voice was wavery and exhausted. He whispered and Thomas bent to hear. William grabbed his collar, "And tell me, Thomas, tell me, if you smell rot."

Aoife had come silently up the stairs and now stood in the doorway. William failed to look up but kept his head hanging, from exhaustion or dread at her reaction to him, it was not possible to tell. She moved to his side. "No, William, I am your wife who loves you, and never was a born lady."

William raised his head, but before he could protest, Aoife said, "I heard, William, and I am here." She reached the bed and laid her cheek against his forehead. "Shhh, love, shhh." She looked up at Thomas. Her eyes pleaded silently as she hardened her voice to demand, "Go, bring warmed water so I may wash him."

He hurried down the stairs. The three men paused in their eating as he passed through the kitchen. As one, they stared hard at him.

The corporal held up his free hand. He took a swig of water and swallowed a poorly chewed mass of food. He coughed once. Putting down his bread, thickly spread with potted meat, he asked, "How fares our captain?"

"He is in the best of hands, those of Mrs. Sprigett, his wife," he continued. "And I will do all I can to help her."

The soldier dropped his voice. "I do not know if Mrs. Sprigett should be told what the doctors say."

"And what is that?"

189

"They say Captain Sprigett has not long to live, which may be a blessing. No man would wish to live as he is now."

Rage rose in Thomas's heart, but he took a deep breath to tamp it down. *Christians should never believe death was a blessing, but simply the will of God.* Still, he did not want to be at odds with these men. Stiffening his back he said only, "I must go to the well. Mrs. Sprigett wants water to bathe Mr. William."

At the well, Thomas pumped furiously, filling the bucket halfway before he paused. The effort had drained away his anger. *These are good, loyal men, risking execution for a man they know to be doomed.*

It was not the soldiers who had stirred his ire, but the truth. He bent to take the bucket's handle.

"Thomas? Has Mr. William returned?" Lettie's voice, from behind him.

"You are up, Lettie? Are you well again?" *She knows, having seen him, so why pretend not?*

"The men who came seem rough. They frighten me." Despite her statement, she was prettily arrayed, her hair neatly up, dressed in a fetching way and adorned with a flower. A sight sure to catch a man's eye.

"Then you best stay in the barn, out of sight." He gestured in the direction of the open door and watched until she left, dragging her feet with seeming reluctance.

He lifted the full bucket and left her peering out from inside the barn.

Once inside the house, Thomas added boiled water from the kettle and carried the bucket up the stairs. He placed it on the floor next to Aoife. A slight, tentative smile lifted the corners of her mouth, to silently thank him. She dropped a cloth into the bucket.

It was her husband who spoke. "Are my men well cared for?"

"Mr. William, they declare Mrs. Sprigett has set out a feast. Their horses are fed and watered, and I will make a place for the soldiers to sleep."

"Soldiers no longer." William's forehead dripped with sweat at the effort of speaking. "No bed. Tell them to go. Not safe for them here."

Chapter 20

BENNY WAS EXERCISING FREDDY by playing ball when Iris reached home. Freddy raced after the ball, his tongue hanging out so far it looked like a pink necktie. *Good dog,* she thought as he stopped without going into the street. *We raised you right.*

Iris pulled into the long drive and parked at the mudroom door. She got out and, leaning against the car, waited for the game to be over. The orange Chuckit was a blur when swung, sending the ball farther than he could send it by hand. She snickered at the throwing device, glad Benny couldn't see her reaction—he'd know what she was thinking. *You always did throw like a girl!*

At last, the dog was so tired and hot that he refused to return the ball, lying on the grass, his sleek black sides heaving as he panted.

Iris got out of the car and walked toward them. "Ben, it's late to start cooking. Would you like to go out to dinner?"

Benny grinned with an impression of exaggerated lasciviousness. "A repeat of that last dinner out?"

"Could be. But you're all sweaty. Want to shower first?"

"Sure." He waggled his eyebrows. "Do we really need to eat?"

Shit, he could have died in bed after their last dinner. In bed with her after sex. But the doctor had given no restrictions on activity. In fact, he'd said, "Anything!"

They were almost inside when he took her arm and said, "Speaking of dinner, we're eating with Jessica Saturday, in New York, at some restaurant she raves about. I already booked Freddy at the boarding place and us at a hotel. We'll have a little romantic getaway, just the two of us, except for that one meal."

She stopped in her tracks and stared at him. Without running it by her, Benny had set up a dinner with Jessica Hartnup!

"I promise, it'll be fun." He expected her to just go along and be a good sport. Be understanding. "I'll go wash up. Lotta drool on that ball and it's damned sticky out." He headed upstairs to the bathroom for a shower.

The water ran noisily into the tub, the sound easily heard in the kitchen. It would take him a while to return because the hot water was slow to reach the upstairs. She hated showering in that ventless, damp bathroom. The previous owners had painted the tub with wall paint, and it was now peeling. The porcelain surface looked like diseased skin. Benny didn't care.

She rubbed her neck to relieve a crick—she'd been unconsciously cocking her head while mulling things over. Benny had never had a woman as a friend, if that's what this Hartnup person was. Sure, he'd been pleasant to the wives of couples they knew—more than pleasant, gentlemanly. But he'd seemed horrified at the thought of conversing with them one-on-one. "What would I talk about? Sports? Cars? Programming apps?" he'd asked.

What were Benny and Jessica sharing? Iris couldn't imagine clandestine sex—Jessica wasn't his type. He'd always favored the willowy; never found large women appealing.

But aren't we too old for that stuff? Having a "type"? Judging by appearance? At our age, it's companionship that's sexy.

Anxiety formed a sweat mustache on her upper lip. She wiped it away with the back of her hand. *Don't make a fuss. Best be a sport about it all, whatever that entails. You've been wrong about so many things.* But the last was a slippery concept for her to hold on to.

Benny reappeared in the kitchen, dressed in a clean T-shirt and a pair of boxers from which his skinny calves, adorned with white hairs, protruded.

"Hey," Iris said, "That weekend in New York sounds like fun. Tonight, why don't I just make a quick frittata? We've got eggs and vegetables to put in it."

"What vegetables?" Benny's voice was wary. "Not eggplant or okra, I hope. They're so slimy."

"Peppers, onions, and potatoes." In this nascent rapprochement, why not show she really cared? "Think there's some Italian chicken sausage left, too. I'll put that in."

As a light rain had started, they ate in the small conservatory off the dining room. An old card table and lawn chairs served as a dining set as the kitchen's eating counter was freshly painted and still tacky to the touch. Iris found some baguette pieces in the basement freezer and toasted them. Together with the egg dish, it was a satisfactory impromptu supper.

"What did you do today, hon?" Benny asked, after a swig of local apple cider washed down his mouthful of bread.

Iris fished in the olive jar for the last Kalamata. "Just went to the morgue…"

"Why'd you go there? The baby's been cremated, so there's no body to view. Did that Charlotte go with you?"

She nodded and, hoping to turn the conversation lighthearted, recounted her feelings about the fast-food snack and the need to shield the leather upholstery. But that didn't succeed in derailing his train of thought.

"It sure seems funny to me that she's doing so much running around for an academic paper nobody will read. At least Jessica wants to write a whole book. That could make a bundle of money. At least money's a good motivation."

"Benny!" Why was he so suspicious of Charlotte's motives and jealous of the time Iris spent with her?

"What?" He put his fork handle down on the dirtiest part of the plate. The meal was over. "Let's at least go to Rita's for frozen custard." He was like a sulking child, demanding a treat.

On the drive to the custard stand, he was silent. Iris thought of placating him, pretending to be enthusiastic about the upcoming trip to New York. If she played her cards right, she could follow with a discussion of how her promise to Charlotte still stood, giving her first crack at Little Jack's story. In the past, Benny had been easy to manipulate.

But after they got a packed quart of vanilla, manipulating him seemed wrong, considering how recently they'd crossed the gap that had separated them for so many years and the truths they'd learned about each other. Considering how close they were to full reconciliation. She couldn't fall back into old patterns, even if they felt safer to her than being exposed.

As they reached home and pulled into their driveway, Iris wondered if Charlotte would be amenable to a similar rapprochement with Jessica. It took years for a book to come out, so something in an academic journal would probably come out first. Charlotte's thunder wouldn't be stolen.

They walked into the house to discover Freddy cowering against the front door. Iris comforted him while Benny went into the dining room.

"Oh, fuck no!" he yelled from the other room.

Iris and Freddy rushed in to find him looking up at the ceiling with dismay. Benny's bath seemed to have been the last straw for the unrenovated bathroom. The wood beneath the upstairs tub had collapsed onto their newly refinished dining room floor. Together, they stared in dismay at the sight of rotted wood and ceiling plaster piled on the floor, surrounded by a filthy puddle, growing amoeba-like from a dangling and dripping pipe. The crash must have been horrendous and scared the poor dog.

"Oh, Ben, thank God I didn't bring my grandmother's table in yet."

But Benny was gone from beside her. He'd run to the basement and shut off the water to the upstairs.

"You okay?" he asked when he returned.

Iris nodded, too numb to speak.

"Well, the good news is we were renovating that bathroom anyway. And don't know how you'll take this, but at least I'm not having a panic attack." He kissed Iris on her temple and went to call Richie, their contractor.

Thomas

1862

"Gentlemen," Thomas said, "I was going to prepare you a place to sleep, but Captain Sprigett desires you be on the move as soon as your horses have rested."

All three looked up from their plates. "Has he now?" said the one with the huge drooping moustache. "We take orders only from his mouth. Are you all there is here with the captain's young wife? And him being bedbound now?"

Before Thomas could answer, their corporal pointed his knife at the man. "You ain't got a right to speak, Matty. You even glance again at Mrs. Sprigett, who's been so kind to us, and I'll gut you like a fish. Captain Sprigett may be bedbound but he's still in charge."

The third and youngest soldier tossed his head in Thomas's direction. "Ain't he been here all along, Matty? Taking care of the place? Ain't he trusted by the captain? You should be burning with shame."

The leader turned to Thomas. "Don't pay that fool no nevermind. We'll be gone…."

"Gentlemen!" Interrupting them, Aoife came down the stairs. In the kitchen, she appeared wan and worn-out as she stood holding the edge of the mantel. "Please let no one dishonor myself or Captain Sprigett by believing he would ever put me in peril, or ever bring danger to our home. Nor should you say a word against Thomas. He gave up helping his people so that Captain Sprigett might fight with a free mind, knowing his wife and his property were secure."

The three soldiers sat with their mouths open in astonishment at her defense of her farm's worker. Having seen Aoife stand up to her husband's mother, her actions did not surprise Thomas.

The youth was the first to recover. "How fares the captain?"

"He rests, as comfortably as possible, worn-out from the journey and his pain. Quiet and loving care is what is needed, but before he slept, my husband fretted for you, his men. He said you'd best be continuing on, as you will be hunted as deserters. He does not wish that his life be saved just to see his saviors with their necks stretched. He thanks you heartily for bringing him home, but this is the first place they will look."

"Captain is right," said the corporal. "Ma'am, is there a fit team here to replace our weary horses? We just barely made our way here, fearing they'd drop from being pushed so hard."

"'Tis sad to say that the farm has only the one horse, a mare, for plowing. I will bring her if you wish."

Thomas placed his hat on his head, preparing to go outside to fetch the men's wagon.

"My husband took a fine horse with him when he left."

"A bright-colored bay?" asked the man.

Aoife nodded. As the men were staring at her, Thomas risked looking into her eyes to give her silent support.

"Beg pardon, ma'am, but that horse was killed when the captain was injured, shot out from under him. We won't take your plow horse. Know you of any good animals hereabouts?"

Thomas dropped his eyes and glanced at Aoife discreetly. She smiled slightly, a small break from her somber mood.

"Nearby is the house of my husband's mother. Mother Sprigett, who would have forced him be brought to her against his wishes," she said.

The two older men looked at each other, and Thomas thought perhaps they knew such overbearing mothers.

"In the stable there are excellent horses, kept from the war by her money. As soon as it is fully dark, you can change your worn-out team for two of hers."

"A team of matched Morgans," Thomas added, "like the ones you brought with you, but these well-fed and fresh. An easy exchange. It will be up to her to explain how two horses disappeared from the army stables only to appear in her barn." He picked up the heavy basket Aoife had prepared for the men's journey, so that they might delay as little as possible.

"Wait at the crossroads a while, and Thomas will lead you to the horses. Do not worry," Aoife said, "I will care for my husband even should I sacrifice everything else. So fare thee well, gentlemen, and may the Lord keep you."

As the men pushed back their chairs and took the food for their journey and Aoife had gone back up the stairs, Thomas went to the barn to get the fed and watered, though only briefly rested, horses.

Aoife

1862

Having left the men with a plan for their escape, she paused on the landing, fearing the lightheadedness that accompanied her pounding heartbeat. The loud whoosh of her heart's blood resounded in her ears, loud as water through a sluice gate. She worried it was loud enough that another might hear. *Dear God, William must not!*

She would not have him more distressed at the thought that she might be horrified by his injuries. In truth, his wounds overwhelmed her, so severe she couldn't imagine how they came to be or how he had survived thus far. It was bad enough when he was carried into the house and she first saw his legs were gone, but now that she'd seen him unwrapped, it was more devastating than she'd imagined. His right leg now ended at the middle of his thigh, his left just above where his knee once was and still should be. From his hip joints down, torn and damaged skin lay in rough ridges, coarsely sewn, though seemingly healing. Below were untidy, folded over lumps at the site of the amputations.

He had fallen asleep before she could do more than wash his face and neck and remove the filthy, reeking bandages from his legs. *Mayhap this was a foolish thing, him insisting on coming here. More time in hospital might have benefited him and the army would have transported him in better comfort after his recovery!*

But hadn't Thomas told her they'd risked their lives and freedom because William had longed to return home? And the corporal's letter had said that more injured men died of contagion in hospital than from their wounds. She could make sure that no contagion reached him here, in his own bed.

His being home was the best thing. She herself, his loving wife, would make sure of that.

Leaning against the wall, Aoife filled her lungs slowly and deeply, several times over.

He will never again walk in the blossoming apple orchard, dreaming of the harvest. They had wandered hand in hand amongst the trees while courting, blooms falling around them like sweet-scented snow, white on the sky blue of his shirt. He had reached up and combed them from her hair with his fingers. She shivered, recalling how his touch, loosening her bun to let her hair tumble over her bosom, had brought out the boldness in her, the wanton girl, heedless of the risk she faced. Trusting that he could—and would—always care for her.

How desperately she'd tugged his linen shirt from his checked trousers, her breasts aching with desire. How eagerly her fingers struggled with the buttons to allow him to be free to give her pleasure!

In the back of her mind Mrs. Sprigett's voice: *Irish slut!*

*   *   *

From the hall, she listened for a while to William breathing, reassured that he was still with her. Heard the slight whistle at the end of each exhalation—a noise for which, in the past, she'd shaken him at night and teased him in the day. How she'd missed that sound while he was away at war! Would it ever again bother her or remain a happy reminder that she had him safe back in their home? *I mustn't think of myself, neither good nor foul. 'Tis William who suffers the most.*

She went into the other room off the hall. It was small; the steep-pitched roofline and the stairs allowing only their one large bedroom and a few built-in cabinets. William had shown the little room to her when the house was his alone but, he swore, would from then on be theirs.

"I will add on, love, as needed," he'd said. "We have time for that. Meanwhile imagine a sweet cradle here, one I bid Thomas make from that chestnut we felled. That wood has a fine, straight grain." He walked to the sunlight coming in the many-paned window and tapped the glass. "You might sew curtains." He turned back to her with a smile. "So my son won't disturb us when I kiss you here and here, and caress…"

He nuzzled her neck while slipping a hand deep in her bodice to squeeze her nipple.

His caresses aroused her, made the damp start between her thighs, but she still wasn't ready to cease their teasing. "The room is for a babe, is it now? For a cradle? William, it takes months to make a child, boy or girl, and, for sure, ours would be too precious to not be but right by my side. For feeding in the night, you know." Laughing, she pulled at his wrist, drawing his hand from her bosom. "And those will be for the feeding!"

He'd grabbed her around the waist and carried her into the other room, to the canopy bed. Dropped her onto the mattress, pushing up her skirts as he did. She kicked off her shoes and wrapped her legs around his slim hips, crying out in her mounting pleasure. With vigorous movements she matched with her own, he'd brought her to an agony of bliss.

No child resulted from their exertions, though the two of them were spent, lying on sweated sheets, and panting like hounds after a chase. Nothing then and nothing for the next few years. The little room was left bare, anticipating a future, a family. And then William went to war.

Well, he was home now. She went to the doorway of their bedroom and gazed at his face, still handsome in the calm of laudanum-induced sleep. And she resolved to try again, as soon as her devoted nursing made him well enough. She smiled to herself, feeling her sex tighten at the thought. That she could cajole him into trying was certain. *Irish slut, indeed!*

Chapter 21

THE UPSTAIRS BATH WAS UNUSABLE. Though the contractor had the tub removed for safety, Benny insisted the floor be ripped up before Iris set foot in it, even to brush her teeth.

"Who knows how much is rotten," he said. "One step in the wrong spot and *BAM!* you're dangling from the dining room ceiling with a broken leg."

"But Benny, if there was really extensive rot, wouldn't the tub have fallen through? It's cast-iron and weighs much more than me."

Benny looked piously up to the heavens. "Praise the Lord, Iris, we are blessed. A renovation miracle."

"But my makeup is in the cabinet…"

He put his arms around her waist and kissed the top of her head. "Iris, you're gorgeous naturally." He winked, exaggerated vaudeville style. "A real classy broad. A fox. Need I say more?"

When she laughed, his hands strayed up to cup her jiggling breasts. She pushed them down. "But Benny, we're going to Manhattan. Much dressier there. We're going to a real upscale place for dinner. I don't want to look out of place."

He looked at her quizzically from under distrustful, lowered brows. "This isn't about seeing Jessica Hartnup, is it? She isn't exactly what anyone would call a sharp dresser."

Silly old Benny, thinking women dress for men! Dressing for them would only mean dropping our necklines and raising our hems.

He was still talking. "And again, she's not interested in me and I'm not interested in her. Trust me, it's the truth."

She looked ruefully into the damaged bathroom, the medicine cabinet far away, feeling like Alice in Wonderland, when she was quite small… and all of Alice's best Victorian-era cosmetics were out of reach. Iris sighed. *If I go in and fall through, I'll never hear the end of it.*

"We have to take Freddy to the boarder's," Benny sighed and scratched his head. Typical that he hadn't done a thing to get ready for their trip.

From his usual spot in the hall, the dog picked his head up at the mention of his name, obviously hoping for a treat or, if that wasn't forthcoming, a walk.

"I'll take him. That way you can pack." She poked Benny's belly. "We all know you wait 'til the last minute for that!"

Benny pursed his mouth. "Guilty as charged." He pulled his small suitcase from the closet and stood looking deliberately pathetic.

Iris put the dog in the back of the SUV. She hopped in the driver's seat and raced to the same place they'd boarded him before, when, with snarls and raised hackles, Freddy had decided the best and cheapest electrician was his mortal enemy. He'd been banished from the house until the wiring was done.

When Freddy saw where he was, he dug his claws into the hatch's mat, attempting to avoid the inevitable, but Iris was having none of that. *If I have to face Jessica Hartnup, Important New York Intellectual, I have to look good at the restaurant, not like a frazzled renovator, an insecure and jealous wife, or a half-crazy PTSD sufferer.*

Sephora was only a short drive away.

She shopped quickly, applying foundation, eyeliner, and mascara, right in the store, despite the rolled eyes of the salesclerks, perky-breasted twenty-somethings plus one very gay boy. She held off on the lipstick, though she'd purchased a pleasant warm terracotta. It would only be chewed off in the city's traffic.

To her surprise, Benny was ready when she pulled up at the house. Not only ready but standing outside with his case and hers. Seeing him lifted her spirits from the low-level fretting of the morning. Breaking a bad habit—in this instance, procrastination—was such a loving thing.

He adored her—she was sure of that now. But she still wasn't convinced Jessica Hartnup's interest in Benny was only friendship.

Iris waved and unlocked the doors. Benny loaded the suitcases, and they took off, heading over the bridge to New Jersey and then up the toll road to New York.

Once in the stream of highway traffic, her guilt worked on her. She wanted time to process what she'd done, all the times she accused him in her mind, and shut him out from her emotions. She wasn't ready to bring someone new into the mix. Didn't want the years peeled back and the past put under a microscope.

Most of all, she didn't want someone saying her attachment to little Jack Doe was pathologic, especially something based on earlier trauma. It may be true, but she still wanted to hold him close to her own heart. She wanted to find out who he was and why he was in her pond.

"Benny," she said outside of Trenton, "forget what we said about couple counseling. I know I've pushed for it, but now we've gotten everything out in the open, I'm sure we can work things out privately, between us. No outsider needed. I was just so deep inside myself, I couldn't tell anyone how I felt, but I figure now I've told you everything, why start with a new person?"

"I don't know, Iris." He furrowed his brow. "Just to talk about the big-ticket items… It might be good…"

Your affair… She was too busy changing lanes to answer.

"Maybe you're right," he said. "We should give ourselves more time to mull it over, now we're open about what's happened. Once we've gotten away from the stress of renovation… It's supposed to be as hard to live through as a divorce. Or it can lead to divorce or something."

He plugged in his phone to get their music on Spotify, fiddling with the buttons on the dash. "While we're in New York, the bathroom floor's going to be fixed. Richie promised. The guys'll get extra for working the weekend. We're putting that house back together, brick by brick, and we'll work to put our marriage back together the same. Brick by brick, stronger than ever before. Love's the mortar."

That sounded kind of hokey. *Is Benny getting poetic on me?*

Iris searched her memory for an old song, one with that concept as part of its lyrics. But she couldn't think of one.

She mused on that the rest of the way to the Battery Tunnel and on into Manhattan. The drive was easier once Benny had selected The Righteous Brothers, Iris's favorite.

The boutique hotel he'd picked was stunning. Their room had floor-to-ceiling windows with views of the Empire State Building and, in the distance, the Statue of Liberty, but you'd need binoculars to be sure. Benny dropped his suitcase on the floor and opened Iris's for her, spread out on the king bed. She changed quickly and applied her new lipstick.

"We don't have much time to get to the restaurant." He tapped his toe on the gleaming wood floor. "Jessica could only get an early reservation at short notice. The restaurant's apparently a hot ticket item."

"I hope it's not too fancy." Iris's best clothes, tailored pants and a contrasting sleeveless linen shirt, seemed dowdy next to the outfits walking in and out of the lobby twenty floors below. Consumed with the house in Pennsylvania, she'd forgotten how always evolving and expensive the chicness of Manhattan could be.

"Iris, quit worrying. Come on, time to go."

To Iris's surprise the restaurant was casual in design, all pale wood, punctuated with ebony and potted bamboo. Even better, it featured creative pan-Asian cuisine.

"Pretty great, right?" Benny said, grinning from ear to ear. "Jess asked what you'd like and I suggested something like this."

Jessica was already seated when they arrived, at a table with four place settings. Benny and Iris joined her. There were bottles of Asahi beer—super dry—as well as sake. A waiter immediately set down a plate of duck spring rolls, neatly cut on the diagonal and adorned with sprigs of micro cilantro. He lifted the sake. "Hakkaisan Tokubetsu Junmai. Aroma of toasted rice cake with a finish of vanilla and mountain herbs. Goes stunningly…"

Stunningly… Iris kept her expression bland. She had, after all, come to the glitzy area of Manhattan voluntarily.

"…with light fare and with more fatty or buttery foods."

"I hope you don't mind my choosing the drinks," Jessica said. "I am very particular to the ones from Japan."

Another waiter brought a huge plate of exquisitely thin sashimi. He placed it near the extra setting. The fish did look good, as good as any they had in San Francisco. It glistened with freshness.

"Is someone else coming?" Iris asked. "We should wait to start."

"No need." Jessica, however, held off taking any. She sipped sake instead and waited until their mouths were full before saying, "I ordered this and a whole bunch more of their best, though if you see anything you'd like, we'll just add that." She tapped the pile of menus in the middle of the table. "By the way, how's work on the house going? Benny says you're making progress."

"Yes, but we just had a setback." Iris laughed to show she wasn't a pain in Benny's ass about the renovations, that she could roll with the punches. "Just before we left to come here, part of the dining room ceiling came down." She described looking up at the bottom of the ancient linoleum bathroom floor.

"Sounds like a real nightmare. Hope things go smoother soon." Jessica smiled in a way that made Iris wary. "Ben also says you've been researching the baby found in your pond with a new friend. A grad student?"

"Yes, a lovely young woman named Charlotte Moore. She's been really a boon companion when it comes to looking stuff up."

Jessica Hartnup leaned across the table to speak to Iris. "And where is she doing her degree?"

"Penn, I think? Not sure she mentioned..." Iris pulled back, realizing she didn't know. Charlotte had only said that she was in school, getting her doctorate, but not what school. She glanced at Benny, who was studiously attempting to pick up his fish with chopsticks. The sliver of maguro slid back to the plate time and again. *Fishy...* Iris cut her eyes back to Jessica. "Gosh, wherever. She certainly is efficient at research."

"Oh? Intriguing. Most Ivy League grad students bore you to tears bragging about their program... Has the investigation been rewarding? Found out any interesting details?"

"Yup." Iris nodded, not wanting to give anything away. She wanted time to think what she should say, how much of what she and Charlotte had discovered.

"Well, as you know, I'd love to be involved in figuring out the mystery. It would be a superb plot device for a new book. Why don't I come down and take you and your friend to lunch? I love students, so I teach a lot of writing seminars in the mystery community."

"Uh, okay."

Jessica hadn't pressed for information on their findings. "You must be having a blast looking into your property. One can't help but find such research fascinating. I certainly do—sorry it took me so long to come back and join in. There's so much work to do, marketing books."

"Even if you're an established author?" Benny asked, joining in at last.

Jessica sighed. "Yes. People think it's like it was in F. Scott Fitzgerald's time and you mail in a messy pile of paper for some editor to edit and some publisher to publish. But writers have to do most of the revising and marketing now."

Iris was getting hungry, and the sashimi wasn't cutting it as a stomach filler. What—or who—were they waiting for?

Then Jessica half-rose, a delighted expression on her face. "Kat!"

A tall and beautiful blonde woman, thirty or fifty—it was impossible to tell—approached the table. She was dressed all in black—leather pants despite the heat, and a black silk shell that emphasized her tiny waist with its ruching detail.

"This is Katerina," Jessica Hartnup said. "My muse." She smiled proudly as the woman slid into her seat. "My wife."

Aoife

1862

Nights she lay awake on a pallet next to the high bed that held William. He needed the entire span to spread out his arms and shift himself to be comfortable. Besides, any jostling of the mattress stuffing pained him—though he bit his lip, drawing blood at times, rather than cry out. Aoife could not sit down but needed to bend over to tend his wounds.

She barely dragged herself through the days, tending the cows before William's midnight dose of laudanum wore off, returning to prepare breakfast and set bread to rising, then bringing down the chamber pot, and doing whatever was needed to make William comfortable. He helped her as well as he could, rolling slowly onto one shoulder and then the other when she changed the bed linens. That exertion cost him dearly and almost rendered her efforts worthless, as he broke into a drenching sweat.

When she was sure he was asleep again, she went down to bake the bread, cook, and boil his linens before washing them. The last thing she did, should he not need her, was to see if there were any light chores around the barn. The townswomen had not returned after the hay was in, so, thankfully, Thomas had the time to tend the kitchen garden.

Lettie did no work, though she could often be seen flitting about the yard. She appeared to Aoife like one of the gorgeous butterflies that feasted on the wild milkweed and smooth blue aster. She was followed by Hero.

Unfaithful dog! What should be tending the sheep. Lettie had done nothing obvious to worry Aoife, but she was no lost lamb to be minded by that dog!

Aoife herself did not stray further than she could run in a minute, checking in the house often.

"Rest," Thomas said as she stumbled by him to bring slops to the pigs, "and I will do without sleep to get the farm chores done, if I must. You are about played out." He took the bucket from her hand and walked toward the pigsty.

Aoife returned to the house. Once inside, she darted up to William, thankful he was again asleep. *Nothing like rest to heal the ill, my dadai always said. Rest and, of course, a dose of home-brewed poitín. He must have always been ill, then.* The last thought made her snort with a laugh of rueful anger. He'd gotten his in America, where he'd been forced to work.

How unlike her father were William and Thomas! One bravely gone for a soldier, the other hardworking from dawn until well after dusk. *Mam would have counted herself lucky to have such men in her life.*

The floor creaked loudly as she went to leave the bedroom.

"Aoife, love?" William opened his eyes, which startled her with their bright blue-green beauty.

"Aye, love? 'Tis me." She returned to the bed.

"I have been thinking. Perhaps it would be best for me to return to my mother's house."

She took a step back. "What? Do you love me no longer, William?"

He put his hands up over his eyes and sighed. "More than the sun loves the morning dew, my darling. More than all the tea in China. And that is why I make this request. I don't want to see you waste away and die, what with caring for me."

She stamped her foot, horrified at the thought of losing him again. "No. No. I'll not have it!"

"At least beg her come to see me. Perhaps she will send a maid to help…"

"I do not want another woman in our house, one who would spy for Mother Sprigett."

"Aoife…"

"I will ask that your mam come, as she should, to the bedside of her son, but I will do no more."

Thomas
1862

The farm was suffering. Not the livestock—the sheep and cattle were fatter than ever, having been turned out into the fields there was no time to tend, and the hay was bountiful for the winter and sold well. But Thomas had been able to harvest little wheat. The merchants were turned away, disappointed.

He was shamed by the bounty of the surrounding farms. William's farm had been among those known for fine wheat and corn, as well as excellent dairy and meat.

Thomas hoped William's money would hold out until Aoife would be free to work more on the farm, or until he could find another worker. A few men had asked to come, but they were too lame or too disreputable to be hired. With the wartime openings for factory workers, the hard toil of a farm was less appealing. The work was the load he carried on his back, like it or not.

He also hoped Lettie, contributing nothing while eating well, would not be held against him. Before the war, William had only known that Thomas had a woman in town, one he called his wife, but no children. Though he might work for the farm until he could work no longer, he still wished a place of his own.

Nights, Lettie allowed him to lie beside her, but when he reached out to stroke her, she pushed him away. He had vowed to never again attempt to take her against her will.

"Do you not want to try again for a child? Family was your heart's desire and what I also wish for." He longed for a bit of happiness, a return to the sweet release of amorous congress.

"A child?" Her voice, hard and bitter. "You could not keep me from harm, Thomas. Less could you do so with a babe at my breast. Leave me be." She rolled away from him.

He lay in the dark, staring upward, but the barn was still and silent. Even the owl was missing. His body ached everywhere from the work he'd done in the day, but the steamy late summer heat kept him from sleep. He lay wondering how Aoife fared in the bedroom where she tended to her husband. Did she slumber on her pallet, or did she lie awake, looking up at the night sky? Did she ever think of how they'd sat at the table, him reading the letters to her in the lamplight?

In the morning, he would fix the thresher's bent blade if he could. Thinking of the next day's tasks, finally he slept.

Thomas awoke in the morning with wetness in the bed and the vague realization of a dream, a dream which, like a sheet of cheap paper floating in a puddle, was impossible to read, becoming see-through, and finally disintegrating.

He wiped off the front of him with his shirt from the day before and headed out to douse his head at the pump. The dream, though mysterious, was about a woman, but who, whether Lettie or Aoife, was unclear.

Working the pump as the cock crowed for the start of dawning, he realized the dream had saddened him. It wasn't sex he craved, or the release the dream had given him, but the conversation and the companionship of a friend, the joy of working as one. The companionship he'd had before Lettie had come—and Mr. William returned—to the farm.

He realized that he was lonely.

Chapter 22

IRIS DECIDED TO PLAY IT COOL, show no surprise, though she was seething underneath. Benny is going to get his fucking unagi dumped in his lap, surreptitiously of course, if he doesn't stop grinning at me in that told-you-so manner.

She held her hand out to shake Katerina's. "I've never met a muse before."

Katerina threw back her head and laughed. "A muse for cozy mysteries." She fondled Jessica's arm. "I was sold a bill of goods. I was supposed to inspire the Great American Novel."

Jessica laughed as well, and the two women kissed. Katerina slid into the empty seat and waved away the menu. "I know what I want! Soba. And sparkling water."

"That's why she looks like she does, instead of like me, a Butterball turkey dressed in Laura Ashley."

Katerina raised one eyebrow and rocked her head from side-to-side. "You could try something a little more modern, Jess."

Jessica stuck the tip of her tongue out. She turned to Iris, with a grin that rivaled Benny's. "She's always trying to make me over. Isn't that just like a wife?"

Benny appeared delighted with the discussion and made Iris wonder if the meal had been orchestrated. But if so, why? Her best guess would be to open the door to the cozy mystery around the finding of Baby Jack.

Their food was brought out, one appetizer-sized portion at a time. The meal's pacing, which would typically have driven Benny into a frenzy, now seemed to stimulate his congeniality. "Jess, soon as our house is done, you'll have to come stay. You, too, Kat."

Kat? Is that her nickname? When did he meet her?

Jessica replied, "We'd love to. Katerina's an artist and the area's great to sketch and paint. The covers she designs make selling my novels a snap."

"An artist?" Iris moved back to let the server put down two more dishes.

"Well, when she's not in her office seeing clients. She likes to keep busy."

Iris turned to look at Benny, who was deep in conversation with Katerina. "Clients for artwork?"

"She's a therapist in Chelsea. Big practice in the LGBTQ+ community." Jessica helped herself to a few more curried lamb meatballs. "You need to have things to keep you busy, right? Or you go nuts. I told Benny that's why it was good for you to look into that baby."

"You did?" Iris hadn't meant it as a question, though it came out that way. She put her fork down. What else did he tell her?

"Yep. Now he won't try to keep you from solving the mystery. And a mighty fine mystery it is. Who were the parents? Why did the baby die? And why your pond?" Jessica looked intently at Iris, as if expecting answers.

Katerina interrupted. "The student who's helping you research the baby is named Charlotte Moore, right?" She slouched in her chair, ignoring the food being brought.

Jessica squeezed Katerina's shoulder. "What a memory. I always tell people I married a treasure!" She looked slyly at Iris. "And she takes all clients, including heteros."

*   *   *

"See, you were wrong to worry about Jessica and me," Benny said when they were back at the hotel.

He never misses an opportunity for a "told you so!" Iris stood over him, debating whether to outright ask him everything he'd told Jessica.

He burped and undid his pants, then flopped backward onto the king bed's silvery gray cover, his feet still on the ground. "I ate too much!" He glanced up at her and smiled. "Come here you, looking all serious and shit." He patted the bed beside him.

"I'm just going to undress so I can relax," she said, taking a half-step away. "Brush my teeth. Put on pjs."

"Oh, no, not pjs! And I want to undress you."

She froze in place. Before she could move again, he sat up and undid the waist of her pants. He let them drop and tugged her panties down to her knees.

She moved to step out of the tangled clothing, but he stopped her, grabbing her buttocks and pulling her toward him. He buried his face between her legs, his tongue licking, his lips nibbling and sucking. The maneuvers had always been something she'd requested but he had been reluctant to try.

His mouth steadily increased the force with which he nuzzled her. The movements were so fierce, his grip so strong, that she didn't sink down, but swayed, moaning incoherently. She was brought to near climax, then he backed off and started again, his tongue thrusting harder. This time she came and was surprised by the liquid her body produced. She'd thought herself past that, too old and dried up.

"There," he murmured. "That's my girl." He stood, lifted her up, leaving her pants behind. Swung her onto the bed and pulled off her panties and slid himself inside her. She came again immediately.

In the morning, awakening unusually refreshed, she could remember nothing past her second orgasm. Benny lay snoring on the bed, his carefully trimmed beard glistening, sticky, and looking quite like a frisée salad that had been overdressed.

Well, Benny, old boy, you still got it. But don't go thinking you can sweet fuck me into doing therapy with Jessica Hartnup's anorexic wife!

She smiled, though, feeling very fond of him.

Thomas
1862

A sudden early storm had coated the world with a clear glaze, beautiful but treacherous. As soon as that sun had reached its zenith, Mother Sprigett's carriage rolled down the drive. "Come here!" she called to Thomas, who was scraping the ice remaining on the stone kitchen steps.

He leaned the shovel against the kitchen wall and walked to her.

"Hand me down," she demanded, holding out her gloved right hand—her left held a fine Malacca cane.

Thomas did as she asked. The movement of her skirt revealed her ankles were now grotesquely swollen. He glanced at her face, which was yellowed and puffy. Dropsy. He'd seen it before, many times, in those whose heart was failing. He nearly laughed. *She has no heart—it is time she came, as her son has been lying here these several months.*

He took the reins to lead the team away.

"Don't unhitch them. Tie them here." She swayed where she stood, the cane taking the weight off her left leg, and pointed to a young tree nearby. "And help me into the house, lest I slip."

He obeyed that, too. The last thing needed was for the old woman to be injured at the farm. Or fly into a rage and upset Aoife and Mr. William.

"Mistress Sprigett comes," he called, to warn Aoife of her mother-in-law's arrival.

Aoife appeared at the kitchen door, holding a dishcloth. "Mother Sprigett, welcome."

"That will do." The old woman said, dismissing Thomas with a wave of her hand as soon as she was safely inside. She turned to Aoife. "I've come to see my son. Let me lean on you as I climb the stairs."

To which Aoife replied, "Perhaps Thomas…"

Mother Sprigett snorted. "You are strong enough."

Aoife sighed. She nodded at Thomas to let him know he could leave the kitchen.

Back out in the yard, Thomas again hefted the shovel and left for the barn, though he longed to hear any further discourse between the women.

Lettie was not to be seen—perhaps she'd stepped out to greet the morning sun. He climbed up into the hayloft to examine the barn's roof from within, seeking any errant ray from that sun. A leak, though minor, threatened to ruin some of his carefully stored timothy. He put the shovel in its place and took up the pitchfork, loosening the sheaves one from another, and tossing them aside. He gazed upward, trying to spy the roof's defect. At last, he noticed a missing shingle and planned to climb up and move the slate about.

"Thomas…" Lettie was climbing the ladder to the hayloft. On top of the sweater given her by Aoife, she had their quilt wrapped about her shoulders. Keeping it from snagging on the ladder slowed her ascent. "Have you a moment for me?"

At Lettie's sweet and conciliatory tone, he stabbed the pitchfork deep into the hay to keep it upright. He helped her up the last rung into the loft to join him. "What is it, Lettie?"

She dropped down, her skirt a dark wave about her legs, and patted the hay. "Sit for a while. The sun has warmed the air here and it is cold below."

He sighed. She never talked to him but to interrupt his work. "The roof needs fixing. It is leaking onto the hay. Do not use up my day for nothing, but tell me, what is it you want?"

"Just to spend time with you." She smiled sweetly up at him. "Husband."

A flame of rage sparked in his chest. He took hold of the pitchfork's handle to keep from striking her. "No, Lettie, I won't have it. You call me husband? No wife would turn away in the night as you do. I'm no husband to you. Not even a man." He was trembling, the corded muscles in his arms clenched tight to keep hold on the wooden handle. "What is it you want from me?"

She looked down, silent.

"I've let you be." He pushed the pitchfork in further as the words tumbled out of him. "Never demanded you do your wifely duties." The rage flared and horrified him, but he was more appalled as longing crept into his voice. "Once you loved me, did you not? Wished for children?"

She didn't speak or look up at him. Instead, she rose and turned her slender back. He looked with regret at the hair tumbling down between her narrow shoulder blades. It was silky again, threaded with copper tresses. "Do not now pretend love or desire. Go away so I can do my work."

She headed down the ladder.

He called after her, "I am a man like any other, Lettie!"

Aoife

1862

Wearing a dress of black silk, Mother Sprigett had entered the house like the empress of China visiting a servant's home. In the time since Aoife last saw her, she'd put on weight and taken to using a cane.

In response to her demand, Aoife had wiped her floury hands, dropped a cloth over her dough—lest it dry out—and put her arm under the fat old woman.

Mother Sprigett leaned on Aoife heavily as they went up the stairs. Their progress was painfully slow, paced by the thump of the Malacca cane. "I do not need your man to go up to my son. You are strong enough." Her voice was thick with arrogance and her cheeks wobbled with angry effort. "You Irish girls always are, with your great rough hands."

There was no benefit in retorting, though angry words formed on her lips. Should William hear, he would be upset.

Mother Sprigett gulped huge breaths like a porpoise coming up for air, like the ones who'd sported in the wake of their sailing ship as her family crossed the ocean.

"They are the steeds of the water fairies," her mam had told her.

When Aoife, knowing fairies spirit children away and leave changelings behind, began to cry with fear, her dadai struck her for her tears. "Your mam is just acting the maggot, so shut your gob, child."

Aoife had hated the sea creatures after that, though those had been sleek and agile, unlike her husband's mother.

Once in the hall, Mother Sprigett shook her off, as if touching each other had been an ugly accident. Banging the walls with her cane as she went, the old woman stumped to William's bedside. Aoife hastened to push her most-prized chair, a wingback upholstered in fine Italian millefleur, under the old woman's buttocks. Mother Sprigett sank down with a loud *ooph!*

William's mother, both hands on her walking stick, bent toward her son. Aoife took in a sharp and audible breath as the tip of that cane lifted the blanket over William's lap. She took a step forward, thinking to strike the old woman's hand away, but William looked at her in such a penetrating way, she knew it was not what he wanted. *Better to get it over with, I suspect.*

"So, 'tis true." Mother Sprigett pulled back her arm.

"Yes, Mother." William smiled, his cheekbones tenting the skin of his face, his eyes like two great green jewels.

How beautiful he is, the flesh worn away with his suffering, he appears like the Christ. Aoife's heart ached.

"If you are ruined, the least I expect is a grandson."

"That we cannot give you." He held up his hand as the old woman glared at Aoife. "'Twill not be my wife at fault but me."

The old woman pursed her mouth. Her chin resembled an apple dried for midwinter pies. "Well, William, first your brother and now you. Robert, to see that widow when her child lay abed with diphtheria, and you gone for a soldier to please a maid. Both my sons, ruined by women."

"I went to fight for the Union, Mother. My wife did not send me. Father would have desired no less."

"Your father was a fool and you after him." Mother Sprigett shook her head, the plumes on her black hat jouncing. "It is not for nothing that I wear mourning."

Aoife could control herself no longer. "My William is not dead!" She moved between him and his mother.

The old woman's jowls quivered with rage, and she rose to stand shakily upright. She raised her fist and shook it at Aoife. "How dare you, you little chit! Take me to my carriage at once."

"So now it is you're wanting escorting on the stairs…"

William tugged at Aoife's skirt, looking up at her, his eyes pleading.

"All right. I shall," she grumbled. "But only for you, love, and for the fact that, should she roll down and not bounce well, we might be stuck with her." She caressed his cheek, then roughly took Mother Sprigett's arm.

*   *   *

Darkness came early. Aoife slipped into the high bed next to William. She turned his face to hers and kissed him deeply for the first time since he'd come home. He tried to twist away, but she hung on tightly. "Don't listen to your mother, love. You are very much alive and here with me."

He groaned. "My legs. They hurt and burn. Don't bump against them."

"My darling, I know you are better. Your legs, healing nicely. Soon they will be strong enough for the wooden limbs Washington provides. We will walk in our orchard again." She slid her hands down his chest, stopping at his waist, uncertain how bold she should be. "We can be as we were before."

He grabbed her hands and held them. He was still strong.

"Let me go," she whispered. "I would lie atop you. William, I want us to have babes. I want to make one tonight." She wrested one hand from his grip, which had loosened as his breaths shuddered in his chest.

"Don't you think I wish for that, too, Aoife?"

Her hand had reached his organ. She took it in her grasp and gently squeezed, but he remained soft. Fear crept into her heart, prickling like a hundred nettles. "Do you not love me? Do you not want me?"

He gripped her other hand hard, as if to crush the slender bones beneath her roughened skin. "Aoife, don't you understand? It isn't just my legs."

She cried out in pain from the force of his fingers wrapped around hers.

"The ball that struck broke into a hundred pieces like spinning knife blades and tore through me. The surgeons said things were cut. My mother is right. I am a dead man or would wish to be."

"Don't say such," Aoife whispered. "It is a sin. Not while I am here with you. Not while I love you with every breath I take." *From now, I sleep beside him, even should he push me away. Surely there will be a way…*

That very night, moonless and quiet, William's nightmares began.

Chapter 23

AT THE EDGE OF THE ROAD, Iris pulled at a thistle, trying to uproot it.

"Why risk getting their little stickers into your hands? Why don't you just poison them?" Benny asked. "Hire a gardener." He believed in bringing in younger men to do yard work, especially since he had passed sixty.

She held up her gloved hands. "Being careful. See?" She loved digging around on the property—it gave her a sense of accomplishment as the continuous construction on the house filled the air with dust and made it impossible to keep the inside clean.

"Aww, c'mon inside and watch TV with me. It's Shark Week on Discovery."

Iris laughed. Sometimes he seemed to her like a teenager or maybe someone entering his second childhood. "Tell you what, I'll be in soon and make you guacamole and chips."

"Yay!" Benny fist-pumped the air. He left for the TV room with the wall-mounted giant screen and the comfy couch.

With him gone, Iris could concentrate on getting out the huge weed. Benny was right, though, she should use herbicide as thistle roots went on forever. But at least she could rip out this plant. She wrapped her hands around the stem and pulled. It moved painfully slowly, but it did steadily give way. And then it released all of a sudden, with a snap. She lost her footing, falling on her behind, the thistle still in her grip. A damp ball of dirt clung to the broken root. No sense putting garden soil in the compost. She banged the dirt off onto the road's surface.

Clink! Something fell from the clump of soil. It rolled across the asphalt, the dirt clinging to it fragmenting and falling off as it traveled. Beneath that dirt was something that gleamed yellow. Iris tossed the plant to the side and chased after it.

"Well, I'll be," she said aloud, though no one was nearby. The thing between her fingers was a ring made of what seemed like gold. She brushed it off further and saw it was more than a plain band. A cabochon red stone, carved, was set in the middle of the gold circle. The carving seemed to be letters, but it was still deep crusted, making it hard to see what they were.

Iris took it to the garden hose and turned the water on slowly. She tugged off her gardening gloves and scrubbed the surface of the ring with the pad of her thumb. It was still difficult to make out the incised letters.

She went inside the house. The TV was blaring. Poking her head into the room, she said, "Guac coming up!" Benny didn't respond, didn't even glance her way. He seemed entranced by a great white trying to snack on a diver in an underwater cage. The *bang, bang, bang* of the monster's snout against the bars reverberated aggressively from their surround sound.

"Jeez, turn it down, Benny! That's how old people go deaf." She went into the kitchen, pulled out the roll of parchment paper she used for baking, and tore off a little bit. There was a Sharpie in her utility drawer—thankfully, it wasn't dried out. Holding the bit of paper over the stone, she stroked the marker's nib on the paper. The engraving appeared in relief, more clearly than she'd hoped. In the center was an elaborate, cursive *S*, with a *W* to one side, and an *A* on the other.

The band was too small for her ring finger, so she slipped it onto her pinkie. While she was mashing the two ripest avocados, she called Charlotte, cradling her phone between shoulder and ear.

"Wait 'til you see what I found in the garden." She moved to the cutting board to chop tomatoes and red onion.

"Send a photo," Charlotte answered. "If you're this excited, it must be something of a wow."

"Nope. You've got to come see. I don't know if it has any link to the baby, but it might. I'll be here all day tomorrow, waiting for the plumber... again. I'll make tea—for you, not the plumber!"

"Okay," Charlotte said. "I'll figure out what time I can be there."

With the sixth sense men seem to have when it comes to food, Benny appeared as soon as Iris had made the guacamole. He wore shorts, which showed that his legs bowed out a bit more at the knees than the last time she'd looked. His arthritis must be getting worse. "Want to see what I found in the garden?" she asked.

Benny held up both hands. "Whoa, whoa! Not after your last find..." He lowered his arms but only to take the basket of taco chips and bowl of avocado dip and head back to the sharks.

Aoife

1863

Night after night when the terror came for William, Aoife clung to him, to keep him warm and his body on the bed. In his dreams, he still roamed the battlefield, whole and healthy and in command.

The one time she'd arisen to use the chamber pot, he had flung himself onto the floor without awakening. Trying to lift him herself had been fruitless, so she wrapped her cloak about herself and darted out through a light and chilling rain, calling "Thomas! I need you."

As soon as she called, he ran from the barn, his shirttail flapping about the waist of his pants. He bolted up the stairs ahead of her, and together they put William back onto the mattress.

"Perhaps it would be better to push the bed against the wall," Thomas whispered, though William remained senseless.

"He asked for more laudanum than usual for his nighttime dosage, so he did not awaken." Side-by-side, they moved the bed, slowly so as not to jar William. The warmth of Thomas's body reached through her thin gown.

William always seemed so bloodless now.

Thomas's breathing quickened, but all he said as he left the room was, "We could pull it back in the morning to help change his bed-clothes."

It was only in the light of dawn she saw the wrap on the left stump was bloodied. Still blurry from sleep, he moved that limb restlessly. "Aoife, my leg hurts anew, as if it was freshly sawn off." He pushed her hand away as she tried to expose the stump. "Did I imagine falling from the bed? Was it a nightmare that I was on the cold floor, and you and Thomas were standing above me?"

"'Twas no dream, William. You threw yourself down and I could not lift you alone. I fear you banged your dear leg on the floor when you fell." Though the chores awaited, she slid back under the covers next to him, put her arms about his neck and kissed him. "Thank goodness Thomas is here to help. And he will be even closer once the lean-to is done and Matthew Gruber delivers the Franklin stove. Soon, all will be snug for the winter." She stood again. "Now, let me run to start the fire for cooking the oats. Then please let me look at your wound."

Upstairs again, she unwound the long bandage. The skin flap had never looked as healthy as on the other leg, and now it oozed blood. "Love, I think the fine wooden legs they sent will have to wait, unless you wish to try the one and crutches."

He shook his head. "I feel too unwell and weak to balance. Less well than a week ago, I fear."

She took long strips of fresh, clean cloth and bound the stump again. "I'll leave you now, for chores I must be doing."

"The farm needs attention, Aoife, and must sadly fall to you. The chance is good that I shall never run it again."

She stood and gathered the dirty bandages. "Don't say that, ever. Whether on two good legs or on crutches or even in bed, you are this farm's master, William."

Thomas

1863

I came when she called and picked him up from the floor, a task I'd never imagined. I stand between him and her. Neither can do without me, just as I need both of them. Would that Lettie felt the same.

Ordering Lettie to help with chores had been met with laughter and a frank refusal. "I'm no one's slave," she declared, unmoved by his plans for their own farm.

Yet he still loved Lettie and couldn't bring himself to abandon her.

When the stove came, they would move from the barn into the lean-to he'd built against the south side of the house. Like the Amish did, he had piled straw high against the sides of the structure to keep in the warmth. It might prove more comfortable a space than the house itself. Some of his savings had gone to purchase a wool-stuffed ticking mattress. Perhaps that luxury would help soften Lettie's disdain.

Now that William was better, Aoife was again sharing more of the farm's work. The fall crops were brought in from the kitchen garden, which she'd expanded while William needed her to stay close. Thomas had tilled the soil for her by lamplight, after it was too dark to work in the big fields. They'd worried it was too late for the crops to succeed, but the fall weather had held warm and the garden, bountiful.

Once the weather turned, and winter was close, she worked every moment tending the produce. Some was taken to market, the rest stored in the root cellar with the potatoes, carrots, cabbages, and some of the apples he'd taken from the small orchard near the river.

He came upon her leaning over the pot in which she was boiling spiced pears, destined for the springhouse, or later an icehouse, should the freezes come, and he had time to dig one. Her face was red from the rising steam and her hair hung in dank and greasy strands on either side of her ears. He paused, holding a basket of string beans for her to hang by the fireplace to dry. The sight of her made his mouth dry and his heartbeat skip. *'Tis strange how beautiful she now seems to me, worn as she is.*

He realized that others might find Lettie prettier, with her well-tended looks.

"Ah, Thomas, thank you," Aoife said. "I planned to pick them myself, but for those." She lifted her chin to the sliced fruit and vegetables already hanging before the fireplace, and then laughed. "You may see bits upon my crown. I keep forgetting to watch where I lift my head."

Fearing his woman's rages, neither of them mentioned Lettie or the help she could be if only she would try. Thomas was grateful for Aoife's silence.

"I have a man who might help with the breeding," he said. "He's old but strong enough to help with the bull. He's to come today to speak with us."

She pulled the pot of pears further from the fire. "That's good Thomas. You are pushed to your limits." Taking a cloth, she dipped it in water, wiped her face and smoothed back her hair. "Now I must check up the stairs." It seemed to him that fatigue slowed her steps as she left.

The worker Thomas knew, a huge mass of slowly sagging muscle beneath skin so black it was nearly blue, rapidly approaching sixty years of age, came while Aoife was tending to William. "I come only out of respect for you, Thomas," he said, "but my wife will not let me work here. Too much gossip has been swirling around you and Mr. Sprigett's wife. 'Tis not true, I am sure, but still endangers our community. You and Mrs. Sprigett alone here for so long, the captain being so grievously injured… They say it was unseemly and disloyal of you." He clapped his hat back on his head and walked off toward the town.

When Aoife returned to the kitchen, he told her they had no one to hire, that the man mentioned earlier had hurt his back and couldn't work. It was hard to tell her a lie but what good would it do her to worry about rumors?

Without another worker, the two of them handled the breeding. Thomas had isolated the farm's fine ram in a pen for more than a month, and the time had come to present him with the ewes. His smell would bring them into season. They would mate in time to birth lambs after the greatest risk of frost was over. Thank the Lord, Hero was skilled, a great dog for separating out the ewes they wanted to breed. The ones not wanted for lambs were destined to be salted mutton.

The bull would be difficult, but bulls ready to mate always were.

229

Chapter 24

CHARLOTTE HOPPED OUT OF HER CAR, ignoring the loud creak of the dented door, yelling, "What have you got? Another body?" She sounded delighted at the thought.

"No. More like buried treasure." Iris took the ring from her little finger and held it out.

Charlotte turned it around and around in her hand. "Wow, whoever wore this must have been small. And the letters! Spencerian script."

"And that means?"

"Dates it. Writing style only from about the mid-nineteenth century on to the early twentieth. That's what's so exciting—same time period as our little guy." Charlotte tried it on her little finger, but it hung up on the second joint.

Iris held her hand out. "What do you think the stone is?"

"Could be ruby. Could be garnet. Bohemian garnets, quite fashionable in Victorian times. I can take it to a jeweler to find out."

A strong wave of possessiveness washed over Iris. The ring was hers, just as Little Jack was hers. And then the feeling subsided. As she slowly pulled back her hand, Charlotte held out the ring. Iris took it back and slid it onto her finger. It went on easily. "That's the advantage of getting old," she said, trying to sound jokey. "The flesh wastes away."

"The letters are so hard to read. No contrast to make them stand out."

"Benny and I went to England a long time ago. I saw this touristy thing where they let you put a piece of paper over the old carvings of knights and ladies, then rub charcoal over the paper. Gives you a reverse image, like the Shroud of Turin. So I took paper and did that with the ring." She held her hand up and traced the letters with a fingernail. "There's an *S* in the center, on one side of it, a *W*, and on the other, an *A*."

"Just a sec." Charlotte pulled her laptop from the capacious hobo bag that always hung, like an extra limb, from her shoulder. She opened it and awkwardly balancing it in one hand, signed in and brought up a spreadsheet. "There was a prominent family here—one with enough money to have such a signet ring—with a last name beginning with *S*. The Sprigetts. But their house was down the road and much bigger than yours, at least how yours was before being added on."

"Any Sprigett first name start with a *W* or an *A*?"

Charlotte pursed her mouth. "Don't know. I'd have to check into people around the time, check the lists of locals." She took Iris's hand and looked at the ring. "It really is a nice ring. If it's a ruby that size, it must have cost a good bit."

"How could someone lose a ring like that?"

Charlotte shrugged. "People lose everything."

Iris walked Charlotte to the pond, sat on the wall, and looked into the water. "I can't help thinking the ring is somehow linked to Baby Jack. At least I feel it." She tossed a twig into the pond and watched it bob up and down until it settled and floated peacefully.

Aoife
1863

In the very early morning, Aoife was in the milk shed, sitting hunched over in the cold, dim light. Her best cow had an infected udder, despite careful stripping of each teat.

The brown and white cow was known to be a sneak, bringing her hind foot up and kicking forward without warning. She had already turned over the pail holding the infected milk that Aoife's hands had sent streaking down. The steam from the pail rose like a cloud around Aoife's head, stinking of ammonia, like the urine-soaked sheets she often changed in the morning, as the laudanum kept William from awakening and asking for the chamber pot.

The peppermint oil rubbed on the udder burned her nose, fighting with the smell of infection. And she was tired, so tired. At last, she was certain the sick quadrant of the udder was empty. She tossed the milking stool against the wall and led the beast back to the stall.

In the yard, Aoife stood for a moment stretching, both hands pressed into the small of her back. It ached fearfully. *Remember, 'tis but one small portion of the pain William suffered.*

The cold air helped keep her awake, but shivering made her stagger. If Thomas had been awake, she would call him, but he was in the lean-to, insensate with fatigue, asleep next to his Lettie. Though Aoife helped all she could, he was still doing the work of two men. The last garden crops had to be gathered, a pig butchered and its hams smoked, firewood cut and stacked, fences repaired. If he didn't do the work, they might not make it through the winter.

Outside the kitchen, Aoife paused to use the metal boot jack, lest she track cow dung into the house. Once inside in her stocking feet, she looked longingly at the tea chest. *How good it would feel to sit and sip a cup with cream.*

Full sunrise was only a brief time away, and, with its coming, William would need his morning meal. She set the kettle to boil in the fireplace and tiptoed slowly up the stairs, shielding her candle's light with one hand, lest she disturb his sleep.

Careful to step where the floorboards were tight, she crept down the hall to their bedroom. She heard William's voice soft and low, relaxed, and amused. *Was he in the midst of a pleasant dream?*

The pre-dawn light kept the room deep in shadows. She could just make him out, upright against the pillows. His eyes glistened, fastened on the high-backed chair in which she usually sat, close by the bed.

"Sweetheart?" She walked toward him. The chair moved slightly. Someone was curled in its seat. Aoife stepped in further and saw William's visitor. Lettie.

Thomas
1863

Next to him, the mattress was empty, the quilt from that side thrown onto him. With that and the stove going, Thomas sweated. Where was Lettie?

He groaned and rolled onto his side. There was not one muscle in his body without an ache down to the bone.

Aoife must feel the same. The two of them, bowed low by the endless work, two beasts of burden like the oxen, yoked together to save William's farm.

William's farm. Thomas resolved to ask Aoife, when he had time to speak with her, and ask would she approach her husband to deed him the portion of land they'd discussed, back before the war, when William was whole. That time felt nigh on a hundred years' past.

He'd proven his worth and waited long enough to make his request. It had not seemed decent while William was away as a soldier, nor when he'd first returned, so grievously injured. But summer had turned to fall, and winter was fast approaching. Winter was the time for dreaming, when snow might come and halt all work but caring for the livestock.

My own farm. Lettie's and mine, alone. But the thought didn't make him as pleased as it once had.

Chapter 25

CHARLOTTE STOOD AND THREW a stone into the pond, aiming at, and hitting, the twig Iris had tossed. The little stick sank below the water. "I always did have good aim."

Iris laughed.

"I know they dredged the water like crazy, but have you looked through the house for any papers or journals or anything that might give us a clue as to who lived here?"

Iris laughed again. "That always happens in romance novels and such, probably 'cause it's an easy plot device. But, like finding buried treasure, it rarely happens in real life. Didn't happen here! No, the damn house was such a wreck, the contractor took it down to the studs, room by room—where there were studs. The old walls are solid stone. Anyway, he found shreds of old wallpaper and loose nails, but nothing remotely interesting."

Charlotte thought for a moment. "So, if there's anything else, it would be in the barn or out here in the garden." Her eyes glittered with possibility as she scanned the wide lawn.

"The barn was completely rebuilt, except for the stone walls, after a tree came down on it in Hurricane Sandy." She winked at Charlotte. "Maybe it's just my age, or maybe I'm short of optimism since I wasted so much buying this place, but I think this is a one-off, honey."

Hoisting her bag over her shoulder, Charlotte said, "I have an idea. One of my loony uncles watched that show about detectorists in England, you know, people who walk around looking for metal things under the ground. He went and got a detector, like he's going to find the Templar's treasure hidden in Philly. I don't think he's used it in five years. I'm going to get it for us, and we'll walk the whole property. What do you think?"

"I think it'll be a wild goose chase… but what the heck. You bring the thing, and we'll give it a try." Iris pictured herself and Charlotte roaming the woods behind the house, the metal detector going *beep, beep, beep.* Benny would get a real kick out of this.

She waved goodbye as Charlotte headed down the drive. She stood for a moment in the warm evening air before mosquitos drove her inside. Benny was still in the TV room watching a shark movie that seemed particularly silly, featuring a shark with many heads.

Iris sighed and went to the kitchen and made popcorn in her old, scarred popcorn pot. After topping the kernels with melted butter and dusting them with truffle salt, she went back and sat next to Benny.

The movie droned on, with the shark making predictable "surprise" scenes, slurping up or chomping down on scantily clad young women.

"Stupid, isn't it?" Benny said,

With the break in his TV trance, Iris seized her chance, holding the ring on her hand in front of his eyes. "This is what I found, Benny."

He took her hand, thumb against her palm, and the image of his hand pressed against her buttocks, pushing her into his mouth, flashed into her mind.

"You found this ring in the dirt?"

Iris nodded.

"Let me see it closer, under the light." He took the ring from her finger and held it under the lamp. He rubbed the stone and turned the ring this way and that. "I don't know much about gemstones but I can photo it and send it to my cousin Izzy."

"Oh, please. Ask him to give any information he can. If I have to go up to his shop in Manhattan, I will."

"I don't want you to go into New York. It's not safe. People are being attacked all the time. Old people."

"There are oodles of old people in Manhattan. What makes you think I'd be picked out?"

He handed back the ring back. "Could you move over? I can't see the screen."

Iris hit the power button. "I will after you text Izzy."

"Not gonna be in his shop now. His loupe is there." He reached for the control.

Iris held it further away. "He doesn't need it to look at an image on your phone."

With a sigh, Benny picked up his phone and took a few photos, inside the ring as well as the outside, and one or two focusing on the stone. Rolling his eyes at her, he sent it to his cousin, grabbed the remote, and went back to watching the screen. The multi-head shark monster movie was over, and he had to be content with *Sharknado*.

Izzy texted back the next day while they were at breakfast:

RE: RING: MOST LIKELY ENGLISH. FIRST HALF 18TH CENTURY OR EARLIER BY STYLE AND SLIGHT CRUDENESS OF CABOCHON. LACK OF PURITY MARKS SO CANNOT DATE MANUFACTURE BETTER THAN THAT. ENGRAVING LATER—

19TH CENTURY. GARNET NOT RUBY
CAN TELL BY SLIGHT ORANGE
TINGE. CAN REPLACE INITIALS
WITH YOURS BUT WILL REDUCE
STONE GREATLY. HOPE THIS
HELPS.

"Good old Izzy always comes through. You want him to put our initials on instead of the ones it's already got?"

"What? Are you crazy," Iris said, hiding the ring beneath her other hand.

"Didn't think so." Benny chuckled and left to turn on the TV again.

I suppose I should be glad it's Shark Week and not Shark Day. He'll be too busy to interfere. But she couldn't help laughing. Their renewed sex life had put him in such a good mood lately.

The next day, Charlotte returned, waving as she hopped out. She yelled, "Look what I have!" A huge grin showed her gums.

"What?" Iris said, walking across the drive toward her.

Charlotte pulled something from the back seat and put it on her arm. At first glance it looked like some kind of crutch or cane, with a cuff up near her elbow and a long metal rod. But the bottom was a circular bit that could never bear anyone's weight.

"The metal detector." Iris had seen them on TV or in photos but never in real life. "That's nice," was all she could think to say.

"Don't look so skeptical." Charlotte leaned the detector against her car. "People have found amazing stuff with these.

Maybe we'll turn up something that will give us a clue to Little Jack's real identity."

It was worth a try. "Is it heavy?" Iris asked. The contraption did look clumsy.

"Not at all. Let's start over there." Charlotte pointed to an area with a few struggling rose bushes, a favorite snack of the deer. They spent the morning walking slowly up the hill one way and back down the next, Charlotte swinging the instrument the entire time, but found nothing.

"Well, maybe tomorrow afternoon," Charlotte said, as she left. "I have some work to do in the morning."

Benny was hovering at the window inside the kitchen, waiting to speak with Iris. "Two things. First, is the tile for the new upstairs bath ordered?"

"No. I've got to pick something out."

"Can't we use the blue and white stuff we already have?"

"Benny, it's not blue. It's *gray* and white in a distressed pattern bought to disguise Freddy's hair and drool spots. It doesn't go with the pale sage green vanity."

"Looks blue to me." His jaw was thrust forward stubbornly in a characteristic don't-want-to-spend-more-money way.

Why would someone color blind have opinions on color? "What's the other thing you wanted to ask?"

He looked a bit more shifty, more wary. "Could you please ask Charlotte where she's taking her doctoral degree? Kat and Jessica have looked at every program in the area and can't find her name."

Aoife

1863

Fury rose in Aoife's breast. "Why are you in our bed-chamber, Lettie?"

Lettie rose from the chair, her face pallid, grayish with fear.

"Leave at once!"

But William raised a hand. "Aoife, let her stay. She does no harm but makes the day pass more easily. The girl has an easy manner and a gift for bright chatter."

Aoife shifted from foot to foot, uncertain as to what she should say, keenly aware of the difference between her disheveled hair and wrinkled clothing and Lettie's charming appearance. The girl wore her pale green ticking dress, neat and well-fitted at the waist, and, as usual, had ornamented her hair with late-blooming flowers. The white sprays of Virginia sweetspire framed the side of her face in a fetching manner, as if they were expensive bird plumage. As she took in the picture, Aoife's shoulders slumped from exhaustion and sadness. She felt as if she was a servant in her own home, unfit for her husband to view.

At William's words, the color had returned to Lettie's cheeks, a pale tea-rose blush. Demure smiles flashed across her lips and disappeared again. Her eyes shone. "I think I shall go now," she said with the poise of a wellborn southern lady. "I'll return whenever you wish, Mr. William." She swept from the room and floated down the stairs, like a sleep deprived dream.

Aoife sat in the chair instead of her usual place on the bed, next to William. "'Tis enough that she has lived here with no duties, no offers to help, but now she makes free with our privacy." Her words sounded to her ears like those of a jealous and querulous wife. She wanted to sob with fatigue but how could she weep in front of William, who was so brave?

"I am sorry you're so burdened, Aoife. I know there are no other workers to be found. It's vexing that my mother won't bend to send us a man from her farm, though she has more than enough hands." He cleared his throat. "The girl's gaiety and bright laughter not only helped the long hours go by, but they also eased my pain. Perhaps she could cook and serve me during the day, saving you running in from the fields."

Aoife shrugged. She wanted nothing more than to let her head fall back and her eyes close.

"And then you and I would more easily relax in sleep together. I know my restless dreams disturb your sleep and even injure you, though I awaken in the morning with no recollection of them. It is a sign of your devotion that you stay by my side."

She moved over to the bed and, despite her dusty dress, stretched out next to him. "Oh, William, I do love you. And I have prayed that you would be healed. I long for us to have a child."

He pulled out her bun and stroked her hair. "Aoife, Aoife, if only that were possible."

"The doctors don't know everything. Not nearly as much as God. Sure, and miracles happened, many times, in the old country." She pinched his side, gently, as she'd done teasingly before he'd gone off to war. "You will soon be like new."

William laughed and pulled her head onto his chest. It was an hour before she woke with a start, the day's chores, still unfinished, on her mind.

Thomas

1863

"Don't be angry with me, Thomas." Lettie's lips drew up in her most winsome smile and her eyes twinkled with high spirits.

"You have no right to go into the house without permission." He took a step toward her.

"Oh!" She backed up, hand over her nose and mouth. "I beg you to wash first, before you approach me. You reek from slaughtering that pig. The steam from scalding has only worsened the smell. Quite makes me ill."

Thomas's chest tightened with anger. The woman before him, the woman he'd taken for a wife, the one he'd protected and supported though night after night she denied him, was acting as if she was vastly his superior.

Her expression haughty and smug, she said, "I do have permission. From Mr. William himself. Or is he no longer the master of this farm?"

He didn't step closer, though he longed to grab and shake her. "If you really wished to help, you would work alongside me instead of Mr. William's wife. Or you'd scrub the floors and set up the great kettle to do the laundry."

Her dainty head was drawn back, and he noticed the white flowers tucked above her ears. "I said long before I'll be no servant."

"No one is asking that of you, but just to be a help, as a wife should. To work together with me to obtain our own farm."

"Do you really mean this is why we remain here? For our own place? I don't believe it, nor do the people in town! And I *am* a help… to Mr. William whilst his own wedded wife neglects him. I care for him like he was part of me, a sickly child, a suffering angel!"

Thomas stilled his tongue. *A crazed light burns in her eyes, and it is best not to cross her. I will speak to Aoife and find out what transpired.*

After she left to return to the house, he stood lost in thought. *All those lost babes, all those times of wishing and longing, all those hopes dashed. Is Mr. William just someone to mother? To care for?*

Chapter 26

"**WHAT THE HELL DOES THAT MEAN?**" Iris was stunned that Jessica and Kat had looked into Charlotte's past, as this seemed to come out of nowhere. "Your friends are checking up on my friend?"

Benny nonchalantly peeled a tangerine. But he wasn't fooling her—obviously, he knew the discussion might lead to another fight about Jessica. "Just what I said. I love you, Iris. We've been together for a long, long time." A flash of color diverted her gaze as Benny tossed the brilliant orange rind into the trash. "I was all ready to accept that young woman. I know what she symbolizes to you. But I can't sit back and let someone lie to you. Misrepresent herself for some reason I can only guess at. Maybe take advantage of you?"

"Why on Earth would you think she's taking advantage of me?"

He chewed a few segments of the fruit before answering. "You're vulnerable, Iris, and there are people who sense that and use it to get what they want." "What can she possibly get out of friendship with me? The right to tell Little Jack's story? It's not like a scoop or anything. He's been in the papers—there are just details left to divulge and right now everything else is just speculation."

He put the rest of the tangerine on the counter and stepped toward her, but she moved back, out of reach. "The two of us have just started to deal with all that long-ago stuff…"

"Don't be such a guy, Benny. Don't retreat back into euphemisms. Say it like this, 'The two of us have just started to deal with our child dying.' Try something honest like that."

He crossed his arms over his chest and took several deep, slow breaths in through his nose and out through his mouth.

"Chest pain?" Fear pushed anger from her mind until he shook his head no, continuing the deep breathing. The internet said that headed off panic attacks, but it made him look like an adenoidal walrus.

He ignored her concern. "Honest? Don't stoop to sarcasm, Iris. It's demeaning. I have trouble expressing how I feel about our baby, same as you do. And conflicted feelings about you obsessing over a dead kid on our property. Not to mention letting a stranger come between us."

Iris pulled at her hair in frustration as tears came to her eyes. "For fuck's sake, we don't know anything about Little Jack. But Charlotte's helping me do the work of finding out, so Jessica can just mind her own damn business. I don't care if Charlotte isn't what she claims to be. I just don't give a shit!"

Benny moved close and, despite her struggling to fend him off, took her in his arms. "Shh, shh. I'm sorry, so sorry. Please, don't let my clumsiness destroy all that we've gotten back, all we've learned about each other, all the understanding."

Iris sobbed, her throat tightening. It was difficult to get words out. "Why did those two women have to interfere? Why?"

Benny half-led, half-carried her to the living room and put her on the couch. "Don't blame them, Iris. They were just trying to be my friends. This is on me. There are all these warnings about predatory young people preying on older folk. Charlotte was spending so much time with you that I worried you were being scammed." He gave a little laugh. "I couldn't figure out how, either, but all sorts of abuse scenarios ran through my head."

A wild laugh tore out of her. "Elder abuse? That's the first time you've admitted we're old, Ben. But even if we're old, we're still not stupid. Do you think I would have given her money or something? Let her move in to this perennial construction site?"

He shook his head.

"She may have been misrepresenting herself—we aren't certain yet—but if so, I want to hear her reasons before passing judgment." She took a deep breath. "I've been misrepresenting myself, too, pretending to be a contented, childless wife. A woman who didn't need to face that she'd carried a dead little girl inside her. Losing any chance of..."

"Iris, I love you much too much to think about you being disappointed again. There have been so many times… And I didn't even realize." Benny reached down to the coffee table and grabbed a tissue from the box. He held it out to her.

She took it and wiped her nose. "And now, becoming attached to a dead boy, as if I'd given birth to him more than a hundred years ago. Becoming so smitten with a young woman the same age as our baby would be if…" The words were muffled as she cried again, buried deep in her husband's chest. "God, Benny, you pointed all that out to me yourself! Ever think maybe I'm just lonely for simple friendliness, or for working together with someone, working for the same goal? That used to be us. Was supposed to be us, renovating our new home."

"Sorry, I'm sorry. It is, it is." He rocked her in his arms until she quieted. "I swear, Iris, if that girl's innocent of any desire to do you harm, you can adopt her, even if she's got parents… does she?"

Iris shrugged. She'd never asked—had never wanted to imagine Charlotte in the midst of a family, her real family—and Charlotte had never said.

"Well, it'll be up to the two of you. I'll just be the support system. I'll put up the Christmas tree and light the Hanukkah candles. Carve the turkey at Thanksgiving. The only one we have to ask about this is Hal. But he's not the jealous sort. He's good at sharing."

Sometimes, Benny made it hard to stay angry with him.

Aoife

1863

Every morning, Lettie came to the kitchen, neatly dressed, clean, and newly respectful to Aoife. "Ma'am, Mr. William's tray ready?" At Aoife's nod, she took the tray up the stairs.

After a while, it came to Aoife that it was a blessing to not need run up the stairs, heart pounding and breath short, worrying William might have knocked over his water and been left parched, or concerned his meal had been delayed by her pursuing a rogue chicken. Or the worst, fear that he'd been in pain and the laudanum out of reach.

Aoife went to the barn to help tend the animals with Thomas. She had grown used to the stink of dung and the burn of urine in her nostrils—it meant the animals throve and, with them, the farm.

Thomas was waiting by a pile of rich manure from the sheep pen. He filled the first bucket for her. Aoife carried it, one load at a time, to the kitchen garden and mixed it with soil, while Thomas shoveled out the heavier cow manure and their urine-soaked straw.

Once, Thomas would have stopped her from the chore of dung-spreading, declaring it too difficult for a woman and too coarse for a lady, but the work had fallen behind during the time she'd refused to go any distance from William. Now, Thomas and she worked together, cleaning the barn, spreading manure in the garden, and piling the rest for the fields come spring. He did not object to any chore she attempted.

In the garden, watching leaves drop from the trees, Aoife paused for a moment to straighten her aching back. She looked at her house, remembering how she'd thought life would be, herself mistress of the hearth, cooking for her husband and keeping his home tidy. How different things were than that. *Why Thomas and I are like two beasts, side-by-side, while my husband lies abed, waited on by Lettie. 'Tis strange, to be sure.*

Stealing a moment from the back-breaking labor, she and Thomas often laughed together at the antics of the animals: the greed of the pigs, the sly positioning of the cows seeking their place at the trough, and Hero's delight having the two people as companions.

When it grew too dark to work, she went into the house to wash the barn stink from her before attending to William, bathing him and changing his bandages. When that was done, she swung her lantern at the window to signal to Thomas. It was time for him to climb the stairs to help William walk the room.

At that time, Lettie was nowhere to be seen. *She must lie abed, waiting for Thomas.*

William made little progress. The mid-thigh limb stump's ragged and thickened scar would not fit properly, even with the new gutta percha cup sent by the army and meant to cushion his skin. He could move one step, and then another. At the third, he'd look longingly at the bed.

Seeing him wince when he attempted to put weight on either limb, despite leaning on both Thomas and the crutch, her heart sank. *Truly, I cannot recall the last time he and I laughed together. But 'tis certain it was before he went off to war.*

Thomas

1863

While they worked together in the barn, Aoife did not recoil as Thomas came close, but after the day's work, when she reverted to being Mr. William's wife, he became aware of the sweaty animal funk that clung to his skin. And he was more than aware of Lettie, who, as soon as she saw him coming toward the house, flitted like a ghost to the lean-to.

Each evening, he pumped water into the bucket, brought it into the barn, and stripped, washing his skin with lye soap. Once clean, he went to the house at Aoife's signal, to help William rise and take steps on his wooden legs.

In the kitchen one night, Aoife was waiting, bosom heaving in anger. "I came to find Lettie had washed my husband and changed his dressings. 'It is part of my work, Mrs. Sprigett,' the chit said, calm as clay. 'Is it now?' I asked her. I looked to William, but he did not object. What say you, Thomas, to your woman so tending to my husband? She is no nurse, nor ever was trained to be. It is indecent." She set a cup of tea and a slice of buttered bread with honey on the table. "Eat."

He slid into the chair, glad Lettie wasn't in the house to hear herself be labeled a chit, as that would surely cause her to fly into a rage. Looking at Aoife by the fire, her color high with indignation, he felt a slight regret that William was upstairs and Lettie close in the lean-to. Wrong as it was, he longed for the days when he and Aoife were alone on the farm and alone evenings, reading letters together. The dangers of that thought shocked him. "I fear that is up to Mr. William. And you."

She turned her bright blue eyes to his with a look of betrayal, and he ceased speaking.

After he ate, he and Aoife went upstairs to help the wounded man into his prostheses. "Put your arm about my shoulders, Mr. William," Thomas said, as he did each night, swinging William off the bed to stand, swaying precariously on the wooden legs. His weight rested the most with one arm on Thomas. Under the other arm was a crutch, its top padded by Aoife's stitching a small, quilted block of cloth.

With each step, William let out a muffled groan. Even after months, he couldn't stand alone or, despite help, walk further than the room. Thomas's heart ached for him, and for Aoife, his thoughts conflicted and tangled. The burden seemed doubly heavy.

Thomas helped William back into bed and left him waiting beneath the covers for his wife. What would happen then, when Aoife slipped in beside William, was something that troubled Thomas's mind. He went to his own bed in the lean-to and to Lettie. Their room was snug and warm, even on the coldest nights.

She was always asleep when he came, though at times it seemed she was play-acting. They rarely talked and then only when necessary. From time to time, he stroked her arm and she rolled away. Play-acting again.

One morning, he awoke with his arm aching fiercely from a wound incurred while sharpening a scythe. The pain cost him his patience and he shook Lettie roughly awake. "Bring me my breakfast as you do for Mr. William. Dress my wound, suffered in the cause of keeping you safe."

"Feed yourself and bind your own wounds, or have that woman care for you," Lettie sat and stretched, as serene as the still, chilly morning.

"No. It is your obligation." He turned her to him and thrust his hand between her legs. "I work to feed you, clothe you, and house you, to keep you safe…"

Her body had frozen, stiff and still as a corpse. The only heat came from the anger in her voice. "Safe? You could never keep me safe. They was coming for me again, like they did for my Sary. It was only the likes of William who stopped them!"

He slapped her across the mouth, hard, splitting her lip. She cried, "Oh," and put her forearm up over her mouth. She pushed him away. "I knew it was him that I wanted. I knew it from the first time I saw him, in that fine blue uniform, riding through town with the troops." She rose and left their room.

Chapter 27

"**SORRY I HAD TO LEAVE YESTERDAY,**" Charlotte said. "It was fun even if we didn't find anything. I'm ready for more today." She wore sensible jeans for their exploration, and hiking boots. The outfit made her younger and more graceful than the skirts she usually wore.

Iris couldn't make herself bring up the discussion she'd had with Benny. She'd have to, sooner or later, but it would be hard to prevent the young woman from feeling that battle lines had been drawn and she was under suspicion. If that happened, she might not return.

A better tack would be directness. "Have you begun to write about Little Jack yet? I'd hate to see too much time go by, and everyone lose interest."

"I haven't. It's important to be careful and have the piece completed before submitting it. Has to be substantive. All we've got now are hypotheses, except for knowing he's mixed race. That's a story in itself for the times, but without some idea of who his parents were and why he was placed in the pond… it's poignant, of course, his body handled with such loving care, but that's a thin and kinda sentimental basis for academic journals."

"Huh." Iris couldn't see a clear way to asking for confirmation of Charlotte's academic credentials or even her school. Maybe she just didn't want to know that Benny—along with Jessica and her wife—was right. She picked up the metal detector. It weighed much less than she'd thought but the long shaft with its bottom coil would easily catch on the downed tree limbs and dense bushes. What would Benny say if adventuring with Charlotte caused his wife to fall on the wood's uneven ground? It would certainly lead to more disputes about her friendship.

As if there weren't enough fights already.

She handed the instrument back and they started up the barely cleared path among the oaks and the dying ash trees. The unusually dry weather seemed to be bringing fall early, leaves turning, the ninebark yellow and the wild viburnum leaves reddish purple.

"We better check for ticks later," Charlotte said.

Iris paused to catch her breath "Well, since they're supposedly worse here late summer to early fall, I sprayed myself with Off. Do you want to go back for some?"

"Nah. It just makes me cough, and the liquid gives me a rash. I rubbed repellent all over my boots. I'll pick the little bastards off when I get home." Today, Charlotte was different somehow, cheerful, more self-possessed, almost cocky. The devil-may-care attitude toward getting Lyme's impressed Iris.

The hill wasn't terribly high, but enough for them to look down on the house's slate roof, where the roofer was busy fixing a leak. On the ground by the pond, Benny was holding the man's ladder, obviously contemplating climbing up to supervise, to prove that he wasn't yet too old.

Well, I'm not either. Iris pressed her lips together, took the metal detector from Charlotte, and soldiered on.

The detector sounded over and over for all kinds of junk: nails and screws, both antique-looking and modern, a broken saw blade, spoons, and the like. Nothing notable or informative, let alone valuable.

The detector beeped again, dully, and Iris reached beneath pebbles covering a mound of hardened mud, breaking her last decent finger-nail digging a metallic outlet cover from the dirt. "Ow!" She nearly put her finger in her mouth before noting how filthy it was.

"Hey, come here!" Charlotte called from behind a dense clump of vegetation.

Iris abandoned the detector rather than try to maneuver it to where Charlotte waited. She pushed aside the tangled bushes and saw weeds, tall weeds. Charlotte was standing in the midst of them.

"What did you find?"

The young woman pointed down and to her left, at an old stone planter containing a woody rosebush, with a few dry yellow blooms still clinging to its stems. "A China rose. Popular the past two hundred years at least. And see?" At her feet was a badly rotted wooden cross. Several more were nearby. "Chestnut, that's why they lasted. Oak's harder but chestnut resists the elements better. The blight got them all. Means the cross is old."

"Old enough?" Iris swept the dust of years from the front of the first cross. All she could make out was the letter *S*.

Thomas

1864

A violent storm, with winds pelting down near-freezing rain, swept through the area in late January, increasing the misery and the work. The puddles in exposed areas froze, the crusts razor sharp when broken through by a foot or hoof. Hero whimpered, running after the sheep to gather them. The already born lambs needed shelter beneath the barn's roof, and several of their best cows would deliver at any moment.

Aoife was more and more careworn from lack of rest. Sometimes Thomas arose from the bed he shared with Lettie, and aching with unfulfilled desire, he stood in the yard, looking up at the dark bed-room window of the house. Through the closed shutters, he could, at times, hear William's screams and orders yelled to the ghosts of the battlefields.

No one could sleep through that.

It seemed as if it took an hour before Aoife could clear the cobwebs from her mind and wipe the great dark circles from her eyes. He begged Lettie to help more but was again greeted with scorn. "I am a slave no longer. Not to that woman and not to you." She turned her eyes toward the second story. "But I willingly care for him."

Yet she remained meek and demure when in Aoife's presence. *Does she fear she will be shut away from her brave and handsome soldier boy? I am whole—how can she prefer half a man?* And then he felt shame. William had been grievously injured and was in so much pain. He had been a friend to Thomas, humble in his desire to learn farming. He had promised land.

Thomas knew he should still crave his own property, a home for him and the beautiful girl he'd loved and wanted, but how could he ask while William was so weak?

And how could he leave Aoife?

The night of the freezing rain, while encouraging Hero, whose paws left bloody marks in the slush, Thomas left the barn where he'd checked on two cows ready to deliver. Both were in the first stage of labor and seemed to be progressing well.

Outside, he paused again to gaze at the silent farmhouse.

And then came a bellow, a cry the likes of which Thomas had rarely heard, one of intolerable pain. He ran to the birthing stall. Adele, the prize Jersey bought just before the war, stood, legs splayed apart, straining. She had labored for hours, with seemingly no problem, but now she was in great distress.

When she saw Thomas, she wailed a long cry of pain, as if asking for help. Tears ran from her large brown eyes and the beautiful fawn coat over her bulging middle was dark with sweat.

Thomas used his most soothing voice as he entered the stall. "Hush, now, hush. You've gone through this before. 'Tis nothing new, here."

Adele wailed again and lowered her head. He went behind her and touched her flank. She raised her leg to kick him. Something was very wrong—aside from her value being the best milk producer and reliably birthing prize calves—she was one of the gentlest of the beasts. Adele had never tried to hurt him before. He moved back and squatted in the corner atop the clean straw, unwilling to leave her alone.

The cow swung her head from side-to-side and again moaned. Her sides heaved and subsided. At last, he realized that, with the intensity of her pain, he had to check inside her. He went behind and, at his touch, she landed a blow on his thigh, dropping him. He rolled out of reach and lay still for a moment, biting down on his arm to distract from the pain in his leg. The area she'd kicked was already swelling. Had she gotten him lower, surely a bone would have broken.

Panting, readying for the effort of limping to the yard's freezing puddles to gather ice for the bruise, he looked at the cow and knew what was wrong. Instead of the calf's head and forelimbs, its hind quarters were coming first, the rear legs now protruding from the mother's body. She needed help and Thomas couldn't do it alone.

Standing, he shuffled rapidly out to the house, opening the kitchen door. Though it might wake William, he yelled, "Aoife!"

The floorboards above creaked and thudded as someone left the bed and headed to the stairs. Aoife appeared, her feet bare, her skin pale as the moon, wisps of hair from her long braid hanging about her face. She hastily tied a robe about her sleep dress. "Thomas, what is it?"

Aoife
1864

"It's Adele." Thomas cried. Each word sounded bitten off as if it stung him, the waking of her. "The birthing is obstructed and I need you to hold her."

"Adele? I'll dress. We can scarce afford to lose her calf." She turned to go back up the stairs, but his next words stopped her.

"There's no time!" He stepped halfway in, shaking from urgency and from the cold. Water ran off him onto the floor. "Not just the calf—she's in danger of rupturing her womb."

She pushed past him to slip on William's high boots, no longer of use to him. Together, they rushed to the barn. Her feet slid inside the boots but, well-waxed, they kept out the cold water. By her side, Thomas was moving rapidly with a heavy limp. She looked at him, silently questioning.

"Adele kicked me, hard."

They had reached the barn and having brought the lantern Thomas had left burning on the dirt floor of the aisle, they entered the stall. The cow's head near touched the ground, and her legs were so wide apart it seemed she would collapse in a heap. She moaned piteously.

"Thomas," Aoife cried. "We cannot lose her."

He limped to the wall where ropes hung. "I'll tie her hind legs together whilst you hold her head. That will keep her from kicking me again."

Aoife put her hands on either side of the bridle and braced her legs. As she did so, her robe tie slipped, the ends dropping to the filthy dung and bloodstained straw. Behind the cow,

Thomas moved rapidly but she couldn't see more than his head above the beast's haunches.

The cow screamed suddenly, with a sound more heartrending than anything Aoife had ever heard before. "Thomas? What has happened? Is she torn?"

He shook his head. "The hips are clear, but the calf is huge, the ribs wide. Come to me now! Her labor has paused for a moment, and she seems too worn to move."

She dropped the cow's head and saw Thomas was right— the great tears continued but Adele was still, only her shallow breathing fluttering her sides. Aoife came to help Thomas.

His arms were deep inside the beast, Adele's blood staining his front. The calf's legs protruded, still inside the birth sac. "Pull gently but steadily on the legs whilst I attempt to move the body. Careful to not force." He moved slightly to the side, giving her more room.

Aoife grabbed the wet slippery little hooves, now freed from the birth sac. She began to pull, aware that the heat she felt came not just from the cow but from Thomas's body against her own. She closed her eyes to keep herself steady as Thomas shifted and grunted, his cheek against Adele's rear.

At last, with a great gush, the calf slid from its mother, forelegs and head coming last. With its exit, both Aoife and Thomas, soaked through, tumbled to the floor, entwined, in a puddle of gore. Laughing with relief.

Chapter 28

"THE S ON THE CROSS..." Iris ran her finger along the old wood. "Sprigett?" She tried to make out more letters. All she got for her efforts was a splinter, which she worked out with her thumb and forefinger. A drop of blood appeared. She wiped it on her jeans.

"Could be," Charlotte said, squinting at the cross. "The other letters aren't clear."

The hum of insects arose as Iris waded into the weeds, stepping carefully among the dry, crackly stems, to examine the other markers. The odor of dry earth reached her nostrils. When she touched another of the crosses, it broke apart, crumbling into dust. None of the others had anything on them but dead bugs and wind-blown seeds caught up in spider webs. She made her way back to Charlotte, calling to her as she went. "We need to check here. Get the detector."

Charlotte pushed through the brittle underbrush, stumbling over the roots of a downed sapling. She returned with the metal detector. "Just stand there and I'll walk the ground. It's full of potholes."

Iris remained in place, rising and falling on the toes of her sneakers, unable to control her excitement. "Sorry. Kind of barked out an order there. Didn't think I could get it myself or carry it past the branches." When Charlotte didn't respond, she added, "Getting too old."

"No worries." The younger woman swung the detector back and forth. Within a few inches of the first cross, the detector emitted a low beep.

"What is it?" Iris straightened to look over the weeds.

Charlotte moved back over the same spot. The noise came again. "Sounds like an iron something, I think. Shame this unit has a crap LED display. Some'll show you what the find might look like." She stepped about two feet away, keeping the shaft in motion. Multiple small beeps sounded along her way and stopped when she went further. When she walked about six feet perpendicular to the first sounds, the detector beeped again.

Charlotte looked at her and grinned.

Iris felt a giggle bubble up in her chest. "God! It's so stupidly obvious what we've found. We won't be digging anything up."

"There might be really valuable information if we do. Things buried with the body in the grave."

"More than one. Graves." Iris pointed at the other crosses. "But still... Is it worth desecrating graves?"

Charlotte shrugged. "DNA could confirm links to people around here. It could fill out a lot of family histories."

"Well, I'll think it over. They're not going anywhere. I looked it up when I thought about burying Little Jack. It's legal to have a cemetery on your property here, so they can stay right where they are. Let's go back to the house."

They made their way back down the hill. Charlotte kept the metal detector turned off.

The house was quiet. The workers had finished early, and Benny was gone. He'd left a note saying he'd taken the dog on a walk, hoping to beat an incoming storm.

"Where should I sit?" Charlotte asked, as they went into the living room.

Iris pointed to her own chair, the one with the fine Italian upholstery. Charlotte brushed her clothes down with her hands and then sat, gingerly. "Are you sorry you didn't bury the baby here?"

Iris thought for a moment. "No. My husband was already freaked out by Little Jack in the pond. And the church cemetery gives me a place to go think about him. It's peaceful. No construction going on."

But maybe Jack should lie at rest with the rest of his family, if that's who are buried here. But the thought of having the urn with his ashes exhumed and reburied was overwhelming and sad. "What if the graves up the hill have nothing to do with him, or have some awful connection, like they were his owners?"

Charlotte shrugged. "We'll never know unless the people buried up there are examined. If *S* is for Sprigett, it might mean the family in the big house down the road—the one I told you about. But there are lots of other names beginning with *S*." The young woman dropped her eyes and looked slyly up at Iris. "I totally doubt Little Jack was a slave. More likely he was free, born to people who were free or were protected runaways."

Iris was surprised. How long had Charlotte believed this—or known this—to be true? "Why's that?"

"William Penn, the great Quaker, who for sure never owned slaves, had a son with an unusual first name. Guess what it was?"

A flash of annoyance shot through Iris. And then she laughed. Even knowing how important this was, making a tease was the kind of thing a grown child would do to her mother. "Spit it out."

"Sprigett. Sprigett Penn. And the Sprigett family down the road had a son named William."

Thomas

1864

Lying against him, Aoife's laughter made Thomas ever more aware of the nipples lifting the thin fabric of her gown, the softness of her breasts, and lack of stiff corseting confining them. Her body was open to him, as a wife's body would be to her husband.

His penis stiffened, pushing against her, but neither of them drew apart. Instead, she gasped and pressed her body closer. Helpless to stop himself, he took her breast in his hand and, as he did, her movements grew desperate.

She kissed his neck and brought her head up so that her lips met his, tightly closed and then opening, her tongue thrusting in.

The heat of her body, the rich smell of hot blood on the floor, made him heedless of the muck beneath them, heedless of protecting her from it, arousing him as it aroused her. The world seemed to have sped in its rotation in the universe, dizzying him, spinning them together as if nothing else existed. They were alone, gloriously alone in a sweet haze of fatigue and relief. They'd worked as one, yoked together in endless toil, and now they moved as one.

Her blood-smeared long hair came undone from its braid, caught against his face, and tangled in his hands. He rolled onto his back and lifted her onto him, holding her hips until her knees bent beneath her body and she knelt atop him. With wild gasping urgency, hands fighting over the buttons, they opened his pants and worked her nightgown up above her sex, and he entered her.

She called out, "Thomas!" and, with his hands clutching her thighs, her body moved in frenzied abandon, rising up until they nearly came apart, but then dropping back down on him.

There was a timeless span of fierce and breathless motion and then, suddenly, they both cried out with a choking sound, and she collapsed against him.

They lay together for a while without speaking, waiting until their hoarse, rough breathing calmed. At last, he had the wind to say, "I could not control myself." *I've been so lonely, so longing for a woman's willing touch, and you are so beautiful.* "Forgive me, Aoife."

"I will not, Thomas, for there is nothing to forgive. I am as guilty as you. And as lonely." She rolled off him and sat, pushing back her wild, disordered hair. She pointed to the cow, lying peacefully chewing, her baby beside her. "Look, the calf there! A fine *fathach* bull worth a fortune. We saved him and Adele, too. Together, we did that. And this was our reward."

Aoife

1864

Aoife felt as if she'd never need sleep again. She didn't deserve rest. *Our reward and our mistake.*

Beside her, Thomas lay looking up toward the rafters. "Look," he said. "The owl is hunting."

In the light of the now-sputtering lantern, she could just make out the ghostly white form of outstretched wings and clever little heart-shaped face. "An evening's amusement for you now, were we, Mistress Owl?"

She stood and moved her weary limbs, sighed. "We best return to the house and our duties. Be again who we are."

She wobbled on stiff legs walking to the stall door. Thomas rose, similarly unsteady. He took the now guttered lantern to the end of the aisle and left its feeble flame to die. They went out into the crystalline moonlight. The steam rising from their over-heated bodies joined in the misty air. To her,

Thomas appeared like some strange mystical creature, a haunter of dreams. When that mist swirled about him, his skin gleamed.

Despite the damp of the congealing blood on her shift, Aoife was not bothered by the freezing air.

"Go into your house," Thomas said, "and I'll bring wash water for you to heat."

She shook her head. "We share the work as we share the blame. I'll carry water myself." She stood by as he drew the water, the light squeaking of the pump echoing. But aside from that, the farm was still, the moon reflecting in the puddles and on the surface of the stock pond down past the field. While he was bent over, his back to her, a great shame came upon her. The cow's blood that had seeped through her gown stuck to her breasts and her sex. She shivered.

She did not have the right to heat the water and so get comfort.

Thomas put a full bucket in front of Aoife and stepped aside. She took it into the kitchen, but didn't shut the door, though the cold air filled the room with mist. At the pump, Thomas stripped off his shirt and poured water over his head and down his back.

She sighed, cupped her hands, and brought up enough cold water to pour on her chest. It ran down, soaking the skirt of her nightgown.

Thomas came to the door with the second bucket, filled to the brim. Aoife moved away, deeper inside her house. "One more bucket, and the night is over. Such will never happen again. Nor shall we ever speak of this night, except to mention the birth of a bull calf."

When he left, she dropped her gown in the bucket to soak and swept the spilled, bloodstained water out the door.

She stuck to her word. The only way she alluded to that night was to look at Thomas when they were alone with the beasts and say, "I love my husband as you love your Lettie."

Chapter 29

"SO, THE SPRIGETTS HAD A SON named William." Iris said to Charlotte as she turned on the living room lights. It had clouded over suddenly.

"But there's no record William had kids. His older brother apparently died young, before him. He had sisters, but of course their children wouldn't be Sprigetts. The local Sprigett line died with William as far as I can find."

"Any chance William Sprigett married someone with first name *A* ?"

"I have to admit I didn't check the marriage records yet. Other duties got in the way. Sorry."

"Well, it was great to go exploring with you. Thanks so much for taking me."

"Iris, it's your property." Charlotte took up her mug of tea.

"I held you back. You're so much younger, bounding along like a little goat." Iris sipped her tea. She looked over the rim at Charlotte and put the cup down. "Why, I'm old enough to be your mother."

"I wish you were."

Hmm... "Oh, dear! I do hope you're not estranged from your mom." *Jesus, I sound like a sweet old biddy in some 1930s film.*

"No, she's just not adventurous. Big city girl. She'd never take off her heels and hike around the woods. Might break a nail or something."

"She must be very proud, you getting a doctorate."

"Mmm-hmm." Charlotte nodded.

Just then, Benny called out from the mud room, "Don't worry, I wiped him off."

Freddy bounded into the room, panting, dripping from his belly, followed by Benny. "Raining out." He did a double take on seeing Charlotte. "Sorry. I didn't know you had company."

Iris's back stiffened. *Is he going to be unwelcoming?*

"Why don't I bring in a plate of those cookies from the Italian grocery? It'll only take a minute." Benny whirled about and left. Freddy followed.

Charlotte laughed. "A dog goes where the food is."

"Do you have a dog?" Iris leaned forward, wiping one of the paw prints with her foot.

Benny shouted from the kitchen, "A dog? You'd be welcome to bring it here. Freddy's great with other dogs." He returned with a plate loaded with biscuits still in their cellophane wrappers. After putting them on the coffee table, he bounced down next to Iris on the couch. "I hear you're writing a scholarly paper on our little water baby."

Charlotte nodded.

Iris's heart froze in her chest. *What's he going to say next?*

"That's great." Benny leaned back, one knee up with his hands wrapped around it. "The more we know about him, the better."

He didn't ask about her school, though he definitely wants to. He really is trying. Iris felt a surge of love. She hid a smile behind her teacup.

"I'm going to do my best to find out everything. I know it means a lot to Iris but it's real important to me, too. Not just the article, which I hope will get people interested in my work."

Iris swallowed. "What else? You said, 'Not just the article.'" Benny squeezed her hand. "I'm... we're curious."

Charlotte hesitated for a moment. "It's this area, I love it. Have for a long, long time. It's why I chose it to study…"
Which school?
"I love this house. I feel so welcome here. Like I belong."

Aoife

1864

The bull calf throve in the weeks after his birth, growing rapidly on Adele's rich milk. Several local farmers, knowing of the quality of their stock, came with an eye to purchasing him, but Aoife was loath to let him go at any price. Every day, she watched him gambol by his mother's side, a reminder of their work saving the farm.

She wove him a necklace of spring beauty and laid it on his brown hide. He quickly shook it to bits, bounding about the muddy pasture, but no matter. He meant so much more to her than the other beasts.

"I would you see him, William. As you wished, we have named him Hercules and inscribed a plaque for his stall door. He will be the pride of the county at the fair. Let Thomas bring you down." Beside the bed, Aoife waited for a reply, but William was silent.

At last, he said, "My love, can I not just see him from the window?"

Aoife sighed and studied him. His face was thinner and his expression fretful, querulous. The face of an invalid, a beautiful sufferer. It seemed as if the bones of his face were visible beneath his too pale skin. An ache swelled deep beneath her breastbone. *If only he'd come back whole or never gone.*

But she couldn't think that. He was a man and she, his wife. Her duty was to honor his wishes. To comfort him and help him heal.

William was living in her world less and less, despite her efforts, despite her attempts at lovemaking, at wooing him into closeness. His nightmares still plagued their sleep, and the most she could draw from him was a gentle smile.

Only Lettie seemed to bring him to laughter, to divert him during the day, but Aoife put that thought aside. The girl was still abed.

She opened the curtains. "Mayhap Thomas can aide you to stand and I'll parade Hercules back and forth below. I can handle him myself."

"Can you now?" William muttered in her very lilt. The imitation of her speech stung. If only she could take back her words! How it must shame him to know that she'd so surpassed him in strength and ability.

Aoife left to return to the kitchen, where the weekly bread was nearly done rising and a joint of pork, seasoned with sage, was browning above the fire, the rich and savoy grease dripping into a pan of onions. She bent slightly to touch the crisp crackling, and had to step back rapidly, bile bubbling up into her mouth, nausea cresting like a wave from her stomach. Spinning around, she vomited into the wash basin.

Her head swirled. She clung to the tabletop to keep from falling and dropped herself onto a chair, face hidden in her apron.

No, no!

She rocked back and forth, thinking back on the past weeks, and realizing the truth. Her monthly course had failed to come, and she'd been wrong to believe that due to exhaustion.

Her mam had told her the peril maids faced from the men of the family they served. How lucky she'd been in not falling with child then. How lucky that William had been different, that she'd found love. And now...

Aoife looked up suddenly.

Lettie stood in the doorway of the kitchen, her demeanor haughty, her expression unreadable. "I seen you two in the yard. You thought I was safe abed."

Aoife dropped her apron's skirt and, mouth open in horror, looked at Thomas's Lettie. "You played the spy?"

Lettie tossed her head and looked Aoife in the eyes. "I woke on and off to the cow's bellows. Then came the sounds of other beasts, such as heard in the quarters when the men visited their wives. Outside my bed was cold and treacherous, ice all about. I stood just in the open door and watched as you two came from the barn, shameless. A faithless wife with her faithless servant."

"Lettie," Aoife began to rise but lacked the will.

"Some of the women were low, just like you, wild when with a man, shameless. But I will never tell *him* and destroy what little peace he has."

"Never tell your own man, Thomas?"

Lettie's mouth turned down with scorn. "Never tell William he has a faithless wife. 'Tis enough for him to know I'd never betray him."

Thomas

1864

Thomas stood, back against the barn wall, looking away from Aoife.

She tore a piece of straw with nervous fingers. "We must act as always, Thomas."

"But you say Lettie knows…"

Aoife stood across from him, her eyes cast down, her voice flat and dull. "She swears she'll say nothing."

"Aoife…" *I do not trust Lettie's word. Her mind is too oft disordered.*

268

"What we did was wrong, but 'twas the heat of the moment, the triumph of saving the calf and his mother, and our sadness and longing."

"*You* did nothing wrong. The fault be all mine, a woman, married in law before God. You are a man wed only in the common way, declaring yourself a husband and your woman a wife. And she has spurned you in your bed." She sighed. "I repented of our deeds but not with confession. With no penance done, so I am punished. I am with child, Thomas. Your child."

He slid down the wall to sit on his heels and hid his face in his hands. "Whatever shall we do?"

"There is no choice but to see it through and trust in the Lord. Keep it from William until we no longer can, hoping he grows strong enough to forgive. I love him, Thomas, and would not have him hurt. Not for all the world. And yet he will be."

"I love you, Aoife."

"And I love thee, Thomas, but not as I love him, not as husband. Not as you love Lettie. You have sacrificed greatly for her."

He rose from his crouch. "You must stop working the farm."

"Phsst!" She laughed. "I remember my mam telling how she worked the croft until the moment she bent over in pain to have me! Why, sure, she crawled to the cottage for the birth, attended only by my gran. All the while, my father was off drinking the day away. No, Thomas, I am of stronger stuff than you think."

"Still..."

"Winter's return delayed the field tasks, and you have things well in hand. Turn the soil for me and I'll start the alfalfa. The great sack will hide my belly and I'll walk the fields until I can no longer, though my apron might rise high and my back ache. But should anyone come, I will play the lady, indisposed, as Mother Sprigett always was when someone inferior stopped to visit. Sure and 'tis a good thing she'll not visit again." Her smile was forced, a grimace. "Your meals will be simple 'til my sick time passes."

Her Irishness comes out more in her speech when she is afraid. Thomas smiled up at her, disguising how afraid he was, himself. *How will I tend the farm without even her to help?* And the worst, how to handle Lettie. At least she had kept no friends in the town, no gossips.

He said nothing more. It was the closeness, the partnership with Aoife that was precious and that he could not lose. His thoughts refused to stray to the child she was carrying. His child.

He no longer wished to tear away a bit of the farm for him and for Lettie. There were too many reasons to remain.

Chapter 30

BENNY PUSHED HIMSELF from his overstuffed chair. "Why don't I get dinner started for us? It was Indian tonight, right, Iris?"

When she nodded, he went to cut the cauliflower in small florets. Iris sat, open-mouthed with wonder. *Is he really leaving us alone to chat? Or did he think that keeping Charlotte here would give him a whole evening to weasel info out of her?*

"I love Indian food but have no idea how to cook it." Charlotte was leaning forward, trying to peer into the kitchen.

"Just making something simple tonight along with a salad. Want to come in and help?"

"Sure."

As they walked into the kitchen, Iris admitted, "I don't have a recipe. Just wing it with cauliflower, potatoes, and a whole lot of spices. It won't be anywhere near as good as a restaurant."

"Oh, pshaw! Stop being so modest." Benny had finished cutting the vegetables and was rooting about in the spice cabinet, setting the containers Iris needed on the counter. He sat in the nook when everything was out.

With Charlotte watching, Iris heated oil in a large, flat frying pan. She set in the cauliflower and potato bits to soften and brown.

Outside, the rain came down with increasing force, but the house felt snug and secure and the glass in the new windows didn't move at all. The newly renovated kitchen was properly set up at last. "A chef's kitchen," the designer had said to Benny's great amusement.

Just as Iris was adding the spices, lightning in the distance lit the treetops, followed by thunder that seemed to roll across the sky like giant oil drums passing overhead. The lights flickered and went out. "Dammit!" Iris exclaimed. She turned the flame down so nothing would burn until she could see.

"Not used to the good old East Coast thunderstorms yet," Benny said. "Didn't have many in California."

"Good thing you bought a generator." Iris knew he was proud that he'd thought ahead back last May.

The room was dark except for the intermittent flash from the jagged lightning, and a faint odor of ozone came from the yet-to-be-replaced mudroom door. The generator kicked in and they resumed making dinner.

The food was on the table fifteen minutes later.

"This is delicious," Charlotte said, taking her first bite.

Benny reached for the jar of mango chutney but before he got the serving spoon in, their phones buzzed, high-pitched and steady. The dog howled.

Surprised, each of them pulled out their phone, as if expecting different, individualized alerts.

"Storm direction suddenly shifted, upgraded to hurricane category one, winds up to ninety miles per hour?" Benny's eyes were wide with disbelief as he read the alert. "Did we move to Florida or some shit?" He read silently for a moment. "Says the worst of the storm is going south of here, as usual." He put down his phone with a loud *thunk*.

"Hurricanes freak me out." Charlotte shoved hers back in the pocket of her hoodie. "I remember Sandy. It was really awful. Worse up in New York. I had an auntie left homeless. And didn't you say Sandy tore up your barn?"

Iris nodded. "It did, before we moved here."

"I better get going if the weather's going to get that bad."

"What direction are you going?" Benny's expression was full of concern.

"Toward Philly."

"That would be south."

Iris glared at Benny's touch of sarcasm, though for him it was pretty mild. She touched Charlotte's arm. "No. Stay. You don't leave a safe spot in a bad storm."

Charlotte looked from one to the other.

"Really, stay," Benny said. His tone had nothing that aroused Iris's suspicions. "They've put out flash flood warnings."

"If you go, I'll fret myself to death. Finish eating."

Charlotte picked up her fork, still looking from Benny to Iris. When they resumed the meal, she did, too. They sat in silence, except for the howling of the wind and the noise of the rain beating down.

They were eating the tiramisu Iris had brought from Costco when the phones alerted again. Landfall of the worst winds had caused a tornado to form just north of Philadelphia, headed northeast.

"Great. Now we're Oklahoma. With our luck, it'll change course, hit and undo every renovation we've made."

Iris let out a nervous giggle. "That's the spirit, Ben. Always look on the bright side of life."

Thomas

1864

He had culled the stock down as low as was feasible to still assure a future for the farm. Some were butchered, the meat sold but for what they needed, which was placed atop purchased ice blocks and covered in hay and sawdust. The better animals they could spare were sold.

Aoife sat in the stall and cried when the bull calf went to a big farm across the river in New Jersey. Tears running down her cheeks, she rocked back and forth as she wailed, sitting, skirts in disarray, on the floor of the stall where the little bull had been born. "I thought a dynasty would be started with him, for sure. He is finer even than his sire."

Thomas resisted the urge to put his arms about her for comfort. Instead, he crouched across the aisle and spoke soothing words. "We still have his sire and his dam. Adele will be bred again and, God willing, breed true. You'll have your dynasty." Ruefully, his thoughts added, *As will I.*

"Are you still often ill?" he asked.

"No."

She was lying so that he would have no excuse to stop her cleaning the animals' manure, even if he found the remains of her meals in the dung when he went to spread it.

"Aoife, I'll finish the work today. Go in, get yourself warm. Drink tea."

She snuffled her tears back up and dropped her lower lip defiantly. "I want to work and so I *will* work."

Thomas pushed himself up, sliding his back against the wall. "This is my baby, too. A child needs a healthy mother to survive. And I will stand here until you agree."

But they were not the only ones who would suspect the child was his. Lettie, the woman who'd failed to deliver him a living child, had seen them come from the barn. *How will she react if Aoife is successful? Thomas, you great coward, you must sound her out.*

Aoife

1864

The barn was still and dim with floating dust motes from the sweet-smelling hay. Cold, but Aoife had little desire to stand and face the remains of the day. She was tired, oh, so tired, as if her structure, her bones, were softening and melting.

It was comforting—yet dangerous—to have Thomas standing across from her. Her thoughts returned to that night, to their triumph over death, to how her fingers had caught in the tight curls on his chest as the wave of desire within her crested.

The memory must have shown on her face from the way Thomas's eyes glittered. She stayed for a while until her hesitation to move seemed craven. She rose and went to the house.

Lettie stood at the fireplace. Her hair was neatly contained beneath a cloth tied at the nape of her neck. The kettle was on its tripod, Aoife's best teapot was open and ready on the table. The kitchen was warm and fragrant with the odor of toasted bread. It was also tidier and cleaner than when Aoife had left for the barn.

"The tea is brewed." Lettie took up the butter and spread the toast thickly.

"Is Mr. William awake? Does he wish tea and not coffee?" Aoife wanted the girl gone.

The butter knife was paused in midair. "No, Mrs. Sprigett. He sleeps. This is for you. You're too thin. We all must keep our strength up."

Aoife gaped open-mouthed at Lettie naming her as William's wife. She was dumbfounded by the words—and tone—of concern and kindness. It was touching, but the turnabout worried her.

Lettie placed the toast and a cup of tea, thick with cream, in front of Aoife. She filled the coffee grinder and said, "I'll be outside, grinding this for the rest of us, lest the smell make you lose your breakfast."

"Wait!" Aoife looked down at her own stomach, to see if it had somehow swelled in the previous hour.

Lettie turned. Her face was serene, her brow unfurrowed, her mouth soft, but her gaze strangely intense. "I got eyes. Saw you washed no cloths for your monthlies. I don't need to see a belly on you. You're carrying my husband's child." She tilted her head like a nesting barn swallow. "I'll be doing all the wash from now on."

That night, Aoife was sleepless, grateful that William slept deeply. Not only grateful but glad there was no chance he'd put his hands on her and perhaps caress the little apple-hard lump in her belly, just above her sex. It was not yet visible to others, but when she looked down at her naked body, it was plain as day.

A searing flash of remorse hit her, and she wished he would dream those awful terrors that led him to beat her in the night. They would be fair punishment by a husband to a wife like her. But he slumbered on.

Morning came and she took the chamber pot into the nursery William had prepared for the child they might have had. She put one foot up on the chair and held the pot between her legs, hoping to see blood. If the baby came this soon and died, it would be a blessing. She pushed hard with the muscles of her abdomen, but her urine came, clear yellow in her candle's light. She dropped her skirts, put the pot on the floor, and returned to William.

As she slid into the bed, something like a captured bird fluttered deep inside, deep down at the bottom of her belly. And she suddenly wanted the baby to live—more than she'd ever wanted anything before.

Chapter 31

"THE BRIGHT SIDE OF LIFE? Are you stooping to Monty Python references?" Benny said.

Iris smirked. "If the shoe fits, Ben!"

Unoffended, he winked at her.

Within a few minutes, the phones alerted again. The tornado was headed their way. Its speed was picking up.

"Do you have a cellar?" Biting her lip, Charlotte looked around the room as if she'd see the furniture and paintings rise and spin off into space.

Benny couldn't resist lecturing on the science. "Hurricanes have spinning winds around a calm center, what's called the eye of the storm. The winds hit land, the land's surface is rough, compared to the water, and... *BAM!*" He pounded his fist sharply on the table, making the women jump. "Local increased friction creates a tornado."

Enough mansplaining! Iris put her hand on Charlotte's arm. "Yes, we have a cellar."

Benny shot her a wounded look. Swamped with guilt, as if she'd joined forces against her husband by mocking him, she looked away.

Her brows knitted quizzically; Charlotte looked from one to the other.

Benny pushed back from the table. "Gonna go follow the storm real time."

As he left, Charlotte said, "I hope he doesn't mind my being here."

"Not at all." At least, Iris hoped not. "He's checking his ham radio."

There was a growing rumble outside, like a roll of thunder that crescendos without end. It sounded like a jet plane approaching, its engines roaring.

Trembling inside but determined not to show it, Iris said, "I'm very glad you're here. We've grown too used to being alone, we two."

There was a subtle change in the room, a feeling of *something leaving*, a vacuum. Breathing was very slightly more laborious, the air thinner. Iris felt anxiety tightening her chest further. Outside the window, the sky seemed to unfurl like a black flower.

Benny reappeared. "Jeez, you hear that?"

"The plane?"

"Plane? For God's sake, get to the cellar!" He ran to the stairs. Freddy bounded after him.

The roaring noise increased. Several lightning flashes broke through the dark. The ozone stung Iris's nose.

Benny yanked the door open, yelling something Iris couldn't hear over the wind. Grabbing the handrail, Iris stumbled down the stairs first, followed by Charlotte. Benny brought up the rear, shutting the heavy door behind him.

In the chilly basement, it was quieter. Benny pulled out plastic lawn chairs, setting three in a semicircle. "Good thing we stored these away. We'll be cozy and safe down here."

Charlotte didn't sit down. Instead, she paced, running one hand on the rough stucco walls. She was shaking slightly. "Would the house withstand the tornado directly hitting it?"

"Sit down," Iris said as gently as she could. "The house has stood for three hundred years. This isn't its first bad storm."

Benny jumped in with, "Sometimes they built the house over a spring, and the basement served as a cool food storage."

Iris's heart warmed, though she shivered in the cool air. Benny had been doing homework on the house! And though he was yelling, the boring facts calmed Charlotte. She sat at last.

Iris closed her eyes and prayed the house would, indeed, stand.

Benny pulled a corkscrew out of his pocket. He went to the wine rack and selected a bottle. He raised his voice even louder to be heard over the screaming wind. "Won't be optimal temperature, but will be very, very good. A Passito di Pantelleria, Donna Fugata, 2008. Limited edition."

"I've been saving this for a special occasion and this is it."

"Glasses?"

"We'll swill it from the bottle, family style! Really get to know each other." He grinned and bounced on his toes like a boxer, glowing with enthusiasm. Or mania. Hoisting the wine in his right hand, he waved the opener. "Maybe we'll be too drunk to go back up the stairs!"

Aoife

1864

A month later, with planting time nigh, Aoife was still sick to her stomach, so unable to keep food down that her vision swirled with black spots and her head felt as if she'd drank too much red ale. Along with fear that the fatigue would keep her from working, she was terrified something had gone wrong with her baby.

Terrifying, too, was William's lack of progress at walking. The prosthesis for his mid-thigh amputation continued to pain him. He couldn't bear to attempt the stairs. He'd not left their second story since he'd returned injured more than a year before. Sitting at the table by candlelight, she'd sewn a little curved sack filled with goose down and padded the cup with lambs' wool, but it made no difference.

She and Thomas continued encouraging him, taking on much of his weight, but his cries and winces, though muted, made Aoife lose heart. "Perhaps, my love, we should move our bed to the parlor so that you can at least walk to the doorway and look out at the world."

But William answered, "No, I'll not be on display should anyone come by, a peddler or a neighbor."

Or Mother Sprigett? For the first time, Aoife grieved that the old woman cared so little for her son, now he was injured, to visit him.

Aoife begged Lettie to change the bandages daily. The painful stump had been poorly sewn and that led it to develop a thick and rough-surfaced scar.

"I would resew such a hem," Aoife had told William when the poor healing had become obvious.

"Such a scar might form again," William said. "I'll have no more butchering."

Lettie sewed larger aprons for Aoife to cover her ripening body, swelling faster than it seemed it should. "Old Lady Sprigett discover you with child, she'll know it ain't Mr. William's. Not with his wounds."

At her words, Aoife was flooded with sorrow. Rue, like a poison working its way through her body, killing her slowly. *It does not matter. Soon there will be no way to keep it hidden. It will be clear to everyone that I carry a babe.*

A week later, as Aoife headed back to help Thomas, Lettie ran from the house and grabbed her arm. "You must come with me."

The girl's demanding words angered Aoife, who shook off her hand. Then she saw Lettie's face. "What is it?"

"He's awful hot to touch."

Aoife's heart felt as if it jumped into her throat. She lifted her skirts and ran up the stairs to find William in a bath of sweat, moaning softly, thrashing his head, delirious.

Lettie stood so close behind, her breath humid in Aoife's ear. "I swear it was sudden. Fine in the morning, saying his leg hurt like always. Then, 'bout two hours ago, it was like a fire lit in him. Cool rags on his forehead... nothing."

Aoife yanked down the quilt. The wrapping over William's mid-thigh stump was loose. She pulled it away, though it stuck to the spot where the flesh had been closed poorly. It was swollen and red, oozing yellow fluid. He screamed when she touched it lightly.

"'Tis infected." Aoife sank to her knees. "Quick, Lettie, bid Thomas ride for the doctor."

Lettie stood still for a moment before leaving. When she returned, she held an extra quilt from her lean-to. "Best you sit in the chair with this on your belly, should Thomas find the doctor willing to come. The visit may not stay secret from the old lady's gossips."

The doctor, a kindly, round little Quaker with an old-fashioned white beard, was more than willing. He followed Lettie up the stairs and came to the bedside.

Lettie pulled a fan from her skirts and, standing between Aoife and the bed, fanned her. "Poor Mrs. Sprigett is beside herself with worry."

After his examination, the doctor said, "She is right to worry."

He took Aoife aside and whispered, though William was not conscious. "The infection is too far gone. Further amputation might have saved him, or bromine applied when it first turned red." He packed his bags. "There is now nothing to be done." He paused, his expression kindly. "I have seen bromine make wounds worse, more prone to gangrene. I fear Mr. Sprigett was doomed from the time he suffered this wound. My condolences to thee, Mrs. Sprigett."

Aoife bit her knuckle to keep her sobbing quiet as possible, wishing she was alone with William. *I married a treasure. But all that is squandered now. The baby is not my punishment. It is losing my true love.* "When?"

"Not more than three days, but more likely less."

*   *   *

Once the old Quaker left, Aoife moved from the sheltering chair to caress William, wiping his brow and kissing it. "Do not leave me, my sweeting," she murmured. "I cannot imagine life without you." But he did not awaken.

That evening, when she returned from her meager meal, she found Lettie sitting vigil in the chair, as instructed, for Aoife would not have him left alone.

In her hands, Lettie held needle and thread, working on a half-sewn garment, a tiny infant's gown. In the basket beside her was another, already complete.

Aoife whispered, "Has my William seen these?" Her breath was tight, her heart pounding as she waited for a reply.

A serene smile was on Lettie's lips and her voice was calm. "He has. I told him they were for a local woman, who will soon enough deliver a colored child."

Thomas

1864

William was doomed. Thomas could tell from the somber demeanor of the doctor as he took the reins of his carriage.

"Thee will be needed here. The infection was not seen to in time. Mr. Sprigett is not long for this world."

Thomas went into the kitchen just as Lettie was making fresh tea. He took her arms in his hands, grasping harder than he'd ever done. "Why did you not notice before today?"

"He wanted to die. Told me was already half in the grave."

The muscles in his arms ached with the desire to hit her. "You kept his despair from his wife? And from me? That was not your right!"

She smiled slyly. "Better this than him finding out what the two of you done. I kept him from knowing what it led to." Her smile faded, was replaced by fear as her gray eyes searched his face. She stepped behind the table, away from him. "How were you going to keep him from knowing?"

"He was her husband."

A wild peal of laughter broke from her. "You didn't know, did you? Couldn't have been his, not with his wounds. She kept that from you, didn't she? And the baby, the baby... never will look like him. 'Less there was another colored man on the farm, the daddy had to be you."

He wanted to kill her.

"And now," she said, "you and me will once again be man and wife."

Chapter 32

THE HOUSE SHOOK AS THE TORNADO ripped through the property—banshee screams of wind circling about the roof.

Freddy, lying at Benny's feet, jumped, threw his head back, and howled.

His hands shaking, Benny uncorked another bottle, when, with a loud *CRACK!* the wood Bilco doors were sucked off their hinges. Fragments flew like shrapnel into the cellar. The rest disappeared into the violent storm. Benny dropped the bottle, to smash and spill on the floor.

Another scream sounded, but not from the wind. Iris felt as if the force of her terror had ripped from her throat. She kept her eyes squeezed shut, unwilling to see what else the tornado could do. And then arms were around her, both Benny's and Charlotte's, pulling her deeper into the basement, further from the steps to the outside.

A monstrous crash resounded. They stood backed up against the stone wall. It held firm. The winds continued raging about the house for what seemed an eternity.

The storm's wail faded slowly away, spiraling into the distance. The rain stopped, and the calm was so complete it seemed unnatural. The birds returned—they could be heard chirping madly—consternated and enraged by the disturbance of their homes.

In the basement, the three humans were still entwined, still trembling slightly, but warm in each other's embrace. Iris peeled open one eye, amazed they were alive, intact. But was the house? Her almost renovated house?

"Benny?"

"What?"

"I'm going upstairs to see what's up."

Benny and Charlotte looked at each other and then at Iris. They dropped their arms and took a step back, Charlotte blinking and Benny shuffling his feet. They seemed embarrassed that they had not been the first to break the storm's spell.

They stood, wearing identical sheepish expressions, as Iris started up the steps. Then they followed. The house was in the same condition as when they'd gone to the basement. Not a single improvement had been undone. All three of them stood gawping at the peaceful living room.

Benny flicked a light switch, and the ceiling light went on—either they hadn't lost power or the generator had kicked in. "It's like we dreamed the storm. So, what was that huge thud?" Benny opened the front door. "Oh, my fucking God!"

Iris joined him at the door and gasped. "Oh, no, Benny!" Charlotte came up behind her and put a hand on her shoulder. They went out and surveyed the damage.

The oldest and largest tree, a white oak, lay deeply embedded in the top floor of the barn, caving in the roof. It completely blocked the north end of their drive and had taken down a smaller hickory that, falling sideways, lay prone across the south end.

Charlotte's car was under the hickory.

Sirens blasted by on the state road at the end of their street. Police, fire, ambulances. Each sound distinct.

Freddy had run out, excited to be free from the cellar, the tornado seemingly forgotten.

Giant puddles filled every hollow in the paving, and down below the emergency vehicles sprayed each other when they passed. Benny stood, fists on hips, surveying the property. *Like an elderly dictator about to tell how we'll proceed.* She smiled to herself. *Cute, if he doesn't take it too far.*

"Well," he said, "good news is, the damage is all under our home insurance. But I doubt we'll be high on the list for downed tree removal."

Iris's heart lifted at a realization. She turned to Charlotte. "I guess you'll be staying with us for a few days."

Aoife

1864

Mother Sprigett sent demands that he be interred in the town cemetery, in the family plot begun a hundred years before. Aoife would have none of it. She had Thomas turn away the old woman's emissaries, even the preacher. They buried William up on the hill behind the house, his grave marked only with a wooden cross.

Aoife visited him daily, climbing up behind the house, through the blackberries, slipping on the early spring mud, her long skirts dragging in the back. In front, her growing belly held up the cloth.

Thomas hacked away the brush, the witch hazel and buttonbush, but it grew back, wild and stubborn. The blackberries leafed and then bloomed, their branches catching at Aoife's clothing.

"They are thorns of penitence," she said to Thomas. "Leave them be. You have more than enough work."

She no longer went to the field or the barn but spent much of the day in bed. Her belly grew bigger than seemed possible for her thin frame. "To think, William found me plump and full of juice, Thomas, and now, but for this…" She put both hands below the bulge. "…A stick woman, bones clanking together."

Bones clanking together… Mam carried me with her to childbirths. The screams, the stench of blood and shit as the babe forced itself out to live… or not, if stuck inside like a leech, sucking away its mam's lifeblood until death. I was too small to stay alone at home, too young to know if those women were sinners. There never was a man about when a woman's time came. They never paid for what had been done. I fear sleep, for dreaming of that time, the faces fixed in terror and pain, for worrying that my time will be like that.

What does Lettie know that she cares so for her husband's strumpet?

Perhaps Thomas forced Lettie in some way, as now she did more than cook for Aoife. She served her in the bed chamber when needed, gathering the dirty linen, and making the bed up fresh. She walked to town and met with the churchwomen she'd spurned before, all to learn tempting foods for a mother-to-be. Puddings and pastries, stuffed with fruit or meat, were on the table at every meal. Lettie even managed to find a worker to help Thomas, the man whose business had failed for lack of supplies.

At the end of her sixth month, in the summer swelter, Aoife's appetite mysteriously reappeared, but at both Lettie's and Thomas's insistence, she stayed in the house. Her only outing was to visit William's grave in the early morning, when the sun hadn't yet peeked over the treetops.

Aoife didn't mind. A great lethargy and feeling of broody content had entered her. The twisting and turning of her infant provided all the company she needed, and a love grew, as great as any she'd ever known.

Curled on the mattress, she whispered to the babe, telling all the memories of her own childhood, singing the songs her mam had. Reassuring the little one, and herself, that somehow things would work out.

Thomas
1864

"It serves no purpose, climbing the hill in near dark. A daft affectation, especially for a woman with child. What if you fall on your belly? Who would be punished then?"

But Aoife persisted, though her feet and ankles swelled until William's boots fit and her breath came short with each step. To Thomas's surprise, Lettie not only took over the household chores, she milked Adele. The cream that rose to the top, she made into custard tarts and pies. Thomas was allowed only what Lettie would give him. The rest went to Aoife.

"She must eat well. She has been thin for too long."

Thomas was happy to hear that Lettie was willing to make life easier. He was even happier to hear her singing and smiling as she worked. Her black moods seemed to have lifted like the morning dew when the sun comes upon it. She had even allowed him access to her body at night, though without showing it pleasured her. He hoped that would come.

Coming down from the cornfield one midday, he saw Lettie dart into the lean-to and followed. *Perhaps the dim light and the heat is making her languorous. Perhaps her blood will respond to my touch at last.*

He moved quicker, as his arousal at the thought of Lettie, compliant, had hardened him and the tightness of his trousers was painful. Hero, by his side, felt his anticipation and circled, barking ecstatically. "Hush! No woman is seduced by a dog's singing!"

He pushed open the door and stopped. Lettie was tying some-thing about her waist. "What are you doing?"

She turned. Laced to the front of her stomach was a pillow. She stared with a cool and haughty look. "I am going to town for rice, for to make pudding."

"No, what is that there?"

"To claim the baby as mine, I need to be seen with child."

His heart began hammering in his chest. Her semblance of sanity had been an act. "It's not your babe, Lettie."

"I did not think you such a fool, Thomas. You realize that you and her would be disgraced and shunned by everyone? You a colored man, married, and her the Irish wife of a hero named Sprigett? Some might even want you dead for fucking his wife whilst he was dying." She put an old corset over the pillow and secured it. "Each month I go to town and each time the pillow is more stuffed with feathers. The women gather 'round me at our church…" Her look was sly and amused. "…Though I am too timid a girl to let any feel my growing belly. All are glad to see the wild girl has got religion, and another little child will belong to the congregation. They are glad a babe has at last stuck hard inside my womb and not come slithering out like all before. They'll welcome my child with open arms." She pulled on her gown. The waist had been let out. "That man Charlie come to help you? Preacher Matthews sent him, just for this baby's sake."

"But Aoife…"

"You must not tell her. Not 'til she delivers. A mother's unsettled thoughts can make a babe come before its time. I will not have the child harmed."

Chapter 33

CHARLOTTE STOOD NEXT TO the driver's side of her car. The front wheel was at a forty-five-degree angle and the fender crumpled like a used tissue. The fallen oak's leaves moved in a gentle breeze. Bits of a squirrel's nest dropped down.

"Looks really bad." Benny ran his fingers through his beard, but Iris noticed the maneuver was mostly to hide a grin.

"Bad?" Charlotte had tears in her eyes. "My poor car's totaled!"

"He's kidding, Charlotte," Iris said. "Our homeowner's will cover it." *But no way she'd get a running car for what her old heap is worth.*

Charlotte was most likely calculating the same thing. She sniffled, going from competent academic to distraught child.

Benny softened right before her eyes. He dropped his hand. "Sorry, sorry, I shouldn't joke like that. Of course, you're welcome to stay."

Charlotte wiped her eyes with the back of her hand and shuffled over to Iris. "Can I use your bathroom?"

Iris took her hand and led her into the house, leaving her in the powder room. Back out in the slanted early evening sunshine and fresh-scented air, Benny was gassing up the chainsaw. "Benny, it's really ok for her to stay? She'll be our first overnight guest. Your heart was set on that being Hal."

He smiled. "It's important… *She's* important to you. But if I can get the drive clear, I'll take her home when she wants to go." Carrying the saw, he walked to the fallen giant, the one Iris felt held mystical powers. The pride of their property, it had been grand enough to inhabit a Hibernian grove, worshipped by Irish Druids. "Come look at the bottom of the trunk. There's an opening big enough for someone to hide in. But the heartwood's gone. That's why it broke off."

Iris touched the gap's edge. How long had that little hidey hole been there? A child might have made it a playhouse long ago, fairyland castle eerie in the morning mist.

"There's no way you can cut up this huge tree with that puny chainsaw." She looked down the south drive. "Maybe the hickory. At least where the trunk blocks the way."

Charlotte came from the house as they walked toward the smaller tree. Her face was shining, newly washed, and once again full of resolve. The sunlight glinted on her russet hair and highlighted her tanned skin. "Can I help?"

"Ever use one of these?" Benny held up his tool, as if it were massive. *As if he's a lumberjack.*

"Yup." Charlotte nodded. She turned her head toward him. "But I'm not strong enough to hold it as steady as a man."

Iris joined them as they picked their way down the drive, through leaves still attached to branches, and hundreds of acorns rolling about. She looked at the other two, wondering if there could be a bond forming after their frightening time in the cellar.

Midway there, Iris stepped on something that slid under her foot and she went down, her ankle twisted beneath her. "Benny!" she screamed, bursting into tears at the sharpness of the pain.

Benny bent over her. He gingerly felt her foot. "Nothing seems broken. But I'd bet on a bad sprain."

"Got a cold pack?" Charlotte said. "Not ice cubes, something more bendable, like a bag of frozen vegetables."

"You can get that from the freezer," Benny picked Iris up.

"Benny, your heart!"

He ignored Iris's protests and started toward the house. "I'm gonna take my wounded sweetheart to the living room to put her little tootsie up."

Iris laughed with tears in her eyes. *Ow, ow, haha! Ow!* The pain was less sharp now that she expected it, but the jostling as she was carried made it worse.

Benny put her on the couch, her foot elevated on an embroidered pillow. Her seat was by a window, but the eighteen-inch-thick sill would block the view of them cutting up the smaller tree. Charlotte placed the bag of peas—which Iris had planned to use in shepherd's pie—around her ankle.

Chattering to each other about the storm and how to safely dismember the tree's limbs, they headed back out to the driveway and got to work. The whine of the chainsaw changed key when the blade was biting into wood, like a weird tribal instrument.

Made as comfortable as she could be with a couple of ibuprofen tablets, Iris fitfully read on the couch, the cold plastic bag cradled around her ankle, rapidly defrosting.

I wonder what they're talking about. Can Benny stick to his promise not to pump Charlotte for information?

At last, the noise ceased. They came in, near bent over with laughter, and seemed surprised to see her. Had she and the now soggy peas been forgotten?

"Iris, how's your ankle?" Benny, recovering quickly, radiated concern. He didn't wait for her reply. "We've got the hickory near cut up and the driveway clear. I'll make you some tea."

"I'll do it!" Charlotte's color was high from the fresh air, exertion, and mirth. She went into the kitchen yelling, "Don't worry, I'll find the cups and such."

"The two of you seem to have had a high old time."

"We did! I didn't realize how delightful she could be."

"Are you driving her home?" Iris pushed the pea bag off her ankle.

"She's going to stay. Said there was no way she'd leave us to handle things, what with the trees down and your ankle. That's real nice of her."

Benny's phone rang. He fished it from his pocket. "Oh, hi, Jessica." His eyes met Iris's. "No, I don't want to know. Not that I don't care to know, it's just that I think Charlotte will tell us herself as soon as she's ready." He nodded. "Uh-huh, uh-huh. No, I'm not worried. I'll tell you if I am." He ended the call and smiled at Iris. "Charlotte says she's not as creative as you, but still a good cook. We're going to poke through the freezer for tomorrow's dinner."

Aoife

1864

The air was sweltering at the start of September, summer's last hurrah after fooling them into thinking the time of humid heat was over. She was eight months gone. Her huge belly left little room for food or for breathing comfortably.

Lettie waited on her as Aoife once waited on Mother Sprigett. She made certain Aoife's bed had crisp white linens and pillows to keep her upright. On the meal tray brought to Aoife's confinement were rich broths, sweet custards golden with egg yolks, and mugs with mulled wine.

Lettie had become skilled at baking—or perhaps had always been. When Aoife's appetite was at its puniest, she was served toast studded with dried apple and raisins; when she felt she could tolerate more, sweet cakes arrived.

Lettie hummed as she served and cleaned the bedroom. Her apron was always clean and ironed, and her hair tied up neatly. Her cloud-gray eyes always like a sea, becalmed. They gave Aoife no hint of her thoughts.

Thomas never ventured up the stairs. When Aoife heard his heavy step, she leaned forward eagerly, hungry for even a small taste of his voice. He spoke in the kitchen but rarely. His voice never raised against Lettie.

While Aoife napped, Lettie was in the wingback chair, sewing little white gowns from fine cotton. Her head was bent over the work, driving a tiny needle in and out of the cloth while biting her lip. Her stitches were neat and even.

Aoife watched her secretly, beneath her lowered lashes. At last, she could drowse no longer. Her fingers itched to work on her babe's garments. The child seemed to approve, little hands patting her insides at the thought. "Get my workbasket and give me a gown. I would tat a lace collar."

Lettie brought the basket but said not a word. Aoife took out her old silver tatting shuttle, sliding it between her fingers before engaging the thread. The surface was cool and worn. The hands that had so thinned the shuttle were her mother's, the only precious thing her mother had owned. *Feeling this is like having mam nearby.*

There had been many childbirth deaths, of mothers and babies, in Ireland, when her mam was called to a neighbor's croft, taking Aoife along, going only when no one else could. Small as Aoife had been then, the women's endless screams when labor went wrong—and later wails of the orphaned children—fixed themselves in her mind.

She put her remembered fear aside with the help of the tatting, staring tight at the thread dancing about the shuttle. In the middle of finishing the border about the rosettes, a small cramp tightened the small of her back. It was like the ache after hours scrubbing the floor. She shifted her hips in the bed, trying to find comfort.

It had begun.

The collar was a masterpiece, her best handiwork ever. The last row had been almost finished when the first cramp hit her belly, small, like one from her monthly. The second contraction was stronger. "Lettie, please you call Thomas to me."

Lettie shook her head but rose from the chair. "'Tis not right for a man. Confinement is women's doings. He got to stay away." She left and went down the stairs.

With the next pain, Aoife breathed, "Lettie," sick with wishing the girl were there, as little company as she'd been. When the contraction began, Aoife's body bucked her upright, supported on her arms. Each breath was a monstrous puff, "Oh, oh, oh."

When it passed, she was exhausted with knowing it would only worsen. She opened her eyes to see Lettie, returned with a basin of cool water. Lettie wrung out a cloth to wipe the sweat from Aoife's face.

I would that it was William. "Is Thomas waiting down the stairs?"

Lettie grunted assent. "Told him stay out 'less I call him."

Another pain, harder, and Aoife cried out again.

"It comes hard now, faster than it should. Let me see." Lettie pushed the quilt down from Aoife's belly, letting it fall careless to the floor.

The next contractions were titanic waves breaking against Aoife's insides. A gush of fluid flowed from her sex, drenching her thighs. She raised herself up again with the pain and saw the bed linens bloomed with blood. "Lettie!"

The girl jumped, knocking into the chair, sending it crashing to the floor. "No!" she screamed. "It cannot be!" She pulled the pillow from behind Aoife's back and pried her legs apart. "It is coming too fast!"

Aoife could smell her own blood, hot and metallic, like that from the pig at slaughter. The room swirled, spots sparkling like fireflies in her head. Another spurt flowed from her, hot against her cold skin. She pressed her knees together, as if that might stop the bleeding.

Her vision blurred and blackened. *Mam, mam! Where are you?* Had she thought that or cried it out? *Is this God's punishment?*

She could not stand Lettie's touch. She fought her off, crying, "Leave me be!" She pulled at Lettie's wrists as her legs were pried apart, her strength now desperate as that of an animal caught in a trap.

Lettie flung the window open and screamed out, "Thomas! Hurry!"

It seemed an eternity, filled with pain and dizziness, seeing Lettie's wide frightened eyes boring into hers. *Why is she fearful? It is I who am dying, unshriven.*

"A priest," she begged.

Thomas ran into the room. "My God, Lettie, I'll fetch the doctor!"

No, a priest!

"'Tis too late, Thomas!" Lettie grabbed his sleeve.

Her pains crescendoed, hitting like a storm at sea, putting aside all thoughts of eternal damnation.

Thomas bent over her face, his mouth moving to speak. But she no longer wanted him. "Mam! Mam! Where are you?"

Thomas's shirt billowed against her cheek.

Consciousness slipping away, she closed her eyes and dreamed of the past, of the croft. She was cold and growing colder.

"No, stay where you be! Hold her knees up and apart."

She felt his hot hands slipping on her flesh.

Thomas's voice, "I can't!"

"You can and must! The babe must live." And Lettie was on the bed, between her legs.

Aoife opened her eyes. Thomas's face was disordered, his mouth opened, as in a silent scream. And then everything was black.

Thomas
1864

With his eyes fixed on her face, he wrenched Aoife's leg apart hard, fearing she might rip in two. Their child, conceived in the violence of lust and joy, was being born in the violence of desperation.

Though her face was still, pale as the moonlight, her belly continued its monumental contracting.

Lettie reached between Thomas's hands, reached into Aoife. His stomach churned. It seemed like an act of revenge, of mutilation.

"I seen many born, but this is too, too fast," she muttered. "Too fast and too much blood."

His heart pounded, roared like a storm raging about his head. *Aoife will die and it will be my fault. Could it be that the hard birth of that bull calf somehow infected us and our babe's conception?*

He threw his head back and looked upward and prayed for the first time since he'd hid behind his mother during the riots. *Lord, this sinner beseeches you. Let them live. If, in your great goodness, you let her and the child live, I will serve you all the rest of my days.*

"Thomas, your knife!" Lettie was screaming. "The babe strangles!"

He released Aoife's now unresisting limbs and pulled his knife from his belt. In Lettie's hands was a gray round bloody thing, grotesque, hanging half outside Aoife's sex. With a gasp, he realized it was the baby's head. Beside it, the limp little arms dangled down. The bluish cord went from Aoife's body and twice around the tiny neck. Lettie slipped a loop from the baby's head. Thomas stretched to thrust the knife blade through it, jerking his arm upward to free the child. She pulled the rest of the body into the world. "'Tis a boy!"

She held the child up, shaking him and then hitting his back with her palm. "Cry, cry." she muttered between clenched teeth. But the little boy was still and flaccid. And yet perfectly formed…

The tiny body seemed a thing of contagion, heralding a fall from grace, inhuman. Thomas turned his head away to look at Aoife's still and colorless face. "He is dead, but Aoife, save Aoife," Thomas cried. "She still bleeds."

Lettie put the child on the chair and returned to the bed. She wrapped the cut cord around her hand and pulled steadily and firmly, kneading Aoife's low belly as if it held a ball of dough, pressing hard with her knuckles. She pulled on and on, with constant tension, then reaching inside as if clawing out contagion. At last, the gray-pink afterbirth was delivered.

Thomas vomited on the floor, desperate with the desire to flee. He wanted to hug Aoife and make her safe. He wanted Lettie to love him without blame.

The bleeding continued.

"Thomas!" Lettie's voice was harsh. "Bring more water from the well and more clean sheets. Quickly!"

Chapter 34

EVENING FELL, THE WANING LIGHT still imbued with an eldritch clarity, making the house like an island, unmoored in time, the past and present blending into one.

They sat in the quiet living room as the shadows moved across the flowered rug. Iris—with her foot still up and ankle now encased in Seapoint Farms frozen peas—Benny, and Charlotte sipped herbal tea and ate lemon muffins.

"We got a lot done, Iris, cutting off the branches. I called the arborist for the trunk—the guy we had take down the yews by the house."

"Such a shame about that grand old oak." Charlotte turned, gazing out the window at the tops of the still standing trees. "I didn't realize this area was so lush. Really beautiful."

She's surprised by Pennsylvania? Was Jessica Hartnup right?

"Thanks for being here, Charlotte," Benny said. "You've become very important to Iris."

Charlotte nodded and looked from Benny to Iris. She tapped one finger against her lips, over and over, before saying, "Iris is super important to me. You, too, after today—I didn't know you before."

He inclined his head. "The fault is all mine."

"I felt you didn't trust me. Yet today you were so nice."

"What makes you think I didn't trust you?" Benny was wide-eyed, almost dewy. *Like that cartoon cat, Garfield, when he's playing innocent or wants a treat.*

Charlotte's eyes were fixed on Benny.

"I knew you were Team Cozy Mystery. But after today, I know you were like that—to protect Iris. I wish my dad cared that much about my mom." She turned to Iris and began laughing. "No joke, Iris. Everything we talked about became about you. Like how beautiful you're making the dump you bought sight unseen."

Benny turned bright red.

"Why are you embarrassed, Ben? It *was* a dump." Iris felt a surge of love warm her heart. She leaned to stroke the unruly gray curls at his neck though moving made her ankle sting like it had entrapped a wasp. "That only makes me love you more." She smiled at Charlotte and winked.

"I want to tell you all about me. I am in a doctoral program, but in Michigan, where I grew up. Combined history and anthropology. I'm here..."

"For a paper." Iris broke in.

"Not really."

"Why then?"

Charlotte sighed. "You've made me feel so accepted, more than anyone has in my life, except my mom. You guys are like family to me, more than my own family. I owe it to you to be honest."

Benny cocked his head as if he was going to say something, and Iris worried. She relaxed as his features settled back into listening mode.

"When I saw Little Jack's picture... I felt a connection, like we're related somehow. He was like a magnet pulling me here. Hard to explain but, whatever the reason, he wasn't wanted. That's the way I felt my whole life. An outsider."

The lace gown and cap... he was wanted, just like our baby was! She thought to challenge the statement aloud, but looked at Benny's sympathetic expression... *It would be kinder to take a soft approach.* "Any family would be proud of you."

"Huh." Charlotte's fingers danced nervously about the rim of her cup, like flies afraid to stick a landing.

A familiar tide of loneliness, of feelings sequestered when thoughts of her daughter arose, swept over Iris.

Benny seemed to sense *something*. He slid closer to her and took her hand, but he spoke to Charlotte. "If our girl had lived, I'd want her to be like you. Smart, educated. Still having time for us old folks."

There was an uncomfortable quiet, broken only by the sound of Freddy licking his privates. Abnormally loud in the silence, it made Iris want to break into nervous laughter.

Charlotte rubbed her temples with her fingertips, quieting them at last. "My father didn't want anything to do with us. No support, no visits—I remember asking my mom about why and she said that his people didn't like him taking up with a white woman. He died when I was six, had a big family who would only let me visit if Mom didn't come. She had a big family, too. Her family hated that she'd gotten *knocked up* by a black guy." Charlotte snorted derisively. "That's what they said, *knocked up*. And I was in the middle, some ashamed of me because I was a shade too dark, the others resenting me because I was a shade too light…" Her voice trailed off.

Little Jack's image, fresh released from the bag in which he'd been hidden, floated into Iris's mind. The little odd man out, the curiosity.

"Anyway, so my father's family came from around here a long time ago. They once owned a farm. But no one living knows how much land or exactly where. All they knew was, farm life was too hard and too isolating. Land was sold off bit by bit over the years until nothing was left. The family scattered. My father's great-grandparent went to Detroit to earn real money in the factories and my mother's family was already there. Norwegian farmers."

"And the rest is history," Benny said, and then, as if he was afraid of Iris's reaction, "Didn't mean to sound flippant."

"Why didn't you just come tell us this?"

"With all the publicity, all the trauma tourists and other gawkers, how could I come and say, 'I want to snoop around your place to see if it once might have belonged to my family, might once have been mine?'"

"Yeah," Iris said, turning her eyes to Benny. "Then *certain people* would have been really suspicious."

Benny narrowed his eyes. "Give it a rest. I'm not that big a jerk. And it's not as if Little Jack lived long enough to be anybody's ancestor."

Thomas
1864

The water sloshed on the pie steps as Thomas rushed back with the bucket. He slipped, bloodying one shin, the pain sharp. Upstairs, the doors to both rooms were shut. He opened Aoife's and found her lying still, pale and alone, her arms by her sides. He sat on the bed next to her, twisting his hands together with such force that his fingers cracked over and over, the only sound in the room.

"She ain't dead yet, husband." Lettie had come in quietly. She took the small hand mirror from the dresser and held it to Aoife's lips. "See? The reflection fogs." She dropped the mirror on the bed beside him and went to the door. "The bleeding is done. I'll leave you with her one last time and go wash the boy's body."

Thomas lay beside Aoife, holding the mirror just above her mouth, to see the in and out of her breath. *I do not care what Lettie thinks, only that you live, Aoife. If you do not, I shall be alone.*

While she remained still and cold, seemingly sinking into death, he held the looking glass. It seemed an eternity, but

302

slowly the cloud on the glass expanded, and grew to fill the frame. Without opening her eyes, Aoife whispered, "William…"

Thomas's arm and hand burned as he put down the mirror after holding it aloft so long. He took her face in his hand, palm over the high cheekbone, thumb caressing over and over the arch of the bone. Her eyes opened and she smiled at him. "My lovely friend." She lifted her head and looked about the room. "The child?"

Lettie glided back in, her long apron stained with blood. She carried the infant's body. "Your babe died before ever he took a breath. Hold your son." At that, she put the body in Aoife's arms.

The tiny body was dressed in the gown and bonnet adorned by Aoife's lace. Aoife touched the cold little cheek as Thomas had touched hers. "My poor little darling." Then her eyes closed, and she slumped, insensate once more.

Thomas went to go to her, but Lettie stopped him. "She will live if no infection come. Look at your boy whilst you still can."

Thomas obeyed. The baby's face was the perfect blend of features, his and Aoife's. Tears welled up in Thomas's eyes and ran hot and silent down his cheeks.

Oh, for what might have been.

Aoife

1864

Aoife walks with William beneath the blooming apple tree, turning to kiss him as he brushes the fallen blossoms from her long, wild blonde hair. The air grows cold and footsteps, resounding on wooden boards, ring in her ears. The spring air is now sick-room stale with the iron smell of blood, the sky darkening into winter.

One single wail, that of a new infant, had pierced the fog that surrounded her. She was sure of it. And someone had lain next to her. Bewildered, her mind still clouded, Aoife sank in and out of consciousness but did not dream again.

Full awareness came, only to bring bitter reminder that her little boy was dead—and the realization of Lettie demanding he be held against Aoife's bosom, clothed in the lace she'd tatted.

"Poor wee mite, never to know the world." She stroked his belly, admired the perfection of his fingers. "Like little rays of light from stars," she crooned. "They will serve you well, sitting at the Heavenly banquet." Certainly, he, an innocent, would join the martyrs at the table, at the Lord's right hand. Had she and Thomas martyred him with their fornication?

Thomas had been reflected in her baby's countenance. She grieved to remember how she'd once dreamed of such a moment, holding a son who reflected William.

But she was sure a cry had come, strong and piercing, no dream hallucination. It had been like the call of a cat in the night, a newborn's wail. At the sound her breasts swelled with an aching pressure. She looked about, desperate.

Lettie read her face. "The child you heard cry is not yours."

Thomas stood. "What do you mean?"

"The one that was yours and hers is dressed in the gown she made. Mine is naked as she came into the world."

A wail again reverberated through the door of the nursery room.

"I knew the Lord had a plan, knew he would put things to right, though her belly grew too big and the morning sickness did last too long. Reached up inside her, felt the second sac, but it seemed too much blood, I thought both were doomed. Should've had faith He would guide my hands to save our child, Thomas." Lettie's eyes gleamed. "We have a babe at last!"

Aoife's hands fluttered uselessly as Lettie unbuttoned the neck of her gown. The cloth was pulled aside and her swollen, blue-veined breast, newly weeping milk, was exposed.

Thomas moved to stop Lettie taking the little body from Aoife's arms but was held in check by her words. "This your doing, husband. You ain't got no right to stop me," she said as she went out the door, carrying the dead boy. She returned with a squirming baby, swaddled in a kitchen cloth. "You'll nurse her, Aoife, but she'll sleep with me."

The living child was a girl, tiny but furiously living. Put to the breast she sucked ravenously.

The babe was smaller, but as perfect as the other, and more alive than any creature Aoife had ever known. Her hair was reddish brown, a mass of still-damp curls, tight against her well-formed skull. Aoife stroked them, feeling the tender soft spot in the center. She clutched the little bundle tight enough for the infant to cease sucking for a moment and squeal indignantly.

"She is not yours, Lettie, and shall not sleep with you!" Aoife pulled the coverlet up to hide her breast and the child's face, as if she concealed a secret.

Her face as fixed as a carven image, Lettie leaned over Aoife, again exposing the nursing to sight. "She was made shamefully, in a cow's byre, by an adulteress and an adulterer. Would you have her know that?"

Aoife put up a hand to ward Lettie away.

But Lettie wasn't to be put off. "Thomas, he put babe after babe into me, all in our marriage bed, and all were lost. I have longed for a child to love. I won't lose her." She straightened her back, cocked her head from one side to the other as if examining the child for the first time. "Just like your dead boy, she's got Thomas's face and color. You wish to blight her life? Everyone will know whose daughter she is and when she was conceived." Lettie's fists balled up digging deep in the sides of her waist, and her features were contorted in anger. "And they will say that, while William Sprigett suffered, while he lay dying, that wife of his was in the barn, like an animal, with the colored field hand. But let her be mine and she'll have a father, a family. I'm of a shade for her to be mine. She'll have a place in the world, a colored missy with a colored mama."

Chapter 35

BENNY BROUGHT UP A BOTTLE of chardonnay and got wine glasses out. "Good thing about our cellar. Keeps the wine the proper temperature for drinking right away." He stroked Iris's foot gingerly. "How about you knock a bunch back? Will help you sleep despite your ankle."

Iris grimaced. "It'll be hard enough getting to the bathroom at night."

"Just wake me up and I'll help you."

"If I get too drunk, I'll never make it, even with your help."

Charlotte was grinning, looking from Iris to Benny as he got up and jingled his key ring, the car fob clunking against the keys. Somehow, the young woman knew he was about to say something jokey, and it might be pretty good.

"Where are you going?" Iris asked.

"To buy your favorite prosecco. Two bottles. We're going to get you drunk. Oh, and I'll stop in at the drugstore for some adult diapers."

Iris gasped in mock anger, grabbed one of the small decorative pillows, and threw it at him. She struck him in the crotch and turned to Charlotte and said, "I always did have dead-on aim. He's lucky it wasn't this friggin' defrosted bag of produce. Those raw peas are like BBs."

Charlotte laughed and Benny did, too. He sauntered out the door, waggling his hips.

"It is so nice to see the easy way you two get along..."

"For an old married couple, you mean?"

The young woman blushed.

Just what she was thinking! But Iris didn't want to embarrass her more than she had. "By any chance, is your family name Sprigett?"

Charlotte shook her head. "Nope. A lot of Jacksons and Grants and other presidential names, but no Sprigetts."

Iris thought for a moment, an idea buzzing around in her head. "Charlotte, do you think there's any way to find anything more about Little Jack? Why he was in the pond?"

"Not unless we get lucky and find letters or a journal. I think you said something about that always happening in fiction..."

"And this is real."

"If his birth and death were secrets, there'll be no announcements or registrations or christening."

The buzzing in Iris's mind grew more insistent. *From the pain?* "Or maybe it's the wine," she said aloud.

"What?" Charlotte looked startled. "Or what's the wine?"

"It's that I just realized, if there's any chance of finding a connection between you and him... We do have that DNA report."

Charlotte blushed. "I was hoping and hoping you'd suggest that. I was afraid to ask—it could have caused trouble between you and Benny or made you both mad at me." She flushed even more deeply. Her freckles stood out, darker red than her blush. "I sent off for my own report—that was routine—and a comparison with his, printed out from my phone. The comparison is a bigger deal and takes a lot more time. But it should be back soon." She stood and came to where Iris reclined, crouched down to be at her eye level. "But don't worry. No matter what it says, it was all a long time ago."

Iris looked into her eyes and saw something that made her smile at the determination and sly audacity. *You're fibbing again, Charlotte. You've already gotten the results.*

Aoife

1864

As tiny as she was, the girl, named Sary by Lettie, fought furiously to live. Her fists beat against Aoife's heart as her eager mouth nursed at the stiff pink nipple and emptied the milk-swollen breast.

Her brother lay in a pine box that Thomas hastily crafted, even as his sister slept in the cradle he'd made at William's request. An unanticipated symmetry.

Lettie stayed in the small bedroom with Sary, sleeping on the floor next to the cradle, attentive to the baby's every murmur. She brought her to Aoife when she woke, bawling like a calf. If suckling didn't calm Sary, Lettie walked up and down the hall, floorboards creaking beneath her feet, singing softly lullabies strange to Aoife.

Three days after the birth, bringing Aoife a supper of pig liver and bacon with cooked greens, Lettie stood waiting, her hands folded over her apron. "Eat while Sary sleeps," she said, her voice soft. "The old ladies say liver builds the blood. Without blood there will be no milk. Then we all will talk."

Pushing with a hand either side of her hips, Aoife struggled upright. Weak, she had yet to leave her room but was ravenous. Her bones and sinews were demanding their due. The two babes inside her womb had drained the flesh from her, and she still needed to nourish one.

She finished the dish of pale pink-gray liver and soft bacon. Lettie took the tray downstairs and returned with Thomas. Without saying a word, she pointed to the little pine coffin.

"The rains have made the ground too wet for burial. Holes fill with water." Thomas said, avoiding Aoife's eyes. "He deserves a proper grave but can stay in the springhouse for the while, until I can dig one."

Lettie shook her head. "You'll not bury here, at Sary's home. I won't allow a grave to stir the curiosity of the idle who happen by."

"We can leave it unmarked." Thomas's voice was filled with yearning.

Drawing herself up, Lettie seemed the largest presence in the room. "The spot would need no cross above it. Would be marked in your mind. I won't look cross the yard and see a damned shrine."

Aoife turned to her in distress. "But he is in limbo, alone, poor dead thing. Do me this good, let him be buried up the hill where I can visit him, as I visited William!"

Lettie seemed lit by fire. "That affronts Mr. William. Too well you know this boy's no Sprigett." She turned to Thomas. "For the sake of our daughter, you will burn the body in this pine box. If you do not, I'll tell the churchwomen you have beaten me. I'll take the girl from here." To Aoife she said, "You won't never see her again, lest you shame her with knowledge of her birth."

In the other room, the baby woke and cried. Lettie went to her.

"Thomas, you won't do such a thing, will you? Burnt and scattered…. He would never be resurrected!" She rose to her knees and tugged on his shirttails, beseeching, "Have you any affection left for me, your friend, for our poor dead babe, you will do no such thing."

He tilted his head and whispered, "Never. I'll find a place by the road far enough away."

But I must have him near, where I can visit. She bit her lip, drawing blood, the pain to keep her tears silent.

Lettie brought the little girl into the room. "Poor darling was wet and hungry." Giving the babe to Aoife, she pushed Thomas into the hall. "Go. Ain't seemly for you to remain. Not no more." Their footsteps clattered down the stairs, Lettie's muttering loud and full of rage.

Aoife put the child to her breast. For the first time, the nursing brought a strange sensation to her lower belly and her sex. She blushed at the pleasure she felt, accompanied by a delicious drawing in her breast.

Little Sary made small murmuring sounds and smacked her tiny rosebud lips after each gulp. Aoife felt a surge of love looking down at the child's face, unlike the simple possession she'd felt before. With that love came the sure realization that no sacrifice was too great. "I swear to do nothing to ever bring you shame. Nor to come between your father and his wife."

I cannot, nor ever will, call Lettie your mother. But I shall not protest when you do, child.

That night, after Sary had been nursed and taken away, Aoife slipped from her bed and went to the cupboard. From a velvet bag, she took the silk dress and slippers William had bought her for their marriage, along with the crown of flowers, now sere and dead. The sight of them on the bed made her cry anew, remembering the joy she'd had in her heart that day. But she was resolute.

Looking down from her bedroom window, her view of the pond was clear.

Aoife took the tiny body from the coffin and, with her mam's rosary laid over his heart, put him inside the bag. So no one lifting the coffin would be the wiser, she replaced the child's weight with her wedding garb and carried the velvet bag down the stairs, barefoot, to keep the stairs from resounding with her steps. All the while, her heart beat loudly with fear she'd be discovered.

Lettie sleeps lightly in the nursery with the baby girl, ever attentive to any whimper, no matter how soft.

The ground was icy and slick from the freezing rain, numbing her skin while leaving a deep ache in her bones. She lurched through the deep, frozen ruts made by hoof prints and cartwheels. Came to the pond, seated herself on the stone wall. "The pond is deep and still, untroubled and peaceful. But how shall I keep you from rising, my little man?"

By the wall lay an old iron, cast off years before, that she tied to the bag with a length of rope. "It may rot, but by then you will be bones and I will be in my grave, unshriven but repentant. Until then, I shall ever keep watch over you." As the bag sank beneath the half-frozen water, she prayed to join him in purgatory. Perhaps William, though not in the true Church, would be made saintly by his final suffering, and be there too. The thought that there was no salvation outside the faith gave her comfort for the first time as she made her way to the kitchen to wash her feet and then upstairs to bed.

Thomas

1864

"Hammer the box shut in the kitchen, Thomas," Aoife said when he came to collect his son's body. "I could not bear to have you trip on the frost and spill him or think his little body will fall out into the flames. The poor babe deserves dignity in death."

Lettie was in the other room with little Sary, napping. Thomas was safe from her hearing as he knelt by the bed and whispered, "What shall we name him?"

Aoife shook her head. "To name him is a way to speak about him, to keep him alive. But Lettie is right. Any shred of his existence will only blight his sister's life. Heaven or no, he is in the Lord's hands and shall remain nameless until I see him again."

Until we see him again. Grief and loss hammered at Thomas's heart. He regretted his lack of faith though knew he could never find comfort in religion. Preacher Matthews was a fine and good man and would surely have wise words, but the close-knit community of strong and clever women might find reason to question Thomas's sudden visit to the church office.

"Swear you will shut him up tight, not expose his poor little corpse to view."

"I swear, Aoife." He gathered up the box, shuddering inwardly as the contents shifted in his arms. "Best I go now, while Lettie sleeps. I would not have her see my sorrow."

He went down the stairs, worried, as his hammer and nails were in the barn. Sary's cry followed by stirring in the room above the kitchen changed his plans. He would close the coffin tight, but not in the house. Treading carefully to the barn, he worried with each step that breaking even that part of his promise to Aoife would hex his way. Their little son might fall out into a manure-stained puddle.

He reached the barn's workroom safely and put the box on the table where he repaired Maisy's harness. The hammer proved a familiar and comforting weight in his hand. He took a nail and positioned it, only to put it down again. He was overwhelmed with the need to see the baby's face one more time.

Lifting the lid revealed a pair of silk slippers, a gauzy gown, and dried flowers woven together. His son was not inside. Sometime in the night, while Aoife was alone with the coffin, the little body had been removed. Somehow, she'd found the strength to hide her child's body.

Thomas looked toward the house, toward the bedroom window. All was still. He vowed it would remain so, though a voice in his head whispered, *Aoife, what have you done? Whatever it is, Lettie must not find out.* He shook his thoughts off and, pushing a nail point into the soft yellow wood, raised the hammer and began.

A short while later, he laid a bonfire in the yard, far from the house and barn, too far for Lettie to want to go in the chill with little Sary. He took a chair from the barn and set it close so that Aoife could watch safely yet still stay warm. Setting the little coffin top the firewood, he returned to the house.

Lettie was at the kitchen table, eating. "Sit, husband."

"What is it, Lettie? What do you want?"

"Come spring, add another room behind the house. A proper room, not a lean-to. With a window and another stove to keep it warm."

He sighed and sat, took a dried apple slice from the bowl and chewed on it. "Are you not comfortable in the room, sharing with the baby?"

"I am and will be 'til she is taken from the teat. But once weaned, you and me will be a family, living together, her mama and papa. A proper family should have a proper home. Room for a child to play on the floor, come winter."

He fixed her with a steady, level gaze. "Don't you wish a cabin of our own, on the land I was promised?"

Her head came up proudly. "That child will be done proud, taken care of here, by me and you, on this farm, not on no little scrap of land."

"What about..." He stopped before he might say *her mother.*

Lettie raised her chin quickly. "I been upstairs while you were in the barn. She was on her knees to *me*, crying like her heart was broke. She vowed to do all I say she must, all I want.

Lay no claim to Sary." She slammed her knife on the plate and bit off each word with her teeth. "So we stay. You do what you must, too. Go burn that boy, like he never was."

Thomas stood. "I'm helping her down to watch the pyre."

Lettie scanned his face for a moment and nodded. "I be watching from the door, should Sary wake."

And to be sure no one will rake the ashes for bones.

Chapter 36

"**THERE WERE STORIES** in my father's family," Charlotte said, perched on the edge of her seat. "Nothing definite, just tales told at gatherings. Mostly concerning some of the family acting strange or even totally insane. Maybe winding up in mental hospitals, or in prison…"

"Prison?" Iris felt herself draw back. With the movement, she realized how full her bladder was. Would she have to ask Charlotte to help her walk to the toilet? Where was Benny when she needed him?

"… for doing crazy shit." Charlotte smiled. "Don't worry, not me. Seems to affect only the men, though they say it started with a woman."

"Yoo-hoo! I'm home!" At last, Benny had returned with the wine. "I'll get the glasses."

"Ben." Iris shifted to greet him. "Help me to the bathroom first."

He put the shopping bag on the floor and eased her from the sofa. On the way to the powder room, Iris said, "We've been waiting for you. Charlotte has something to tell us, then she has something to show." Letting him think they'd held off until he returned would help soften any reservations of his when he saw the DNA report.

Once she was back, her ankle elevated again, Iris told Charlotte to begin.

"My family told stories every time they got together, especially at barbecues on warm Midwest summer evenings when getting sloshed on beer was most appealing, and everyone was lolling about in deck chairs, barefoot, laughing. Bellies hanging out—'cause after all, it was dark, and no strangers would be there. Everybody having a wonderful time, reminiscing about the past and their own aunties and uncles and grandparents."

Benny uncorked a bottle with a loud pop. "Sorry. Should have bought screw tops. Quieter." He poured them each a glass.

"Go on, Charlotte," Iris said quickly, a bit afraid he'd continue explaining the benefits of bottle closures.

The young woman took a sip. "I used to sit under the picnic table when I was little, playing with my cousin Jameel, and listening in. That's when I first heard of an estate back East, lost now, sold off when the family got tired of the hard work and poverty of farming and yearned for city lights, factory work with days off, diners, cinemas, and dance clubs... You know, what passed for a better, or at least an exciting, life. Still, there always seemed to be something in the air..." Charlotte looked up as if the poetry of her words embarrassed her. "A kind of collective memory of country quiet, the joy of growing things and caring for animals, owning everything you can see. Being independent, standing on your own two feet. That whole mix of old ways and new, of choices and regret, gave me my love of history and started me on my journey here."

"You said it started with a woman? The, as you put it, crazy shit?" Iris said.

"The woman would have been my five- or six-time great-grandmother, but that's mostly my guess."

"Was she maybe Little Jack's mother? Were there stories of her doing something to a baby? Putting a body in a pond?"

"Nothing like that but just vague stories, and no proof of anything hinted at."

"There is now, right, Charlotte?" Iris knew the answer. "What does the report show?"

"The report?" Benny said, his tone suggesting he suspected something had been kept secret.

"The DNA report that proves Little Jack is related to Charlotte."

Aoife

1865

She was besotted with the living child, the little sprite, Sary, who seeped into every thought, from early dawn before Aoife rose, to the candlelit nights. The delicate fingers pale as sweet alfalfa honey. Fingers she longed to kiss. The little feet, bottoms not yet soiled by walking. They were still as tender pink as the inside of the conch shell that had sat atop Mother Sprigett's mantle. Like the shell, Sary was something rare and exotic and out of reach, though tantalizingly close.

Her daughter glittered always at the edges of her mind, a tiny burning flame of what might have been.

"Here, go be comforted," Aoife said as she finished nursing and, careful of cooing and petting the babe, handed her to Lettie. Though it broke her heart, she turned away when Sary reached out for her, not wanting to leave the warm and generous breast.

Lettie often watched the suckling jealously, a scowl like a storm cloud on her face. But she bit her tongue.

"Thomas, what more can I do to ease things?" Aoife asked when they met in the barn in the midst of chores.

"Give her time." Thomas was bent over, cleaning the dung-bedecked straw from Maisy's stall. He paused and straightened with a groan, one hand against his back. He seemed to have aged a decade. "She is happy again, believe it or not, though she hates to show it. 'Tis the longest she's been calm, since before her losses. She is a mother at last."

"A mother at last." Aoife knew the echoed words were bitter seeds spat from between her lips.

Thomas sighed and leaned his weight on the shovel's handle. "We know what we know, though no one else shall. And the child remains here for you to watch grow."

And you still here, to be known as her father. Aoife sighed. But it would do no good to resent him. She abandoned her work and went to the pond's stone wall. "Boy," she whispered, "at least you I have to myself, if only in memory."

Over the next days, she brought her needlework to the pond and stitched in the shade of a redbud. All the while, she conversed with the dead, bringing him news of his twin. Keeping him alive. "Your sister grows apace and is now twice the size when you were with her. Greedy little boy, inside me, you took the lion's share…"

A ripple crossed the surface of the water. An errant breeze. *Oh, 'twas quite like the laughter of a child.* It filled her with a burst of delight as if the sun rose in her bosom. "You little rascal!" she exclaimed.

The breeze grew chilly.

Talking to a phantom. I grow as near daft as Lettie. That would only be harmful to Sary. At that, she gathered her skirts and went to the barn where Thomas sat oiling the harness.

Aoife leaned against one of the stall's posts. She spoke with careful laziness, stirring the dust with the toe of one boot. "Had the boy lived, sure, and we'd call him Thomas."

His hands stopped moving.

"After his father."

"Aoife, you cannot." Thomas wiped his hands on his trousers and stood to place his hands on her shoulders. He looked into her face. His eyes were wet, but no tears came to track down his dusty face. "I feel it, too, Aoife. It stabs in my heart like a knife. I never will now have a son. But we're not the first to lose a child."

She made her gaze hard, looking into his eyes. "The difference betwixt you and I, Thomas, is you still have one." With no further word, she left for the house. Her breasts were beginning to leak. It was time to nurse again.

I will call him Sean after my granda. For God is gracious. He will be mine alone.

Up the stairs, the little girl sat in the crib Thomas had made her once she'd outgrown the cradle. She reached toward Aoife, who turned away, her heart aching, as Lettie rushed to be the one bringing the child to nurse.

The months passed and things eased. Sary crawled and then walked, unsteadily at first, holding on the edge of chairs when in Aoife's kitchen, and then with increasing boldness. She ran to Lettie when she was hungry or had fallen, calling "Mammy, Mammy," but mostly was uncannily solitary. She played on the kitchen floor, banging wooden spoons on tin plates while Lettie cooked or cleaned. At night she slept in the room Thomas had added on the lean-to.

"Our child is happy." Thomas smiled at Lettie, who was at table, busy spooning porridge into Sary's mouth. The little girl was babbling her own private speech to no one in particular.

Smiling, Lettie reached out and took Aoife's hand. "Our child, though none may know it. Thank you. You ended my loss."

From that moment on, an unspoken agreement had been reached. Lettie and Aoife shared chores, hung the wash together, tended the kitchen garden, each keeping watch on Sary. Aoife had no private time to sew by the pond, though she glanced at it often.

Little by little, the four of them became an object of great curiosity and discussion in the community.

Thomas

1869

"Thomas!" Pastor Matthews cried, "It pleases me so to see you. It has been quite a while." The stubby, round-faced man walked along the roadside. Nan and Mamie, the two churchwomen who had helped Thomas take the raving Lettie from the town, were with him. "What are you carrying?"

Thomas pulled Maisy up short and the wagon clattered to a stop. He tipped his hat. "Reverend. Ladies. Just taking some vegetables to market."

Mamie, her broad forehead beaded with sweat from the warm sun, peered into the baskets. "Brother Thomas, I see some mighty fine greens."

Nan joined her. "Nice corn and beans, too. Could go to make a succotash."

"Do you wish to buy some, ladies?" Thomas asked.

Mamie didn't answer his question directly. "Nan and me on our way to Mrs. Johnson. She been real poorly lately, what with her husband's passing and having five children. Everyone in the church been chipping in."

Thomas could see where this was going. He nodded. "I have enough to spare. Take what she needs."

"Sure is a hot day," Matthews said. "I'm going to the church. Long way to walk in this heat."

Thomas sighed. "Climb on up. I'll carry you all."

Pastor Matthews helped the women onto the wagon bed and hoisted himself to the seat beside Thomas. Matthews pulled a starched white cloth from his pocket and wiped his face. "I see you have water. If I might wet my throat...."

Thomas held out his bottle, and the pastor drank deeply, handing it back.

"Thomas, we all have been so pleased with your actions of late. Are we not, ladies?" Matthews turned on the creaking wooden seat to check with the women behind him. They let out a chorus of uh-huhs, nodding vigorously. When he turned to face front again, the reverend said, "Since you and Lettie had your beautiful little girl, the dangerous gossip has ceased. We could all breathe easier, no fear of any mob."

Thomas didn't need to ask what gossip he meant.

Managing to look both modest and sly, Matthews said, "Perhaps it is because I preached to them Proverbs 20:19."

Thomas took a long swallow from his water bottle and clicked his tongue at the horse. "He who goeth about as a slanderer reveals secrets, therefore do not associate with a gossip." Matthews again took the bottle and swirled the contents, a little smile of self-satisfaction on his lips. "And Proverbs 16:28, 'A willful man soweth strife, and a whisperer separates chief friends.'"

Much as he liked the pastor, Thomas could hold his tongue no longer. "Did you forget 17:28? 'Even a fool, when he holdeth his peace, is counted wise...'"

Matthews chuckled. "And even the Devil can cite scripture."

Thomas couldn't help but laugh. *Pastor Matthews is too fond of himself to be easily offended.*

"No one faults your behavior now, Thomas," Nan said, poking him in the back. "Our community has found in you a model for our young colored men."

"Hardworking and loyal. Real Christian," Mamie added.

Maisy, flicked on her rump with the reins, picked up her gait for a moment and then settled back down in an ambling walk.

Matthews reached down and pulled a long stem of grass. "And a most excellent employee—dare I say, friend—to the widow of Captain Sprigett, a hero who fought for our cause? And you stuck by your wife and made her whole again." He leaned against the seat's wooden back and put the stem in his white teeth. It waggled as he continued speaking. "Though I admit to being disappointed..." He spat out the grass before continuing. "When an educated colored fellow could have had a position of honor, teaching in the new land-grant universities..."

Thomas had not thought of his lost opportunities for a long while. The chance to be a man of importance, buoyed by the education he'd received in Philadelphia. *No good will come of musing on that. It all is gone, flowing downstream like a river. But perhaps I learned so much more on the path taken.* "That would have afforded little time for family. I stayed a humble man because it was best for Lettie, calm surroundings, good wholesome food. And now, motherhood."

"Perhaps we'll see you and Lettie? All the ladies would like a chance to make much of the baby." Nan's voice was soft now.

"Lettie has said she has no desire to rejoin the church. Even she knows her black moods might return. In knowing herself, she is far better. Quiet suits her. Quiet and the little home we share."

"Courtesy of Mrs. Sprigett..." Matthews said.

Nan broke in again. "Please give the church's regard to the young Mrs. Sprigett. So unlike the old one who passed. The modest young woman, still in widow's weeds."

"Does she never wish to marry again?" Matthews's question surprised Thomas. It seemed to surprise the women, too, as Nan hastily said, "Reverend, that's not our business!"

The pastor didn't seem admonished. Plucking a crease in his trousers from under his buttocks, he settled more comfortably on the seat, and said, "She, like you, is also forgiven."

"Forgiven?" Thomas pulled forcibly on the reins, halting Maisy. The mare's head jerked up and she whinnied her confusion. "What on Earth has Aoife Sprigett done to be forgiven by the colored folk hereabouts?"

Matthews opened his mouth to speak. One of the women quickly reached forward and put her hand on his arm. The preacher's mouth snapped shut.

"No," Nan said, "we never condemned her!"

"We would not," Mamie spoke up. "She was a good and faithful wife who nursed her husband and saved his farm."

"And she took in Lettie," Nan added, "when even *we* wished to be shet of her, if honestly said."

Thomas tried to suppress it, but he burst out in laughter at her words. Lettie had, indeed, been a sore trial for the church's community. "I do remember she cursed at the Quaker elders."

Both women joined in his merriment, but the reverend seemed bewildered by it. "'Twas horrid!"

Nan wiped her eyes, giggled a few more times with her work-worn hands covering her lips, and said, "I walk 'bout the town daily, mostly I go unnoticed, and hear women talking. Even Quakers, though they are meant to be prohibited from gossip. Why, I even overheard the Sprigett sisters, those grand ladies, in the dry goods! They forgive that young Mrs. Sprigett for once being their mama's Irish servant and for stealing away their only brother and his land."

Thomas geed up Maisy, who had lapsed into grazing the weeds. The wagon creaked and groaned before lurching forward.

"The Quaker ladies particularly praise Mrs. Sprigett for her affection to your little Sary. Why, they say she is like a kind, even loving, auntie to the child."

"And your girl!" Mamie added. "It will gratify you to know what is said about that beautiful child, Thomas. They call her charming. Why her beautiful coloring…" They were coming to their destination, a clapboard house that sorely needed painting. Mamie hastened to finish her thoughts. "… lighter even than her mother's, and her hair, curly as Lettie's, with streaks of the most fetching reds and ambers, like the maples and oaks in fall."

Pastor Matthews could stay quiet no longer. He had never tolerated the strong-willed women in his church taking over a discussion. "Heard tell she takes after her mother's sister Sary. We never met her, of course."

The churchwomen nodded slowly. They knew the story of the murdered young woman.

"Shame we only seen the child once or twice over the year, next to you on this here wagon. We'd've loved to visit with her today… Or any Sunday in the church." The reverend had never been above nagging to increase his flock.

And Thomas wasn't above bragging. He had few enough opportunities to do so, as Lettie rarely let him take Sary off the farm. "Bright as a firefly in the night, reading when not yet five years of age." He wanted to discuss his little girl's odd behavior but couldn't bring himself to so as to expose her. Sary spent every free moment chattering away and gesturing as if another child was with her. He even suspected that she'd learned her letters just to read the prayer book to the imagined friend.

That she might be talking with the spirit of her twin had strayed across his mind, but he'd firmly put it aside. That was so much harder to believe than a simple made-up companion.

"Well, this here our stop," Mamie said, lifting her basket. "We thank you for the charity."

Matthews wasn't ready to give up the ghost. "You and Lettie bring the child, come Sunday. She will do our community proud."

Chapter 37

"**THE KITCHEN'S ALREADY SUCH** an amazing improvement!" Jessica Hartnup's mouth was opened in amazement like a carp's when pulled from a pond. Amazement that Iris hoped wasn't faked. "It was so dark and dingy with those disintegrating wood cabinets. So much better since I first saw this house. It's beautiful now…"

"The white cabinets really make this space light and clean," Jessica's wife, Katrina, said. "From the description Jess gave me, the difference is really something."

Benny opened a drawer and pushed it in just far enough for the soft close drawer slides to catch. Iris suppressed a giggle. The mechanical things, even the silliest little ones, meant more to him than the light sliding across the slate floor, highlighting all the subtle colors in the stone, or than the upper cabinet glass fronts displaying her art deco vase collection.

"I gotta show you the master suite we built over what was once a deck." He could scarcely contain his enthusiasm. "Remember the old bedroom? The tiny closet?"

"The one with the mouse carcasses along the baseboard?" Jessica laughed.

"Yup. It's now a big walk-in and a new bathroom. Come up and see it."

They trooped up the stairs, Benny talking the whole time. "Of course, you don't see the really important stuff I did…"

I? Iris controlled her desire to challenge his taking all the credit. She'd been the one cleaning up the plaster dust and the plumber's mucky footprints, while her husband had traded stories with the men setting up the mini splits for the HVAC. Benny was inordinately intrigued with the difficulty of getting them to the rooms outside the eighteen-inch-thick stone walls.

"… the most important stuff, like making sure the foundation was repaired. Three hundred years of water messes with mortar. Very important to me, the foundation for anything…"

They'd reached their new bedroom. Benny took Iris's hand as if he was leading her in for the first time. She had the weird feeling he might do something outrageous, dramatic, like sweep her off her feet and carry her in like a new bride. But all he did was say, "Yup, no matter what, you have to make sure the support structure's secure. Even if you have to constantly work on it. Anyway, look at the antique tiles Iris found!"

Ten minutes later they were back in the kitchen having coffee and sweets.

"I don't suppose we'll ever find out how the baby's body came to be in the pond," Jessica Hartnup said as she took another slice of lemon-glazed cake. "Pass the whipped cream, Kat. Without any editorializing."

Katerina grinned at Iris. "Her cholesterol's sky high but she just won't listen."

Benny passed the bowl of cream to Charlotte, who handed it to Jessica. "Don't worry, Jess. Iris says the same thing about me."

"Well, remember why I care about your cholesterol." Iris spooned freshly washed raspberries onto his plate, perfect little red jewels glistening with droplets of water. She looked at the others gathered around her table and smiled to herself. *Summer's sweetness.*

She'd decided it was nice to have Charlotte and the two women from New York visit. Have them sit at her antique oak table in the dining room, with orchids blooming on the deep windowsills. Her surrogate daughter and Benny's friends. It had been months since they'd trekked to the house.

Benny winked and put a hand on Iris's knee under the tablecloth. A stirring of desire tingled in her belly. Flustered, she turned to Jessica. "Okay, so what did you dig up about our house and Baby Jack? Benny says you did a lot of research. Still planning on a cozy?"

Jessica had the grace to look down, blushing. The color was unnatural on her face, heating up her city-pale skin.

"Direct, isn't she?" Katerina laughed. "Giving Jess a taste of her own medicine." She poured herself more coffee. "But yeah, if you and Ben agree, Jess thinks there's a book to be written... one she'd sure as shit like to write."

"Only with your permission," Jessica said. "And yours, Charlotte. You both play a big part in this story. But not a cozy. No, the scope of this story is far more than any genre tale...." She sighed. "To be honest, I'm a little scared when I think about writing it. I've always relied on doing what I know. Formulaic. I wonder if I'm up to the task... but I'd like the chance to try."

Iris just managed to suppress a gasp of surprise. *Jessica Hartnup, who bulled her way into my house to become my husband's buddy is intimidated about something? What the hell did she find out?*

"To tell you the truth, I've become obsessed with the story that was hidden in your pond. Little Jack's story. Charlotte's proven connection to this property, to him. From what I've found, it's a grand, sweeping American story of friendship and loyalty, about working together to build something worth saving..."

Iris's left eyebrow lifted skeptically. "About putting a baby's body in the pond to maybe save face?"

"See," Jessica said, "that just might be the hasty conclusion. Might be wrong, taking away the complex common humanity of the situation."

"Be fair, Jess!" Benny rose to Iris's defense. "Despite flinging around lofty—but vague—concepts, that's a totally logical conclusion."

Iris reached under the table and squeezed his leg in gratitude. A bit higher than he'd squeezed hers. His eyes widened in surprise.

"I think Benny's right." Charlotte pushed back a long curl of reddish-brown hair from her eyes.

With her freckles all darkened by the sun, she looks lovely, naturally so.

"Not only logical but typical," Charlotte went on. "For sure my family would jump to that conclusion. If it's wrong, I'd like to know why. Knowing what you found would mean a lot to me."

Jessica shifted back and forth in her seat as if her panties were riding up. "I spent the past months combing through old news accounts, school records and essays... There was a treasure trove of anecdotes from local church records. And journals from the period, oh, I just looked at anything and everything that might shed light on the situation and got lucky enough to find a good bit of material. I'm embarrassed to say that this became an obsession."

"I can vouch for that," Katrina said. "Night and day, barely spoke about anything else. Uninterested in food." She giggled in a surprisingly inelegant manner. "Why, she almost lost weight."

Kat's banter was familiar to Iris, relaxed and irreverent, making her so unlike the big-city creature she'd seemed at first. Likable. Jessica shot her partner a look that would have made Iris hold her tongue. But Katrina only rolled her eyes and said, "Sorry," drawing it out like a petulant teen.

Neither Iris nor Charlotte said anything for a long, awkward moment.

"So what's the story, Jessica?" Charlotte asked. "I'm dying to find out."

Jessica hesitated. "Before I start… Charlotte, you're an academic writer and I'm not. I tend to the stickily sentimental, the meet-cute situation. It would be great to have your perspective… even your collaboration. This needs to be a literary mystery, almost a nonfiction novel like Capote's *In Cold Blood*. I fear that's beyond my skill level and I'm not even sure how to frame it."

Wow, Jessica Hartnup eating humble pie! Or is she manipulating Charlotte? Benny and Iris exchanged glances and Iris sent him a mental message. *Don't say anything about Charlotte's made-up credentials, Ben. Hopefully Jessica doesn't want Charlotte just to have a black coauthor.*

Charlotte might have been mulling over the same things as she took a moment to answer. When she did, it was to say, "I'd love to be involved."

"So…" Jessica sat back in her seat. "I can't guarantee one hundred percent that what I've cobbled together is about this particular property. They sometimes played fast and loose with deeds and births in those days. People didn't go into the hospital to deliver and often didn't have time to register anything we now take for legal requirements. Graves were often unmarked…"

"Enough already," Benny said. "Get to it."

Iris shot him a glance and he added, "Please."

"Well, I really do think what I found relates to this piece of land. Along with other properties, it was bequeathed to a son of the Sprigetts, who as you know, were important landowners around the county, at least in the early 1800s. The young man was named William, like Penn's son. He was gravely wounded in the Civil War and died soon after coming home—there's firm documentation of that. He married but he and his wife were childless.

"The interesting and maybe most pertinent thing is that young Mr. Sprigett had a worker who saved the farm for him and his wife. Aside from William Sprigett's service in the Union army, not much was to be found about his wife or the worker and his family after Sprigett's death. The only thing of note was that the worker was African American, married to an escaped slave and they had a daughter. There were no official records of her birth, just copious anecdotal bits as, apparently, she was quite a character.

"When the little girl was born is uncertain, but she was named Sary. She must have been homeschooled and the stories written about her all had to do with odd behavior. We kind of have to take those stories with the proverbial grain of salt. It seems the local kids loved to spy on her, and they were the source of the rumors, though she may really have been seriously mentally disturbed.

"Instead of playing with the other kids, she chattered away to someone no one else could see, possibly an imaginary friend. At first, the local children were urged to include her, as their Christian duty, but that was unsuccessful. They wrote how she simply walked away like they weren't there, holding the hand of… nobody."

"Sounds like the local ghost story," Iris said. Benny kicked her shin to quiet her.

"Over time, it was decided the girl was crazy and it was feared she'd become violent. Told to stay away, the kids, being kids, were more determined to follow Sary and find out what made her act so strangely.

"Come summer, the other children spied on her at the farm. And here's the creepy part. Every day, Sary took her food and a book immediately to the pond behind the house, sat on the low stone wall, reading aloud or chattering away, frequently looking into the murky water as if a water sprite lay beneath the duckweed.

"The children never investigated the pond itself. Several describe a bullfrog living in the pond. You know how creepy they can sound. This frog's croak was said to be the voice of the Devil waiting to pull an unwary child under."

"Probably saved a lot of kids from drowning. Bet our pond was a fertile source of nightmares," Benny said. "Sorry. Go on. No more asides from me!"

"The adults in the community tried to have the girl put away as insane, but never actually did so. It was mentioned very often that she was extremely pretty and that might have had something to do with them not wanting to commit her—surprising how the beautiful can get away with things. Or maybe it was just that she kept to herself and never did anyone harm.

"Anyway, when she was eighteen, a young man came to work with her father. He was apparently quite a catch—tall, strong, black—but without a nickel to his name. Poor as a church mouse. He worked for a summer and then asked for Sary's hand. That she seemed to be haunted by a spirit didn't deter him at all. Her parents allowed the match.

"Sary and her husband had eleven children, all of whom lived to adulthood, married and had children of their own."

"And Sary might be my ancestor." Charlotte half-rose with excitement, her freckles burned on her cheeks.

"But nothing about Little Jack? No baby that died?" At first, Iris was disappointed. "How did he come into the picture?"

Benny's soft gaze let her know he guessed her feelings. But then another emotion intruded. *He is no one's but mine, and I am richer for that.*

She held her hand out to Charlotte, who grasped it in her own. "Whether or not this is the place in the story, you belong here with us."

"Let me just tell you one more thing," Jessica said, "about the ownership of the property, whether it's this one or another of the Sprigett family holdings. Sprigett's widow apparently treated the children as if they were her own grandchildren and, when she died at the age of sixty-two, she left the farm to Sary and her descendants. As Mrs. Sprigett had no living relatives, the will went through without challenge. Here's what was said of her at the time: 'Truly was a marvel of selfless love and Christian kindness to have taken so to a colored woman's child.'"

*   *   *

Jessica Hartnup and her wife had left on their way back to New York City. Seen through the kitchen's bay window, Benny and Charlotte were busy chatting up a storm while cleaning. Iris went out into the balmy evening to hear the frogs sing. She sat on the stone wall, still warm from the sun that lingered low on the horizon.

The evening breeze ruffled the water. Funny little amphibian eyes poked up to check if she was still there. The pond seemed a living thing.

A sudden flash of regret hit her. *Little Jack is gone from here.* If only he'd waited to be found. She might have let him slip back into the pond, where he'd been laid to safely rest, in his fine and lovingly made clothes. A baby, sleeping for one hundred and sixty years.

The mystery of Little Jack would never be solved, not completely. But it was enough to know that he was genetically related to Charlotte. He had real family, no matter how distant in time. And the story Jessica Hartnup had told was so intriguing.

Maybe she should go to his grave in the morning. It had been a while since she'd been to the cemetery. *Or maybe...*

The breeze came up again and stirred her hair—a strand fell across her eyes. She had been still long enough for a frog to clamber out onto the grass. It sat, throat pulsing, until its tongue shot out and caught a beetle carelessly trundling past. Iris laughed; the startled frog leaped back to hide, submerged under the water.

The water rippled again. Maybe the secret wasn't Baby Jack, but, instead, the pond. A place from which there are secrets buried so well, you think you'll never have to face them—only to have them rise, dripping from the depths and covered with muck, into the light.

With both hands, she pushed the hair from her eyes and turned back home.

About the Author

Rachel Callaghan, a retired physician, writes for relief from the seemingly endless renovation of a pre-Revolutionary house. She is helped by her husband, their German shepherd (a tracker in search and rescue), and a small black imp of a cat.

For more great books from Empower Fiction
Visit Books.GracePointPublishing.com

Made in the USA
Middletown, DE
29 March 2024

52300414R00205